The Orphans of Amsterdam

The Orphans of Amsterdam

Elle van Rijn

Translated by Jai van Essen

bookouture

Published by Bookouture in 2022

An imprint of Storyfire Ltd.
Carmelite House
50 Victoria Embankment
London EC4Y 0DZ

www.bookouture.com

*For Betty's nursery children, those who lived
and those who were killed.*

PROLOGUE

In the hallway downstairs, I pass preschoolers holding hands in line, ready to cross to the other side. Rucksacks on their backs, stuffed animals under their arms. Mirjam is accompanying the group.

'Weren't you supposed to help clean up?' she asks in her whispering voice.

'I'm on my way.'

'Come, children, move along.'

The line starts to move. I try not to take in the faces. I have too many images in my head already of children who were deported. Too many questions that threaten to drag me down into the depths because of their possible answers. *Don't think about the conditions they're now living in, if they're even still alive at all. None of that! It's done, over with. It never happened.*

Through the open door, I see Virrie in the preschooler room busy folding the linen from the camp beds that were taken away.

'Have you already arranged someone for the new package?'

I ask when I enter. I'm referring to the baby that was brought here at the last minute.

'Everyone's busy with the group that's still at Plantage Park-laan.' She's talking about the twelve children we'd arranged to be picked up immediately yesterday. Most were a bit older and had been hiding here for months already.

'Otherwise I'll just take him myself.'

The surprised look on Virrie's face is hard to miss. 'Where to?'

I shrug. For weeks, I've been asking myself who I'll go to when the time comes. Friends and acquaintances have told me I can go into hiding with them, but I don't know if the offer still stands in this phase of the German occupation. It's getting harder to know for certain if someone is good or crooked. People are afraid to speak out, for fear their words will land them in trouble. Or worse: that their actions will.

'Virrie, we're not giving the Germans this little boy. You should see him.'

'I know, but we may not have another choice.' She sees me hesitate. 'Or do you want to put us all in danger?'

I shake my head. 'Of course not.'

'If it's too much for you, I can bring him across the street.'

'No, that's not necessary. I'll make sure he stays well hidden today. There's a chance we'll get him out of here tomorrow, right?'

'Maybe,' she answers, unconvinced.

CHAPTER 1

THURSDAY, 4 SEPTEMBER 1941

In 1906, the Infants' Institution and Children's Home Association founded a nursery on Rapenburgerstraat for Jewish mothers seeking regular care for their child. Since most people from this part of Amsterdam had to work hard to make ends meet, many mothers were unable to stay home with their offspring. Because of this, the nursery for Jewish mothers came as a welcome solution. The costs for this nursery were no more than a quarter per child per day. This, of course, did not cover all costs, and so as not to have to rely solely on donations it was decided the nursery and the training programme for nursery teachers be merged so the childcare would be financed with income from the training. In 1924, the nursery moved to the stately building on Plantage Middenlaan number 31, where previously the Talmud Torah association had provided religious education in the small shul on the top floor. After relocating, the nursery was opened up to non-Jewish children as well and went on to become the largest and most modern nursery of the Netherlands. One renovation contributed to this: the building was given central heating, running water in each room and actual children's toilets.

. . .

I get on the blue tram in my nurse's uniform and matching raincoat, my back straight. I'm not just proud of the uniform, which makes me an official nursery teacher, but also because the work dresses and aprons have been made by Oudkerk Manufacturen, my family's own fabric shop, for years now. For me to be wearing one of these light blue nurses' uniforms, which I'd always see hanging in our shop, all at once makes me an adult. Even if I'm only seventeen years old, it seems as if all of Amsterdam suddenly sees me as a lady. A lady carer. I notice it commands respect. A cyclist on the pavement lets me pass, while he might as well have knocked me off my feet the day before. In the tram, a handsome young man with wavy black hair gets up for me. 'Please have a seat, sister.' In turn, I politely offer my seat to an old rabbi I vaguely know from the *shul*. I feel the young man leering at me as we hold on to the same steel rail. I keep my eyes cast down on our hands that don't quite touch. He's not wearing a wedding ring, which is why I look over my shoulder and give him a modest smile just before getting off at Plantage Middenlaan. He casts me a meaningful glance in return. Who knows, I might run into him again.

I was told the nursery front door is only used by visitors. All the parents and their children go through the side entrance, where the little ones are handed over through a hatch. It's only 7.45, but the entrance is already teeming with families.

'Pardon, could I pass? Excuse me.' I squeeze past all these people and go inside. In the reception room, I see toddlers of barely two years old taking off their coats and shoes themselves, which they then put in a bag with their name on it. They then hang the bags on the small coat hangers mounted on the various walls. It's a happy sight. From the reception area, I pass through a long hallway with the front door at the far end on the left and on the right the back door that leads into the garden. There are cipal said there was a 'particular reason' for this that she couldn't elaborate on. I looked around the room. That's when the penny dropped for me: we were all Jewish girls. The 'particular reason' was that we were no longer welcome at the Christian Domestic Science School. I'd heard enough and turned towards the door, but the principal called me back and handed me my diploma.

'You'll be needing this, Elisabeth,' she said. 'I'm sorry. This is all I can do for you people.' I was already starting to get used to people saying *you people*.

Though I felt like tearing my diploma to shreds right in front of her, I held my breath and walked out.

That same afternoon, when I heard they were looking for girls for the nursery teacher-training programme at the Jewish Nursery, the day took another radical turn. It had always been my plan to do something with children, so I applied immediately.

More and more girls are entering the staff room. I know several of them quite well because they're also from the domestic science school, like my friend Sieny Kattenburg. The mood is cheery and carefree. Maybe because we're all Jewish girls among ourselves here and don't feel we have to be ashamed, defend ourselves or be self-effacing. The cheery chatter among the girls is a sign I'm not the only one who feels free for a change. Director Pimentel enters. She's a stocky older woman in a white smock with silver-grey hair that sits on her head like a small ocean wave. A little white dog sneaks into the room together with her and sits down right beside her legs, like a real guard dog. When Pimentel claps her hands, all conversation stops abruptly.

'Welcome, all of you. As you may have understood by now, the nursery is a training school and charitable organisation in one,' her talk begins. 'You'll be getting your practical training during the day, and three evenings each week you'll be instructed in children's play, nutrition, general childcare, paediatric illnesses, hygiene, music, applied kinesiology and religion. I was put in charge here several years ago and allowed to put my stamp on how we work. I subscribe to the ideas of the educationalist Friedrich Fröbel, who believes a child's development is optimised if it is stimulated both creatively and actively. Equally essential are rest, cleanliness and routine...'

I'm getting even more excited as I listen. Thank goodness I ended up here!

'When the children arrive, they're first checked for diseases, like mumps, measles, rubella—'

The animal beside her immediately starts yelping at the word 'rubella'.

'Bruni, hush!' Pimentel orders. 'Where was I? Oh right, the children are checked for diseases and of course for bugs like fleas or lice. It's important you do this with great care, otherwise the children give it to each other and before you know it the building is a hotbed of infections. Babies and toddlers all receive white clothing from the nursery. Children between two and a half and six years old only receive an apron.'

The little dog jumps up against her legs. She doesn't tell it off this time but takes it in her arms.

'Though we may have started as a Jewish institution at one point, we also welcome non-Jewish children. That the Germans are now making us go back to being a nursery for Jews exclusively isn't just a nuisance for all those other children we took care of, but also for all the non-Jewish nursery teachers who came here every day.'

There's genuine outrage in her voice. Then she composes herself. 'We have more children coming in now than ever, so I'm glad you're here to help.'

'Sorry, director...' There's a nursery teacher in the doorway.

It's the friendly girl who pointed me in the right direction earlier. 'There's a bit of an issue with the combing.'

'Excellent topic – thank you, Mirjam.' Pimentel turns towards us again. 'Combing is done every morning. Does anyone know what this entails?'

Sieny raises her hand. 'Checking for lice?'

'Very good.'

There's giggling behind us, and I see Sieny turn red. I give her a little nudge and wink. Never mind. The Kattenburgs are the most decent, pious people I know. Even lice would wipe their feet on the doormat and say a *berakhah* there, if they even dared to go in at all.

'Lice, they're a terrible pest,' Pimentel continues. 'We have enough mouths to feed here, so we don't need parasites looking for a free meal.' Everyone laughs out loud. Laughter that lightens the mood a bit. More people are nervous on this first day.

'So that's why we start each morning with combing. If the child has a lot of these little bloodsuckers, the mother will have to take them back with her. As you've just heard from Mirjam, there's some congestion by the door. So, which of you is willing to help?'

Not much later, I'm wearing an apron over my blue dress and a white cloth on my head, and I'm delousing children according to painstaking instructions. I was the only volunteer to raise my hand. The director chose three more girls besides me. Oddly enough, Sieny didn't have to go. Maybe because she hadn't been ashamed to answer earlier. 'We do what we must,' my mother always says. And so I find myself going over the little ones' heads with a small comb. It's not easy because it takes me ten whole minutes to first brush out the tangles if it's a girl with long hair. Once the hair is tangle-free, I have to run my fingers through to look for nits, which are easily mistaken for dandruff or other filth. When I'm sure the hair has nits, I run the fine-tooth comb through. After each stroke, I clean the comb in the sink and check what I've caught. The full nits burst open when you crush them with the top of your fingernail. That's still amusing, but I can't bear crushing lice, especially the fat, fully engorged ones that leave a red trail of blood on the white porcelain. The number of lice each child has is recorded in a little notebook. If there are more than twenty living lice, the children get sent back home with their mother.

'It's a nuisance, but it can't be helped,' the certified nursery teacher Mirjam had added.

My final patient is a cute girl with golden hair. I immediately see her head is crawling with the critters. The girl's mother watches me anxiously. My own mother had warned me it's often the poor who have to bring their children to a nursery. The proof is right in front of me. The woman has done her best to dress her daughter somewhat decently in a loose-fitting burgundy dress. The mother herself is wearing a grubby dress that's been darned in four places. Despite her sunken face, I can tell she must have been quite a beautiful woman, though not much of that endures with a mouth full of rotten teeth.

'Is she ready? I need to go to work,' she says, almost pleading.

'I'm doing my best, madam. Do you also delouse her at home?'

'I do, but I also have two sons. My hands are full already. My husband is out at sea.' She glances anxiously past me at the notebook, which already counts sixteen marks. She hopes to be gone before I'm at twenty, of course, so I can't call her back anymore.

'Where do you work?' I ask to distract her.

'On the market.'

'Here on Daniël Meijerplein?'

'The Albert Cuyp, sister. We sell potatoes, carrots and onions.'

'Everyone needs those, right?' Meanwhile, I've plucked three more lice from the girl's hair. There's a good chance I'll find more, and then I'll have to send this child off to the market with her mother all day.

'Done!' I say, abruptly ceasing my combing. 'Not quite twenty, but you'll really need to work at it yourself tonight, otherwise we won't be able to keep her tomorrow.'

The woman looks grateful. 'I'll certainly do that, thank you, miss... I mean, sister.' She hurries out the nursery.

'Alright, and you're coming with me to your friends,' I say as I put the girl down on the floor and take her hand. 'What's your name?'

'Greetje,' she says in a hoarse voice.

'Well, that's a pretty name!'

'Momma wok.' She squints up at me.

'Yes, your mama's off to work. But you know what, Greetje? You and I are going to have a wonderful time here.'

'Momma wok, Greetje play,' she says with a broad smile.

'That's right.' I take her to the toddler room, which is on the ground floor, adjacent to the garden. I'd already heard I was assigned this room. Pimentel has divided the new girls between the different departments.

As soon as we enter, Greetje starts scratching her head. Maybe I'd have done better to give her back to her mother after all. How on earth do I keep myself from being the instigator of a lice outbreak on my very first day? As I wonder how, my own head starts to itch a bit too.

I keep a close eye on Greetje the rest of the day, jumping in when she gets too close to the other children. I'll distract her with a toy or read her a book. She keeps saying: 'Momma wok, Greetje play.'

Director Pimentel, who walks in now and then, comes up to me and asks how it's going.

I have a frantically scratching Greetje on my lap as I rattle away about how great it is to be with the little ones and how happy I am to be able to start my training already because I have a thing for children. Always have. Even when I was still a child myself. I rattle on until she interrupts me.

'Elisabeth, isn't it?'

'Everyone calls me Betty, ma'am.'

'It's miss, but please just call me director.' She gives me a stern look. 'Betty, I notice you're very much focussed on one child. We can't allow you to have favourites. Every child is equally precious here, and we don't favour one over another.'

'No, of course not, miss... I mean, director.'

'Momma wok, Greetje play,' the girl on my lap says again.

'You've combed her well, I hope. This child is always covered in lice.'

'Of course,' I bluff.

Pimentel strokes the girl's blonde hair. 'Good, because we don't want an epidemic breaking out here.'

'I totally understand. Who would?' I laugh nervously and ignore the itch on my head. 'Why don't you go do a puzzle?' I tell the girl, sliding her off my lap. The child gives me a bemused look.

'The blocks are over there in the corner,' says Pimentel, turning Greetje in the right direction. This she understands, and she skips over to the corner. 'Greetje is mentally handicapped, but surely you'd figured that out already.'

I feel cut down to size and shrug. 'I guess.'

'She's small for her age. She should actually be with the preschoolers, but that would be too much for her, mentally. Anyway, I want you to treat each child equally, even if one might be a bit more vulnerable than the next. The strong ones have a right to care and attention too. Look at those two children with the drip candles over there. That needs to be cleaned.'

'Drip candles?'

'The snot running from their noses.'

I get off at Tweede Jan van der Heijdenstraat to walk the last bit and pass the grocery where we do our shopping these days. The Plantage area, which is also where the nursery is, was historically a Jewish quarter, while our district, De Pijp, has more non-Jews than Jews living there. We used to always go to the grocery opposite our house, but we don't any longer since they – just like the Zwartjes shoe shop and the City theatre – put up a sign that says FORBIDDEN FOR JEWS. I didn't like those people already, and I'd expected this. Mother hadn't seen it coming herself and was flabbergasted. These people had been some of our best customers, for crying out loud. Piqued at this injustice, I felt like throwing a rock through the window, but my brother Gerrit firmly told me not to and asked if I'd gone completely *meshuga*. Only when I saw my mother's tears did I understand this was no eye for an eye, tooth for a tooth situation. I could handle her raising her voice, bulging her eyes and speaking harshly. I enjoyed going along with that, but her tears left me at a loss. The following day, it was as if the scene had been a melodramatic figment of her imagination, and with her head held high she told us that from now on we would be doing our grocery shopping at Tweede Jan van der Heij-denstraat.

The grocer raises his hand at me from inside the shop. I greet him back and only then notice the white swastika painted on the wall next to the entrance. Could it be he hasn't seen it yet?

The man comes towards me in a hurry. 'Betty, wait! Your

mother asked for grapes. I just got them in,' the man says kindly. I can't help but look at the still-wet paint on the wall.

'Oh, that,' the grocer says. 'I'll paint it over tonight. We shouldn't give the idiots of this world any attention. Otherwise we stand to lose a whole lot more.' I know what he's thinking of: the more than four hundred Jewish boys who were sent to Mauthausen after the uprising against the anti-Jewish measures, not a single one of whom has returned. It's really hard to believe that all these things are happening while everyday life just goes on.

'How was your day?' Mother asks when I enter our shop. I'm met by the familiar smell of freshly woven fabric rolls, a typical scent I'd instantly recognise anywhere. Mother is just busy closing shop.

'Great!' I say, handing her the bag of blue grapes. I give her a vivid account of how my day went. For convenience sake, I leave out the story about the lice. Mother wouldn't get a wink of sleep all night thinking about the itch. 'They have a piano at the nursery too, by the way,' I say, chipper.

My mother looks up from her bookkeeping. 'That's great, my dear. Then you'll be able to keep up with your piano playing.' My mother would have preferred to still be a pianist herself, rather than be the owner of a fabric shop. 'You did tell them you play, I hope.'

'Yes, because for the next six months I'll be in the red room with the toddlers, and I'll be teaching them all kinds of songs. Oh, the little ones are so lovely I could almost eat them.'

'Best you don't.' I look up, surprised. I hadn't seen my brother Gerrit yet. He's come down the ladder in the back of the shop and gives me a friendly pat on the shoulder.

'Hey, Sister Betty, patron saint of children,' he quips. 'Just as long as you don't have any yourself before you're twenty.'

The man I'll one day marry has to be just as handsome as Gerrit, with broad shoulders, dark hair combed back, a strong jawline and gentle eyes.

'Hey, cut it out,' Mother says, pretending to be peeved.

'Know who I ran into the other day?' Gerrit goes on, teasingly. 'Our old wet nurse. She has two teeth left in her mouth, and she's lost it a bit up there.' He points his finger at his head. 'But she assured me we could still hire her as a wet nurse. So, Betty, when you do have a child, at least that's taken care of.'

'Ugh, no. You can hire her yourself.' Mother never fed us herself because she wanted to keep her good figure. She'd always been proud of her slim waistline, which she still has. Add to that her delicate features and long, wavy dark blonde hair and that's my mother. She probably hoped she could get back up on stage as a pianist eventually. After going to the conservatory, she played at the Concertgebouw concert hall several times, but ever since we were born she's only worked as a piano and singing teacher. There are quite a few rabbis who became cantors – *chazzanim* – thanks to my mother. Some were utter rubbish and a waste of effort. I used to sit in the hallway, secretly listening in on my mother trying to teach those shrill crows to sing somewhat in tune.

A career as a performing musician seems unlikely to happen anymore. The growth of Father's fabric business meant Mother had to help out more and more. At first, she only handled the hiring of sales clerks and seamstresses, but ever since Father died she and Gerrit run the whole business themselves.

The shop bell rings, and the door swings open. All three of us look up. Japie, my thirteen-year-old brother, enters. He's a typical adolescent with spots on his face and a body that hasn't quite shot up in height yet but already has enormous hands and feet attached to it.

'Oh, you're still here,' he says drily.

My mother's bright mood suddenly turns sour. 'Well, what were you thinking? That you could just sneak by unnoticed?'

'No, why would you say that?' He makes a face that's supposed to convey innocence but in fact proves the opposite.

'For God's sake, Japie. Tell me it isn't so!'

'I don't know what you're talking about, Mother.'

She goes up to him and runs her hand through his hair. My brother winces.

'Wet!' For ultimate proof, she also gives his head a quick smell. 'Jaap, if you go to the swimming pool one more time, you're grounded for three months.'

'Why am I not allowed to swim? I think it's ridiculous other people can go to the swimming pool but I can't!'

'It's not fair indeed, but if you're caught you'll be in a whole lot more trouble.'

'Why would I get caught? No one can tell I'm Jewish by looking at me, can they?'

'They can if they pull your swim trunks down,' says Gerrit, further stoking the fire.

'You really need to shut up!' And he's gone, upstairs.

I try to catch my mother's eye, but she's looking at Gerrit. 'Did you really have to make a joke about it too?'

'If I can no longer joke about it, I might as well hang myself, just like those people down the street.' He walks to the back, shuts the ladder and goes upstairs, whistling.

My mother sighs. 'We're no longer allowed to swim or listen to the radio, we have to put our money in certain banks, and in *The Jewish Weekly* I just read that as of this coming week we're no longer welcome in parks, hotels, museums and whatever else. How do I explain this to a thirteen-year-old child?'

'Did you deposit our money in the bank?' I ask to be sure I heard her correctly.

'They wish. Lippmann-Rosenthal hasn't been a Jewish bank for ages now. I'm not bringing them a single penny. Come, dear, I'm closing up.' She locks the shop door and puts her arm around me. 'It's good that you're learning a trade, Betty. Whatever situation we end up in, nursery teachers are always needed.' We walk up the stairs to our home together.

Later when I'm in bed, I hear the sounds of Mother playing the piano from the living room, which is next to my bedroom. Those stolen minutes when she thinks she's alone and loses herself in her playing are sacred to her, and to me. As a child, I would sneak out of bed and go to the landing to listen in secret through the open door. To see how her upper body swayed along to the melody as her fingers danced briskly across the keys. Tonight, she's playing my favourite piece, 'Songs without Words' by Mendelssohn. Music I could disappear into. I drift off into a dreamless sleep.

CHAPTER 2

FRIDAY, 5 SEPTEMBER 1941

Earlier this year, not long after Father died of a brain haemorrhage, cafés near Rembrandtplein continued serving their Jewish customers anyway, even though by then this had been prohibited. Consequently, the WA, the paramilitary arm of the Dutch National Socialist Movement NSB, brutally struck at a café at Thorbeckeplein where Jewish artists were performing several days later. Afterwards, as the WA marched towards its next target full of bravado, the communists came up for our people. The fight was brief, and the WA had to retreat, tail between their legs. But one of their leaders, Hendrik Koot, a real Jew hater, was found lifeless alongside the road. The rumours going around about how he'd died were grotesque. Jews had supposedly bitten off his nose and ears, licking the blood off their lips afterwards and biting his larynx to top it off. But Koot had been knocked down with a single blow to the head – that's what the police officer who found him had stated. My brother Gerrit thinks it was all staged and Koot was killed by the Germans themselves so they could use his death for propaganda purposes, because the place where Koot was found was a good way off from where the fight had taken place.

This was where all the trouble began. Not long after Koot's death, a number of people received notes in their mailboxes that read: TEN JEWS FOR EACH NSB MEMBER THAT IS KILLED. A well-known Jewish sculptor who went to post a letter in the evening was stabbed in the back three times. Several days later, trouble struck again on Van Woustraat, where we live, at Koco, where they sold the best ice cream in all of Amsterdam. The ice-cream parlour was frequented by Jews and non-Jews alike, and for this reason was often targeted by the Nazis. The two owners and several customers had banded together to defend themselves. Well, it didn't end well. I remember walking past the shop the day after the confrontation and seeing the wreckage. In retaliation, over four hundred Jewish men were arrested at random and rounded up together on Jonas Daniël Meijerplein. They were beaten up, and then put in trucks for deportation to Mauthausen, a prison camp in Austria. This was cause for tens of thousands of workers and students from greater Amsterdam to organise a strike on 25 February as a show of solidarity against the persecution of Jews. Unfortunately, the strike lasted only two days and was brutally suppressed by the Germans.

Out of all the young men who were captured, not a single one returned from Mauthausen. Though more and more death notices are coming in.

Mr Cahn, one of the shop owners, who always gave me an extra scoop of ice cream, was shot in April.

The sky is clear blue. Still, my head feels cloudy after a night of trying to process all the impressions of my first day. With my handbag on my shoulder, I get on the tram and squeeze past the other passengers to the back in order to stand on the balcony. I get a fright when I see two German soldiers in uniform standing there.

'*Kein Problem, Fräulein, hier ist Platz für drei,*' the tallest of the two says to me in German, smiling politely. If there's anything I've learned recently, it's to be as inconspicuous as you can and just to play along. Anything else can lead to trouble. So I nod back politely and take a seat on the balcony. I make an effort to look the other way and not to listen in on the conversation the men are having. It's moments like these I wish I didn't understand German, but we learned to speak the language perfectly back home thanks to the German maids who lived with us. The last one was Annie, who belonged to the Dutch Reformed Church. This girl was so pretty everyone wanted a piece of her beauty for themselves. I was allowed to brush her hair sometimes, my older sister Leni learned how to apply makeup from her, and my gangly brother Nol would play cards with her for days on end. Not because he was so fond of games, but because he was head over heels for Annie. Even Father wanted to ask her to be a fit model for the clothes we made. But Mother felt that went too far. It was also no longer possible because she had to return to Germany. Non-Jews were no longer permitted to work for Jews.

'We're lucky we're not on the Eastern Front,' I hear one of the soldiers say.

'You bet. Especially now winter is approaching,' the other one says in a high-pitched voice that makes me involuntarily look back to see if it's really a man. 'I heard the extreme cold causes your limbs to freeze.' It's a man alright. His shrill voice gives him a clownish quality, and he's wearing short service trousers with two thin, hairy legs sticking out from underneath. I struggle not to laugh and turn my eyes back to the street.

'That's supposed to be really painful,' I hear the other one say. 'Especially if your willy freezes off.'

'Stop it, Kurt. I don't want to think about it,' the high-pitched voice says.

It seems they assume I don't understand what they're saying, because they keep talking.

'Poland and Russia have more Jews living there than here, so you have to work even harder,' the tall one says.

'Did you know they just put them down over there?' the high voice says. 'First they have them dig a ditch, then they make them line up at the edge, and then, rat-tat-tat-a-tat-a-tat, they're all mown down.' The shrill laugh that follows so sickens me that I nearly throw up. I hold on tight to the iron grip to keep myself from falling.

'Pardon, miss, could we squeeze by?' The tram comes to a halt.

I take a step back and try to keep a straight face.

'Have a nice day, ma'am.' They give me a courteous nod.

I'm all shaken up when I reach the nursery, where Mirjam is the first person I run into in the staff room.

'Wow, you look pale. Are you okay?' she asks, looking concerned.

'I'm alright,' I say. 'Just a bit short of breath today.' I put my bag in the cupboard and grab a clean apron from the stack when I hear Sieny enter.

'Good morning! Lovely weather today.' Then she looks at me. 'Betty, are you not feeling well? You're as pale as this tablecloth.'

'That's what I said,' Mirjam says.

I can't lie to my friend. 'I just heard something awful in the tram...' They gather close. Faltering, I tell them what the two German soldiers were saying to each other.

'I bet they knew you're Jewish,' Mirjam says sympathetically. 'They were trying to rile you up on purpose.'

'Or maybe they were talking about a prison camp,' Sieny

says. 'I heard they shoot Jews there, but they only do that in the east, certainly not here. It's against the law.'

'The law? Does the law still protect us, then?' I ask, sounding more naive than I intended.

'Of course,' Mirjam says with a conviction I've never heard from her before. 'My father established the Jewish Council to unite us, because we may be powerless individually, but together we're strong.'

'Is your father the Jewish Council chairman?' I ask, surprised.

Sieny gives me an almost imperceptible nudge. 'Yes, together with Abraham Asscher. My father has always tried to help Jewish refugees from Germany and Poland.' There's pride in her voice.

Director Pimentel enters. 'May I ask why we're not combing?' She doesn't wait for us to answer. 'This isn't a tea party here. There's a whole queue of children waiting again.'

The combing and counting has a calming effect on me. Plus no one is talking about lice outbreaks among the children, so that's reassuring too. I did pull out a louse from my own hair last night, but I don't mention this. With utmost concentration, I attend to each child until the three of us have taken care of no less than sixty-three children's heads. Just when we've put away the combs, someone brings in another child. A boy with short-cropped blonde hair.

'That should be fine, no lice hiding in there. What's his name?' Only then do I look up and recognise the mother.

'Greetje,' she says. 'Can I go?'

'Umm... yes.' As the mother speeds off, I look at Greetje, who I'd mistaken for a boy. Her mother really went to work on her with the trimmer. With her scabby head and crossed eyes, she's lost every bit of cuteness she had.

'Come, Greetje, let's go play.'

'Yeah, play, play!' she cries out with excitement.

Even though Director Pimentel won't allow it, I feel I have to take extra good care of this girl.

CHAPTER 3

FRIDAY, 20 FEBRUARY 1942

I was given an identity card with a big letter J on it. The Jewish Council had to have all Jewish people living in the Netherlands registered. This includes people who according to traditional Jewish law – which dictates Jewishness is passed down through the maternal line – are not even Jewish. But the Germans have different ideas about that. A boy from my class had no idea he was Jewish, but it turned out he had a Jewish grandfather who'd been registered in a Jewish municipality at some point. The fact the man wasn't practicing and that my school friend, like the rest of the family, had been baptised doesn't matter according to the Germans. Jewish is Jewish.

The cartotheque *issued the identity cards. The detailed registration makes it easier to keep track of how many Jews there are and where they live. Or rather, where they lived, because except for a few major cities all Jews have had to move to Amsterdam.*

These past few days, even if it's still light out when I come off work, spring still seems a long way off. Dark grey clouds pass over the city, and sleet is falling from the sky. A bit of a nuisance, because I don't have an umbrella with me. Thankfully, the dark blue tram stops right in front of the door at the nursery, and when I hear it coming from behind the window I make a dash to catch it. I'm able to get my foot on the step just in time and hoist myself up before the vehicle starts moving. *Made it.* I greet the driver, who I've got to know from my daily rides.

'Hey, sister, didn't we agree you wouldn't be bringing any more snow.'

'Oh dear, it must have slipped my mind,' I answer, playing along. He suddenly pulls the brake because a man on a bicycle steers in front of the tram, and we halt so abruptly I almost go flying through the windshield.

'Dumb fool, look where you're going!' the tram driver yells. Not that the cyclist can hear him, but the gesture he makes with his arm is clear enough.

'Idiot!' Then he turns towards me again. 'You alright, love?'

'Sure, I can take a beating.'

'It drives you mad, all these provincials here. They don't know the rules, most have never even seen a tram.'

'They'll catch on eventually,' I say, trying to lighten the mood.

'Had one under my wheels just yesterday. Also thought he could just cross over quick. Well, his front tire got caught in the rails alright. They had to take him to the hospital.'

'How awful!'

'He was lucky it happened right by the NIZ. They wouldn't have admitted the chump at a normal hospital.' The NIZ – Dutch Israelite Hospital – on Keizersgracht only treats Jews these days. We're no longer welcome in other hospitals, even if it's an emergency.

'I really don't get why they have to squeeze everyone together in this neighbourhood,' the talkative tram driver continues. 'Plenty of room in Amsterdam, isn't there?' He gives me a meaningful look, as if to say: *You get which side I'm on now, don't you?* Of course he knows I'm Jewish. I get off at the Jewish Nursery every day. Just like I know he isn't Jewish – just from how he talks about us.

It's true there are a lot more people out in the street these past few weeks. I never had to stand in the tram before because there were always plenty of seats. But ever since Jews from all over the country had to move here, it's much busier. The nursery is bursting at the seams as well; there are almost a hundred children there now, and Pimentel is considering a halt on new admissions.

But it also has its advantages for all of us to be lumped together in this neighbourhood. It's lively and cosy. Opposite the nursery, there's the Hollandsche Schouwburg theatre, now renamed Joodsche Schouwburg, which premieres one new play after another. I went there with some girls from work a little while back. I absolutely adore theatre. My parents always used to take me to the Royal Theatre Carré, where the Netherlands' greatest artists performed. Afterwards, I would imitate the actresses. My family called me a natural actress, and that's how I felt too. I used to fantasise about one day getting on stage and causing a sensation. But when I once carefully broached the subject of making this my profession later on, they all burst out laughing. Artists were far too *achenebbish* according to my parents – not of our class. With that, our conversation was cut short and my dream shattered.

Jews are no longer allowed to visit Carré these days. Thankfully, the most famous Jewish artists now perform in the theatre here. The piece I went to see with my colleagues starred a wacky Heintje Davids, who I'm a big fan of, the handsome actor Siem Vos and the beautiful German-Jewish actress Silvia Grohs. The show consisted of different sketches from box-office hits like *De Jantjes*, *Fortissimo* and *Naar de Artis*. It was such a cheery performance that we left the venue singing out loud.

wooden children's benches on both sides. Two wide stairways spiral upwards halfway down the hall, where they lead to a balustrade on the first floor.

'Can I help you?' asks a small nursery teacher with curly brown hair and round spectacles.

'I'm, errm... looking for the staff room.' I sound like a spring chicken.

'First door on your left,' she says in a soft voice.

The room is full of tables and haphazardly arranged chairs. There's a pale pink sofa and an armchair with the same fabric at the far end, near the window. The furniture gives the room a homely feel, and the walls are covered with framed drawings and photos. Many have a large group of nursery teachers posing and smiling for the camera. It seems new group portraits are made every year because there's a different date on each one. I'm giddy at the thought of soon being on one of these photos myself, in the middle of a group. Another series of photos sees them all dressed up. 12 MARCH 1932, 25 YEARS OF INFANT CARE, it reads below. For the rest, there are several diplomas on the wall with different names on them.

It reminds me of my own training at the domestic science school. I still can't believe they gave me my diploma just like that. This past July, a few days before the summer holidays, I was called out of class. I had to report to the principal and wondered what I'd be punished for. There were several reasons I could think of; I was certainly no goody two shoes in class.

I entered the principal's office and joined a group of girls already waiting there.

'Ladies, you'll be getting your diplomas today,' the principal announced bluntly. Everyone was so surprised they fell silent.

'But we haven't even graduated yet!' I exclaimed. Ordinarily, I'd have another year and a half of school to go. The prin-

When I told everyone about it back home, Gerrit said he'd never voluntarily let himself be packed in there like a bunch of sardines.

'If they're out to get us, they'll have five hundred all at once,' he added. I hadn't thought of that, and I even got upset at Gerrit for being so negative. At which Gerrit took me aside and confided he was planning to skip town. He didn't know how yet, and first he would marry Lous, his beautiful girlfriend – who I was secretly jealous of because she needed more and more attention from him – but that he wouldn't sit around and wait was certain.

I walk the last few blocks home through a veil of white flakes. All day, I've been looking forward to the honey chicken my mother traditionally makes every Friday. She used to have the poultry shop make it, but in the past few years she has learned how to prepare the chicken herself. I always go upstairs through our shop, but today I find the door is locked. It's not that late yet, is it? I take the key from my purse and try to turn the lock with my cold fingers, but it doesn't give. Maybe because of the cold. Or is it possible my key no longer fits because I hardly ever use it? Whatever I try, I'm unable to turn it. I take a few steps back and see there's a light on in the kitchen. My mother always turns off all the lights when she leaves, she's very careful about that. I get an ominous feeling something is wrong.

That's when I see the gate is open. I go via the path to the side entrance, which takes you directly to our upstairs maisonette. I brush the snow off my coat and take off my wet shoes in the hallway. In my stockings, I walk up the stairs to our home. The first thing I notice when entering is that I don't smell any chicken. I run into my sister, Leni, in the hallway, who's just coming out the door of my mother's bedroom.

'Shhh, quiet!' she hisses immediately. 'Mother's just fallen asleep.' She drags me into the kitchen.

'Is she sick?' My mother going to bed during the day, that's not right. It has to mean she's in an awful state.

My sister shakes her head. 'They took over our shop.'

'Took over? What are you talking about?'

Leni rolls her eyes like it's my fault I don't understand. 'You know we were given a *Verwalter*, don't you?'

'Yes, a kind of overseer – and now they want us to pay more taxes or something?' I still don't quite get what this is about. Jewish businesses are administered by the Germans now, allegedly to make sure they're being honest.

'They took the whole shop from us. They've already changed the locks downstairs, and the new owner moves in tomorrow.'

The news doesn't seem to register. The family business my father grew and made more successful each year by working day in, day out, that's well known throughout Amsterdam and the surrounding area, was taken over by someone else?

'So Mother sold the shop?'

'No, of course not. We didn't get a penny for it. Everything was given to the widow Koot. As compensation for her husband's death.' *That WA member's wife is now in charge of our shop? Of Oudkerk Manufacturen?* I sink into a chair.

My brother Japie enters the kitchen. Immediately, he pounces on the breadbasket and tears off a hunk.

'Hey, no snarfing,' Leni says.

Japie shrugs. 'I can help myself if you're not cooking.'

'I'm starting now,' my sister says. 'Chicken soup is a cinch. Betty, will you cut the leeks?' She puts a board and two leeks on the table in front of me.

I push it away from me immediately. 'It's Shabbat, the food should have been prepared already,' I mutter.

'Don't be childish,' she sighs.

'Where's the rest?' I ask.

'Granny and Engel just left for the *shul* on Gerard Dous-

traat, and Gerrit and Nol went to Linnaeusstraat to talk with
the People's Rebbe after widow Koot's visit. They've been gone
for hours.' She turns around to give her attention to the pot on
the stove.

I realise I'm not helping anyone with my attitude. I'd best
follow my sister's example and keep my head straight. I take the
knife and start cutting the leeks.

'Did Granny give out chicken today?' My grandmother lives
with us, together with Engel, her old housemaid. Every Friday,
she heads out with two chickens in each hand for poor Jews in
the neighbourhood, all out of charity. She hides her pearl necklace under a shawl and never takes it off. 'Pearls should be worn
on your skin,' she claims. 'Otherwise they lose their shine.'

'Goodness, Betty, how should I know?' my sister says,
annoyed. 'I've been working all day myself. What difference
does it make?'

'Granny had just come home when widow Koot pulled up
in a car with her new boyfriend,' Japie says.

'New boyfriend? So that's how deep her love for her
husband was,' I say cynically.

'Same type,' my brother says, shrugging. 'A pleb just like
Hendrik Koot, but they acted like they were king and queen.
He had one of those top hats, and she was wearing a thick fur
coat.'

'She likely stole that from someone too,' I say contemp-
tuously.

'I'm not afraid to get rid of her,' Japie says, dead calm. 'I
know where I can borrow a gun.'

'And then we'll all be dead! Is that what you want?' My
sister suddenly loses her cool and raises the knife menacingly,
chicken meat still hanging from it. 'Cut it out now!'

The whole situation feels so unreal that I don't feel
anything at all.

. . .

I gently knock on Mother's bedroom door. When I get no reply, I carefully enter. My mother is lying on her side in the double bed with her back to the window, her long hair in a braid that follows the arch of her back. She looks so small. Like a baby in a giant crib.

'Mama, I have chicken soup for you...' I walk around the bed so I can see her face. She's closed her eyes, but I know she's not sleeping. By now, I'm an expert at recognising whether a child is pretending to sleep or if it's actually sleeping. It's not just the shallow breathing but also the tensed eyelids that show someone is awake. I put the soup on the nightstand and sit down beside her on the bed, gently running my hand through her thick blonde hair, which has more and more grey locks.

'Mama, I heard about what happened, and that's awful, but we'll get the shop back one day.'

She then opens her eyes and gives me a sleepy look. 'I don't know, Betty...' she rasps.

'All things crooked are straightened out in the end, Father always said. And I believe it too, Mama.'

She raises herself a bit. 'Do you know she sent home all the staff as well?'

'Everyone?' We have more than ten people on the payroll. How are they supposed to survive what's coming? 'She can re-hire them, can't she?'

Mother shakes her head. 'Only Gerrit can stay as manager, until she's found a new one.'

My comforting words from a moment ago sound hopelessly naive suddenly.

'But, Mama, this will stop eventually. They're suffering huge losses on the Eastern Front. The Russians are stopping them in Moscow. That's what someone at work said. She'd heard it on the English radio broadcast.'

Mother takes my hand and plants a kiss on it. 'Good thing Father isn't alive to see this anymore.' Then she lets go of my hand and feebly lets herself fall backwards. With her face to the ceiling, she says: 'I'll go on living for all of you, and to care for my mother, but I don't see the point for myself anymore.'

The following day, the morning light comes as always. The roofs are white with frost, and the pavement is slippery. Still, I decide not to take the tram but to ride my bicycle to work. I just can't bear to have people around me now. I cast a last glance over my shoulder at our beautifully decorated shop window. Then I pedal out of the street as fast as I can.

I have all my old childhood dresses in my bag, for Greetje. She's suddenly shot up in height these past few months, and I can no longer bear to see her faded dresses reveal a little more of her mended tights each day. When I slip her mother the bag of clothes, she looks at me, startled.

'I can't ever pay for this.'

'You don't need to. They're for you.' She walks out the nursery without saying thanks. She's likely too taken aback to be polite.

I kept one dress to put on Greetje today. It's a mossy-green winter dress made of heavy wool with a straight top and a pleated bottom. These past years, Mother had all our clothes made from the fabrics of our shop, but as children we were dressed by Maison de Bonneterie. I had so many clothes that hardly any were worn-out. Luckily, I guessed the size correctly because the dress fits Greetje perfectly. She spins around like a princess, even drooling a bit. She likes it that much. When Pimentel enters, I act as if it's her own dress and tell Greetje she has to go join the other children in a far more detached voice. But Pimentel knows, because she gives my arm a quick pinch. 'Just so long as the other mothers don't find out, alright?'

I nod, relieved.

Today is my last day with the toddlers. I think it's a pity, of course, but I also look forward to going to the infants. Mirjam is in charge there, and at least I know her already. More girls, and children too, have been joining us recently, so it's really hard to remember everyone's name. Sieny and I requested we work in the same department in the coming six months, and the director thought that was fine. I've already learned Pimentel is best placated with a sense of humour. She'll say she thinks my jokes are a bit silly, but meanwhile be unable to contain her laughter. She has a good laugh at the jokes I get from Gerrit and Nol especially. It's fine with her, so long as the children don't hear them. I often think up fairy tales for them, which I perform as a kind of play. I can't wait until I can work with the preschoolers; you can dream up all kinds of things with them.

The day isn't half over yet when Pimentel calls out to me in the toddler room: 'Betty, your grandmother rang. You need to go home immediately.' I'm startled; Granny never rings. I don't think she even knows how to use a telephone. I take off my cap and apron and hurry towards the exit.

As I fumble with my coat, Pimentel stands beside me. 'Betty, I don't know what's the matter, but it's no problem if you need a few days off. Let me know.'

'Thank you, director,' I stammer. Nerves make me give her a big, unprompted hug, at which her dog, Bruni, starts barking immediately. 'Oh, sorry...' I say, letting go of her.

'Bruni, sit.' Pimentel pats me on the shoulder. 'Let me know if I can help, alright?'

As I ride my bicycle into Van Woustraat, I can see the sign in front of our shop window from afar: FORBIDDEN FOR JEWS. I throw my bicycle against the wall and run to the side entrance. The first person I run into upstairs is Gerrit, who's bringing a jug and bowl to Mother's bedroom.

'Mother had a nervous breakdown. Granny wants to have a word with you.'

My regal grandmother is in the kitchen, chest out, mouth tight, eyelids raised. Her old housemaid, Engel, sits beside her, a woman with frizzy chalk-white hair who can hardly be said to be of any help because she's half-blind and crippled, but who nonetheless is indispensable to Granny. My brother Nol is hunched over at the table opposite them, Leni leans against the kitchen sink and Japie is looking out the window.

'Granny, what's the matter?'

'Have a seat and take a breath, child.' Granny's calm only makes me more concerned. 'Your mother had a... moment of weakness today.'

'What do you mean?'

'That she tried to take her own—' says Engel, hoping to clarify what Grandmother is saying.

'Be quiet, Engel! I'm telling Betty.'

Suddenly, my head starts spinning.

'Your mother took some sleeping pills. Nol found her frothing at the mouth.'

I'm so dizzy now I have to sit down. I move the kitchen chair back, my hands tingling.

'She drank so much water that she threw up in her sleep. The doctor has been already, and he says she shouldn't have any lasting effects. Except that she'll have to get her nerves back under control. We all have to help her with that.'

She'd said so just yesterday. She'd said she'd do it if she didn't have us. But we're here, aren't we? So then why did she... I squeeze my thighs. 'Because of the shop?'

'Worse still. They took Granny's houses from her,' Leni says.

'All four?' I squeak. Grandmother had inherited two of

those houses from her parents, after which rental income and a frugal lifestyle allowed her to buy two more houses herself. The houses were meant for us, for when we left home.

'The SD came in the shop this morning at widow Koot's request,' Granny goes on. 'They found the eight thousand guilders your mother had hidden in the shop, but which she hadn't been able to retrieve yet. Apparently, this *malveillante* still didn't think this was enough, because they then searched the entire upper floor and found another ten thousand guilders.'

'We have nothing now.' All of a sudden, Japie starts to weep. 'I hate them. I hate them so much I'd like to kill all of them with my bare hands.' He looks at us, holding his long, thin child's fingers in front of him.

I get up and put my arm around Japie. So long as I can comfort my little brother, I can suppress my own feelings of panic.

'Japie, we've discussed this already,' Granny says sharply. 'We can't lose our heads now. Not your mother, and not you either.' One by one, she gives each of us a stern look. 'What your mother did today is understandable, but it's not allowed. Us Jews don't do that. Only God's will be done!' The silence that follows is so oppressive I can hardly breathe.

Suddenly, I hear music coming from Mama's room. It's Gerrit, who's playing his violin for our mother. No one says a thing, everyone just listens to the high-pitched notes emanating from the room. Then I can't control myself any longer and start screaming for it to stop, that this can't go on any longer. All of this. I press my hands against my ears and run to my room.

After two days of bed rest, our mother shows up fully dressed in the kitchen again and snaps at us for not doing the laundry. As if dirty laundry is a capital offence in a life she'd been ready to turn her back on several days before. The human spirit is apparently so flexible as to allow us to forget major grief in exchange for minor grief. But I'm relieved; rolling up your sleeves is always more productive than worrying.

Under Granny's watchful eye, my sister and I get to work on the pile of dirty underwear, shirts and linen. We do everything as meticulously as possible, though it's really never good enough. Granny's standards are higher than what's humanly possible. Good thing I only understand half of the comments she mainly dispenses in French, and she always rewards us afterwards with fresh butter biscuits or Chelsea buns that she gets at Blom, the pastry shop in Rijnstraat.

My mother is slowly picking her life up again too. She fills her days as she used to with piano and singing lessons, as if using music to iron over her nearly fatal act. We have our emotions under control again and don't talk about what happened. The world keeps spinning as usual, and that's what matters most in the end.

CHAPTER 4

MONDAY, 4 MAY 1942

Jews can no longer marry non-Jews, Jewish butchers are being forced to close their doors and Jews are no longer allowed to sell furniture from their own house. This last rule is to prevent Jews from having sold all their belongings when they have to leave their homes so they can't be plundered by the Germans. Since yesterday, we're required to wear a six-pointed star with the word JEW written on it in Hebrew-like letters. The cotton stars only went on sale yesterday, and Nol queued up for hours to get them for us. Each person is entitled to four stars, for which you have to pay one textile stamp and four cents. You're expected to wear the star visibly on your outside clothes.

With the greatest precision, Granny spent several hours sewing stars on all coats, overcoats, vests and suit jackets until her fingers blistered, then she told us we would have to do the rest ourselves. I'm so repulsed by this hideous yellow rag that I spent all Sunday inside and only today, just before having to leave for work, picked up a needle and thread to sew the unsightly thing on my raincoat. When I go out a little later wearing it, I'm mortified. All seats in the busy tram are taken, so there's nothing for me to hide behind. Standing in the aisle, I feel like everyone is looking at me. I keep looking outside, where spring is well underway. The trees all have bright green leaves, and birds are singing happy songs. It's a stark contrast with the oppressive mood in the tram. Only right before we turn onto Plantage Middenlaan do I have the nerve to look around me, and I see I'm not the only one wearing the yellow Star of David on their clothes. I catch the eye of an older woman, who nods at me, as if to say: *Welcome to the club.*

No one at work talks about it at first. After all, what can you say? We already complained amongst ourselves when the star ordinance was announced in the newspapers. I'd even announced I'd refuse, but as with all new rules and laws we felt were wholly unreasonable and absurd on the first day, it only takes a few days for you to start to think it's normal. Any rebelliousness on my part is vanquished by that point. But this doesn't seem to be the case with everyone. From her room at the front of the building, Mirjam sees a dog wearing the yellow star on its tail. The man walking the dog isn't wearing a star himself and looks around, smiling kindly. A little later, there's a pregnant woman walking by who's sewn the star in the middle of her enormous belly. An older gentleman is wearing it on his hat, which makes him look like an English police officer. All these stars in odd places are a cause of great hilarity, and not just with us. The actors from the theatre are coming outside to clap for every non-Jew passing by with a fake protest star.

I pull Sieny along. 'Come on, we're clapping too!' A group of children are wearing the stars as jersey numbers on their coats. A street sweeper has one stuck on his cart. Some ten dashing young men saunter by with fake stars on their satchels.

'Whose idea was this?' I ask one of them.

A tall blonde boy grins at me. 'This is a protest of Amsterdam citizens declaring solidarity with the Jews.'

'That's great!' I say, impressed not just with what he's telling me but also his light blue eyes.

He reaches in one of his pockets: 'Look, a few days ago they dropped thousands of these pamphlets from the roof of De Bijenkorf department store on Dam Square.' He hands me a pamphlet picturing a yellow star with the words below: *Jews and non-Jews united in struggle!*

'And who are you, then?' Sieny asks with a sceptical look on her face.

'We study at Vrije Universiteit and feel we can no longer ignore the German measures against the Jewish population,' the boy says with a voice that betrays he's spoken this sentence before. 'Excluding Jews and branding them like this goes against every single convention.'

I'm surprised how deep his words touch me, and I have to keep myself from cheering and throwing my arms around him.

'I need to get going,' the boy says, pointing at his fellow students who've already moved on.

'Of course. Thanks!' I watch him walk off, brimming with pure gratitude. I also wish I'd got to know this handsome boy a little better.

Sieny nudges me. 'Betty, don't stare!'

Someone is tapping on the window behind us. It's Mirjam; we have to get back to work.

Meanwhile, our life with the children in the nursery continues with its regular rhythm of playing, eating, sleeping, playing and bathing. I listen to babies trying to form their first words, to the short and often incoherent sentences of the toddlers, the wisdoms of the preschoolers. The war stays outside, and it seems as if nothing is wrong. Still, reality slowly seeps through here as well. Everything children say is unfiltered and reflects what's actually going on in their young lives. What can't be said out loud, but is said anyway.

'My father says Germans are very bad people.'

'I shot a kraut in my sleep!'

'My mama cries more than me. Odd, isn't it?'

'Mother says the star is pretty, but I'm not wearing it when I'm six.'

'My grandpa and grandma took a pill and now they're dead.'

No one at home is talking about what it was like the first day wearing one of these stars. As if it doesn't exist. I miss Gerrit; he would have talked about it. He would even have got so worked up about it that sweat would pour from his forehead as his cheeks turned purple. But Gerrit no longer lives here. Immediately after marrying on the first of April, he moved in with his wife Lous's family. While I can't imagine a better sister-in-law, I'd have preferred if she'd been from a poor family and Gerrit hadn't moved into his in-laws' imposing house straight away. But I understand Gerrit. As the oldest son, he would join Father on his travels to do the purchasing for the shop from a young age. And when they weren't travelling through the country, he would be at Father's side behind the counter in the shop downstairs. After Father died, Gerrit worked very hard to secure our income, which he managed quite well despite the war. Now he's lost his job and is no longer allowed to visit the place where he spent the greater part of his life. Understandably, he doesn't want to live with us above the shop, where at any moment he might be confronted with the hoi polloi downstairs, the widow Koot.

. . .

Rather than having a discussion at the table, we now eat our dinner of boiled potatoes and vegetables in silence. The seven of us – Leni, Nol, Mother, Granny, Engel, Japie and myself – still manage to fill a large table, but it feels empty without Father and Gerrit.

'Have you heard anything about Gerrit's emigration plans?' I ask not just to break the silence but also to remind everyone that there's at least one family member trying to swim against the current.

'That's not happening,' my mother says, listlessly picking at a few beans with her fork.

'Why not? Didn't they have it all set up?'

'They recently implemented a travel ban for Jews looking to move abroad,' my brother Nol says. 'I'd already heard it was coming, but now it's official.'

Nol, who now works at the Jewish Council's bread distribution department, increasingly acts as if he knows more than we do. I might have tolerated such an attitude from Gerrit, but from Nol it's infuriating.

'If you already knew, couldn't you have told Gerrit?' I say accusingly.

'I did, but he wasn't able to get it together in time. Besides, he wanted to wait for my wedding.'

Engel chokes on a bite of food.

'*Allez*, Nol, you can break the news a bit more gently,' Granny says, patting her old housemaid on the back.

'I thought you all knew I'm getting married,' says Nol.

'We did,' Granny says, 'but I didn't have time to tell Engel yet.'

'Or me, apparently,' Japie says drily.

'Or me,' Leni says.

'Or me,' I say at last.

'Mother?' says Nol, turning towards the only one who hasn't said anything yet. 'You knew, didn't you?'

'Of course, my dear,' Mother says flatly.

I doubt it's true.

'To Jetty?' I ask to rattle him some more.

'Yes, to Jetty.' He rolls his eyes and then gets up from the table. 'I'm going to her place.' He leaves his plate on the table.

After dinner, I join Japie in looking for a better place to hide the food Mother stockpiled, sort out the rationing coupons that go with each person's registration card and do a bit of piano practice. Afterwards, I go to bed and sleep like a log.

CHAPTER 5

FRIDAY, 10 JULY 1942

Since the beginning of the year, unemployed Jewish men are being summoned by the National Service for the Expansion of Labour in the North and East Netherlands. They have to work in different villages like Nunspeet, Ochten, Putten, Ede, Hummelo, Ruurlo, Lievelde, and so forth, developing land and doing forestry work. Because ever fewer Jews are allowed to work in commerce, or because they can no longer get work permits, unemployment numbers are rising and these labour camps are filling up by the day.

The weather is so nice today that we decide to get the foldable paddling pool from the attic and fill it with water. The preschoolers are allowed to take turns in groups of six. After twenty minutes, the whistle is blown and they have to get out again. It's a lot of work for us. We help them dry and get dressed, make sure there's no mud on their feet or sand in their bottoms. And then the whole song and dance starts from the top with the next group. When you see the children having fun splashing about, you almost forget there's still a world outside this building.

One boy who likes to make others laugh gets back in the water right after he's fully dressed, much to the amusement of the other children. Mischievous children get on Sieny's nerves, but I really like them. It's how civil disobedience starts, and if we were all civilly disobedient we wouldn't stand for all these ordinances, right? I feel indolence and docility are far more damaging in the long run than defiance. I always have heated discussions about this with Nol. He says it's actually better to go with the wind because the wind can change direction by itself at some point.

Towards the end of the morning, when the sun is at its highest, I've slogged away at water games so much that I'm drenched down to my underwear.

'I might as well get in the pool myself,' I say.

'I don't think that's a good idea.' Sieny laughs. 'I don't think they want to see you naked.'

Her words are picked up immediately by a pair of children's ears. 'Yeah! Betty's swimming naked!' they howl, and soon enough everyone is chanting: 'Betty naked! Betty naked!'

I play along. 'Shhh! I promise I'll swim in my birthday suit if none of you move for five minutes. Not even a teensy-weensy bit.'

Sieny gives me a disapproving look. She's such a prude that she feels even bare ankles are naked, and she prefers to wear long socks even on warm days like this.

Not that I'd actually get undressed here, but I know the children just aren't able to sit still, even if they wanted to. It has to do with their muscle tension.

They make a few valiant attempts anyway, and every time they fail they all start screaming: 'Again!'

I'm startled to see Pimentel in the doorway. She beckons me.

In my sopping wet shoes, I walk up to her.

'What do you think you're doing?'

I don't know how to answer her question and just shrug. I'm never lost for words ordinarily, but with Pimentel I never know quite how to respond. I see Sieny chat with her regularly, but it's as if my words falter in her presence.

'We don't want this place to start looking like the monkey house at the Artis zoo. Do you understand?'

'Of course, director.' I try my best not to avert my gaze and keep looking in her light eyes. We're both small, but her personality is so much bigger. Not to mention her authority.

She then shakes her head and lifts her eyebrows. 'My goodness, where do you get all this malarkey from?'

'My grandmother always says I have an overactive imagination,' I say, shrugging apologetically.

A tiny smile appears on her face now after all. 'I'm sure you do, but inside these walls we don't want to have it rub off on the children.'

'I'll make sure that doesn't happen, director!' I give a salute, hoping that's the end of it.

'But they are affected, young lady,' she says again, sternly. 'I found this.' She takes a piece of paper from her apron and unfolds it in front of me. I immediately recognise my own handwriting.

If you were my little piggy, I'd scrub you down.
I'd put you in a little cage and always keep you around.
I'd teach you to poo on a little pot.
And clear your snout of all the snot.
I'd poke you, prod you all the time.
Rinse your mouth, you little schwein.

'Did you write this?'

There's no point denying it's mine. 'Yes, just a little rhyme. That's not so bad, is it?' I say, feigning innocence. 'Apart from the word "poo", of course.'

'Betty, you're not stupid. You know very well what's wrong with this. It doesn't say swine, it says *schwein* – in *German*. It's an implicit indictment of the occupiers.'

I raise my chin and look at her. No longer shy, or apologetic, but impudent. A look that can infuriate my mother. 'So? They can do whatever they want, and we're expected to obey.'

'You're putting the children in danger!' she says in a voice that will take no lip. 'If they repeat what you taught them, they could be arrested just like that. You do understand, don't you? A hundred times, I want you to write: *I, Betty Oudkerk, will not come up with silly nursery rhymes anymore.*'

I hadn't thought of that. 'My sincere apologies...' I stammer, ashamed.

'Regret always comes after the fact,' she says, then strides off.

After the Sabbath, Gerrit comes home with us. I have my arms clasped around him nearly the whole time because I've missed him so. Then he turns towards my mother and says he wants to have a word in private with her. Mama, who was busy making a grocery list, looks up immediately.

'What's this about?' I inquire.

'None of your business, Betty. Shoo.'

Begrudgingly, I leave the kitchen. I try to hear what they're saying on the other side of the door, which I've left ajar on purpose, but I can't understand them. All I pick up on is my mother's shock when she exclaims: 'My dear God... Why didn't you tell me sooner?'

Gerrit makes her lower her voice with a firm 'shhh.' Afterwards, I hear only agitated whispering, but I can't make out any words. Then Mother begins to sob. I consider barging in or stomping up the stairs to my bedroom. But maybe it's really best not to know what was said; I've had to hear enough bad news already.

'What are you doing here?' It's Leni, who catches me hunched over with my ear to the door.

'Nothing,' I stammer, but Gerrit has noticed us already and calls us in from the kitchen. Nol, Japie and Granny are summoned as well.

Mother sits at the kitchen table with a mottled face and teary eyes. She's holding a letter in her hands.

'I wanted to inform Mother first,' Gerrit says, 'that's why I asked you to leave us alone for a moment.' His accusatory eyes dart at me, then he goes on. 'A few days ago, like so many others, I was summoned to work at a labour camp—'

'Dammit, why didn't you say so?' Nol says. 'I'm sure I can get you a job with the Jewish Council.'

'I don't want a job with those two-faced scoundrels.'

'Calm down now,' my grandmother tells Gerrit. 'I don't know the chairman, David Cohen, but Asscher happens to be a fine gentleman.' I can tell Gerrit disagrees, but we never contradict Granny.

'Mr Cohen's daughter works with me at the nursery. I could ask if she can do something?'

Gerrit ignores my words. 'Lous and I already discussed it with her family,' he goes on. 'We want to escape via France to Switzerland. We would have gone already, but I wanted to wait for Nol's marriage. This changes things.' Gerrit pulls the letter from Mother's hands and lays it down before us.

NOTICE TO APPEAR, TO GERRIT OUDKERK.

'In connection with your possible participation in the

expansion of labour in Germany under police supervision, you are to report to the transit camp Westerbork for a physical examination and medical assessment,' I read out loud.

'Where's that? The village of Hooghalen?' Japie asks.

'Somewhere in Groningen,' Nol answers.

'In the province of Drenthe,' Leni corrects him.

The letter is from the Central Agency for Jewish Emigration and has a date and time when Gerrit is expected to report. At the bottom of the letter is a list of belongings he can bring: a pair of work boots, drinking cups, a food bowl, bedding and wool blankets and so forth.

'I heard at the nursery that lots of people aren't going,' I say. 'A colleague's father and sister—'

'Betty, please be quiet,' Gerrit huffs at me. 'This isn't about who you know or what you heard. This is about a notice I have to comply with, or else I'll end up in a prison camp.'

'In Mauthausen, you mean,' Leni says.

Gerrit ignores Leni's remark and, with a stern look, says, 'I've come to say goodbye. I'm sorry, Nol, I can't be at your wedding.'

Japie runs towards him and grabs him by the waist. In tears, he tells Gerrit he can't leave. It's what I'd wanted to do, but I'm grown up.

A little later, my brother leaves carrying his violin, which until now he'd left at home because he didn't want to burden his in-laws with his scratching.

CHAPTER 6

TUESDAY, 14 JULY 1942

Every time we think the last ordinance has been announced, there's something new again. Everyone is affected. My brother Japie absolutely hates the fact we won't be allowed to fish anymore from the end of May. He could spend hours with a friend and a fishing rod in hand by the Amstel river. My grandmother is upset when she reads we have to hand in all art and precious metals to Lippmann, Rosenthal & Co, also known as the robber bank. She immediately hid her jewellery, beautiful heirlooms passed on from generation to generation, including her pearls. I think it's especially tough that public transportation is now off limits to Jews and I can no longer take the tram.

Walking through Sarphatistraat on my way to work, I can hear the screaming from a distance. I'm on my guard immediately. It would be wiser to turn around now, but I'm too curious. As I approach, I see the German police dragging people from their homes and taking them to the crowd waiting outside. Fifty, maybe up to a hundred, people have been rounded up; they're all wearing a Star of David on their coat or waistcoat. The police have them surrounded with their rifles drawn, like they're a herd of wild animals.

I join a group of people looking at the spectacle from a distance and ask if they know what's going on. A small, plump woman looks at me and says, nodding at my bosom: 'Put that thing away, they'll arrest you in a second.'

I quickly take off my raincoat with the star on it and drape it over my arm.

'Those Greens will take you without a second thought,' she adds for emphasis. The German officers of the *Ordnungspolizei* are popularly known as the Greens because of the colour of their uniforms. I thank her for warning me, but her attention is already drawn by something happening further down the street. An elderly man trips and falls on the cobbles, his hat rolling on a bit. I feel I should go help him up and brush off his hat, but one of the Greens is already standing beside him.

'Get up!' he yells. The old Jew slowly gets back up on his feet, but just before he's standing upright the officer kicks him in the stomach. 'Faster, idiot, faster!'

A woman starts to scream out her window: 'My husband isn't Jewish. He's married to me. Let him go!' Her breaking voice echoes off the housefronts. There's no reaction. I wonder which of these people is her husband, and why he doesn't say who he is.

All of a sudden, one of the officers looks back at the group of onlookers around me. It takes effort not to avert my eyes and keep looking as if this isn't about me as well. More than anything, I'd like to break away and run into a side street. Away from this horrible sight. For fear my escape would give me away, I remain frozen in my tracks.

The officer is distracted by a child that suddenly escapes the crowd and runs off. He curses in German. A dog is set loose and gives chase to the boy.

'Lex, look out!' a woman cries. She's immediately hit in

the head with a rifle butt. Down the street, the aggressive animal has grabbed the boy by his coat. Still, he doesn't give up. In the struggle, he's able to take off his coat and runs off into an alley.

More cursing in German, and the arrestees are getting stirred up now. Woeful moaning from the woman, then suddenly and with renewed vigour she screams: 'A child, how dare you!'

A man siding with her: 'You'll never catch him, you hear? You hear?' He then tries to comfort the woman.

A loud order to stay calm. Warning shots in the air. All of a sudden, everyone is silent.

'Dirty krauts. I'll scratch their eyes out if I get the chance,' hisses the plump lady next to me. She then gives me a quizzical look. 'What are you still doing here? If I were you, I'd get out of here.'

Without saying a word, I turn around and quickly flee this awful scene.

I'm late arriving at the nursery. Even the long detour I took didn't quite calm me down from what I'd seen earlier. I hope to run into Sieny so I can tell her my story, but in the staff room, the girls have circled around a new colleague who's in tears. Her sister was arrested. When Sieny sees me, she says: 'Her sister had a *Sperre*, for crying out loud. That should exempt her from being summoned, shouldn't it? But now she's been arrested anyway.'

The randomness of notices leaves us at a complete loss; there's no rhyme or reason whatsoever. One of the girls says it depends on the district, and I suggest it might have to do with surnames, in alphabetical order.

'Our neighbour works for the Jewish Council,' another continues. 'His adult sons didn't get a notice. So it's more a matter of having the right ties to the Council. It's nepotism, plain and simple.'

There's no shortage of opinions or speculations. Only Mirjam remains silent. I don't know if the others noticed, but I see her hiding her folded hands in her lap and blinking a lot behind her glasses.

Then Pimentel enters and puts an end to the discussion. 'Ladies, get to work! The children are waiting, and they have nothing to do with the suffering taking place outside this building.'

I find that hard to believe. I suspect these children have to deal with this every day, but I know this isn't the moment to act smart.

I'm one of the last to leave the staff room, when I see Pimentel take a young colleague aside for a moment.

In the baby room, I deliberately stand next to Mirjam, and we simultaneously change two babies on the long changing table. 'Does your father ever say anything about things like this?' I ask as breezily as I can.

She jerks her head towards me. 'He's not allowed to talk about it,' she says defensively.

'I understand. I'm sure it's hard for you. I think I'd be nagging at my father all day to try to know more,' I say, still in a tone that doesn't fit the seriousness of what I saw today.

'My father is a religious and good man. He's always done everything he can to help others.' She tosses the soiled diaper in the basket and slides a clean cloth under the girl's bottom.

'That's great. Helping others, I mean. My father is dead.' I see the boy I'm changing only has a wet diaper.

'I'm sorry to hear that,' Mirjam says. With that, our conversation ends and we focus entirely on our work.

. . .

With a tense face, my mother slides an extra edition of *The Jewish Weekly* towards me across the table.

'Have a look at this.'

'Seven hundred Jews were arrested today,' the front page reads. 'If the four thousand designated Jews do not report for the labour camps in Germany this week, all seven hundred arrestees will be transferred to a concentration camp. Signed, the chairmen of the Jewish Council, A. Asscher and D. Cohen.'

I immediately realise the group of people rounded up like cattle earlier this morning are among those seven hundred prisoners.

'Gerrit left just in time,' my mother says. She wipes the table with a cloth, seemingly also brushing off the question whether others should have to pay for his departure.

'Dammit, he should have taken my offer to work for the Council,' Nol says in frustration.

'Calm down!' Granny folds her arms under her breasts, as if rearranging them. 'Whether we work for the Council or not, they won't spare our family if they intend to eradicate the Jews.'

'Shhh, the children are here,' says Engel, trying to calm things down.

'I'm not a baby anymore,' Japie says indignantly.

'They're setting us all against each other.' Leni has her suitcase open on the dresser and puts some extra food in it. Tomorrow, she'll be leaving for the Dutch Israelite Hospital, where she'll be a resident nurse from now on.

'Eat something, Betty,' my mother says.

'Not hungry,' I say. 'I'm going to sleep. I had a busy day.'

In bed, I try to forget the image of all those desperate people I saw this morning. The mother whose child escaped, the old man who tripped. The screaming from the window of the woman who cried that her husband wasn't a Jew because he was married to her.

CHAPTER 7

THURSDAY, 16 JULY 1942

In The Jewish Weekly, *we read that Jews will no longer be allowed to practice sports. Bicycles and other forms of transportation have to be handed in. From now on, I can only go to the nursery on foot. There's a curfew between eight o'clock in the evening until six in the morning. We're no longer allowed to use the telephone or visit non-Jews. Fish markets are now off-limits. And we can only grocery shop between four and six in the afternoon, when everyone else has already been and the shelves are empty. I wonder when the newspapers will say we're no longer allowed to breathe.*

The director's room is furnished like a cosy living room, with on one side a seating area with two old leather armchairs and a dark-green velour two-seater, and on the window side a large desk that Pimentel sits at doing paperwork. It's like she lives here, because every time I'm here she's somewhere in the building. Even when my shift is until closing, she's often here with visitors – men as well. I know she lives a little further down the street with her two sisters, but still it feels like this is her home and I'm visiting her here.

'One moment, Betty. Please have a seat,' says Pimentel, writing something on the piece of paper in front of her.

I'm not quite sure where she wants me to sit: on the chair in front of her desk or in the seating area?

She notices my hesitation, it seems. 'There, on the sofa. Go ahead.'

I go to the sofa and sink in deeper than I expected, which makes it difficult for me to keep my back straight. Pimentel puts down her silver fountain pen and gets up to have a seat in one of the armchairs opposite me.

'Alright, Betty. I'm satisfied overall with your performance. The meeting with my staff also confirms you're a highly optimistic and cheerful young lady, always willing to help out. And the children adore you, which is great to see. But...' There's a long silence. 'We find it hard to tell sometimes who's the child and who's the adult here.'

'Oh, that's not good,' I say contritely.

'Well, you can keep the playfulness,' Pimentel continues. 'But make sure you also know exactly how far you can go. We have a great responsibility here; people are bringing us what's most precious in the world to them. Always keep that in mind, understand?'

'Yes, director, I'll make sure I do,' I say solemnly, managing to put a smile on her face.

'Right, what I called you in for... I understand your sister works at the hospital, right?'

'Yes. Leni. She lives there now too.' Even though my sister and I don't have a particularly strong bond, I feel it's a pity she's left home. For one because I'm now the only girl to help with household chores.

'I'd like to ask you to drop by the hospital every now and then. To pick up medicines, or when there's something wrong with one of the children. Mirjam, for instance, took a baby to the NIZ hospital on Nieuwe Keizersgracht yesterday. But I'd rather she stays here, as head of the department.'

'I understand,' I say.

'So, Betty, do you think I can trust you with this respon-sibility?'

'Of course.'

I walk to the hospital later that afternoon with great pride. The beautiful weather means it's busy in the streets. All the chairs and tables are out at the coffeehouse on the corner. Some actors in front of the theatre are handing out pamphlets. I recognise the red-haired German actress Silvia, who I saw perform last year, and raise my hand at her. Foolishly, because of course she doesn't know who I am. But she kindly waves back.

On the corner of Plantage Kerklaan, I can smell and hear the animals in the Artis zoo, and I pass a group of excited chil-dren. I'm here more often, of course, but never at this time of day. This unexpected walk feels like it's my day off. Like when I was a teenager myself and I would wander further from home all the time, looking for adventure. On the bridge of Plantage Muidergracht, I pause for a moment to look at the boats. Then I turn right alongside the canal and walk along the water, which glistens in the sun. An elderly lady gives me a kind nod. 'Some weather, huh?' In front of the bridge by the hospital, I'm suddenly confronted with the war again. A large sign that reads JEWISH QUARTER leaves no question as to who this open prison is for. The city is no longer a place for me to freely wander.

In the foyer, I'm asked to wait a moment. Most people don't like the smell of hospitals, but I rather like that typical smell that's a mixture of detergent and medicines. I look around to see if I can spot my sister anywhere.

'Betty Oudkerk, right?' There's a boy in a white doctor's coat beside me, surely not much older than myself. His eyes are a blue I've never seen before, like the ocean on colorized post-cards. Several locks of his otherwise combed-back hair hang nonchalantly over his forehead.

'Errm, yes. My sister works here,' I say thoughtlessly, impressed with his handsome appearance.

'Oh, and she is...?'

'Leni Oudkerk, but we don't look alike. I'm the cutest of the two,' I blurt out, extending my hand. 'Betty. Oh no, you already knew that.'

'My name is Leo,' the boy says, laughing. 'Leo de Leon, no joke.'

'Really?' I say in surprise.

'Yes, my parents thought that would be a laugh. So now I always have a great opener. Even when I'm bringing bad news.' He contorts his face, making me burst out laughing instantly.

'There should be some medicines for me here, for the nurs-ery,' I say, pulling myself together.

'That's correct. For Miss Pimentel, right? Please come with me.'

'Do you work here as a nurse, or a doctor in training?'

'The latter,' he says, opening the door for me. This takes us to a small room full of wall cabinets. 'But I really only just started. I still have a long way to go. And you?'

'Nursery teacher in training, and a short way to go,' I say with my cutest smile, which I've practiced often in front of the mirror.

'Well now,' he says, and opens a drawer, standing beside me and briefly touching my arm with his. When he pulls open another drawer, he touches me on purpose. I'm sure of it.

'This is it,' he says, and hands me the brown bag of medicines. 'Miss Pimentel already has the instruction leaflets.'

'Great. And if she doesn't, I'll just come back again,' I say off the cuff.

'Please do.'

Leaving the room, I could nearly cry and jump with excitement. That was definitely the cutest and funniest boy I've ever met.

CHAPTER 8

MONDAY, 20 JULY 1942

At present, 480 people have reported voluntarily with the Zentralstelle on Euterpestraat, where the Germans do all the paperwork for the deportation of Jews. But because still too few Jewish men have complied with the request, the raids continue. Hunting Jews isn't too difficult with such a high concentration of yellow stars in Amsterdam.

From the room at the front of the nursery, a colleague and I are looking at the expensive Mercedes parked in front of the theatre's door. A car I've seen before. The black paint glistens in the sun, and the German officer behind the wheel has taken off his hat and is leaning back in his seat, enjoying the warmth on his face. You have a good view of that pompous white building from the baby section at the front. Mirjam turns a blind eye to us peeking out every now and then. 'Two at a time!' she says in a stern voice. 'And stand in the corner by the curtain.' There really isn't much to see, but the fact that this high official's posh car is parked there in front of the door with two other army vehicles is unusual. Especially because there's a matinee show being staged, and none of us can imagine a German commander coming to watch Jewish actors. Early in the war, we would still see German soldiers go in for some entertainment, but this is no longer appropriate. Now it's only someone who comes to check whether the pieces aren't political or provocative every now and then.

The girls' speculations about what might be going on are getting increasingly far-fetched. 'Maybe the commander has a crush on an actress?' 'They're bringing all actors to Camp Westerbork to cheer things up over there.' 'They're auditioning for a part.'

At last, there's some movement in front of the theatre. Germans in grey SS uniforms exit the building, followed by a bigwig indeed, a tall man with a thin face. My colleague thinks it's Lages, the head of the SD. But Mirjam tells us it's Hauptsturmführer Aus der Fünten, the man who is sending all the young people to labour camps.

The driver has sprung up and walks around the car to open the door for his superior. He then gets back in and steers the flashy Mercedes onto the street, followed by the two other vehicles.

In the afternoon, I have to take a toddler for a visit to the hospital. The small boy is terribly constipated, with nothing whatsoever coming out of him. Pimentel made an appointment with the doctor at the NIZ to have him checked out. Maybe the poor child needs something to become unblocked.

I've put the boy in a stroller and feel like a young mother when I'm pushing him out the door. There are several actors on the other side of the street, smoking. This is my chance to ask what those Germans wanted from them today. I wait until a horse cart and two cars pass and then cross the street. The red-haired actress, Silvia, is there too. She sucks on a cigarette with her painted lips, listening to the conversations her colleagues are having.

'There's nothing we can do!' one of them says. 'That's the whole problem.'

'Then what about the shows?' the other asks. 'The tickets were sold already.'

On the posters hanging next to the entrance, I see she's playing in the matinee show *Wiegelied* this week.

'Is the show not going on?' I ask the pretty actress.

She looks at me in exasperation, which makes me feel uncomfortable, like I've said something wrong.

'Apparently not.'

'Was it cancelled?'

She leaves the group and takes two steps in my direction. Before talking to me, she casts a quick glance over her shoulder to be sure no one is near enough to listen in on us. 'We've been banned from performing,' she says with that dramatic facial expression so typical for stage artists. 'You didn't hear this from me, but Hauptsturmführer Aus der Fünten got on stage with his tall boots and claimed the theatre.' I smell her strong perfume mixed with the cigarette smoke on her breath. 'The theatre will be serving as a deportation centre from now on.'

At the risk of coming across as foolish, I ask: 'What's a deportation centre?'

'All Jews who are summoned for the labour camps have to report here. That's all I know,' she says, shrugging. 'We're not allowed to ask questions. We're not allowed to go home or contact friends or family, and we have to wait here for further instructions.'

'But there's no one keeping you prisoner here, is there?' I ask. 'I'd just leave.'

'To be put on a transport as a consequence? No, thanks. They've taken down all our names, so there's nowhere for us to go.' Silvia throws her cigarette on the ground and stamps it out with her elegant heel. 'Too bad you won't be able to see *Wiegelied* now,' she says with a sad smile. 'It was a great show.'

At the hospital, there's no sign of Leo, the cute doctor in training. After the doctor on duty examines the boy and I'm given medicines for his intestinal problems, I make my way towards the exit again. Nearly twisting my neck looking for Leo, who really has to be around here somewhere, I fail to see my sister approach.

'Betty? What are you doing here?' she says so loud several people look at us. I'm irritated at how she always just sees me as her little sister.

'I had to stop by the doctor with this little man. What about you?' I ask.

'I work here, obviously.'

'It was a joke,' I say drily. 'How do you like your room here?'

'It's great. I really needed this,' she says, smoothing her nurse's uniform with her hands. 'It's not getting any merrier back home.'

'No, tell me about it. Then again, I can finally go to sleep without that reading lamp of yours shining in my eyes now.'

'Well, so it's all for the best that I'm gone,' my sister says indignantly.

'That's not what I meant.' My sister and I don't speak each other's language.

'This must be your sister!' Leo is suddenly standing beside me and extends his hand to Leni. 'Leo, doctor in training.'

Leni brightens immediately in his presence and gives him a coquettish smile. 'My sister never told me she knows a young man here.'

'Well, we've only seen each other once before,' Leo says.

'But that's about to change,' Leni says flippantly. 'She'll make up an illness to see a cute guy if she has to.'

I'm utterly mortified.

'I'm sure she'll be fine, right, Betty?' Leo says before I can react.

I'm burning with shame, but I bounce the ball back: 'She's talking about herself. My sister is desperate for a man. I need to get going. Have a great day!'

I push the stroller between my sister and Leo and make my way to the exit without looking back. Behind me, I hear Leo say: 'Nice sister you've got there.' Well, that certainly hushed her up. My sister thinks I'm flirting, but I'm not. I just have a better sense of humour. And bigger breasts, but I can't help that now, can I?

CHAPTER 9

WEDNESDAY, 22 JULY 1942

Each day, trains full of mainly young men depart for Camp
Westerbork in the village of Hooghalen, a former Jewish refugee
camp that was set up several years ago by the Dutch government
to shelter refugees from Germany and Austria. However, the
government demanded the Committee for Jewish Refugees pay
back the one million guilders in construction costs in
instalments.

Nol and Jetty's wedding is going on as planned today, despite
the raids. I waver a bit in front of my wardrobe. Clothes are in
short supply these days, but as a child of parents who owned a
large fabric shop I'm not wanting for anything. Still, I feel I have
nothing to wear today. The dress my mother left out for me is
too tight around my bosom, and it's too late to do anything about
it now. The suit I wore at Gerrit's wedding is too warm. In the
end, I go for a light blue silk blouse with short puff sleeves and a
dark blue ribbon. Below, I wear the dark skirt I wore at Japie's
Bar Mitzvah. Thankfully, I haven't gained any weight around
my waist and thighs. Not that I could have, as there's less to

snack on all the time. The fact that my breasts got bigger despite this might have to do with my genes. Or maybe fussing with all those babies has given my body ideas, and it's already set up a milk factory.

When I come downstairs, I see the women are all dressed up. Mother is wearing a dress with a tight-fitting top and a dashing flared skirt made of an ornately decorated pink fabric with silver threads. Granny wears a greyish-green A-line dress that somewhat covers up her curvy build. The cuffs of the sleeves have pieces of soft fur, and she's wearing nearly her entire collection of jewellery. Engel is also dressed festively in a sparkly dress of sorts that looks like something you'd wear at a carnival. I exchange glances with Japie, after which he burst out laughing and chuckles his way to the front room. Mother gives me an irritated look: 'What's the matter?'

'I think it's odd,' I say.

'What do you find odd?'

'That you're all dressed as if it's the King's birthday at a time when we're being treated like lepers. That we're off to celebrate a Jewish wedding and keeping silent about the fact there's absolutely nothing to celebrate here.'

'*Tais-toi!*' my grandmother says. 'You still have to sew on your star.'

I actually wanted to go on – *That's what I mean! Why would we celebrate love when there's so much hatred? If Gerrit can't be there because he's fled? Something we should do ourselves before it's too late. No, we cling to our daily lives, or what remains, and try our best to keep our balance on the narrow ledge we're left to move around on.*

But I only think these words as I pull the yellow star off my raincoat and go get a needle and thread to sew it onto my blouse.

My sombre mood is mainly due to the fact we haven't heard from Gerrit yet. Surely he must have arrived in Switzerland already? We're no longer allowed to own a telephone, but we'd agreed he would call the nursery. Pimentel arranged for us to be allowed to keep a phone there, for emergencies. Maybe he lost the number, or maybe he hasn't been able to access a telephone in Switzerland yet. A postcard will take a long time now, but surely he could have sent a telegram? I feel it's unlike Gerrit not to contact us somehow on the day of his brother's wedding. And no one is talking about it, like he doesn't exist.

'Can we finally go now?' Nol, who's been biting his nails in the front room this past hour, peeks around the corner impatiently. Mother and Granny are busy solving the complex puzzle of fitting all the dishes of food they've cooked in the refrigerator. Once at last they succeed, they yell in unison: 'Yes, let's go!'

Since Jews are no longer allowed to rent carriages, Nol has no choice but to pick up his bride on foot. He leads the way in his striped grey wedding suit. Even though Mother had the suit taken in, it still looks too large around his round shoulders. The top hat Father wore at his wedding with Mother sits on Nol's head. It's much too warm for such dark headgear, and I see sweat run down his cheeks. The wedding bouquet in his small hands is starting to wilt from the strong sun. Japie, who doesn't seem to know what to do with his fast-growing body, slouches alongside him. Mama and Granny walk behind them arm in arm, their frivolous hats bobbing up and down with each step. I was tasked with holding Engel by the arm, which is nearly unbearable because of her musty smell, but if I don't keep her firmly pressed against me I'm afraid she'll trip and not get up again. Some aunts, uncles and cousins have joined us at the back, so we're quite a crowd walking in the July sun together. It seems grotesque, and I feel embarrassed when we pass people on the way. De Pijp has more non-Jews than Jews living there now, which makes it extra risky for us to be parading through the street here. Some people react with good cheer: 'Congratulations!' and 'Mazzeltov'. A jolly man on a bicycle asks if we lost the bride. An overgrown teenager yells: 'It's still a long walk to Jerusalem!' at which his friends burst out laughing. From a balcony, we hear: 'Jew rats!' A small girl points her finger at us and says: 'Mommy look, dirty Jews.' She's cuffed on the ear straight away by her mother, then starts to cry and says: 'That's what Papa always says.' But worse than all these remarks are the condescending glares from people passing by silently.

At Nieuwe Achtergracht, Nol veers off to ring the doorbell of his bride's family home. We continue onto Rapenburgerstraat, to the *shul* in Beis Jisroeil, the Joodsch Ons Huis Association building, where Leni is also going straight from the hospital. I haven't seen her since the incident with Leo, and honestly I'm not looking forward to it either. She made a total fool of me in front of him. As if I were some schoolgirl in desperate need of a boyfriend. The more I think about it, the more I have to conclude she was trying to flirt with him at my expense.

I already see her in front of the entrance. The suit she's wearing looks good on her. All at once, she looks like a grown woman. I feel a pang of jealousy.

Once Leni has greeted everyone, she comes over to me. 'Hey, sis, that Leo sure is cute.'

'Congrats. You can have him,' I say sourly.

'I knew I'd ruffled your feathers,' she says with a laugh.

'Me? Are you crazy? I really don't care.'

'Well, if you don't care, I guess I don't need to tell you what he said about you,' she says, feigning disinterest.

'Yes, you do! What did he say?'

Mother interrupts our conversation; we have to go in.

'What did he say?' I whisper as Mother ushers us to the front row seats.

She looks at me, knowingly.

'Leni, please...'

'Stop it, ladies,' Mother says. I fold my arms and give my sister an angry look. She's not intimidated in the least, it seems, and stares back at me with a triumphant glare, which only enrages me more.

'They're coming!' cries Japie, who has remained by the door.

'Be a good sport, Leni.'

'He thought you were a very pretty lady,' my sister says when she's done teasing me. 'Funny as well. I put the latter in perspective, of course.'

'You didn't!'

She smiles mysteriously. 'Just a wee bit. Don't worry, he can't be persuaded otherwise anymore. He even asked if you're seeing anyone.'

My sulky mood lifts at once.

Just then, the choir sings 'Baruch Haba' – Blessed be all who come – and Nol comes walking through the *shul* doors locking arms with Jetty. My brother gleams with pride next to his bride, who decided to ignore the war and wear an exquisite wedding dress with a wide skirt, large puffed sleeves and a tulle veil. The yellow star sewn on her side is barely visible.

CHAPTER 10

THURSDAY, 6 AUGUST 1942

Over 6,600 Jewish men have been transported from Amsterdam to Westerbork at this point. Westerbork is a transit camp and consists of a bunch of barracks, which together form a village of sorts. They say you can take courses there, that there are shops where you can buy things using a special kind of money, that you can play sports and that they even have a football competition. Children go to school as normal, and there's also a nursery for the little ones because all the parents have to work. There's a need for teachers for the schools and medical personnel like doctors and nurses for the large hospital. Germans are highly concerned about diseases breaking out. There's a greater chance you'll be allowed to stay in Westerbork if you have a specialism they can use, like making and repairing shoes, welding, carpentry, nursing or teaching. Because no one wants to be sent to the east.

There's an SS man by the door of the white theatre all the time now, overseeing the people coming in. So many people go in, you'd almost think there was a show. And it's not just young men with duffle bags anymore. I see a pregnant woman and her husband, who's lugging along a large steamer trunk. A father with four grown-up sons with only two small suitcases. Two women who go through the revolving door holding hands and get caught with their luggage. The guard lends them a hand. A woman in a fur coat over her summer clothes and a floor lamp in her hands. An old grandpa with his dog. Even though Pimentel insisted we don't look, it's impossible not to cast a glance outside every now and then to see all these people disappearing into the building. Especially as we've never seen anyone come out.

It's two o'clock, and most of the children are sleeping. Pimentel has asked everyone – if work allows it – to gather in the hall. Within minutes, the room is filled with more than thirty trainees, carers and teachers. The director addresses us from the balustrade.

'Ladies, many of us here at the nursery are feeling a bit on edge of late because of the theatre, which now serves as a gathering place for Jews who are about to depart. I understand everyone is affected by this. Maybe you have family there, or close friends. Still, from what I understand the living conditions in Westerbork are reasonably good.'

'But what's happening in Poland, where people are being sent on from Westerbork?' It's Sieny asking the question.

We all grow restless, and chatter fills the room.

'I'm aware of the rumours circulating myself,' says Pimentel, raising her voice. 'My source – who's in direct contact with England – tells me these horror stories are incorrect. People are put to work in the Auschwitz concentration camp, just like in Westerbork. But the facilities are quite a bit worse, this is true. Everyone knows rumours get blown out of proportion when they come from hearsay. And I don't think we should go along with this hysteria.'

I raise my hand on impulse and start to speak even before

I'm given permission: 'I once heard two SS men say how in Poland they're lining up Jews in front of mass graves and shooting them.'

'Betty, I'm expressly asking you not to sow panic and spread rumours.'

'Sorry, I'm just saying what I heard...'

'I want to have a word with you in a moment.'

Sieny takes my hand and gives it a quick pinch as a sign to not let it bother me.

'Why would the Germans want to waste free labour? They need us to keep the factories running. So there's no sense in doom-mongering. We have to sit this time out, but I'm sure it'll end at some point. The Allies are slowly gaining ground, and the rest of the world now also understands human rights are being violated here. The world won't let this happen!' The group erupts in applause.

Pimentel ends by saying something about children and their mental flexibility, which allows them to survive in even the most difficult circumstances. 'They don't have the physical strength or verbal prowess of adults. But still, they're able to survive by being inconspicuous thanks to their ability to adapt. Something we adults might learn from them by closely observing the little creatures we work with every day.'

My anger has subsided, and I wonder what sort of scolding I'll be getting from Pimentel later.

'Come in!' she says from the other side of the door.

I take a deep breath and press the handle down. 'You wanted to see me.'

'Have a seat, Betty.'

Pimentel points at the chair in front of her desk. She closes the folder in front of her and leans back. 'So, you still don't understand.'

The words 'understand what?' nearly come out of my mouth, but I keep my lips sealed.

'When will you learn that it doesn't help to always just say whatever pops into your head? You're a smart girl. It isn't too difficult, is it?' The grey curl on her head moves with every word she stresses in a sentence. 'How do you think we'd be doing if I only ever said what I thought?'

I assume it's a rhetorical question, so I don't answer.

'Well?' Pimentel says.

Ah, so it seems I am expected to say something. 'I, errm—'

But then she cuts me off again. 'Freely venting our first thoughts at a time like this isn't just unwise, it's outright stupid.' She suddenly gets up and looks out the window. 'This here!' She points at the theatre. 'It's a shameful, disgraceful, monstrous operation. But us Jews are public enemy number one already, so whatever criticisms I might have, it would only work against me to voice them.' She abruptly turns to face me. 'You, I, all of us here can only hope to buy time by staying one step ahead of them. And how do we do this?'

'Errm... by thinking?'

'That's right. By keeping your head. And that means not only thinking for ourselves, but also for those around us who are vulnerable. Girls whose families aren't as good as yours. Who might be less intelligent.'

All at once, I understand. She thinks highly of me, she has all this time and only wants me to act more responsibly. For me to grow up. 'I understand completely, Director Pimentel. And I promise I won't disappoint you anymore.'

'I hope not. You can go now.'

As I can't show my gratitude by hugging her, I take a small, ridiculous bow. 'Thank you, director.'

Feeling special, chosen, I'm about to leave her office but then hear Pimentel behind me say: 'You know who you could take an example from? Your friend Sieny. She knows how it works.'

And just like that my high spirits plummet.

'I'll do that.'

'Oh, one second.' She gets a list from her drawer and hands it to me. 'We need these medicines from the NIZ.'

It's raining outside, and I'm met with the sickly smell of damp hair and unwashed fabric when I enter the hospital. I haven't seen Leo since that time with Leni, and I really hope I'll run into him again at the pharmacy. It's much busier than normal, like everyone chose this place to shelter from the variable weather in the middle of summer. The hospital staff diligently make their way through the crowd of visitors. Three times, one of the patients grabs my arm, and I have to explain that I'm not a nurse here. I finally reach the medicine dispensary and see Leo at work beside a male colleague. My heart skips a beat or two immediately. In the days since I last saw him, my daydreams about him have taken on a fairy-tale quality. I've rehearsed different scenarios in my head in which I not just respond to his fictional questions with witty answers but also catch him off guard with my self-assured look.

'Hello, a very good day to you,' I say cheerily. Unfortunately, it's not Leo but his colleague who comes over to ask what he can do for me.

A bit too confident, I say: 'Your colleague usually helps me. He knows what I need.'

'I can help you just as well if you give me the prescription slip.'

I have little choice but to hand over Pimentel's order. As he goes over to the medicine cabinet, I turn towards Leo, who sits stooped over his work. 'How's Doctor De Leon doing?' I ask as nonchalantly as I can.

Leo looks up, irked, but then sees me standing there and jumps up. 'Betty, great to see you! Sorry, I was busy with this order list. It's a painstaking task.'

'I was starting to wonder. Did I not leave an impression on him?'

'Oh no... No...' Leo seems a bit taken aback by my candour.

Boldness isn't just my greatest strength, it's also my main weakness. Especially when I try to fill the uncomfortable silences I cause myself.

'Oh, that's alright. I've already developed a good relationship with your colleague.' I point past him at his colleague, who's rounding up the various medicines.

'Oh, but you're in good hands with him as well,' Leo says, coming towards me on the other side of the counter.

'Perhaps, but he's wearing a wedding ring, and you're not.' I sometimes don't even know myself where I get the audacity from.

'That's entirely right,' Leo says with a crooked grin on his face. 'Both you and I aren't wearing one.'

The colleague joins us. 'Pardon me,' he says to Leo, who's standing in the way.

'Of course,' Leo says, stepping back and making a funny face behind his colleague's back. I have to force myself not to laugh.

'This is everything that was on the note. If you could just sign here.'

I write my ornate signature and start to think I've advertised myself plenty already. If Leo doesn't take the bait now, I should probably just let it go.

'Thank you kindly,' I say to the colleague. 'Have a great day! You too, Mr De Leon.' I throw him one last smile, turn around and walk off. Not too fast, so he can still come after me. Unfortunately, this doesn't happen. When I'm by the exit, I take a deep breath and step over the threshold out into the open air, where I can let the persistent rain wash off this enervating encounter.

I open my umbrella and start to walk, when behind me I hear: 'Betty, would you like to meet up some time?'

Leo, in his white coat, is standing behind me in the pouring rain. He gives me a helpless look. 'Sorry, I was afraid to ask before.'

CHAPTER 11

SATURDAY, 8 AUGUST 1942

There's another extra edition of The Jewish Weekly. *It says everyone summoned to be deployed for work and failing to report will be sent to Mauthausen as a consequence. The same goes for Jews not wearing a star on their clothing or who move house without permission. Because most parents of boys sent there last year have received a notice of death by now – their son was allegedly shot while attempting to escape or perished from some illness – anything is better than to be sent to Austria.*

I'm nervous as I wait for Leo, who's picking me up at four o'clock. The rain puddles from this morning have dried since, and the weather is perfect for walking. I'm wearing my favourite dress, made of mint-green silk with dark-green woven leaves. The dress is several years old already, but it fits me better now than it used to, and I feel confident wearing it, and pretty. With a short coat on top – which also has my star on it – my choice of clothes isn't too conspicuous. I don't want to arouse Mother's suspicion. I lied to her about going to meet my old friend Tineke Baller from Amstelveen. 'She's still allowed to ride a bicycle and is coming our way, and then we'll go for a walk along the Amstel river.'

Mother looks at me in surprise. Were Tineke and I still in touch? How was her family doing? And could I please give her father her best regards? I regret not thinking of a different cover story. One that would raise fewer questions.

Tineke was my best friend at the domestic science school and was from a strict Dutch Reformed Christian family. Her father worked for a trading company in Vijzelstraat, and when he was dispatched to a subsidiary in Germany in the thirties he was so shocked by the open anti-Semitism that he decided to move back to the Netherlands in less than six months. He would have nothing to do with it. The last time I visited Tineke's home, her father took me aside and said, with an insistence I'd only known from teachers and rabbis before, that I could always come to them, should it be necessary. That was a year ago now. I remember thinking this was an overly worried reaction from Mr Baller at the time.

The doorbell rings. I tell Mother she's here and run downstairs. Instead of Leo, there's a cousin of Mother's at the door, a disagreeable woman who's always looking for gossip. The last time she visited our home, she'd heard the shop had been taken over by Mrs Koot. Mother told her cousin how humiliating it was for her to have to slide Koot's mail under the shop's door each morning. This cousin said: 'It's awful what they did to you. To go from being that rich to this poor! You don't have anything anymore?' When Mother confirmed this was the case, the cousin once again threw a fit of over-the-top sympathy. It felt disingenuous. As if this woman were roused by our misery.

'Betty, is your mother home?'

'Yes, just go upstairs. I'm waiting for someone here.'

'Is that right? For who?'

'A friend. Nothing special.'

'Have fun, child,' she says, pulling me towards her by my

arm. 'Enjoy it while you can. Especially after what happened to your oldest brother.'

I'm startled. 'To Gerrit? What's happened to him?'

'You don't know?' she says, looking shocked. 'Is your mother home?'

I nod. My mouth is suddenly so dry I'm incapable of swallowing.

'Come with me.' She continues to talk as she walks up the stairs. 'I was wondering whether to come here, but then I said to myself: "Suppose they don't know. I'd never forgive myself... Because if I were a mother..."' I follow her up and look under her skirt at the bumpy skin of her fat thighs staggering up the stairs. Will I always see this image when we're talking about Gerrit's fate?

'Betty just told me you don't know yet,' she says to Mother, who's busy kneading dough.

'Know what?' Mother holds her two doughy hands up, as if she's surrendering.

'Someone ratted on Gerrit and his wife, and they were arrested at the French border, two days after they left. I know from hearsay. Someone got a letter from one of the people in the same group. They'd taken a boat down some small rivers to the French border. Someone from the resistance was supposed to be waiting for them there. The guy turned out to be crooked. They're all in a prison camp in Drancy now. I'm sorry, Jet.'

My mother continues to stand there with her arms raised, as her face twists up and her eyes swell with tears. I clench my hands into fists. I'm consumed with hatred for this cousin who felt it necessary to come tell us this. The meaning of the message doesn't seem to sink in.

'Oh my, how awful. You didn't know!' the cousin exclaims. 'Jetty, wash your hands. Come, let me help you.' She pushes Mother towards the sink, where she opens the faucet. My mother shrugs and lets her cousin wash her hands. And I can't believe it. I can't believe it's really true. It's only a rumour. Something this gossipy cousin either grossly exaggerated or made up.

The doorbell jolts me from my thoughts. I run down the stairs and see a happily smiling Leo standing there. I'm so shaken by what's happening upstairs that I haven't yet put on my usual veneer of cheery audacity.

'Good morning, Miss Oudkerk, care for a walk?' I apparently look so shocked that he becomes uncertain. 'We had a date, didn't we?' I smell his aftershave lotion, fresh and spicy.

'Errm, yes, of course...' Should I tell him? Should I tell him what I just heard about my favourite brother?

'If it's inconvenient, I can also come back another time.'

Rather than his usual doctor's coat, he's wearing a sporty polo shirt that shows off his big arms.

'No, it's fine.' I slam the door shut behind me. 'Let's go.'

I start to walk, quickly pulling myself together. I want to remain as ignorant as I was a quarter of an hour ago and focus all my attention on the first official date in my life.

'Koot? Wasn't that your shop before?' Leo says, now walking beside me.

I explain how it came to be that Mrs Koot took our business from us.

'What a story,' Leo says sympathetically. 'And did she steal all your stock too?'

'Yes, all the stock from the shop, but early in the war my mother stockpiled hundreds of food tins, which were in the shop's basement. When we heard Mrs Koot would be a *Verwalter*, we brought the tins up to where we live. Mrs Koot caught us when we were moving all the packs of toilet paper upstairs. "Oh well," my mother said, "on second thought, you can keep them. Just so you'll know what it's like to wipe your behind with paper made for that purpose, rather than the *Volk en Vaderland* Nazi magazine."'

Leo has a good chuckle at my story.

We pass the beginning of Albert Cuyp market, which now also has a sign that says FORBIDDEN FOR JEWS. I tell him that several years ago a third of all merchants here were Jews. That we would always buy our meat and bread here, but that there's not a kosher crumb to be found now.

'Number 54 at the Bakker café is where the Dutch Nazi Party members meet. That tells you all you need to know. Only the diamond polishing factory at number 2 is still working over-time to provide goods that the Germans can use to help fund their weapons industry.'

As we continue on our walk, I talk about my childhood here in De Pijp. How as a child I'd scour the market every day, looking for fruit and vegetables that had fallen from the carts. I'd brush them off, and when I had a bag full I would go inside the shops and give an apple to the butcher, a pear to the poul-terer, prunes to the tobacco salesman, and so forth. They would give me a few cents for my kind gesture each time, which in the end earned me more than if I'd sold it. If I saw a beggar who wasn't drunk, I'd sometimes give him the whole bag of food. Or I'd give him the money I'd received, but only if he promised not to buy alcohol.

Leo looks at me and laughs. He says I'm an unusual girl; I'm not sure the remark is meant to be a compliment. But still I thank him. Better to be an unusual girl than a boring girl.

I tell him I always count the Jewish stars in Van Woustraat on my way to work, so now I know the number of Jews here has gone down by seventy percent since the stars were imple-mented. Leo, who lives in Rivierenbuurt himself, is quite upset over our neighbourhood's metamorphosis. For me, it was a more gradual process, but when I look at our neighbourhood through his eyes I realise this part of town has turned into a district of Jew haters in a short time. I point out the Pronker draper's shop to Leo when we walk by. The window reads:

JEUGDSTORM UNIFORMS ON SALE. They don't just make the Nazi youth movement's uniforms here, but also the black shirts that the NSB and WA wear. There are a lot more crooked tradesmen here, like Abraham Puls's moving company, which deploys trucks to clear out all the homes of Jews who fled or were deported. No one doubts he's collaborating with the police anymore, who are also in the neighbourhood, after all. The PBA, Police Battalion Amsterdam, has confiscated the monastery on Cornelis Troostplein. Everything seems to have a different use now. Even some street names were changed because the Germans don't want to honour Jewish painters. For example, David Blesstraat was turned into Marius Bauerstraat, and Josef Israëlskade is now called Tooropkade.

Walking next to Leo calms me down a bit. The conversation we're having is a lot more serious than the dialogues I'd made up in my head, which didn't include the phrase 'German occupation'. It's a subject I'd hoped to avoid, but it turns out to be impossible to get to know someone without talking about how the war impacts our lives. Unlike at my home, where it isn't spoken about. At work, we whisper about what's happening, but it goes no further than sharing the latest news and gossip in between tasks.

Leo and I have passed the sign that reads JEWISH QUARTER and are at Waterlooplein, which these days is called Hollywood because it's rife with yellow stars. I've never seen it this busy before. Jewish shops are allowed to open no more than two hours per day now, and it's peak rush hour. Market stalls are prohibited, but there's lots of business being done under the awnings. I notice lots of people are wearing rags. This area is quite a bit poorer than De Pijp or the Plantage neighbourhood. Houses are poorly maintained, many windows are broken and the outer walls are sooty. The pungent smell of rotting waste makes me nauseous. I involuntarily start to move closer to Leo so I can smell more of him and less of my surroundings.

Leo talks about how he wants to be a really good doctor later on, and how frustrating it is for him to be unable to continue his studies now. When he was ten, he'd decided he wanted to make people well again when he grew up. Not by giving them pills, but by operating. It was no coincidence that this ambition came about shortly after his sister died. He'd heard his father tell his mother how she would have survived if they'd had a better surgeon. That made him decide to become a surgeon, even if he didn't know this word yet at the time. I spontaneously take his hand, but then let go again after a minute or two because our hands are getting sweaty. I have no idea if it's him or me who's perspiring so much, but both possibilities make me nervous.

We're met by the smell of roasted chestnuts.

'Want some chestnuts?' Leo is already about to order some.

'You'll have to finish the whole bag yourself, because I hate the things.'

'Doesn't everyone like chestnuts?' Leo says, surprised.

I shrug. 'I'm not everyone. We used to eat them quite often during dinner, and my father would make me finish them.' I still recall the chewy chunks in my throat nearly making me retch as I tried to finish my meal. 'Thankfully, my brother Gerrit would sneak a few chestnuts from my plate when my parents weren't looking...'

After saying his name, I'm suddenly no longer able to contain the recent news and start to cry. Leo is taken aback by my unexpected sadness and puts an arm around my quivering shoulders. He leads me through the crowd to a doorway, where he takes a folded handkerchief from his pocket to dry my tears. I'm ashamed of my tear-stained face and the surely unflattering way I try to explain what I heard right before he'd come.

'Why didn't you say so immediately?' Leo asks. 'I'd be grief-stricken myself if I'd got a message like that. It's nothing to be embarrassed about.'

'It's not that...' I'm stumbling for words. 'I didn't want to think about it.'

'But, Betty, horrible things don't disappear when you don't think of them.' He gently dabs my cheek with his handkerchief.

I look into his azure eyes and then bend forward slowly. Even before my lips touch his, there's a police whistle, then swearing: 'Stay where you are!' Children begin to cry, a woman screams. Through the crowd, I see a skinny man running in our direction, followed by two police officers. A final warning. One of the officers pulls his firearm and shoots twice. The running man falls on a cart of onions, which roll across the ground as the owner curses. He gets back up and tries to stagger off, but the officers are on him already and give him a terrible beating with their truncheons. They then tie his hands behind his back and pull him up. 'You're lucky we didn't blow you away.' The crowd has split in two. The liveliness of hundreds of people all going about their business has turned into an almost static image. The sound has died down. Then I see what they're looking at. A group of Jews with suitcases in hand and wearing rucksacks are coming our way through the crowd. They're being held at gunpoint by four Dutch officers. When I look behind me, I see where they're headed. There are army trucks on the corner to take them away.

'Move along, people. Nothing to see here!'

'Dammit, a raid,' Leo whispers. Like an animal backed into a corner, he looks around for a place to escape.

'But you have an exemption for your work, don't you?'

'I'm not wearing a star. It was on my coat. But the weather was so good I took it off at the last moment.'

Now I get why he reacted the way he did. I hadn't even noticed he wasn't wearing a star.

'Everyone who isn't wearing one is sent to Mauthausen,

even if you have a *Sperre*.' Leo pushes me further into the doorway. 'Don't look at them,' he hisses and forcefully presses his mouth against mine. My first impulse is to free myself from his grasp, but then I understand. As long as we stand close together, no one can see his star is missing. I surrender to him. To his hands clasping my head, his mouth kissing me feverishly, making it hard for me to breathe, let alone return his kisses. Then he sticks his tongue in my mouth. I turn my face away from shock. 'Betty, please...' he whispers.

'Alright, but slowly, slower.'

Again, he presses his wet mouth against mine. This time I'm prepared when he touches my lips with his tongue. I open my mouth and almost automatically our movements flow into each other. This is what my sister always meant by a 'real' kiss. This is what the girls at the nursery would giggle about when someone had kissed a boy. This intimate interaction between two mouths against each other, tongues dancing around one another. Disgusting and highly enjoyable at the same time.

Only once we hear the trucks drive off does the never-ending kiss stop. Minutes that could have gone on for hours, as far as I'm concerned. Afterwards, I feel like I'm a different person.

We walk back to Van Woustraat in near silence, where he says a formal goodbye and extends his hand. He thanks me for the wonderful afternoon and apologises once again for the 'emergency measure', as he calls the kiss.

'Who was that, Betty?' Mother asks when I come in. She must have seen us approaching through the window.

'Just a friend,' I say, then disappear into my room. When a little later Mother calls me for dinner, I say I'm sick. And it's no lie. I'm so nauseous I could throw up. Elated and miserable all at once. That's what being in love does to you, apparently.

CHAPTER 12

FRIDAY, 2 OCTOBER 1942

A Sperre *is a provisional exemption from deportation to the labour camps on the rationale that these people aren't available because they're already being deployed for the German labour market indirectly through the Jewish Council. Pimentel has arranged such a* Sperre *for all nursery teachers at the nursery. However, it's only valid for one person, not for family members.*

I've tried to visit Leo at the hospital twice already. He wasn't there the first time. He'd be coming in any moment the second time, and I waited more than an hour for him, leaving him a note in the end.

> *DEAR LEO, CAN WE MEET? YOU CAN FIND ME AT THE NURSERY. LOVE, BETTY.*

I couldn't think of anything better. That was three weeks ago now. The silence is maddening. I talk about it with Sieny, who says I should forget about him. If he's showing this little interest, there's really only one conclusion to be made. But I can't be wrong about what I feel, can I? This was real and has to be mutual, right?

We celebrate Yom Kippur, the day when Jews atone for their sins before God and celebrate forgiveness. Although 'celebrate' is a big word for a day on which nothing may be eaten and you're officially not allowed to wear shoes all day. In fact, work isn't permitted either, but thankfully the nursery was open as usual today.

Granny thought it important that we observe it anyway, but she's the only one wearing a white robe and walking barefoot all day. She's hung a sheet on Engel, which makes her look like a ghost. Mother, who ordinarily goes along with her to keep the peace, pays no mind to her praying mother and has no qualms about eating from the stew on the kitchen table beside her.

It's a relief for me that she's letting go of the rituals imposed on us. But it frightens me at the same time. Mother isn't Mother anymore. It's as if someone else has crawled inside her skin. She no longer plays piano, and she's constantly busy with house-keeping, something she used to prefer leaving to others. All damn day, she's frantically washing, ironing, dusting, sweeping and mopping. She starts her task of getting the home in tip-top shape earlier every morning, when it's perfectly fine already. Even in the empty rooms that belong to Gerrit, Nol and Leni, she'll wipe down the furniture every day. She lets Japie do the groceries, or Granny, who'll use the opportunity to let Engel get some fresh air, something she felt was unnecessary before, but even she feels our home is becoming a bit suffocating. All the roles have been reversed. No one is their old self anymore. I'm happy to be able to leave home in the morning to go to the nursery, which at this point has far fewer children and fewer and fewer beds, tables and seats being used.

. . .

People aren't even notified anymore like they were before the summer. Most Jews have a bag of clothes, food, shoes and toiletries ready by the front door for weeks already. You never know when they'll ring your doorbell, so it's best to be prepared. Because of our work, Nol, Leni and I were given an exemption stamp in our identity cards, but we were unable to get one for Mother, Granny, Engel and Japie. But still they don't have any suitcases ready in the hallway. Mother refuses.

It's ten o'clock in the evening, and I'm just about to go to bed when I hear trucks approaching. We're alert to each and every sound at this point. At this same time a week ago, someone rang the bell at the neighbours' house, at the Overvliet family. 'Child nurse', the neighbour always calls me. My parents were always on good terms with the Overvliets, who often bought things from our shop when this was still allowed. They had a Jewish husband and wife living above them who were arrested by the Dutch police, who are now widely deployed to assist the Ordnungspolizei. The next day, I immediately wrote a letter to my old school friend Tineke Bakker in which I asked if she could talk to her father. I didn't dare commit the phrase 'go into hiding' to paper. I still haven't heard from her yet. And maybe it's too late now.

I dart over to the window to peek behind the curtain. 'Betty, wait!' Mother yells anxiously. 'Turn off the lights first.' Once the ceiling light and floor lamp are off, I pull the curtain a bit to the side. Apart from the trucks' headlights, I can't quite see what's happening because of the unlit streets. I open the window just a crack. I've become very good at listening at this point. Footsteps walking in a specific direction, some thirty, forty metres from our home. Knocking at a door.

'Open up!' says a man's voice, echoing in the empty street.

I let go of the curtain. 'You have to hide, before they come here.'

'Forget it,' I hear Granny say in the dark.

'I can't see anything,' Engel says.

'You never see anything, Engel,' Mother snaps.

Granny flicks on the floor lamp.

'Mother, cut it out,' my mother says.

'Engel can't see anything.'

Mother wants to turn the light back off, but Granny stops her.

'Never mind, Mama,' I whisper. 'The curtains are closed.'

Again, the screaming from Dutch police officers.

'Police, open up!' Then a loud bang. I hear excited women's voices, men cursing. Officers warning they'll have to use force if they try to resist.

Japie starts nervously pacing up and down the room. 'We're up next. They're coming to get us.' I walk towards him and push him onto the sofa. 'Calm down, Japie. I'm sure they're not coming for us.' Mother wipes down the coffee table and dresser for the umpteenth time as Granny prays and Engel stares blankly into the distance.

The sound of pounding on doors, barked orders and panicky reactions is getting louder. No one in the room makes a sound. I hold my brother's trembling body close. Our anxious hearts beat against each other. Then, all of a sudden, the voices sound very near.

'Good evening, we're cleaning out the street.'

'Good evening, gentlemen, how are you?' Mr Overvliet says amicably to the officers. 'Not too many living here anymore, are there? How many are on your list?'

Then there's some mumbling back and forth that I can't understand. Until I hear our name. 'The Oudkerks. No, haven't seen them. Didn't they leave already?' The man knows very well that we're home.

'Do you have a key?' he's asked.

'A key? No, I don't. I can lend a hand if you want to break the place open.'

Why is he offering to do this?

'But it's a bit inconvenient now,' the neighbour says. 'My wife is in bed. She's been a little feverish these past few days. I'm not quite sure what's the matter.' His wife isn't ill. I saw her walking outside just this morning. I hold my little brother closer still. He lets out a sob. 'Shh, I'm here with you. It's going to be okay,' I whisper, bracing myself for the sound of the doorbell. But nothing happens. We hear some more screaming, and then the truck's engine starts to hum and slowly the sound dissipates from the street.

Only when I see the truck's taillights getting smaller do I dare breathe again. Dizzy from the sudden rush of oxygen, I let go of my brother. No one says a thing. Still a bit shaky, I get up and turn towards Mother. 'See? You have to flee, or do you really want to be deported to a labour camp with Granny and Engel?'

Granny is still rocking back and forth in her chair, praying. Engel looks at me with squinty eyes. 'Don't talk to your mother like that!' She rarely raises her voice, but now she's flexed her vocal cords to tell me off.

I give Japie a hopeless look, and he looks back equally hopeless.

'I'm not going,' he then says resolutely. 'You can do whatever you want, but I'm not going.'

CHAPTER 13

MONDAY, 5 OCTOBER 1942

The railway in Westerbork built by prisoners is finished, so now there's a direct connection on the Meppel-Groningen line. In the night of 2 October, on Yom Kippur, all the other labour camps in the Netherlands were cleared out, and the men were reunited with their wives and children who were already in Westerbork. We've heard that these families were sent on to Germany and Poland by the hundreds from the already overcrowded camp. We in the Netherlands don't know what exactly goes on there.

When I get to Plantage Middenlaan, there's a queue in front of the theatre's revolving door. One by one, people disappear into the black hole. The monster is being kept well fed again. Families with children, the elderly, pregnant mothers, babies. They all disappear into its mouth. I can't bear to look at it and flee into the nursery.

This doesn't improve my mood. I'm met with crying nursery teachers whose parents, brothers and sisters were arrested over the weekend. We talk to each other, but what's there to say?

Sieny says it was the biggest raid so far and that the entire Dutch police force was deployed. She heard this from the Jewish Council's couriers, boys our age who deliver groceries here and sometimes help out with things. They, in turn, heard from someone in the Expositur, the Jewish department of the Zentralstelle – the Central Office for Jewish Emigration. Pimentel says we should just get to work. Our tears are upsetting the children. We need to bring cheer, like we normally do.

'We're not machines,' I counter.

'No, Betty, but you're professional nursery teachers now, aren't you? Not amateurs.' A grim look on her face gives away her anger. 'Alright, ladies, get to work!'

Before leaving the room, she takes me aside. 'Eleven o'clock in my office.'

I've flown off the handle again. Maybe this is the last straw before she fires me, and then I won't have a *Sperre* anymore either.

In Pimentel's room, I'm surprised to see Sieny and Mirjam on the sofa as well. Mirjam, slumped on the sofa and looking calm, pales in comparison to Sieny, who looks proud and has a grace about her with her straight back, her legs folded under her, her classic face. To them, I'm spontaneous, voluptuous and funny, but Sieny is elegant, mysterious, unapproachable.

I plop down on the sofa next to Sieny, who gives me a slight nudge and casts a glance that says she doesn't know why we're here either. It's a bit of a relief that Mirjam and Sieny are here too. The director didn't call the three of us in to fire me.

Pimentel seats herself in the armchair opposite us and starts to talk. 'You've noticed yourself that there are a lot of children leaving this building.' A brief sigh escapes her mouth. 'A situation we're not at all pleased with, to put it mildly. I don't need to tell you that all this has to do with what's taking place in the theatre.'

'I've already seen children go in there who used to come here,' Sieny says.

'That's right, Sieny. Lots of children who unregister with me are brought into the theatre several days later, where they have to wait for days, or even weeks sometimes, until they're deported. This while the place lacks the necessary facilities, especially for little ones under six years old. Mirjam can confirm this because she's been there several times already to bring a sick baby to the hospital, isn't that right, Mirjam?'

'Yes. The theatre is overcrowded and dirty... Certainly not a place for children,' she says flatly.

'We'll spare you the details,' Pimentel continues, 'but in any case, be prepared for horrible squalor. I've spoken with the theatre's manager, Mr Walter Süskind, and to make a long story short: we have permission from Hauptsturmführer Aus der Fünten to take in the children waiting to be deported here for the time being. It's an odd situation: my nursery for working mothers is closing and will now serve as an annexe to the theatre for the children waiting for their train to leave.' Pimentel briefly shakes her head, as if a fly is bothering her. She then takes a deep breath and continues. 'Anyway. Not much will change in practice; you already know some of these children after all. What will be changing is that from now on we'll be taking in children from seven to thirteen years old too. To ensure everything runs smoothly, I wanted to ask the three of you to supervise this. On top of your normal tasks here in the building, you'll be a contact person for the parents across the street, you'll be given clearance to walk back and forth between the theatre and nursery, and you'll be picking the children up and bringing them back again when it's time for them to leave. So only the three of you will have clearance to enter and exit the theatre. Any questions?'

Sieny raises her hand. 'When does this take effect?'

'The day after tomorrow. That means the nursery in its current form will be open for exactly' – she looks on her small gold wristwatch – 'one more day and six hours. Anything else?'

All three of us are silent. When Pimentel takes a deep breath to start talking again, I quickly ask: 'Why us?'

Pimentel looks at me with an odd expression on her face. The grey curl her silver-grey hair invariably forms on her head resembles a question mark, with her frowning forehead as the dot. 'Are you fishing for compliments now, Betty?'

'No, no,' I mutter, embarrassed. 'I just want to know why you think I'm up to the task, so I can better prepare.'

'But, Betty, don't you know yourself? You're afraid of no one. Not even of contradicting me.' She goes on without pausing. 'Now let's get back to work, girls.'

The three of us get up, but I topple backwards immediately because I had my feet too far back under the sofa. I feel clumsier than ever.

As Mirjam and Sieny are walking out the door already, Pimentel says: 'Ladies, there's one more thing I forgot to mention. These children will be here at night as well. That means you'll be living here too from now on. Do you think your parents will agree to this?'

My first thoughts are of Japie. Living away from home means abandoning Japie. My little brother who I've looked after since he was born, who I took along in my doll carriage, who I taught his first words and who I got up to all sorts of mischief with. What will come of him if I'm not there to comfort him or cheer him up...? But still, the longer I think about it, the lighter it gets in my head. I can leave our gloomy home. I won't have to pass the window of our old shop every day, where the widow Koot will often be changing the clothes on a mannequin and giving me a haughty look. Where the large portraits of Mussert and Hitler behind the counter can be seen through the shop window. Where she's twiddling her thumbs because she doesn't have a quarter of the customers we had. And where after closing she is picked up in an expensive race car that belongs to her Nazi boyfriend, who spat at me once. I'll no longer have to keep myself from throwing a rock through the window each day. No longer be kept up at night by the adrenaline coursing through my veins because of the murders I'm plotting. No longer have to see Mother's sadness, a mother who's now just a shadow of the beautiful woman who made my childhood so bright. Or Granny's ridiculous pride, which makes absolutely no sense whatsoever. Because there's nothing for her to base this pride on, because we're sinking down deeper, deeper and deeper. Each and every day. I'll no longer have to see the empty beds of Father, Gerrit, Nol and Leni. I'd much, much rather leave behind an empty bed myself.

I've rehearsed my story very well. To support my plea, I was given a letter by Miss Pimentel that says it was her request that I live in the nursery from now on and that it's important for reassuring the Jewish children in these troubled times. She also wrote how my flexible attitude and solution-oriented way of doing things makes me the right person for this.

I walk home with her letter in my handbag to get permission. I walk the route that normally takes me nearly forty minutes in twenty. When I approach our house, I keep my hand next to my left eye, forming a kind of blinker like horses have, and walk past the shop. Then I run through the doorway and up the stairs, where I expect to see my mother behind the stove and Granny and Engel at the kitchen table with a bowl of green beans and potatoes.

But the kitchen is empty. 'Mother?' I hear a thump in the living room. 'Watch out!' I hear Granny say.

I stick my head around the corner of the room. 'Granny, do you know where Mama is?'

'At the *shul*,' Granny says, hunched over a woollen quilt. 'Could you lend me a hand, Betty?'

'Why did Mother go to the *shul*?' She hasn't gone in weeks.

'I sent her there. Help me, Betty, Engel had a fall.'

'She fell?' I hurry towards her.

'I thought I'd put a blanket over her. I wasn't able to help her back up with my back...'

Only then do I see the small bag of bones underneath the blanket, next to Father's smoking chair.

'How did this happen?' I ask as Granny and I lift Engel's frail body up.

'If I knew, I'd tell you,' Granny replies, matter-of-factly. 'One moment she's sitting in that chair, the next she's on the floor next to it.'

We carefully put her back in the chair.

'*Lellit, po lellit*,' Engel moans.

'Do you understand what she's saying?' I ask Granny.

'*Aucune idée!*' No idea.

'Are you hurting anywhere?' I ask Engel.

'*Lellit, not lellit*,' Engel murmurs again, then puts her hands over her face.

'Maybe she's having a brain haemorrhage,' I tell Granny.

'I don't think so. For that, your blood has to be able to run through your veins and not be clotted yet.'

'Now, that's not nice!' I'm surprised at how fierce my reaction to my grandmother is. It's an unwritten rule never to contradict her, even if she's talking utter nonsense. I automatically brace myself for her sharp retort. But Granny remains focussed on Engel, who makes a valiant effort at lifting herself up from the chair.

'Now stay seated until you've calmed down, Engel. *Allez!*'

Something on the parquet floor grabs my attention. 'Is that a mouse?'

Granny immediately falls back on the sofa and throws her legs in the air. She's scared to death of mice because her late husband – my grandfather I never knew – once had a mouse shoot up his pant leg, straight up to his crotch, but Grandpa didn't let it get that far. Because – smack! – he struck it dead on his thigh. It was quite a mess according to Granny, but the critter never reached his family jewels.

'Where? Where?' Grandmother asks, panicking. I point at the ashy grey thing next to the sofa Granny is cowering on. Granny bends forward to get a better look at it, then happily exclaims: 'There's your denture, Engel!' Then to me: 'We've been looking for it all afternoon.'

After Granny rinses the dirty prosthesis under the tap, she sticks it in her old housemaid's mouth. 'There, now you can prattle again,' she says, giving Engel a reassuring stroke on her white hair.

'Poor Gerrit,' Engel says immediately. Gerrit is her favourite. She took care of him the longest.

'*Tais-toi*! We won't talk about that anymore, remember?'

'What's the matter with Gerrit?'

Granny shakes her head furiously. 'There's nothing wrong with Gerrit at all. Yes, he's alive. That's good news, isn't it?' She keeps her face close to Engel and once more repeats, at the top of her voice: 'Good news!' As if the poor woman isn't blind but deaf.

'Granny, what have you heard?'

She takes a deep sigh, then walks over to the dresser with that waddling gait of someone dragging along too much weight, where she picks up a postcard. 'He's dropped us a line. All is well, he just needs a suit. Here, read for yourself.'

Gerrit is alive! He made it! See, my brother won't let himself be caught that easily. He's always outsmarted people, and he's braver than anyone I know. My hero! Granny hands me the tattered card with the crooked handwriting, which I recognise as my brother's without a doubt, but sloppier, cruder. DEAR MOTHER, WE'RE IN DRANCY, it reads. COULD YOU ARRANGE A SUIT? GREETINGS TO EVERYONE ELSE IN THE FAMILY. Not a single word addressed to me. He never even mentioned my name. And what's with him needing a suit? What in the world does Gerrit need a suit for in Drancy? 'Where is Drancy?'

'Near Paris. I already asked myself.'

'But that's good news, then, isn't it?'

'France is also under German occupation, Betty. Read a paper for once! And Drancy is a concentration camp just as well.'

A word that instantly makes my stomach turn. Engel starts to cry.

'But he needs a suit,' I say, thinking out loud. 'So maybe he was given a good position...'

'That's what I said to your mother as well. But she just kept moaning "bad news, bad news." I said: "You don't know that, Jetty. Stop it!" So I sent her to the *shul*.' Granny sinks down on the sofa with a groan and folds her arms under her bosom. 'That's what you get when you turn your back on God. He'll abandon you too, and you won't be able to keep it together. Do you see what I mean, Betty? The only reason I'm able to hold out here is because I know God is on my side, and I'm in regular contact with Him. But it seems I'm the only one here keeping her head on straight somewhat.'

Only at around eight o'clock, right before the curfew starts and we're having a meal of dry bread and pickled fish with Granny, Engel and Japie – who's since come home – does Mother enter the kitchen. Her face is blotchy, and several tufts of hair stick out from under her hat. 'Children, Gerrit was caught,' she says to Japie and me.

Japie, who's heard the news already now, seems unconcerned. 'It can't be all that bad if he needs a suit, right?'

I don't know if Japie believes this himself, but in any case it's what Granny told him.

'I heard at the *shul* that he and Lous went to the cinema in Paris. That they ate at a brasserie near the Eiffel Tower and that they met Lous's family on the Avenue des Champs-Élysées. Do any of you understand this?'

None of us answer. I push my plate away, no longer hungry.

Mother goes on. 'Why didn't he have time to phone us if he was able to have a vacation in Paris? Why are we only hearing from him now that he's in a camp and needs clothes? This story makes no sense at all!'

Engel starts crying again.

'Child, sit down and have something to eat. That's more sensible,' Granny says, pulling back a chair for her daughter. 'It's a good sign that you were praying again. That's where it starts. Everything will turn out well as long as you keep your faith in God.'

Mother casts down her eyes and joins us at the table. For the first time, I don't see my mother, but Granny's child. A headstrong daughter like myself, who's being forced to listen. She disagrees with her mother, but she's too tired to argue back.

'Mother, I'm moving out.' My mother's passive demeanour turns active instantly, and she assumes the role I'm used to from her.

'Away from home? Don't be silly, Betty!'

I take out Pimentel's letter, which I'd kept at the ready all this time in my kitchen apron, and unfold it. 'It's a request from the director,' I say, ceremoniously handing her the letter. 'Only three girls were chosen, so it's quite an honour. And I can stop by on my free days...'

Mother gives me a perplexed look, as if the meaning of my words doesn't square with the bad news the letter contains.

'You'll have to sleep at the nursery from now on?'

'You can't do this!' my brother says. 'Then I'm the only one left!'

'I'm sorry, Japie.' I feel genuinely bad for him. Should I turn aside from my mission for him?

'You're one of the youngest nursery teachers, let them choose an older one,' Granny says in a tone that can't be argued with. 'Anyway, who else is going to help out around here? Or do you think Engel is still able to do much work?'

'I can scrub,' Engel counters. 'And pickle.'

'You haven't been able to pickle for ages, Engel. Apart from the fact that there's little pickling to be done of late. But for that you need to boil everything down first, and that's too dangerous for you. Remember when you had those prunes on the stove so long they were boiled dry? The whole house nearly burnt down, and if I hadn't smelled something wasn't right upstairs from the shop this could have ended very badly...'

As my grandmother goes on lecturing Engel about all the things she's no longer capable of, I keep my eyes focussed on my mother, who's still staring at the letter. Then she raises her chin and says: 'It's alright. Go pack your bags, Betty.'

Granny immediately halts the speech she's giving her housemaid. 'I don't approve. Or don't I have a say anymore in this house?'

'If it's about this, no. Betty is going,' Mother says calmly. 'It'll give her a better chance of being allowed to stay in Amsterdam. End of story.'

She then gets up and starts to clear the table. I'd like to walk up to her and embrace her, but that would only add to Granny's insult. So I stay seated and ask if anyone would like another cup of tea.

'I hate you!' Japie screams, then runs to his room all riled up.

I want to visit him in his room later, but when I try to pull the handle of his door I find he's locked it. 'Japie, please open up.'

All I hear back is: 'You're stupid, go away!'

CHAPTER 14

TUESDAY, 6 OCTOBER 1942

The nursery on Plantage Middenlaan for the care of Jewish children of working parents is closing its doors today.

In all the excitement of the final day, the nursery is still just a nursery, and I have little time to think, let alone for being distracted by that stupid Leo. It's tactless for him to make me think he likes me first, and then avoid all contact. I'd even call it outright rude for him not to even quickly show his face after my note. Okay, I'm rather upset about it. Still, my heart jumps when a colleague calls to tell me I have a visitor. I rush to the restroom to take a look at myself in the mirror. I run my tongue over my lips to add some shine, pinch my cheeks for added colour and put my cap on straight. Then I go to the front door.

Instead of the handsome doctor in training, it's the friend I haven't seen in a year and a half. 'Tineke!' I spread my arms, but she's a bit standoffish and stays where she is.

'Can I come in?'

'Of course, please,' I say, a little confused as to why my

spontaneous gesture isn't answered. Has my friend changed too?

Thankfully, she relaxes a bit in the staff room, and soon she's back to the old Tineke I always had so much fun with at school.

'I can't believe how tall you've got,' I say. 'Did they feed you beets?'

Tineke bursts out laughing, revealing her irregular teeth. 'Well, you've grown quite a bit yourself, Betty.'

'Yes, on the side and in front,' I say, with my hands first demonstrating the width of my hips, then the size of my chest.

Tineke shakes her head. 'You haven't changed a bit. Amazing when you think...' She casts down her eyes.

'When you think of what's happening here?'

She nods and then looks at me again with her light blue eyes. 'I got your letter and talked about it with my father. He's promised to help.'

I hold her hands. 'Thank you, Tineke. I knew I could count on you guys.'

'But Father did say there can be no more contact between our families. When the time comes, come to our house through the back door. You know how to get there.'

'Yes, via our secret path.' While this path, which we made ourselves by pulling bushes out of the ground, stomping on weeds and breaking off branches, is undoubtedly overgrown again, I'd be able to find the back of her house blindfolded.

When we've gone over everything, Tineke leaves as hastily as she came. The encounter was a small upswing, a silver lining to this gloomy day. At the same time, Tineke's visit has made me even more aware of how much my life has changed compared to hers. She's still more or less living her old life, while we're being pulled further and further towards the dark side of existence, until we're surrounded by total darkness. My mood is further exacerbated by having to say goodbye to the children, many of whom have been here every day since they were babies. There's a lot of whimpering among the preschoolers. The sadness also proves contagious to the toddlers, who don't quite understand what's going on and start bawling their eyes out. A young nursery teacher, who's only worked here for a few months, cries every bit as much until Pimentel takes her aside and I hear the director sternly tell her she has to get a hold of herself. The poor thing is so taken aback by the rebuke that she furiously wipes away her tears and clams up completely. But as soon as Pimentel leaves the room, she starts to sob again, her shoulders quivering.

When the moment comes for me to say goodbye to Greetje, I choke up a bit myself. The girl keeps yelling: 'Greetje stay, Greetje stay with Betty!' After which she holds me so tight that she nearly squeezes the life out of me.

'Ow, Greetje! Let me go, sweetie.' I try to pry her strong fingers loose. 'Greetje, that hurts Betty.'

But Greetje is so overcome by misery that she doesn't hear me. With eyes squeezed tight, her hot red face thrown back, she wails at a volume that makes my ears ring. 'Greetje, shh. Greetje...' How do I get her out of this state? I take a deep breath and exhale in her face so hard that she's startled. Leaving her bewildered, I quickly say: 'We'll see each other again! When the war is over, you can come visit Betty every day.' She's already gasping for breath to sound her siren again, but just in time the meaning of my words sinks in.

'I promise,' I say to add weight to my words.

She softens her grip and looks at me with her crossed eyes.

'A promise is a promise?'

'Yes, Greetje, a promise is a promise.'

She then grabs onto my head and pulls me close, her face wet with tears, snot and saliva, smothering me with kisses.

. . .

I don't say a word about the day's dramatic events during
dinner. It's my last evening at home, and Mother has really
outdone herself cooking a meal with extra vegetables and some
kosher meat she managed to get hold of. But the mood is far
from festive. Japie avoids my eyes on purpose, hoping to make
me feel his indignation.

Mother fills our plates with a dour look on her face, struggling to keep her feelings in check.

'Mmm. You've really got better at cooking, Jetty,' Granny
says, who never waits to dig in until everyone is served, yet
always requires the rest of us to. 'You were a bit rubbish before.'

'Thank you, Mother,' my mother says curtly.

Engel, who's always served last, holds her hands over her
plate. 'I'm sorry, Jetty,' she says, 'I'm afraid I don't have much of
an appetite.'

'You're going to eat something, Engel!' Granny says, firmly
pulling away Engel's hands and letting Mother fill her plate.
'You'll weigh less than a cat in a week or two if you keep fasting
like this. And then who'll take care of me if I have a fall? Well?'

Engel lowers the corners of her mouth to indicate she
doesn't know either, then starts to eat, crying.

I really can't bear any more tears in one day. 'Listen, Engel,
I have some good news.'

'Why for Engel?' Granny asks alertly.

'It's good news for all of you,' I hurry to say. 'I spoke with
Tineke Baller today. Her father, Karel, wants to help us find a
place to go into hiding.'

Mother puts the water pitcher on the table. 'We're not
discussing this over dinner. Do you hear me, Betty?'

As I pack my suitcase, Mother enters my room.

'We can't go into hiding,' she says, sinking onto my bed on
top of the clothes I'd gathered. 'Granny doesn't want to, and

she's diabetic besides. Engel is visually impaired and has difficulty walking, and Japie is an adolescent, you can't lock him up.'

'No, not in a camp either!' I take her hand and press it against my chest. 'Please, Mama, it's really what's best! And you can't leave me here in Amsterdam all by myself either, can you?' I give her a pleading look.

'How often do I have to tell you "no"?' She angrily pulls back her hand. 'We're not hiding in some tiny attic or shed. It's not happening, and that's that.'

'But, Mama—'

'And you'll stop this now!' She springs up and starts to walk out the room, turning around once more in the door opening. 'Don't you ever think you know what's best for us, Betty. Do you understand?' She slams the door shut behind her. I kick my old nightstand, causing the lamp on top to fall over, and then, at once, my childhood room goes dark.

The following morning, it seems as if all the arguments from the night before have been forgotten. After Granny, Engel, Mother and even Japie hug me, they wave goodbye from the window. Mother dabs her eyes with a handkerchief, the nearly blind Engel stares into space and Granny sticks her chest out. Japie is the only one who doesn't move his raised arm back and forth but holds it still, which makes it look more like a 'halt!' gesture than a farewell greeting. With a forced smile, I wave back at my family and try to ignore the cramp in my stomach. I then continue along the way I've walked so often, only never before with the intention of not returning in the evening.

My suitcase isn't even completely full, but I have to switch hands constantly or else it gets too heavy. They should make suitcases with wheels underneath. My arms are numb when I get to Plantage Middenlaan.

There's a truck in front of the door of the building. On its side, in big letters, it reads: G. MARCHAND AND SON, BED AND MATTRESS MAKERS. Small beds are being unloaded from the truck and carried into the nursery. I recognise some boys from the Council who they got to help out with this. Even though I don't know all of them by name, we greet each other politely. There are some really cute ones too who – now that I've put Leo out of my mind – I wouldn't mind getting to know a little better. As elegantly as I can, I make my way past the boys and carry my luggage inside, making a joke to my left and extending a hand on the right. I feel their eyes linger on me as I disappear into the staff room.

Sieny is by the table, bent over a drawing and muttering.

'Good morning!'

'Just a second...' Sieny replies without looking up. I look over her shoulder and see her shuffling all sorts of little cut-out rectangles around on the floor plan. These, apparently, are supposed to represent beds.

'Where's that?'

'The *shul* is going to be the dormitory.'

The largest room at the front of the first floor hasn't been a place of worship for some time now, but that's still what we call it.

'Are you managing?' I ask.

'I have to make a layout, but that's tricky if you don't know exactly how many children there will be.'

'Didn't they say how many?' I ask, taking off my coat and hanging it on the rack.

'Sure, they gave me a list. But Mirjam is in the theatre counting them now because there seem to be a lot more of them.'

'Wouldn't Pimentel know?'

'She's out haggling for sheets, blankets, pyjamas, you name it.'

'Let her shuffle things around.' From what I've heard, Pimentel knows a lot of wealthy Jews.

'This is pointless,' Sieny says at last. 'I'll need to know the specifics first – like how many beds we're really getting because that's still unclear too.'

I hear the boys from the Council laugh in the hallway.

'At least they're keeping themselves busy...' I say suggestively.

But Sieny doesn't take the bait. 'How did it go at home?'

'Oh, saying goodbye is never fun,' I say. 'Especially not in my family, where everyone's emotions are always so close to the surface.'

Sieny looks up from her plan. 'My mother acted as if I was off to get a pack of flour.' She shrugs. 'There's always something.'

Her family is so respectable it sometimes feels like I'm from a family of animals where no one is able to restrain themselves in the least. Including myself.

'I'm bringing my things to my room, and then I'll come help you,' I tell Sieny.

Sieny's bedroom is at the front of the building, where Mirjam's room is too. I was given the small attic room in the back of the building. It's a humble little space with a single bed, a small writing table and a wardrobe. I put my suitcase on the bed and go over to the dormer window. Through it, I can see the courtyards of Plantage Middenlaan and Plantage Fransenlaan. Everything looks neatly raked. This will be my view for the foreseeable future. Quite different from the only view I ever had from my bedroom window on Van Woustraat, where I could see horse carts, cargo bikes and roaring motor vehicles passing by below. I was so used to the bustle in the streets that I always had a hard time sleeping during those first nights of my summer vacation in Putten because of the lack of noise outside. I'm suddenly struck by a feeling of great loneliness. Like I've been cut off from my childhood for good.

Even before I enter, I can smell coffee in the staff room. 'Where did you get that?' I ask Sieny. Hardly anyone drinks real coffee anymore because it's too expensive. We drink *Pitto* instead, a kind of coffee substitute made from roasted plant roots.

'One of the boys just gave it to me. I don't know how they got it either.'

'Seems like they wanted to make an impression,' I say to tease her.

'Yeah sure,' she says without much interest. 'Oh, Betty, you'll need to wear that band around your arm from now on.' She points to a small piece of cloth on the dresser.

'Did the letters fall off?' I ask, holding up the white band. 'This doesn't mean anything, does it? The boys from the Jewish Council at least have "JC" printed on theirs.' Mine says nothing, apart from a number.

'Just so long as it works.' Sieny ties the straps around my arm and turns the smooth side to face out. 'Beautiful!'

'So with this rag around my arm, I'm free to walk in over there?' I ask Sieny.

'Essentially, yes. Oh, and if you could also sew a star on your uniform, for when you need to go back and forth.'

'Guess I'll be off then,' I say cheerily after I've sewn on the extra Star of David Sieny gave me. 'Let's see if it works.' I'm headed for the door already.

'But what are you going to do there now? We don't have to pick up the children until tomorrow.' Sieny gives me a questioning look.

'I'm going to help Mirjam count. There's no harm in that, surely? See how much food we'll be needing tomorrow while we're at it.'

There's an SS man by the theatre entrance who I've seen before: a slim man with a young and thin face. His hair is dark, almost black, and sticks out from under his cap, which he wears cocked to the side on his head. He looks around with eyes that express boredom and impatience all at once.

'Good day, officer, sir.'

His demeanour changes instantly. He gives me a startled and defensive look.

'I'm from the children's nursery, and I have permission to go in here.' I show the band around my arm to back this up.

He lets me through with a quick nod. As soon as I go through the revolving door, I'm disoriented by the sheer number of people and the stench. I bump into a young man immediately. 'Pardon,' we both say at once. I recognise the band that reads JC around his arm.

'Betty Oudkerk, from the nursery. I have to report to Wouter Süskind.'

'*Walter* Süskind,' he says.

Oddly enough, I'd pictured Süskind to be older than this boy with the large eyebrows and stubble in front of me. 'Well, that was quick,' I say.

'Oh no, that's not me. My name is Joop. You'd best ask over there where Süskind is.' He points to the foyer, where amid all the people I see a row of tables. I thank the boy and squeeze my way past the people hollering in Yiddish, German and Dutch all at once. I only catch snatches of what they're saying: 'We're entitled to a *Sperre*!' 'Help me, my children are still home by themselves!' 'I don't feel well, where's the sickbay?' 'I wasn't given time to pack my belongings!'

I manage to reach the side of the row of tables, where two women and a man are seated behind typewriters. 'Your registration has been taken care of. You may continue to the foyer, to the left here,' one of the typists tells a Jewish husband and wife. 'You can hand in your house keys there.'

'I'd prefer to keep my house keys myself,' the husband says.

'We understand, but unfortunately this isn't permitted. Don't worry, we keep good track of everything on our lists, so when you're back you can come collect your keys again.'

The man wants to object, but his wife drags him along.

'Could you tell me where I can find Mr Süskind?' I ask before she attends to the next person in the queue.

'You're from across the street, I suppose?' the typist asks in a friendly tone.

'Yes, I'm here to help my colleague Mirjam.'

'Mr Süskind is probably in the *cartotheque*. That's the ticket office on the left, which is also where the SS is.'

The woman sees me hesitate.

'It's also fine if you just continue to the auditorium, that's where your colleague is. Take the doors here on your left, then go through the foyer and continue on through the hall until you're there.'

As I make my way through the foyer, the stench gets worse and worse: a foul odour of sweat, excrement and rotting food. The hubbub of people talking all at once makes my ears ring. The dim lighting makes it difficult to tell people from shadows. Someone grabs hold of my arm, and I jump. It's an elderly woman who looks at me with eyes full of fright. 'Sister, I don't know where to go. Where's the stage?'

The woman must have just come in because she's still wearing her rucksack.

'Come with me. I'm headed there myself.'

The opening bell rings, as if there's a show about to begin. 'This is a message from the Jewish Council,' a voice says through the PA system. 'You are prohibited from receiving letters from outside, as well as from sending letters. If you wish to contact friends or family, you may dictate a message to the Jewish Council in the foyer.'

'I left a letter on the table for my family back home,' the woman says, now holding my arm tight with both hands.

'That's better. I'm sure your children will find it,' I say to comfort her.

'I don't have any children,' she says, 'or a husband either. The neighbours brought me.'

I immediately feel sorry for her. 'Did your neighbours tell on you?'

'Oh no, they're wonderful. I was summoned and was afraid to go by myself. So I asked them to take me.'

'Ah, I see.'

We find ourselves in a bit of a jam. The German guard by the foyer exit barks at us to keep moving.

'Perhaps it's best if you walk behind me.'

'Yes, of course.' She lets go of my arm and gets behind me.

The crowd starts moving again. There's a bit more room in the hallway, and I head straight for the large swing doors. I look back to see if the woman is still following me and trip over the extended leg of a mother who's on the floor breastfeeding her child. 'Can't you look out?' she snaps.

UNEVEN NUMBERS, it reads above the auditorium. When I push open the heavy door, I hardly recognise the theatre that once had rows of red velvet folding chairs, balconies on both sides and a grand stage with a golden arch, heavy velour curtains and beautiful sets. What I see is a kind of human pigsty. The chairs are arranged haphazardly, and there are people standing, sitting and lying down all over the place. Children run around amid the people on the stage. A cacophony of voices fills the large, tall hall. One woman is screaming non-stop. Children are crying. Angry men's voices. Laughing. I'm tempted to turn around immediately, but I can't go back now. I'm already here with my feet in the muck. Besides, the woman is holding onto my arm again like someone drowning clamps on to a lifebuoy.

'Can I take your rucksack?' I hear a voice next to me say. It's the boy from before, with the stubble – Joop. 'The luggage racks are at the back of the stage.'

'Umm... Yes, is that necessary? I'd prefer to keep it with me,' the woman says anxiously.

'They should have told you during registration that all luggage is centrally transported. But you can keep your handbag on you.'

'No one told me anything,' the woman says. 'Where do I register?'

The boy looks at me like I'm responsible for the fact that this woman failed to register.

'I just met her here,' I say. 'I think she must have walked right past it.'

'Did I do something wrong?' the woman asks apprehensively. 'I'm not used to this...'

'No one is used to this,' I say. Then I turn towards the boy again. 'If she didn't register, she could still leave, right?'

His facial expression doesn't show what he's really thinking. Maybe it's a mistake to suggest this so openly. He then bends towards the woman. 'Do you have someone you could stay with?'

Frightened, the woman looks at me, then at Joop, and back at me. Then, softly but audibly, she says: 'I've worked as a book-keeper for an office furniture company all my life. My old boss said he was willing to help me. But I didn't want to get him in trouble.'

'Go, please,' I say. 'Most people here don't have that chance.'

I see my words have an effect. The fright in the woman's eyes makes way for decisiveness. 'But then how do I get out of here?'

'I'll take care of that,' the boy from the Council says. 'Come with me.' Like a son looking after his mother, he takes her with him.

When I look into the hall again, I see Mirjam walking by on the stage. I make my way to her as fast I can. 'Mirjam!'

'Where's the fire, sister?' says a man, blowing his cigar smoke in my face. I ignore him and pass a man with only one leg, an elderly woman talking gibberish, a rabbi praying with a group of people around him, two teenagers having a laugh, a family grooming each other and a small girl crying with a face full of tears and snot. 'Mommy, mommy, poo...' I can't ignore her.

'Where's your mother?' She gives me a questioning look. 'Come, let me bring you to the toilet.'

'Down the hall on your left over there,' a proper gentleman says. 'It might take a while as there's often quite a queue.'

'We'll have to find out for ourselves,' I tell the child, which can't be much over four years old. 'And then we'll go look for Mommy, alright?'

She nods and sticks a thumb in her mouth.

The man wasn't joking. There's a line of at least fifteen ladies in front of the toilet. 'Could this girl here go first?' I ask. 'She can't hold it any longer.'

I hear some muted grumbling, but thankfully the two ladies in front move to the side to make room. There are only two toilets, and the stench is unbearable. It's as if stale urine, diarrhoea and vomit are struggling with each other for prominence.

Even the girl is holding her nose with her little hand. I pull open the door and witness the personal catastrophes that took place here. Even the walls are covered in faeces. 'Listen, sweetie, I'll be pulling down your knickers and then lifting you up and holding you over the bowl. Alright?'

She nods with a serious little face. Only when I've lifted up her dress and pull down her tights and underwear do I understand what this look meant. She's already soiled herself.

I dispose of the dirty underwear and return the girl to her mother. But, of course, now Mirjam is nowhere to be found. I then see a man in a white coat speed by. I go after him, as he hurries up the stairs and opens a door that reads: *Nursing Ward – authorised personnel only*. When he's about to close the door behind him, I call out to him. 'Doctor, may I—'

The man looks at me. 'Are you—'

'Nursery teacher from across the street,' I quickly say.

'Betty? Betty Oudkerk?'

It's only then I recognise him. It's Doctor De Vries Robles, who used to visit our home often before the war. Or rather, before Father died. 'Doctor De Vries Robles, how are you?'

'Well, considering the circumstances...' He quickly looks around. 'How's your mother?'

'Stubborn as always,' I say, smiling. I'm in no mood whatsoever to give a serious answer. 'Would it be alright if I wash my hands? I just had to deal with a little accident.'

'Of course.' As he takes me through the nursing ward, he begins to talk in an upbeat voice. 'You can say it's a miracle we haven't had an outbreak of typhoid or dysentery here yet. Though I'm not so certain about the latter. I've complained to Walter about it because something has to be done. They're installing a few showers now, but even then.' He points to a washbasin. 'It's much better for the children if they can be with you from now on. I really take my hat off to Pimentel for arranging this!'

'I'll tell her,' I say, lathering my hands with soap.

'Please do! And also tell your mother, and certainly also your grandmother, that I said "hi".' He laughs. 'She's quite a character.' He goes through the swing door to the nursing ward, where I catch a glimpse of the people lying in bed. At least the windows on the front allow daylight into the room.

Downstairs, I pass the booth where they used to sell tickets, but which now serves as an office for the SS guards. I glance through the semi-circular opening, which a few months ago still had a cashier behind it selling tickets for the show. There's a man in a herringbone suit with a yellow star sitting with the SS men. This has to be Walter Süskind. With his round head and ginger hair combed back, he looks like any other German. But a Jewish German? I find it hard to imagine. He seems quite at ease among the SS men, with one leg nonchalantly crossed over the other, leaning back comfortably and supporting his neck with folded hands. 'Makes sense, agreements have to be kept,' he says in High German. 'Otherwise, we might as well not make them.' The man whose back I'm looking at is filling the shot glasses on the low table. 'I'll pass, Ferdinand. I might not keep everything under control here otherwise,' Süskind says. A remark that once more sparks facetious comments. 'We have to ship them off alive,' one of them says. 'But it would make piling them up a bit easier,' says the man called Ferdinand.

Who is this Süskind, I wonder? What kind of Jew sits around having a laugh with the Germans?

Suddenly, he directs his attention at me. 'Hey, sister, come in,' he says in German.

I'd been ready to walk off. Begrudgingly, I open the ticket office door and walk into a room that reeks of cigarette smoke and disinfectant.

'Good day, gentlemen,' I force myself to say. 'You must be Mr Süskind.'

'Entirely correct.'

'And aren't you curious who we are?' says a voice behind me.

I turn around and look at the narrow face of the man called Ferdinand. He ogles me with a crooked grin. I recognise him as the bigwig I first saw this summer when he got out of his Mercedes. The SS man whose name is spoken of in hushed tones among the girls at the nursery.

'Hauptsturmführer Aus der Fünten, right?'

'Correct. Pleased to meet you, sister.'

'Elisabeth Oudkerk, pleased to meet you.' I give a little nod and bend my knees a bit.

'Well now, a well-raised Jewess,' he says mockingly. 'That deserves an applause.' He starts to clap, at which the rest start callously clapping along with him. I keep my eyes cast down and brace myself for whatever comes next.

'Did you want something?' Süskind asks.

'I'm looking for my colleague, Mirjam.'

'Mirjam is usually at the side of the stage, where she's made a kind of play area for the little ones,' Süskind says.

'Children play while we sit on our hands,' the chief commander laughs.

'We're making an inventory of the number of children so we can bring them to the nursery tomorrow,' I say.

'Then you'd best have a look in the *cartotheque*,' Aus der Fünten says. 'They're all in there.'

Süskind gets up. 'Come with me, Betty. I'll show you.' He ushers me out the door. Outside the office, he's accosted by people immediately. 'Mr Süskind, help me. Please.'

'You can file your requests in the lobby,' he kindly says.

'You're lucky,' Süskind tells me. 'Aus der Fünten isn't so tolerant normally.' He leads me to the other side of the lobby, where there's an identical ticket booth. Three Jewish secretaries are working at a desk, monitored by a fat, slouching SS man. Süskind kindly greets them, at which the SS man tries to stand to attention so fast that he loses his balance and falls back in his chair. The secretaries giggle, covering their mouths with their hand. Süskind tells me I have permission from Aus der Fünten to see the lists and pulls open a cabinet. He shows me the card indexes and explains how the children are registered. 'Mirjam has been busy all morning, but it's easier if you count them on paper,' he says. 'Then tell her the correct number afterwards. At least you'll know for sure if you got all of them. Here.' He hands me a pen and paper.

Mirjam is backstage, where she's talking to a group of mothers and children. 'It's quieter in the nursery for the children, even if it'll be hard to be without you at first,' she says, visibly struggling to raise her voice above the din.

'Is it mandatory or can I also just keep my child with me?' asks one mother with a toddler on her lap.

'They've made it mandatory. Unless your child is sick or has some kind of ailment.'

'Wonderful,' a different mother sneers. 'First they take our homes, then our luggage and now our children too.'

'We're really not taking your children from you, I promise,' Mirjam says. The way she sits there with her eyes enlarged by thick glasses and her right hand on her chest would make even the greatest cynic believe her. 'If you have no further questions, I'll see you all tomorrow.'

Only then does Mirjam see me. She gets up and walks towards me. 'It's impossible,' she sighs. 'I still haven't numbered everything.'

The voice sounds through the speakers again, like some kind of god. 'There's a delivery for S. Levi which you can collect

in the lobby. There's a *Sperre* available for the Weil family.'
There are cheers from several people in the hall. 'From now on,
lunch will no longer be provided by the Jewish Invalid Care
Institution but by Café de Paris, and can be picked up for a
small fee in the foyer upstairs. Please be sure you do so in an
orderly fashion, or else we will have to take measures. Thank
you and enjoy your meal.'

I follow Mirjam, who seems to know her way around this
place quite well already. 'I can give you a tour.'

'I think I've seen it all already,' I say.

'Well, I'm sure you haven't been downstairs,' she says,
giving me a knowing look. 'That's where the defiant ones are
who are sent east straight away. They're not even allowed out to
get some fresh air or to... you know. And then there's the prop
storage and the space below the stage. I've had to pull children
playing hide and seek out from there on countless occasions.'
She pinches her nose. 'The only upside is it's so filthy that you
won't see anyone from the SS or SD there either.'

'Blink against the light!' she warns before we walk out the
door. In the small courtyard, the bright sunlight hurts my eyes
indeed.

'Not one ray of light comes in at the theatre,' Mirjam says.
'Those who are never allowed out don't know if it's day or night
within days.'

'Don't they turn off the light at night?'

'No, otherwise the guards can't keep an eye on things.
People are complaining that they can't sleep because of it.' She
produces a pack of cigarettes from her skirt and holds it in front
of me.

'Not now, thanks.' I'm not used to smoking, and to be honest
I don't even like it, but I don't want to admit this. Mirjam taps a
cigarette out from her pack, takes it out and puts it between her
lips. She asks another smoker standing there for a light. I notice
she's nervous, as if her constitution isn't up to this place, though

she always seems calm and composed as head of the baby section.

'How many guards are there in this place, actually?'

Mirjam shrugs. 'Quite a few. Fifteen, maybe twenty. It's the Dutch branch of the SD who help out here during the day. In the evening and at night, it's just the SS guarding the place.' She waves her smoke away and leans in towards me. 'They're most agreeable when they're drunk. Not tipsy, then you'd best get out of here if you're a woman, but really drunk.'

'And this Süskind – isn't he a Jewish collaborator?'

'Seems like it, doesn't it?' It's the first time a hint of a smile appears on Mirjam's otherwise always serious face.

I shrug. 'Could be, right?'

'The main game here is to navigate between what's expected of you and what you can arrange unnoticed.'

I try to commit her sentence to memory to mull over later and come to grips with what it means.

'I copied the children's names from the *cartotheque*.' I fold open the sheet of paper, on which I've listed seventy-one children's names with twenty-seven different family names.

Mirjam pulls it towards her. 'How can that be? I counted seventy-five already, and I suspect that's not even all of them.'

'They're not all in the card index then, in any case.'

'I'll consult with Mr Süskind on what we should do,' Mirjam says.

Again, there's a crackling sound from a loudspeaker. I expect to hear another announcement, but music starts to play instead. The sound of the gramophone is coming from an open window of one of the surrounding houses. *'Wenn du jung bist, gehört dir die Welt,'* goes the well-known German song. The people in the courtyard start to sway along while looking up, as if Joseph Schmidt himself were up there singing from the window. Mirjam and I have stopped talking and listen to the cheery song: *'Let's enjoy our lives. Worries are for when we're*

old... Let's dance and sing, now we're still young...' How bitter
these lyrics are in this place, at this time. But maybe that's just
why it's mainly the younger people singing along out loud. To
let it be heard that this goes for us too. That we also have a right
to be young. I don't look at Mirjam and would prefer to go back
to the nursery.

'Shall we go?' I say when the sound dies down.

Mirjam puts out her cigarette against the wall and tucks a
loose strand of hair back under her headcloth. 'I'm making one
last round.'

The door is blocked by a wheelchair being pushed outside.
The girl sitting in it is using her hands to protect her eyes.

'There we go, a bit of sun will do you good.'

I know that voice. It's Leo. Could it be he works here now?
Even before I can think of a good opening line, he's spotted me.

'Betty, what a coincidence!'

'Well... The nursery is right across the street,' I say.

'That's true,' he laughs.

'Umm... Yes. This is Mirjam. Perhaps you two know each
other already?'

'Who doesn't know Leo?' Mirjam says, deadpan.

Leo lets out an uproarious laugh. 'It's really not that bad.'

Is Leo known for being a flirt? Or has Mirjam gone out with
him herself? I find it hard to imagine.

A shrill bell rings. The guard springs into action. 'Time is
up. Everyone line up, double-file.'

'Will we see each other again?' Leo whispers in passing.

'Who knows,' I say haughtily. But really I'm thinking: *Stuff
it*. First he gives me the silent treatment for two months, and
now he wants to meet again. No way.

CHAPTER 15

WEDNESDAY, 7 OCTOBER 1942

The large dance hall in what used to be the shul *was turned into a playroom and dormitory for children from six to twelve years old. The beds were put together as close as possible to leave room for the children to play. A dormitory for the little ones from two and a half to five years old was made in the back. The youngest sleep in the baby room downstairs. In the basement next to the laundry room, a space was cleared for when the children need to take a little rest or if they don't feel well. The large back room on the ground floor was turned into a large dining room, where we'll be feeding the children in shifts. As before, all the regular nursery teachers come during the day. Only Mirjam, Sieny and I are residential.*

The three of us cross the street to the theatre, which now has a different guard in front of the door. His posture is even less formal than that of his predecessor. He leans against the building, legs crossed, a cigarette in the corner of his mouth and his hat cocked forward on his head, which I imagine makes it hard for him to see much, let alone guard anything. He nods even before we ask permission to enter. It's less busy than yesterday. The din of voices resounding all at once has died down a bit as well. Or is that just how it seems to me, now that I'm over the initial shock?

'Wait a second,' Mirjam says. She goes over to the ticket office on the left. Süskind's face appears behind the glass, and he slips her a sheet of paper folded in half.

'This is the definitive list. Good luck, ladies.'

There's an SD man blocking our way when we want to continue to the foyer. 'Hold on, sister, who's ill here?' He's Dutch.

'No one. We're coming to get the children,' I say.

'By orders of your superior,' Sieny adds.

'Another little nurse,' the SD man says, feigning surprise. 'I think I may have to lie down now so you can give me an examination.'

His colleague on the other side of the entrance finds this so funny he lets out a boisterous laugh, revealing his uvula.

'Stop dawdling, move along!' barks a German SS man who apparently doesn't share his Dutch colleagues' sense of humour.

It's mainly women with children and infants in the foyer now, which yesterday was still jam-packed with men looking to make their case.

'Children, will you all please queue up in pairs or threes and stand next to your brothers or sisters,' Mirjam says firmly. 'You can give us your babies or toddlers, or you can quickly come with us across the street.'

'Can I come too?' asks a woman right beside me. A toddler is clutching at her leg, crying its eyes out. 'We just got here...'

'I'm afraid that's not possible,' I say. 'But don't you worry. We'll take great care of him.' I crouch down so I can look the boy straight in the eye.

'Hi, I'm Sister Betty. What's your name?' The child has no intention of answering. 'Will you come with us?' The young boy stubbornly shakes his head. When I try to take him from his mother, he starts screaming bloody murder.

'Silence!' the German guards snarl.

But instead of settling down, he's joined by other children crying at the top of their lungs. Sieny and I look at each other. How on earth are we going to manage this?

'Just take the girls,' the mother says, taking her hollering son back from my arms.

'And what's your name?' I ask the little girl holding onto my hand.

From the corner of my eye, I see Sieny taking a baby that can't be more than a few weeks old from its distraught mother.

'Look, there's Betty!' a voice behind me says. I turn and recognise Loutje, a young boy I've known since I started working at the nursery. The dark-haired boy ordinarily has a mischievous face, and his eyes fix upon me the instant he recognises me.

'You'll come along with Betty, won't you?'

The boy nods and takes my free hand.

The pack of children slowly starts to move, still sobbing relentlessly. When we cross the street, there's a girl of about fifteen years old who recognises Loutje. 'Hey, Lou, big guy! I'll see you soon back home, alright?'

'Is she a friend of yours?'

'That's my sister,' Loutje says. I wonder why she's not wearing a Star of David if she's his sister. The mystery is resolved soon enough. 'Anna doesn't have to go because she has a different mother,' the boy says. 'The mother is Catholic, just like our father.'

We have to go back and forth three times to get all the children to the other side. I notice the smell of warm urine coming from all the little ones who've wet themselves from fright. I see the older children's faces contorted with grief; they understand they need to stay strong so as not to add to the tragedy. 'Shh,

Miem, we'll see each other again when we're transported,' one girl tells her mother, who's beside herself. 'I'll be good, Father. I promise,' I hear another child say. As well as: 'Please, Mother, stop crying. I'll pray every day.'

Several children are so upset it's impossible to get them to come along. When the racket nearly makes our eardrums burst, Süskind and his friendly secretary come to our aid. He says we'll have to leave the 'difficult cases' with their mothers. We'll deal with those tomorrow. I feel like telling him all children are difficult cases because they're being separated from their mothers and have to come along with women they've never seen before in an already threatening situation. But I keep my mouth shut. Thankfully, lots of colleagues are ready to take the children from us when we've crossed the street. Pimentel said we should stick to the usual routines. So first, they're all checked for lice and given a bag to keep their belongings in. The youngest are given aprons from the nursery and a handful of raisins as a reward before they're brought to their designated rooms.

CHAPTER 16

FRIDAY, 9 OCTOBER 1942

The number of nursery teachers is being increased mainly with German Jewish girls, who would otherwise be the first to be put on a transport and in this way are entitled to a Sperre. *Every day, Pimentel sees mothers come by her office with their fifteen- or sixteen-year-old daughters. They beg her to give their daughter a job.*

The extra hands make our work a bit lighter, but it's also difficult because the girls are still children themselves. On top of this, the carers are increasingly speaking German among themselves, which is something the Dutch nursery teachers don't appreciate, resulting in rising tensions. Trouble sometimes also emerges between students who've had a decent upbringing and those from less well-off families.

'Stick your grubby little fingers in your nose one more time, and I'll chop them off!' a new nursery teacher says in her rustic accent.

I see Pimentel turn red. 'That's not how we talk here.'

I exchange glances with Sieny. We can barely keep in our laughter.

'The names of all trainee carers to get extra tutoring in proper manners will be on the bulletin board this afternoon.'

This is so like Pimentel. She'll identify a problem and immediately come up with a practical solution. Thankfully, I'm not part of the solution this time. Now that we're living here, Pimentel groups us with the senior staff, which feels wonderful. Sieny is also growing into her role with each day.

Pimentel turns towards us. 'Ladies, which of you can number the beds and make a plan for which child is in which bed?'

I volunteer even before Sieny can react. 'I'll do it!'

'Great, I want it done before twelve.'

When she's left, Sieny gives me a look and shakes her head. 'Always overzealous.'

'Oh, did you want to do it yourself?' I ask, feigning innocence.

'No, don't be silly,' she says, waving off the suggestion. 'I have enough on my plate already.' She then walks off, laughing.

But I felt her having a dig at me.

I love bookkeeping. I used to enjoy helping Father keep track of our stock and placing new orders. Maybe it's because of this experience that I know when it doesn't add up. The extra children we discovered in the theatre are suddenly no longer there. One or two names I'd seen before on the lists have disappeared. It's clear something is going on that they're keeping from us. But I don't ask any questions, no matter how curious I am.

I learn why it's so important to know which child is in what bed soon enough. It's because we're getting the names of children set to be put on the transport tonight. About a third of the children we picked up the day before yesterday will have to leave with their parents today already. I wonder what the use of this dramatic separation was if they're going in the train today. But I don't ask questions about this, either.

Mirjam enters and looks over my shoulder to see what I'm doing. 'Are you managing?'

I wonder if I can trust her with my doubts but decide not to say anything. 'Oh sure, it's going fine.'

'I had to give you this.' She puts a folded-up note on the table in front of me. 'Good luck,' she says mysteriously, and then she's off again.

I unfold the note and read:

HI BETTY! GREAT TO SEE YOU AGAIN THE OTHER DAY. FEEL LIKE GOING FOR A WALK WITH ME AGAIN? LOVE, LEO.

I read it one more time. Why does he first ignore me for months on end, only to start pursuing me again afterwards? Did something change in the meantime? It seems a bit noncommittal. My mother always says: 'Men have their fill soon enough when they can eat whatever they want.' Well, let him go hungry then! I crumple up the piece of paper and toss it in the bin.

At ten o'clock in the evening, Sieny and I wake the children from our dormitory. 'Come, get out of bed. But be quiet. You can go see your parents.' This last word in particular works like magic, and within minutes they're standing next to their camp beds with their stuffed animals, toothbrushes, books and extra clothes in their rucksacks.

That is, until I wake a boy whose reaction is quite different from the other children's. 'Did you find Mama and Papa?' he says, looking at me with big eyes.

I instantly realise I've made a mistake. This boy of about ten years old with a wan face hasn't said a thing all day. It's only now I remember he'd been in hiding separated from his parents and was betrayed by the neighbours. The boy's parents are in hiding somewhere else and likely aren't even aware their son is here. He's not seeing his parents again at all.

The boy quickly gets dressed, all the while continuing to ask questions. 'And does Mama know I'm here? Where are we going? Is it safe there? Can I stay with Mama and Papa all the time now?'

I don't know how to tell him I made a mistake and that he'll have to be transported by himself.

The children sit at the table eating a warm bowl of porridge, so at least they won't be hungry when they get on the train, when I see Pimentel walking down the hall and quickly go up to her. I tell her about my blunder. 'You could have known. It says what family in the theatre they're with right next to their name,' she says, irritated. 'I've already requested they pair him up with someone to accompany him on his journey. Just hurry up, there isn't much time.'

I'm about to walk off but then think of something. 'Why should a ten-year-old go to Westerbork all by himself? What's the point of that?'

'The point?' She gives me a still more agitated look. 'Has anyone been able to explain the point of this whole situation to you? No? Me neither, so don't ask any more stupid questions and do your job.'

It's pitch-black outside. Sieny and I had the children queue up in a long double-file line on the pavement in front of the nursery. Mirjam, who dressed and changed the babies, waits inside with them in order to hand them over to their mothers at the very last moment. The streets are empty because of the curfew. The lack of street lighting means we'll have to make do with the moonlight. Only the contours of windows not quite blacked out are visible. Pimentel has instructed us to wait until we get a sign to cross the street and reunite the children with their parents. The group of thirty-two children we're waiting with here is surprisingly quiet. As if they're holding their breath for the moment they'll see their parents again. Two lights, moving independently from each other, are coming our way. They turn out to be boys from the Jewish Council riding their bicycles. 'We'll escort you across the street,' one of them says.

'But we're supposed to wait for the director's instructions,' I hear Sieny say. 'So we'll go only when she's here.'

They head into the theatre. Clouds obscure a crescent moon, and a freezing gust of wind hits our faces. The sound of horse hooves in the distance. A girl behind me starts to sob.

Suddenly, the headlights of a small truck parked in front of the theatre go on. It moves forward a bit, and now we have a clear view of the theatre entrance. There's a light on behind the revolving door. A flashlight being waved back and forth comes our way. It's Pimentel. 'You can go when all the parents are outside. It's important that the children remain calm. We don't want a panic.'

All of a sudden, I see something move. Dark silhouettes come out the revolving door. Like a meat grinder turning out sausages, the door keeps spitting out people. A rising murmur. Flashlights pointing the way. German orders. 'Form a group!' 'Stop at the gate!' 'No talking!' The truck has turned around and shines its headlights on the people waiting. A pair of mounted policemen cast long shadows on the street as two trams with an illuminated number 9 on the front edge closer.

We're then allowed to let the children rejoin their parents. Despite orders from the SS to be quiet, this is accompanied with lots of moaning and crying, both from parents and children. One German screams that if they don't quiet down, he'll make sure no one says anything anymore. The sound dies down, but one child keeps whining. 'Shut up!' a mother hisses at her child, and cuffs him on the ear. Mirjam comes over to the queue with two babies in a pram. She calls out their names, then hands over the children to their mothers. I go back into the nursery with her to go get two more infants. Holding a swaddled baby in my arms, I head back to the theatre. 'Lena Papegaai's mother?' A tall, skinny woman raises her hand. I hand over the girl, and I'm about to walk away when the woman, panic-stricken, gasps: 'This isn't my child.' I realise we've mixed up the babies by accident: I gave her the boy. I quickly go over to Mirjam: 'Who did you give the other baby to?' Mirjam points to a mother who's put the baby in a carrier.

'Why?'

'Nothing.'

I walk up to the mother with the baby boy in my arms. 'I'm sorry, but I gave you a girl by accident. Here's your son.'

The woman turns pale, looking at the child in her carrier and the child in my arms. 'For heaven's sake, how incredibly stupid of you!' she hisses. She's likely embarrassed she failed to notice the mix-up herself.

'Yes, it is,' I say, feeling guilty. 'Thank goodness we have people who are paying attention.' I hand her the boy and then take the girl from her sling. 'Alright then, let's go find your mama now.' I give the mother a quick nod. She's holding her son close with a look that says: *No one is taking him from me again.*

What if the girl's mother hadn't been so alert? They might have only found out tomorrow the child wasn't theirs. Who knows if they'd have ever had their own children back? I may look like a certified nursery teacher, but I'm no less prone to making serious mistakes.

The boys from the Council are carrying all the luggage to the transport car. A lampshade clatters onto the street. The muted voices go silent for a second. Then, a small, hunchbacked man walks away from the group.

'Halt, stay where you are!'

A mounted policeman blocks his path. But the man just walks around him and keeps going, undeterred. The officer draws his revolver.

'Stop or I'll shoot!'

The man doesn't even look around and continues to walk, hunching forward. Two shots ring out. The people waiting in line gasp in horror. The man does a kind of nosedive onto the pavement and then remains motionless.

'I warned him,' the Dutch officer says in his defence. I look at the formless heap on the pavement and get the strange sense none of this is real. That it's a scene from a film or play, and that the actor playing the hunchbacked man will get back up in a moment and take a bow.

A low, German voice booms through a megaphone: 'Another escape attempt like this and you'll all be put up against a wall!'

I pinch my hand. This is definitely real. I need to stay calm, do what I'm told and suppress any other impulses.

'We're opening the trams. Everyone, get in quickly and sit down,' the megaphone orders.

People run towards the footboard and squeeze in like it's a game of musical chairs. I help a nervously trembling mother wrap her baby in a sling. I pick up a blanket that slipped off a shoulder and put it back on the grandmother. I stroke a girl's head and promise we'll sing together again when she's back. One of the last passengers to board the tram is the boy who is leaving without his parents and is holding an unknown woman's hand. When my eyes meet his frightened gaze, I look the other way.

Within ten minutes, the coaches fill with over two hundred people. The trams depart as menacingly as they came, but now packed full of Jews, slowly gliding along the glistening tracks like giant caterpillars. The truck filled with all their belongings starts to move as well. Lastly, the horses absurdly trot after the procession. 'Everyone back to your stations!' the Germans order. The screeching tram, the horses' clattering hooves, the hum of engines, the SS men's orders, it all slowly ebbs away until all is silent. Finally, a gust of wind blows away any remaining traces of what took place here. Apart from the lifeless man, who lies in a heap on the pavement, nothing remains of what just happened here. I look at Sieny, who's staring at the man as well.

'What'll happen with...' I point at the man.

'They'll come get him in a moment, I think,' she whispers. I see her softly mutter a prayer.

I wonder if I should do the same, but then I hear Mirjam's voice behind us.

'Are you coming in too?' she asks flatly.

I hook arms with Sieny, and together we go back inside the nursery.

CHAPTER 17

FRIDAY, 6 NOVEMBER 1942

'Primacy of the Germanic Idea', *reads the headline of the periodical* De Waag. *'The expanding empire – which is more than a political conception, and which will be the embodiment of a life philosophy – this Empire not only offers every possibility for such a development, but needs this for its existence. Provided above all else that the Germanic brotherhood of blood is recognised as a condition for the individual life of all.' The front page of* The Jewish Weekly *advertises handicraft courses for people who want to learn clay modelling, drawing or woodwork. Another article recommends three different translation agencies for people who wish to send letters to those deployed to work in Germany.*

Things have settled down a bit in the nursery this past week because fewer people are being brought to the theatre. Could it be the worst is behind us? In any case, the calm gives me the opportunity to take a day off. It's my first day off since becoming a resident of the nursery, and I got up early to walk to my family home. Last evening, I baked a cake made of semolina and bread-crumbs. I know I'm not the world's best cook, but I copied the recipe from Mirjam, who made one a few times when one of us was having a birthday, and I have to say it turned out rather well. I've been looking forward to visiting my home so much I hardly slept. Nol and Jetty also said they'd be coming for tea, and Leni asked for the morning off as well. It feels like a little vacation after all those days and nights blurring into another. When just about every week saw the deportation of children I'd only just got to know. Weeks of sleeping whenever I could, but with an alertness in my veins to spring out of bed and into action at any moment.

I wrap the baking tray with the cake in a teacloth and put on my winter coat. The weather is grey and autumnal.

'Hey, lady, what do you have there?' There's a man cycling beside me who instantly reminds me of my father. The same balding head, the furrowed cheeks, the big dark eyes.

Is he a plainclothes policeman, or what does he want from me?

'This is a cake, sir.' I keep a steady pace.

'I love cake,' he coos.

'Sorry, sir, this one is for someone else.'

'Is that right? For who? Surely he's not as nice as me, right?'

'Obviously, I like my father more than you, sir.' I have no idea why I said the cake is for my father.

'I can come over and introduce myself to your father, then you and I can get on with expanding the family right after.' His laugh gives me the chills.

'My father wouldn't like it if I came home with someone older than him.'

The man immediately gets that I'm insulting him.

'You should be happy if a Dutchman doesn't think he's too good for you, little bitch. I should give you a proper spanking.'

'Are you aware that you can be prosecuted for touching a Jewish girl?' I give him a haughty look, hoping he'll clear off now.

But instead of cycling on, he blocks my path.

'This is why everyone hates you people. It's because you're an arrogant bunch.' He grabs me by the wrist. 'I could report you in a second, you filthy Jewess! I can make sure you're put on a train tomorrow. Or you can come with me now.'

The sudden realisation that I'm trapped makes me freeze with fear. I can tell from the creep's blank stare that he's serious.

"I'm sorry... Let me go.'

'You'd like that, wouldn't you? Come here!' Holding me by the wrist, he starts tugging at me. The man is completely insane. I need to get away before he drags me off to his house. Apart from a few pedestrians and cyclists, the streets are empty. Who'll come to my aid if I start screaming? *Stay calm, don't show him I'm afraid. Think.*

'Sir, you can take me with you, but then we'll both be in trouble,' I bluff.

The man looks at me, uncomprehending. 'What's that?'

'You, because it's a criminal offence to rape a Jewess, and I because I already have these painful sores down there. The doctor said it's best not to because it's transmissible...'

The man's weather-beaten face goes blank for a few seconds as I hold my breath. He then produces a smile, parting his lips and baring a set of rotten teeth. Through the dark gaps in between, he hisses: 'I'm on to you, you filthy whore.'

He then knocks the cake out of my hands and cycles off. I see the baking tray roll out from under the teacloth. Only when it comes to a halt do I dare move again. I pick the tray up off the street, my hands shaking. I bite my lip almost to the point of bleeding just so I won't show up at my home with a tear-stained face. I keep a fast pace, realising it could have gone horribly wrong had I not just learned what venereal diseases are during my medical training.

Still shaking from the incident, I get to Van Woustraat at last, where Mrs Overvliet, our neighbour, is just coming out of Koot's shop. I notice her appearance has become neater in recent years: her hair curled and styled, a tailored wool coat, elegant heels. I hope she doesn't see me.

'Hi, Betty, great to see you here on our street again,' Mrs Overvliet says. 'How's life as a nurse?'

'Nursery teacher. Yes, it's great.'

'You always loved children,' she says, smiling at me. 'Remember when you came by our place with your doll carriage?'

I remember quite well. I mainly visited the childless husband and wife because they always gave me chocolate.

'I got such a fright that time you had an actual baby in your carriage.'

'Japie used to be my big baby doll,' I say.

She moves closer to me. 'That shop of Koot's, it's not what it used to be,' she whispers conspiratorially. 'Nothing worth your money, and don't even get me started about the dreadful service. No, it's an absolute disgrace you had to move out.'

'You can say that again,' I say weakly.

'Oh well, I won't be going there anymore myself. We're moving to Weesperzijde this coming week. Number eighty-seven.'

I'm alarmed immediately. Up until now, she and her husband at least served as a thin shield against the SD. 'That's too bad...' I whisper.

Then, so softly I can hardly understand her, she says: 'Betty, if there's ever anything you need from us, now you know our address, alright?'

'Baking isn't your greatest talent, is it?' Leni jokes when she sees me remove the mangled cake from the baking tin and attempt to knead it back into its original shape.

'Just wait until you've tasted it.'

I serve my creation on the floral porcelain plates Granny brought back from Paris when she'd stayed there a month. This was before she moved in with us, and when Engel was still an actual housemaid rather than part of the furniture.

I cut and divide the cake, and I'm just about to have a seat when Japie enters.

'Just in time. Cake?' He nods.

'Where have you been?' Grandmother asks in a stern voice.

Japie shrugs. 'With Jur.'

I'm taken aback by his deep voice. 'Well now, someone's voice is changing.'

'Yeah, can't you hear?' my brother sneers.

'You wouldn't know it, but our little brother is becoming a man,' Nol says, teasing him.

'Japie is turning into quite a Jaap,' Leni chimes in.

'A strapping young Jaap,' I say.

'If only the changes were limited to his voice,' Nol says suggestively, at which Japie turns red instantly. This has the three of us rolling in the aisles.

'Don't let it bother you, Japie,' Nol's wife says, sticking up for him. 'Later, when they're old and wrinkled, you'll still be a handsome man.'

'Well, he could act like a man once in a while and lend us a hand instead of going out and about all day,' Mother says.

'Jur is being put on a transport this evening,' my brother says flatly. 'It was the last time I could see him.' He goes to his room and shuts the door behind him. We're not laughing anymore.

'How was I supposed to know?' Mother says, grimacing.

'More tea, anyone?' my sister asks.

'*L'absence ne tue l'amour que s'il était malade au départ,*' Granny lilts. 'Absence doesn't kill love, unless it was already ailing when leaving.' Then, turning to Leni: 'I'll have another cup, dear. Top me up.'

'How are things going over there at your work?' Nol asks when we're all through the lighter subjects.

'Oh, I don't notice too much of it,' I answer evasively.

'Come on, Betty, you're right there,' my brother says.

I shrug. 'We just take care of the children. I don't know what else is happening.'

'I heard from a colleague that the nursery is now only open for children set to be deported,' Nol says. 'He couldn't get care for his own children anymore.'

'Yes, that's a nuisance,' I say. My eyes dart to Leni, who gets up and pours more coffee. She knows, like I do, that much worse things are happening.

'Is it true that foundlings are brought in too sometimes?' Jetty asks.

'Yes, sometimes,' I say.

'Can you imagine? Abandoning your newborn child just like that?' she sighs.

It's only now I notice my brother's wife has plumped up a bit. Her hand rests lightly on her lap. Could that be what's piqued her interest? Because she already fears for the embryo growing in her belly?

'Unless you're set to be put on a transport yourself and want to save your child,' my sister says.

'Some days ago, a baby was brought to the nursery, a boy. He'd been found on the doorstep of a villa in Bloemendaal. They named him Remi van Duinwijck. Remi from the book *Nobody's Boy*, and Duinwijck because that's the name of the street where he was abandoned.'

Remi is a rosy-cheeked baby of about six months old. I was instantly smitten when I saw him on Pimentel's arm, looking around so seriously with those big brown eyes. As were all the other nursery teachers. He might well be the most beautiful baby I've ever seen. 'This fellow is living with us from now on,' Pimentel said. 'His name is Remi, but he's far from nobody's boy because he has no less than thirty mothers and a hundred brothers and sisters. Isn't that so, cutie?' Remi answered with a belch. Everyone laughed.

'So, you don't even know his name?' Jetty asks.

'No, not a thing about him.'

Engel raises her hand.

'Yes, Engel, go ahead,' Granny says.

'Then how do they know he's Jewish?' she asks quietly.

Granny rolls her eyes. 'Engel, you do know what men have in their pants, don't you?'

'Yeah, yeah...' Engel says tentatively.

I doubt if Engel knows, and from the looks of everyone else I'm not the only one.

'Well, you can tell straight away by looking at it!'

'Remi isn't circumcised,' I say.

'His schnozzle must be half a meter long then.' Nol laughs at his own joke.

'He has a tiny little nose. But an NSB doctor examined him, and it seems he has Jewish ears.' They all stare at me in disbelief.

'Jewish ears? What are Jewish ears?' Mother asks.

No one knows the answer.

I look around the room at my family. Everyone seems lost in

thought about what remains unspoken. Mother is incessantly rubbing her hands across her legs, like it's some kind of tic, and every now and then, looks back at the hallway door that Japie walked out of. Granny, who's a full foot taller than the hunched-up Engel, stares at the wall, her arms folded under her breasts. I wonder what she's looking at. The photo of Father that's still hanging there? The landscape painted by a distant cousin? Or the dried flowers that Mother framed?

Nol runs his finger across the dessert plate and licks it. Jetty has her eyes on her hands on her lap. And Leni stares out the window.

Mother gets up and starts clearing the coffee table. 'Who's staying for dinner tonight? Because I'll start cooking already.'

I help her clean up and follow her into the kitchen.

Even though her answer last time was quite clear, I decide to try one last time. 'Mother, I just saw Mrs Overvliet. She's moving.'

'Yes, I know,' Mother says in a voice devoid of emotion.

'She told me they'd be willing to help us if we're in trouble.'

'That NSB lot?' Mother shrieks. 'Fat chance! I'd rather let them take me.'

'But didn't they help us a few times?' I whisper to tone our conversation down a bit.

'Do you really think so? Do you know where they're moving? To a large house of Jews who were deported. They're not on our side, Betty. And you're an absolute fool if you still think they are.'

I'm now so frustrated I raise my voice too. 'But, Mama, you don't have any other choice. Don't you understand? Those camps in the east aren't ordinary labour colonies. They're prisons where they might well lock you up for the rest of your life. Please...'

'Can you settle down a bit in here?' Granny peeks around the corner.

'It's alright, Mother. Betty, are you eating with us?'

'No, I need to get back.'

Grandmother casts me an accusing look as I walk past.

'I know, Granny,' I say curtly. 'I need to know my place.'

CHAPTER 18

SUNDAY, 29 NOVEMBER 1942

One journalist writes: 'There are still many who, whether or not they consider race science to be foolish, regardless do not recognise as such the world view that gave rise to the rebirth of race science from skull-measuring armchair scholarship to life and culture-engendering science. They feel there is much to commend in national socialism, like for example the combating of abuses, the fight for social justice, the revival of national awareness, and because of this they feel drawn to it. But that national socialism is not merely a combination of the old socialism and the old nationalism, but rather a new worldview that is based on the conscious experience of our own nature, this is something not many are willing to comprehend. Is this because there are too many consequences? This half-hearted attitude is typical of the people's unseemliness.'

I take a breath of relief when we step out into the cold wind blowing outside. We all cross the street together at the same time. 'Hey, little man, what's your name?' I ask a crying boy who resists being forcibly taken from the theatre.

'His name is Jacob. Jacob Meijer,' Mirjam says.

'I didn't see that name anywhere,' I say. 'How do you know?'

She shrugs. 'Officially, he doesn't exist.'

'What do you mean?'

'Do I have to spell everything out for you?' Mirjam quickens her pace and goes inside without saying another word. I look at Sieny, who waves her away. 'Never mind, she's in one of her moods.'

Even if Mirjam is in a bad mood, she rarely shows it. I think it's something else. 'I think she knows more,' I tell Sieny. 'Only she can't talk about it. And she blames us for that.'

'What does she know?'

I shrug. 'You'd know if I knew.'

Two days later, the small boy is still crying. Holding his wooden jumping jackrabbit in his arms, he keeps screaming for his mama and papa. I decide to try again at getting through to him. 'Jacob? Hey, little man. You'll see your parents again soon!' The small boy gives me a skittish look and continues to sob.

'They're there, on the theatre,' he says, huffing and puffing and pointing his little finger at the theatre.

'Do you mean on the stage? In the main hall?' He nods. For the first time, he looks straight at me with those dark eyes of his. 'And who brought you to the theatre? Your mama and papa?'

He shakes his little head. 'No... I was with Aunt Juf, but she's ill.'

'You were with your aunt when the soldiers came to get you?'

'And with Uncle. But they had to stay home.'

'And then you had to come along by yourself.'

'Yes...' He gives me a look that says: *Finally someone gets it.* 'But Mama and Papa are over there, and I want to be with

them.' Now that we've returned to the subject of his mother and
father, he starts crying again.

I decide to bring him to Pimentel.

'This child really needs to go back to his parents,' I say as I enter
Pimentel's office with the preschooler and his jumping
jackrabbit.

Pimentel is holding little Remi in her arms. The boy seems
to have become an extension of herself. The first few weeks, her
dog was so jealous of its master's new friend that the slightest
thing would make it growl like a cranky, jealous husband. It
even bit Sieny's hand. Not very hard, but that was the last straw
for Pimentel, and she locked the unruly animal in the shed for
two days. Now that it's back inside, it seems to have resigned
itself to its new place and acts overprotective towards both its
master and Remi. Instead of growling, it now barks whenever
someone enters. Perhaps it followed the example of the German
Shepherds guarding their territory on the evenings of the
transports.

'Bruni, sit! What were you saying, Betty?'

I push the boy shrugging his little shoulders forward. 'Jacob
was rounded up at his aunt and uncle's place and saw his
parents again in the theatre. But before he could go to them, he
had to come here.'

Pimentel looks at the little boy and bends down. 'You're
Jacob Meijer, aren't you?'

He nods.

'Why don't you come here with me, dear.' Pimentel hands
me Remi, who's far from shy and immediately grabs onto my
nose. 'He needs a clean pair of pants.'

. . .

I get Jacob back an hour later, and he's still crying. Pimentel gives me an exasperated look that says: *Stubborn as a mule.* Then she turns towards the small boy and says: 'You promised you'd be good and go to sleep now, right?'

Jacob nods, teary-eyed.

'Then I promise you can go see your mama and papa afterwards.'

Jacob doesn't seem entirely convinced, but he sticks his thumb in his mouth and lets me take him with me.

When I put him in one of the beds, his body is still shaking with unceasing grief, but in an effort to keep his promise he squeezes his eyes shut.

'It's great you're willing to bring him to his parents,' I say to Pimentel when I pass her in the hallway.

'Not to his parents,' she says. 'They're gone already. But he'll be picked up this evening.'

'To go to Westerbork as well?' I ask.

'No, not there,' she says, going into her room. 'Somewhere else.' She then turns towards Remi. 'Alright, little man, you come here to Aunt Henriëtte again.'

The following day, Jacob is gone.

CHAPTER 19

FRIDAY, 4 DECEMBER 1942

The sick bay is in the theatre's former coffee corner. It's one of the few rooms in the theatre where daylight enters. Just a few years ago, there were chairs and tables in front of the window instead of beds, and the wealthiest Jews from Amsterdam would be drinking their coffee or tea here with their pinkies raised. You could hear the chatter and laughter from outside. Granny also came here regularly to see and be seen. With a fox collar draped over her shoulders, chaperoned by my mother in her most expensive silk dress.

It's getting dark outside. The room is filled with a pale hue and seems drained of all pigment, like in a photograph. 'Could you go get the things for Betty?' Doctor De Vries Robles asks the young man who's busy in front of the cabinet. It's only then that I notice it's Leo. I haven't seen him in months.

'Oh, hi, Betty,' Leo says cheerily when he turns around. 'Pimentel said you'd come.' His hair has grown longer and curls playfully about his neck.

I try not to let on how physically affected I am by his presence. 'Funny how other people know more than me sometimes,' I chortle.

'Indeed,' Leo says, then gives me a wink that makes the hair on my arms stand on end.

'Here's the package. If you have a second, I'll get my coat. I just finished my shift anyway.'

'Your shift was over an hour ago,' says Doctor De Vries Robles. When Leo walks off, he teasingly whispers: 'He's waited a whole hour for you.'

I'm confused. What did I do to deserve this renewed attention from Leo all of a sudden?

'Would you like to go for a little walk?' he asks when we step outside.

'Like this?' I point at my uniform.

'I can wait for you to get changed,' Leo says. 'An extra half hour won't make a difference now.' His mischievous smile once more sends shivers up my spine. A response that doesn't fit with how I feel about him at all.

He sees me hesitate. 'I'm sorry I haven't been in touch after our date. I was really busy and, well, maybe I wasn't ready for anything serious just yet.'

'Jeez, that's a lot of information in one sentence,' I say, genuinely surprised.

Leo takes my hand and plants a kiss on it. 'Believe me, I've tried to get you out of my head, but I couldn't.'

Ten minutes later, I've dropped off the medicines inside, flung on a cute dress, quickly brushed my teeth and draped my winter coat over my shoulders.

'You did that a lot faster than my sisters,' Leo says, satisfied. He holds up his arm so I can lock mine with his.

Our conversation is a bit stilted at first, but gradually we're both able to relax. Leo asks a lot of questions, showing that his interest is genuine. When he asks about my brother Gerrit, I let go of my last reservations.

'The odd thing is I never thought they'd get the better of my brother,' I say softly. 'And I still hope that's the case, but I'm afraid—'

Leo has turned to face me and puts his finger on my lips. 'Shh, don't say it. You need to hold on to that hope. You know your brother better than anyone. Surely, he's smart enough to get himself out of this, even if he's unable to tell any of you yet.' He gives me a serious look. His eyes seem the same dark blue as the sky now evening has fallen. A puff of warm breath escapes his mouth. Then, slowly, he leans in and kisses me. Not like that first time, rough and pushy, but gently, softly. He wraps his arms around me as we continue to kiss ever more eagerly, passionately. Our intertwined bodies form a cocoon of warmth against the cold wind as he lovingly runs his hand through my hair. Only when someone whistles behind us do I return to reality.

Leo's eyes glisten, just like his lips. 'How would you feel about coming over to my student house? It's a lot warmer there,' he says.

'But the evening curfew...'

'It's only half past five. We could also go to the nursery, just as long as the heater is on.'

'We're not allowed to have male visitors.'

'Really? Then we have no other choice...' He looks at me, almost pleading. 'I won't bite. Nor will any of the guys in my house.'

'Or growl?'

He laughs. 'Not that either.'

Holding hands, we walk along Herengracht to Leo's student house. He can't get over the fact that men aren't allowed to visit at the nursery and calls it puritan.

'It's not that unusual, is it?'

'I just hadn't expected it from Henriëtte,' Leo says. 'She's rather... how to put this, progressive herself, as far as love goes.'

I give him a searching look. 'What do you mean, exactly?'

'Well, let's just say she's not into the traditional boy-girl thing. More like girl-girl...'

There have been whispers, but still I find it offensive to be talking about Pimentel in such a disparaging way. 'Maybe she used to be, but you couldn't tell by looking at her now.'

'I've known her all my life through her brother, who's the director of the hospital in Amstelveen. He's good friends with my grandfather. It's because of him that I went on to study medicine.'

'And it's because of her I went on to work with children. It seems the Pimentel family brought good things to both of us.' With that, I hope to end the conversation.

A life among students in a canal house is quite different from what I'd expected. Five boys are playing cards when we enter, and the room is full of smoke. The waft of cigarettes, sweat and chimney smoke gets deep inside my nose. The floor is littered with old newspapers and magazines, while the furniture is covered with clothing items. There's an empty and a half-empty bottle of *jenever* on the table. The atmosphere is heated. Not because of my entrance or the two other ladies looking bored on the sofa, but because they're playing for cash and food coupons. It looks decadent and disgraceful. I give them my friendliest greeting, but I'm wholly ignored.

'Don't mind my housemates,' Leo says. 'They're barbarians.'

I think I'd have turned around and left if Leo hadn't immediately apologised. 'Do you want to see my room?' he says. 'At least there we can have a chat in peace.' He gives me a look like that of a dog that thinks he'll be getting a piece of sausage. The fluttery feeling in my belly is giving off mixed signals. Should I

come with him to his room or leave it at this? Again, I remember
my mother's remark about men having their fill. 'You have to
keep them hungry and feed them small bits at a time.' Only, my
mother isn't here. 'Sure,' I say.

'Welcome to my little palace.' Leo flicks on the floor lamp.
His room is shabbier and smaller than I'd expected from this
enormous house. It barely fits a bed and a wardrobe. The paint
on the walls is peeling off, and there's a blanket draped in front
of the window. He pulls me onto his bed and once again presses
his mouth to mine. A kiss I return, but which doesn't quite over-
whelm me like the last time. He then gently pushes me back
onto the mattress. Kissing me all over, his mouth seeks out my
neck, and I try hard not to wince from the flutters it's giving me.
His hands slide over my shoulders, down to my breasts. 'You're
so soft, so beautiful,' he pants, stroking the fabric of my dress.
'Can I feel them naked? Your breasts really turn me on.'

It seems a bit impractical with my dress and bra. 'Yes, but—'

He doesn't wait for my objections. It's like I've given him
the go-ahead. He hastily unbuttons my dress, pulls down the
sleeves and reaches behind my back, where he skilfully unhooks
my bra. I'm surprised at how fast it's all going, and how, just like
that, I'm now lying here with my top off. I try to surrender to his
hands. 'Oh, Betty, it feels so good,' he moans in my ear. 'Do you
like it too?'

'Yeah, yeah, great,' I mutter, but it feels like little more than
him squeezing my breasts. Isn't this what I fantasised about
before? What once made me wake from a dream feeling excited
and with a sensation between my legs I'd never felt before? Still,
I fail to get that same feeling now. Or even just to keep my mind
on things. I'm reminded of a time when I was spending the holidays on a guest farm and I was allowed to milk a cow. I
remember what it felt like to touch its udder, with those long
teats you had to pull on really hard. I asked the farmer if I
wasn't hurting the cow, at which he laughed out loud, never

answering my question. I think of the cotton pieces Engel puts between her breasts against chafing when they rub up against each other, of my mother's soft bosom where I leaned my head as a child.

'I'll go on, okay?' Leo pants.

'Alright.' I try to sound as if I'm just as excited to spur him on. I'm sure I'll feel more if I manage to focus. If I no longer look at this banal game from a distance but try to be inside my body. As he continues to knead my breast with one hand, he tries pulling down my stockings with the other. His racing breath tickles my neck. I could help him, but I don't want to come across as lascivious. Which, of course, makes no sense, considering what I'm doing now. I feel him press his crotch against me harder and harder. His hand is now reaching around in my panties, nearly breaking the elastic of my garter.

'Do you want to? Do you want it?'

I'd like to say no, but his glittering eyes, like magic, do something to me. They glisten with yearning, with a desire to possess me.

'Alright, but don't finish...'

'I understand.'

Could it be this is his first time like it is for me?

He unfastens my wool stockings from the garter, but then the hook gets caught on the lace of my panties. As adept as he was at first, he's clumsy now. He moves downwards, and I feel like giggling from nerves. When the elastic comes loose at last, it hits him right in the eye. 'Dammit!'

'Jeez, you're such a klutz,' I laugh.

He suddenly stops what he's doing and raises himself with one hand on his eye. 'Like you're much help!'

'Sorry, are you alright? Is your eye still there?' I ask, hoping to lighten the situation.

But Leo turns away from me.

'Hey, Leo, it was a joke. Shall we continue?'

He has his back towards me. 'Not if it's going to be like this,' he says to the wall.

I'm confused. Did I blow it somehow?

Only when I'm making myself presentable again does he turn back towards me. 'I'm sorry, Betty. I got ahead of myself.'

He brings me home, but we're silent nearly all the way. When we say goodbye, he kisses me on the cheek. 'We'll be seeing each other, alright?'

'Sure,' I say.

'Were you out on a date with Leo?' Sieny asks in a suggestive tone when I enter. She nudges Mirjam. 'We'd already figured it out!'

'Will you be seeing each other again?' Mirjam asks, taking a draw from her cigarette.

I shrug. 'Couldn't say.'

Mirjam blows out the smoke. 'I wouldn't bet on it.'

'What do you mean?' Sieny asks.

'I don't know,' Mirjam says. 'I feel he's a bit arrogant.'

CHAPTER 20

FRIDAY, 18 DECEMBER 1942

The well-known philosopher Victor Manheimer has jumped out of a window from the top floor of the theatre. The colleague who saw him jump said he looked like a bat because of how his coat flapped behind him.

The new Christmas song 'I'm Dreaming of a White Christmas' can often be heard coming from people's houses. Could this be an act of protest, with 'white Christmas' as a metaphor for peace? The Germans merrily hum along, even though they don't like American music. The song would be banned if they knew it was originally written by a Jew.

Harry is the courier from the Jewish Council who can be found in the nursery most often. He's a good guy, and pretty cute as well, but with his Rotterdam accent and crude jokes he tries a bit too hard to seem attractive. He enters alongside a lanky girl with a big pink bow in her hair.

'Hello, ladies, look who I have here. This is Roosje Poons.' The child doesn't look frightened so much as curious. 'These are all sisters who'll take good care of you. Especially this one here.' He puts his arm around Sieny. 'She's really nice.'

'I'd have all of them under my wing if it were up to you,' Sieny says, shaking her head. 'Come with me, sweetie. I'll bring you to your playmates.'

'No time for a little chat today, I suppose?' he calls after her. But Sieny is gone already. 'All work and no play, that girl,' he says in his thick accent, which makes me laugh.

'I wouldn't give up just yet, Harry. Maybe she'll have a bit more time this evening.'

'Oh well,' he says, pulling a face. 'Sparta Rotterdam never wins the national league title either, but I keep believing that'll happen too.'

The girls whisper that he has a crush on her. I've hinted at this several times myself already when I spoke to Sieny. But she waves off any such suggestion, claiming he's this nice to all ladies. I know she secretly feels he's too common to consider him a serious candidate. Even if she liked him, she could never take a boy like that home. I couldn't care less myself. I'm now convinced it's better to meet a guy who'll go the extra mile for you rather than someone who's full of himself. I haven't heard from Leo again.

'Where did this Roosje Poons come from?' I ask Harry. I've grabbed the notebook to write down her details.

'I don't really know,' Harry says. 'She'd been placed with someone who got cold feet and left her at the clothing depot around the corner here. There was only a note that said her name is Roosje Poons and that she's four years old.'

Later on, I go look for the little girl because I need more details than just her name. I find her in the main toddler room, where she's at a table colouring by herself.

'Hey, Roosje, sweetie. Do you like it here?' I say, taking a seat beside her.

She shyly casts her eyes down and continues to colour.

I try to catch Sieny's eye. She's by the sink filling drinking cups but then comes to me when she sees me.

'I was curious how Roosje is doing,' I say. 'And if she could tell me a little more about herself.'

'Roosje told us she's going to a holiday camp, isn't that right, Roosje?' Sieny says.

Roosje suddenly looks up and nods, wide-eyed. 'Mama said.'

'That's great! And what's your mama's name?'

'Manja.'

'And you have a brother too, right?'

'Izak. But he's too small to go on holidays.'

'Oh, how old is he?'

She shrugs, then folds in her thumb and holds up four little fingers. 'I'm this much already.'

'I can't get more out of her,' I say when I'm at Pimentel's desk with the notebook a little later. 'But I can ask around in the theatre if there's anyone with the same last name. Maybe she has family who can tell us more about her.'

I expect Pimentel to be pleased with my thoroughness, but instead she tears the last page from the notebook and tells me to write it all down again, only without Roosje.

'She doesn't exist.' She gets up and walks around the desk to the foundling Remi, who's lying in the playpen. 'Hey, little man. Did you fall asleep again? This is for you to play in. Your bed is for sleeping. You don't quite get that yet, do you?' She covers the boy with a blanket and moves some toys to the side. While Pimentel takes care of Remi and pampers him like he's her own child, she seems less involved with the active care of all the other children, as if they no longer interest her as much. Or is it just my imagination? I look at the dark, handsome boy sleeping on his back. His head tilted to the right, his little arms beside his head. 'Doesn't Remi have to go on a transport too?'

'No, the very little ones don't have to go,' she says, testy all of a sudden.

'Thank God, I was afraid—'

'You'd best be on your way,' she cuts me off. 'And close the door gently so he doesn't wake.'

I swallow my annoyance and get up. Just before I'm out the door, she calls me back for a second. 'Betty, the way things are going now may seem a bit haphazard. But it's not. That's all I can tell you.'

The way she looks at me, with both motherly warmth and natural authority, wins me over again.

Sixty-three of the eighty-seven children will be put on a train this evening. It seems this will be the last transport for the time being, so they also want to take the children who are here without their parents. Only babies and children whose parents work at the hospital or for the Council are allowed to stay. Mirjam and I wake the older children. I cross off each name to be sure they're getting the right children. When they've got dressed and are wearing their rucksacks, they go to the dining room to eat a bowl of porridge. One thirteen-year-old boy is missing. NIZ, it says behind his name. Pimentel brought him to the hospital today. Which seems odd because the child was in perfect health just yesterday. I suspect Pimentel of having 'made' him sick so he won't have to go to Westerbork.

We've got all the children ready. Mirjam is standing by the front door at the beginning of the hall, while I'm last in the long line. Only I don't know where Sieny is now. As we wait for a sign to take the group outside, I hear someone whisper my name. 'Betty, here. Betty.' I recognise the voice as Sieny's but have no idea where it's coming from. 'Upstairs. Come here!' I look up in the stairwell but don't see her there either. I hurry past the children to the front. 'Mirjam, we need to wait until Sieny is here.'

'Sieny?' Mirjam asks, surprised. 'She's in her room. She wasn't feeling well.'

That's odd. 'Try to stall a little longer, two more minutes.'

I quickly run to the back again and go up the stairs to the first floor.

'Sieny? Sieny?' I get no reply but then hear a child softly weeping. It sounds muffled, as if someone is trying to mute the sound. I walk towards the source on my toes. It's easiest to hear on the landing between the first and second floor. When I put my ear to the panelling, I feel one part is loose. I slide it to the side easily, creating a gap. The sound is clearly coming from here.

'Hello?' I say through the gap.

'Betty!' the voice replies immediately. 'We're here. Please come.'

SS men must have entered down in the hall because I hear loud voices. 'Is everyone ready here?'

I can't hear Mirjam's answer, but I hear the German's. 'How so? Surely we don't need to wait for a teacher? If all the children are here, we can start walking. Forward, march!'

From the inside, the panel is now fully slid to the side, and out crawls Sieny.

'You'll have to do it,' she pants. 'She doesn't trust me, and I can't get her to quiet down.'

'Let me handle this. You go back down, quick,' I say.

I'm far less slim than Sieny, but I'm able to crawl into the dark hole of just a metre high with greater agility than I'd come to expect from myself.

'It's Roosje,' Sieny adds before sliding the panel shut.

'Where's the dyno torch?' I manage to ask.

'It's broken.' Then all goes dark.

I bump my head against a beam, try to ignore the pain and
make myself smaller in order to reach the crying girl. No light
whatsoever comes into the cramped space, and I can only follow
my ears. The crying sounds so close I must be near her. I fumble
around with arms outstretched until I feel her hair. 'Roosje. It's
me, Betty. Shhh, it's alright,' I say, trying to calm her, stroking
her head. I understand the child is terrified. This space makes
me claustrophobic myself. 'We already saw each other today,
remember? Listen here, your mama...' The crying dies down a
bit when she hears the word 'mama'. 'Remember Mama told
you you'd be going to a children's holiday camp? Well, aren't
you lucky, because this is the first game at camp, and it's called:
hiding in the dark. And do you know what people do when they
have to hide?' I sit down on the floor and pull the girl onto my
lap. 'They tell each other wonderful stories in the dark.' The
child takes short, shallow breaths like kids do after having a
crying fit. 'Come put your face against me.' I gently direct her
head towards my chest. I'd often lie against my mother like this,
enjoying the way her voice resonated even more than the story
she was telling me. 'Now listen closely, Roosje, because this is a
story that you don't just hear but also feel. There once was a
beautiful princess. She lived in a castle with beautiful roses
growing all around. One cold winter morning, the girl woke and
all the flowers had turned into ice cream. The princess thought
they looked so delicious that she picked one...' I hear men's
boots stomping up the stairs, not one, but several people's.
Roosje has stopped crying.

'I'll tell you what happened next in a second...' I whisper,
holding her ear against my beating heart. 'But now we need to
be really quiet...' A small peep escapes her mouth, but then she
holds her breath.

'How dare you!' I hear Sieny scream. 'Commander, the children are sleeping. You'll wake them up with all that stomping.
This isn't a place for soldiers, get out!'

Good heavens, where does she get the nerve? She could get put on a transport for this herself. I hear the commander – Aus der Fünten? – yell something, then more stumbling on the stairs.

I feel Roosje go limp in my arms. 'Sweetie, don't forget to breathe! Hey! Roosje?' Then I hear her take a deep breath in and out again.

Quite some time passes before Harry eventually frees me from my hiding place. Getting out of the crawlspace with the half-sleeping girl isn't easy. Stumbling and fumbling, I manage to reach the exit. Harry is surprised to see not Sieny but me come out. 'Where's Sieny?'

'I'm here,' Sieny says. 'Alive and well.'

Harry takes her by the arm. It's a spontaneous gesture that clearly takes Sieny by surprise. 'My God, girl. I was so worried about you,' he says, relieved.

Sieny looks at the hand on her arm, then up at his face. I see it happen, the change in her eyes.

'That's sweet you were worried, Harry,' she says softly.

'Good to know you were all a bit worried about me as well,' I say flatly, stretching my stiff limbs with the heavy child still in my arms.

They both at once look back at me. 'Sorry, Betty, you saved my life.'

Harry takes the child from me, and Sieny puts her arms around me.

We all talk about what happened in the kitchen afterwards. 'I was busy loading the luggage,' Harry says, 'when I heard them talking about "that cheeky woman". I thought they were talking about Pimentel, but it was about you?'

'Yes, I'm afraid so,' Sieny says.

'But she's *your* cheeky woman, right?' I say to Harry.

He takes her hand. 'Yes, I sure hope so.'

Sieny turns red.

'Alright, you lot can do whatever you want, I'm going to bed,' Mirjam says.

'Yes, me too.'

I carefully close the door behind me, knowing he'll be kissing her and that she'll let him. Suddenly, I feel all alone.

CHAPTER 21

SUNDAY, 3 JANUARY 1943

The British Foreign Secretary Anthony Eden gave a speech on the BBC in which he said tens of thousands of Jews have been gassed or used as test subjects in Polish concentration camps.

They've cleared out all care homes in the city, so there are now almost exclusively elderly people in the theatre. As a consequence, it's surprisingly quiet at the nursery. I'm looking for the only two children in the theatre. When I find them in the wings and deliver my usual speech to the parents about how the children have to go across the street, the father is unexpectedly curt. 'You're not taking them. The time we still have together before we're gassed is too precious to me.'

I don't quite get what he means but decide to leave it, and I'm just about to leave the hall when an SS man enters.

'Dammit, is everyone in a sour mood here too?' he screams. 'What's the matter with you swine?' I recognise the guard as the dreadful Grünberg with his square head and broken teeth. 'I want to see happy Jews! Understand? I want you to sing. Sing!'

The soft murmur in the background dies down, and

everyone goes silent. I'm standing right by the swing doors, but still it seems best to wait a few seconds before I go outside. What if the door creaks? I'd draw more attention to myself than I want to.

'So, what's the hold-up?' says the SS man.

A man then stands up – hesitantly, but in tune, he starts to sing the first notes of *Hatikvah*, the song of the Zionist movement.

'There you go! Sing!'

Others join in with the singer. First a woman, but then more and more people start singing and humming along to the well-known melody. The German laughs sardonically, though he has no idea what the words being sung mean.

'Our hope is not yet lost, the hope of two thousand years...' the man sings in Hebrew.

I run into Joop in the hallway, the tall courier with the sympathetic face, big eyebrows and dark brown eyes who I've now become well-acquainted with. He often comes by with Harry to bring things to the nursery. 'Betty, did you hide all the children?' he jokes. I'm too shaken by what I've just seen and heard to answer.

'Are you alright?' he asks, leaning towards me.

'Is it true?' I whisper close to his face. 'Is it true they're gassing us?'

'Gassing? As in sticking our heads into ovens?' he asks with a smile on his face. 'I highly doubt it. Where would you get that many ovens from?'

'But someone just said—'

Joops takes me by the arm and pulls me into a corner where no one can hear us. His facial expression has changed, and he gives me a solemn look. 'Keep quiet, but it's true.'

'How do you know?'

'I've heard an illegal radio recording through people I know in the underground.'

'The underground?'

'The resistance. There's a whole bunch of resistance groups now, people doing things in secret to help Jews and thwart the Germans. They distribute illegal newspapers, copy food coupons and identity papers. They arrange hiding places for Jews looking to escape deportation.'

I knew there were things happening in secret, but I had no idea large groups had organised.

'But gassed? How?'

'They didn't say, but later I heard people are made to shower, only it's not water coming from the faucets but gas...'

It's such a bizarre story that the words don't really sink in. Instead, I feel a void open up inside me, from my toes to the top of my head. An infinitely large hole of nothingness, filling out with still more nothingness. Until I slowly start to lift off, like a balloon being carried away by the wind. A Zeppelin sailing through the sky, off to another world.

'Betty.' He gives me a concerned look. 'Are you alright?'

'I just can't believe people would be capable of that...'

Joop shrugs. 'Neither can I, but you wouldn't have believed any of the things happening now half a year ago, would you?'

'This resistance, do they need anyone else by any chance?'

He puts his hand on my shoulder and gives me a piercing look. 'You stay and care for these children. They need you a lot more.'

Now I know what's in store for us, I need to make sure my family gets an exemption before it's too late. This is why I've been waiting for over an hour in front of the Expositur on my one free afternoon. There's cursing and fighting in the long queue. When a woman comes out in high spirits and tells a

friend it's been taken care of, someone in line says she likely had
to spread her legs for it. One gentleman with a cigar manages to
rile everyone up when he says he knows Mr Cohen, the
chairman of the Jewish Council, from Leiden, where they both
studied classical languages. He shows a photo of the two of
them as proof. When it's my turn at last, I passionately argue
that my whole family is doing things for the Council: my sister
at the hospital, my brother in food distribution, me in childcare,
and that each of us deserve one extra *Sperre* for our mother,
granny and my brother. I leave Engel out for simplicity's sake.
The clerk looks fatigued and says they'll look into my case.
They can't promise anything.

CHAPTER 22

MONDAY, 18 JANUARY 1943

The latest ordinance states that all foundlings will be labelled as Jewish from now on, irrespective of their appearance. By doing so, the Germans wish to put a halt to the large number of foundlings turning up in recent months. All these babies are now brought to our nursery.

A colleague just said there's someone on the phone for me. The crying from the baby section, which is right by the staff room, makes it hard for me to hear who's on the other end. 'Hello, Betty speaking. Wait a second, I can't hear you.'

I quickly close the door and return to the wall phone in the corner. It's only then I hear that the person on the other end is crying too. It's the weeping not of a child but of a grown man.

'Betty... I... It's Mama,' the voice sputters.

My heart starts racing. 'Japie, what's the matter with Mama?'

'They were arrested... All of them.'

I lean against the wall and clasp the phone with both hands. 'Japie, where are you?'

'In the café across the street, it was... It was... awful,' I hear him say, hyperventilating.

'Calm down, Jaap, calm down. Breathe in, and back out, slowly. One more time.' I hear Jaap sigh. 'Now tell me what happened.'

'I'd just come home, and Mother was cooking dinner, and I was looking out the window when all of a sudden I saw a raid van. I told Mother so, and then right after the doorbell rang. Green Police. I knew I then had to run to the attic, but there wasn't any time because I would have run into them in the stair-well, so I fled into the side room and hid under the bed.' He stops to take a deep breath after his flurry of words, then goes on talking in a choked-up voice. 'I heard everything, Betty. How they stomped up the stairs and went into Granny's bedroom. She was screaming her lungs out... They dragged Engel out the room as well. Of course, she can't see anything, and I think she fell over because there was stumbling and more screaming, also from Mother. She cried that those Germans were insane, all of them. Didn't they have mothers themselves? Did they also treat them like this? Granny cried: "Keep your hands off me. I won't let you grab me. I'll walk myself." But they grabbed her anyway because then...' Japie is unable to go on.

'What Japie? What happened then?'

'I... never heard Granny scream like that...'

I almost can't bear to listen to him. I press my head against the wall hard so the physical pain overrides his words.

'And then their voices disappeared, and all I heard were heavy boots stomping through our house. Also in the side room where I was. I thought: *This is it, now they'll come and find me...*'

He lets out a sob.

'I was so scared... I was afraid to breathe...Then the door was pulled shut with a bang. The footsteps died down, and the light was turned off. Then it was quiet. But I was afraid to come out. I had to stay down, I thought, in case someone had stayed behind. Or maybe they're still out by the door. And when a half hour had passed and I was about to come out of hiding, I suddenly heard someone come down the stairs. They really were still waiting! So I stayed down a little longer and only came out and went here when I was sure it was safe.'

'Did anyone see you go in? Widow Koot?'

'I don't think so...'

'It was her. I'm sure of it. She called them and told them there were still a couple more here.'

I hear my little brother cry on the other end again. The quivering sound of his young man's voice. 'Betty, what should I do?'

'Japie, you have to stay calm.'

But my brother won't be calmed. 'Did you see them in the theatre?'

'No, I don't think they're here. The place is jam-packed. I know they then bring people to Amstel Station directly.'

'I'm going there. I need to see Mama...'

'Jaap, wait. What are you going to do there? They'll arrest you. Is that what you want? I hope not.'

'I'm going.'

The line goes dead.

Sieny is standing behind me. 'Betty, are you alright?'

I just shake my head. *No. I'm not, dammit.* They got them, they took them before the Expositur could tell me if my requests were granted. My family, my beacon. It's happening again. It's as if the growing void inside me is causing me to lift off into the air. I'm being filled with air that lifts me off the floor like a balloon, and I see myself. I see Sieny putting an arm on my shoulder. She's talking to me. I'm listening and nodding. I see myself wiping the tears from my eyes and saying I'm alright. Promising not to go to Amstel Station myself and trying to focus

on my work. The children who need me. I see and hear all this,
but it's like it isn't me.

Koot's shop is closed. I walk past our old shop window with cold
indifference. My time will come. I go up the stairs to our home
and turn the lock. It's so dark inside I need to give my eyes a
second to adjust before I can see anything. I think I hear something upstairs, and I'm suddenly gripped by fear. Suppose Japie
isn't here anymore but rather someone from the SS with glistening eyes, waiting to get me? Or the man on the bicycle who
wanted to drag me to his house. Should I say it's me or instead
sneak around the house in silence to be sure the coast is clear?
There's a sudden creak upstairs. Someone's walking around. On
impulse, I call out, 'Jaap! Japie, is that you?'

'Shhh!' a voice upstairs says. 'Don't let them hear us.'

He's standing at the top of the stairs like a ghost. We walk
towards each other, and I grab hold of him halfway up the stairs.
His shoulders are shaking from holding back tears. 'Sweetie,
shhh, it's alright.'

The electricity has been cut off, but thankfully the gas hasn't
yet. By the light of two candles, I make my brother some soup.

'I went to the station to see Mama, but there was a guard
from the Green Police with a rifle on his shoulder,' Japie says,
his voice breaking.

'I was afraid of that,' I say, putting the chicken broth in front
of him.

'I was able to see something on the side. People were being
dragged from the stairs onto the platform. Some of them tripped
and toppled over each other. I didn't see Mother, Granny or
Engel.'

'I don't think they fell. They look out for each other, I'm sure of it.'

Still, I can't get the image out of my head. Granny and Engel, their arms interlocked, losing their balance on the stairs and falling forward. Maybe even dragging Mother along as they fall.

Japie sits there, hunched forward as he eats. He then holds his spoon still, tears dripping into his soup.

'Hey, Japie.' I sit down beside him and stroke his back. 'I'm sure they'll be alright. Really.' I don't believe my own words, but so long as I'm able to comfort my brother I can keep from breaking down myself.

Japie looks up with his red, teary eyes and says: 'Betty, what am I going to do?'

'You can go to Karel Baller. I already arranged it. Here's the address, and make sure you go in through the back.' I take the note out from my pocket and hand it to him. 'Memorise it, then throw it away. Alright?'

Japie reads the note and then holds it over the fire.

'Hey, shouldn't you keep it just a little longer?'

Japie shakes his head. 'No, I took a photo with my eyes.' He's nervously scratching his chin, which now has whiskers growing on it. 'But I'm staying here. Nol says he can get Mama out. He's also brought me some food, so I can stay and wait here until she's back.'

'Our house is very likely to be pulsed,' I say, referring to the removal firm Puls, which is emptying out all the houses.

'They won't do that with our house because you and Leni are still officially living here.'

'And what if Koot hears you?' I ask, concerned.

'She won't hear me. I walk around in socks.'

'I'll also try to get Mother released through Director Pimentel.'

Japie nods. 'It's bound to work if it's coming from two sides,' he says, trying to convince himself.

Here we are, two children without their parents. Still, we're no orphans. Not yet.

I've put him to bed, and I'm about to leave when I think of something. Did Granny take her family jewels with her, or was there no time for that? I tiptoe over to Granny's room, which is to the back of the house on the first floor. Her large wooden bed is neatly made, presumably by Engel, who always sleeps on the small single bed with the mesh base on the other side of the room. The grey dress with fur pieces Granny wore at Nol's wedding is hanging from the wardrobe. I put the dress on the bed, open the wardrobe's doors and search the secret compartment in the back. I know that's where she keeps her valuables because she showed me once. 'So you'll know my secret hiding place if I die unexpectedly,' she'd said. You can only open it by first fully pulling all the drawers out and then removing a panel from the top. I see straight away Granny never had the chance to hide her treasure under her dress and take it with her. The box is full of necklaces, rings, diamond pendants, earrings. Fingers trembling, I take everything out from the compartment and put it in my uniform's apron pocket.

CHAPTER 23

WEDNESDAY, 20 JANUARY 1943

They cleared out the prison camp in Amersfoort, which mainly held people opposing the Nazi regime and young men trying to escape being deployed to a labour camp. The prisoners were brought to Brabant, where they will have to help with the construction of the so-called Herzogenbusch concentration camp in Vught.

I pass by the queue in front of the Expositur entrance. 'Hey, get back in line!' a woman calls after me.

'I have an appointment,' I say.

Every day, I've been asking Pimentel if she can do anything to help my family, and she just came to tell me I should report here. The head of the Expositur supposedly has news concerning my mother. The clerk I talked to a week earlier looks up in surprise. 'I still have no confirmation as to a *Sperre* for your family, Miss Oudkerk.'

'Too late, they're in Westerbork already,' I say flatly. 'Mr Wolff, your boss, is expecting me.'

The man gets up without saying anything and disappears into the long hallway behind him.

'Betty? Please come with me,' says the head of the Expositur when he turns up shortly after. A dull man with narrow shoulders and a drooping head.

He leads me to a small office so full of files you can barely make out the desk.

'I'd offer you a seat, but as you can see...' He gestures towards the piles of folders stacked high on the two chairs as well.

'That's alright, I can stand.'

'I'll come straight to the point: I have good news. I can get your mother back.'

I feel my legs go weak and only just manage to grab onto the hatstand beside me.

'Are you alright, dear?'

I wasn't prepared for good news. 'Yes, I'm fine... When is she coming back?'

'I've come to an agreement with the camp officials, so she'll likely be put on a train to Amsterdam tomorrow.'

'What about my grandmother and our housemaid, Engel?' I ask.

'I'm afraid I can't do anything for them.'

I look at the files, all these stacks of documents: they're all people. Thanks to Pimentel and this Mr Wolff, my mother ended up on the small stack, while my grandmother and Engel are on the tall one.

'I have other things to tend to now, I'm afraid,' Mr Wolff says.

'Yes, I understand. Just one last thing... My fifteen-year-old brother.'

'He'll fall under your mother's care again. And because she's getting a *Sperre*, he's exempted from deportation as well.'

Japie has his bag on his shoulder and is about to leave when I enter. 'You can stay. Mother is coming back.'

'Mother?' He looks at me with hollow eyes. As if I'm talking about a ghost from a distant past.

'Yes, she'll be taking the train tomorrow.'

'And Granny?'

I shake my head. 'No, but Mother is.'

I can tell Japie doesn't believe me. 'I don't want to stay here by myself anymore. Nol has an address for me that's further from Amsterdam than where that Baller family lives. I'm going there.' He looks dejected, with his sunken cheeks and uncombed hair.

'Japie, I swear Mama is coming back tomorrow.'

First, I couldn't get him to leave our family home, now I'm unable to keep him here.

Japie looks at the toes of his shoes. He seems unwilling to change his mind about leaving.

'Do you not have enough to eat?'

'I do, but I...' He hesitates. 'After six, when it's dark, it's as if they're all still here. Father, Mother, Gerrit... I could have sworn I heard Granny in her bedroom yesterday. I know it's impossible, and that it's my imagination, but... I can't stand it any longer.'

'You'll be alone just one more night, Japie. One last night.'

He takes off his rucksack again and sinks into Father's armchair. 'Alright. But I'm going to the station tomorrow morning, and I'll be waiting there until her train comes in.'

It's rather dangerous to wait for her to arrive at the station, but I know I can't stop him. 'Alright, so long as you're careful.'

I rush down the stairs. It's half past three. I have to go back to work. I don't look where I'm going in all the excitement and run into the widow Koot. I could kick myself for being so careless and not first checking if it was safe.

'What are you doing here?' she shrieks. I feel her hand press against my shoulder, smell her sweet perfume, look into her eyes with heavy makeup. 'Didn't they come get them already?'

I'd like to dig my fingernails into her powdered face and spew bile on her skin. But instead, I say: 'My apologies, Mrs Koot. I had to come get something.'

She eyes my hands and sees I'm not carrying anything. 'Like what?'

'It wasn't here,' I say, showing my empty hands.

'They've had to bring all their money and gold to the bank. That's required of you people,' Mrs Koot says.

'That's probably it, madam,' I say. It's a good thing I secured the family jewels a few days ago. 'I have to return to work now.'

'Best get going,' she says. 'You have no business here anymore.'

'No, madam.' I walk off, but then I can't resist. 'Mrs Koot, how is the shop doing?'

'Oh, just fine,' she says.

'That's odd,' I say, feigning surprise.

'How so?'

'Well, because our Jewish customers are no longer allowed to come here. And I heard many of our non-Jewish customers no longer want to come here. So then who does that leave?'

'Plenty of people, plenty!'

It's only as I'm walking back to the nursery that I realise the footsteps Japie thought he'd been imagining were real. They were Mrs Koot's as she was looking for valuables.

The next day, I'm so nervous I'm unable to focus on anything, and I accidentally drop something on three separate occasions.

Then Pimentel comes in to tell me there's someone on the phone for me. Not in the staff room, but in her office. *My mother is back! She's back.* But when I put my ear to the phone, it's not my mother's voice I hear but Japie's.

'She hasn't come,' I hear him say.

'What do you mean she hasn't come?'

It takes a second before he answers. 'There was only one train from Westerbork, and she wasn't on it. I thought...' His voice breaks.

'You thought what?'

He clears his throat. 'I thought maybe she'd come tomorrow, so I asked someone from the Jewish Council who'd been on that train himself if he knew anything. He had a list of passengers and said Mrs Oudkerk was on it for today, but that she'd decided not to come because she didn't want to abandon her mother.'

'Dammit!' I swear under my breath, but I'm so angry I could curse out the entire world. How could my mother do this? How could she choose her old mother over her children? I'm moving heaven and earth to free her. Is the message she's needed here still not clear enough? What was she thinking? She must have gone completely *meshuga*. You don't abandon your child, do you?

'I'm out of here,' I hear Japie say before hanging up.

Pimentel looks at me. 'You can take the day off, Betty.'

'No, thank you,' I say with icy composure. 'That won't be necessary.'

Pimentel follows me with her eyes as I walk out the office. The sounds of children echoing in the hall are almost unreal, as if they're coming from the walls and have nothing to do with the little creatures sauntering around at less than a metre tall. Carefree sounds from another world that's pure and beautiful and has nothing to do with life outside. I jump when a child smacks my backside with his little hand and then runs off mischievously. 'Wait 'til I get my hands on you!' The sound of my voice doesn't seem like my own either. Is this the moment I discover the real world is exactly the other way around? That it's me who's trapped inside a camera obscura, who's been living in an upside-down reality all my life?

Everything I do here, every risk I'm willing to take is based on the assumption that children are what's most important. So, then, why did my mother choose otherwise? Why?

I throw up in the toilet, then rinse my mouth and get to work.

CHAPTER 24

MONDAY, 25 JANUARY 1943

In the night between 22 and 23 January, the Jewish psychiatric hospital Het Apeldoornse Bos, which still had nearly a thousand patients and nurses residing there, was cleared out. Hauptsturm-führer Aus der Fünten led the operation, aided by a large group of SS men and the OD, the Jewish Order Police, from Wester-bork. This latter group made sure about a hundred people were able to flee.

The morning is bleak with an icy draught entering our stronghold through the cracks, when Greetje is brought in. My dear, unhappy Greetje, who's still wearing my old clothes even though she's long outgrown them. She's panting because of a neglected case of bronchitis, and there's a big snot bubble hanging from her nose. I ask around in the theatre if anyone knows how she got here. A boy from the Council says she was likely with the large group that was brought in this morning and who are now in the orchestra pit. I head straight to the orchestra pit, a place I've only visited once, when it made me gag and want to get away as fast as possible. Looking down over the edge at the lowered area between the stage and the rest of the hall, I see some thirty people in various states of desperation. For a moment, I think this is where they put the people who've had nervous breakdowns. It happens often enough that someone in the theatre suffers a bout of hysteria. But when I take a better look, I see that they're psychiatric patients. One is rocking back and forth and shouting, while another stares wide-eyed into space and keeps calling for his mother. Another one again is lying on the floor and turning his head left to right.

'They cleared out the nuthouse in Apeldoorn,' says a woman next to me. 'It makes no sense. They put most of them on a train to Westerbork straight away. This group here managed to escape. That's what that nurse told me.' She points at the man in a white coat, who I hadn't noticed yet. He's going from one wretch to the next, trying to calm them. 'But after escaping, they ran into a roadblock and were captured anyway. From the frying pan into the fire, we'll just say,' the woman remarks drily, then walks off.

Distraught by what I just heard, I knock on Pimentel's office to ask if she knew Greetje had been in Het Apeldoornse Bos. When I open the door, I'm face to face with Aus der Fünten. He's holding Remi by two little fingers as the boy takes small steps.

'Please excuse me,' I say. 'I came to see the director.' Little Remi suddenly lets go and falls on his backside.

'Now look! You've made this little man cry,' Aus der Fünten huffs. He sees my startled face and starts to grin. 'Madam Pimentel will be back any moment.'

I see a big teddy bear with a red ribbon sitting on Pimentel's chair behind him.

'Thank heavens,' I say. 'I was afraid she'd turned into a bear for a moment.'

Aus der Fünten looks back and bursts out laughing, his head thrown back and his Adam's apple going up and down.

'That's a good one. No, that would be something alright.' He lifts Remi up. 'I brought this little man a present.' Holding Remi up like an aeroplane, he presses his face against the stuffed animal, at which the little man starts gurgling. His long nose and dark eyes might make you question Aus der Fünten's Aryan origins, but with his hair shaved on the sides, the grey SS uniform full of medals and nervous twitch in his eye, he's a ticking bomb that can go off any moment.

'What's the matter, Betty?' says a voice behind me. It's Pimentel, giving me a stern look.

'Nothing. I wanted to talk to you about the... errm, night shifts,' I say. 'I'd be willing to do those,' I quickly add.

'I'll get back to you about that later, but if you could leave me and Hauptsturmführer Aus der Fünten alone now, please.'

'Of course.'

I return to the room with the slightly older children, where my simple Greetje has to find her feet. You can't immediately tell her level of thinking isn't quite that of her peers, so the other children find her odd. This was already so when she was still with the preschoolers, but she's an even easier target for bullying now. I'm glad at least she still knows who I am so she'll stay near me. The thirty children between seven and fourteen currently here are restless and difficult. Sieny and I try to teach them Dutch and arithmetic, but it's as if their attention spans are no longer than five minutes. It's hailing outside, so we can't let them run around in the garden either. I'm expected to keep them quiet because I have the most experience with this group. I clap my hands. 'Listen! If you can be silent for more than fifteen minutes, I'll stand on my head for five.'

'We want to see if you can do that first,' one boy says.

'You'll see if you're able to be quiet,' I say. But the boy doesn't accept this.

He gets the whole group to chant: 'Show us! Show us!'

'Alright then!'

I kick off my shoes and put a folded-up towel on the floor in front of the wall. I ask Sieny to hold my legs and push myself up, then feel gravity pull my skirt down to my waist, to the children's great amusement.

'Pull my skirt down,' I cry, standing on my head.

But Sieny says: 'Down? It's down already.'

Still upside down, I see the door open and two boys enter. I quickly swing my legs back to the ground. It's Joop and Harry.

'Wow, that's impressive!' Joop says. 'What do you think?'

'Very acrobatic!' Harry confirms.

'Maybe she's willing to do it again,' Joop says, fanning the flames. 'So we can have a closer look.'

'Yeah!' the children scream in unison.

'Oh no! Only if you can be quiet for fifteen minutes!'

They're going to try. While the children sit in their seats, hands folded and lips pressed together, I ask, whispering, what the boys have come for.

'There's going to be another transport tomorrow morning, and the chief commander wants things to go more smoothly than last time. So if you could make sure there's some reserve children on standby for if there's any extra room on the train.'

I look at him, wide-eyed. 'Reserve children?'

'Children who are here without parents,' Harry clarifies unnecessarily.

'I got that much.'

My eyes go to Joop, who sighs in frustration. 'That's what we were told. The Jewish Council backs this, apparently.'

'Unbelievable. And who decides which children go on the reserve list?'

Joop shrugs. 'Pimentel? But her door is locked, so we couldn't ask.'

'We thought it would be handy to make some preparations,' Harry says mysteriously. 'We've installed a light in the mezzanine, and there's some blankets.'

I have to think of Roosje again and how we hid the girl in the dark. Several weeks later, she'd suddenly disappeared. Sieny had grown attached to her and was inconsolable, which prompted Pimentel to lecture us about how we really shouldn't get attached to these children, because then this is what happens. She pointed at Sieny, normally so composed, sitting in a corner, teary-eyed. We weren't told where the child was taken.

'We could also hide children between the collar beams,' Harry suggests in a muted voice.

'But if we hide everyone, they'll know something isn't right straight away...' Sieny murmurs.

'Then we'll just hide some of them,' I say. A quick glance at Joop tells me he agrees. He has a determined look on his face.

I hear a child behind me laugh, which other children react to immediately. 'You're talking!' I say. 'Again!'

Mirjam's head appears around the corner. 'Betty and Sieny, could you come see Pimentel?'

I plan to complain immediately about Greetje and other so-called reserve children being sent to labour camps. But it's not Pimentel behind the door but Walter Süskind with a fedora covering his hair.

'Ladies, thanks for making time to see me.' He closes the door and puts his hat on Pimentel's desk. 'Henriëtte will be here any moment.' With his hands nonchalantly in his pockets, he starts to talk. 'We've organised some things, and we need your help. We've already spoken with Mirjam Cohen, but we want to involve you as well.' He seats himself in the armchair Pimentel always sits in when she's not working behind her desk. 'Henriëtte tells me you know how to handle yourselves and aren't afraid.'

'Well, clearly she's the bravest of the two of us,' Sieny says, pointing at me.

Süskind ignores her remark. 'We're able to get children out of here through several different channels. We're not going to say what channels because the less you know, the better.'

I try to get my legs to stop shaking. Sieny takes a seat, and I follow suit.

'We have to act fast to limit the damage,' Süskind says, switching from Dutch to his native German. 'You may have noticed already, but every now and then children disappear. We'll be going about this on a larger scale now. Priority will be given to children who were abandoned and those who were captured in hiding. This is because their parents had already decided to find a safer place for them before. Also, children coming into the theatre with their parents will no longer all be registered with the Expositur, so if people show up with three or four children, for example, we won't register one of them. Their names are still registered with the main office, but we also have people there who can hopefully get them off the books in time.'

Pimentel enters carrying Remi with the dog trailing behind.

'I was about to explain that we often get specific requests,' Süskind says.

Pimentel puts Remi in his crib and takes over from Süskind. 'Right, suppose we have a place to shelter a blonde-haired child of four in Friesland – because a child has died in that family, for example – then we specifically go looking for a child like that. Then there are children who are relatively easy for us to keep off the list, like Greetje, because she came in with a large group and it was all a bit chaotic. We like using confusing situations like these, and then we look for a family that—'

'I'll do it. I'm in,' I say before she can finish.

Süskind laughs, but Pimentel keeps a straight face. 'I didn't yet say what exactly I need you for,' she says in a stern voice. 'We can't use rashness, Betty.'

'I'm sorry.'

'What we're asking of you is to hide children in the nursery every now and then,' Süskind says.

'We're doing that already sometimes—'

'Let him finish, Betty!'

'We're also asking you to speak with parents to get them to let us find a place for their children,' Süskind says, lighting a cigarette.

Sieny raises her hand. 'Can I tell them anything is better than having them go to the camps too?'

'No. Many people want to believe Westerbork and the camps in the east as well offer them a future as a family,' Pimentel answers. 'Who are we to shatter this illusion?'

'Besides, we can't funnel off all the children, otherwise there wouldn't be any children left to fill the trains and make the enemy think everything is going as planned, as awful as this sounds.'

'We'd also thought of that ourselves,' I say smugly.

Which instantly gets me a furious response from Pimentel: 'Under no circumstance will you be acting on your own authority. Do you hear me?'

'No, but Harry and Joop—'

Sieny nudges me. 'Shhh!'

'Harry and Joop know what we're up to,' Pimentel says curtly. 'But they can only create the conditions. In the end, it's up to you to actually do it.'

Süskind turns his face away to blow out smoke, which the draught blows right back. 'Pimentel is coordinating everything on this end, so you'll be listening to her.'

Pimentel goes on. 'The families who do end up going on a transport are a cover for the children we're helping to hide. You'll have to convince the parents without pressuring them, and without telling them the whole truth that, once they're on the train, their chance of surviving is slim. And make sure no one else hears you. If they find out what we're doing, we're all done for. Do you think you're up to this?' Pimentel looks each of us in the eye.

'Yeah!' a voice from the baby bed says all of a sudden. Remi has pulled himself up and looks at us with a happy face.

'If he can do it, then so can we,' I say, perhaps with too much confidence.

'Thank you, ladies. I'm glad I can count on you.' Süskind grabs his hat from the desk and leaves. Pimentel lets him out.

Sieny looks at me, her face pale. 'Gee, I'm not really sure if I'm capable.'

'Sure you are. I'll help you.'

That same evening, Pimentel instructs us to hide seven orphaned children in the nursery.

When Aus der Fünten comes in during the round-up to ask where the reserve children are – he still has room for eight more – there are only two orphans on hand. Those ones insisted on going to their parents, who are already in Westerbork.

Aus der Fünten is surprised about the small number, but Pimentel waves his doubts away.

'Oh, Mr Aus der Fünten, the total number of people deported today is so high already that Berlin really won't be complaining there should have been another two or three,' she says, amicably patting him on the shoulder. 'Besides: it is what it is.'

I hold my breath for how she's speaking to him, which doesn't reflect the balance of power between them at all. But Aus der Fünten's response is nothing out of the ordinary; it seems he recognises her authority as the nursery's director.

CHAPTER 25

MONDAY, 1 FEBRUARY 1943

Joop has shown me a stencilled copy of a resistance newspaper called Rattenkruid, *in which an appeal is made: 'The joint underground press in the Netherlands hereby appeals to the true Dutch people with a call to join forces in actively resisting the German occupier and its so-called Dutch lackeys now more than ever. Apply yourself with all your might and wherever possible to the great task of liberation!'*

I enter the kitchen in a daze after yet another night shift. Sieny pours me a cup of coffee and toasts a piece of bread for me on the coal stove, spreading it with butter and a few drops of honey. She's sweet. She's been working all morning herself, but you'll never hear her complain.

'Pimentel asks if you can have a word with Liesje Katz's parents,' Sieny says.

I know this means she's found a place for her. The child smuggling goes in two directions. Sometimes, there's an 'order' for a child of a certain sex, hair colour and age, and then Pimentel will ask us to have a talk with the parents in private.

At other times, it's us making a request to find a child a hiding place because we've managed to convince the parents. Supply and demand don't always match.

Liesje is a girl of three with blonde curls and an angel's face who'd already been going to the nursery before I worked there. She only arrived at the theatre with her parents yesterday, and because she knows us already it was rather easy to get her to come to the nursery. We're always happy with children who've already been with us as this makes saying goodbye to the parents far less dramatic. Only thing is we're having fewer and fewer children we already know come here now.

It takes some searching in the constant chaos of the theatre before I find Liesje's parents. People all look alike in this pale yellow light. Even if I know all the occupants of the theatre are 'replenished' each week, it seems like they're the same people all the time. It looks no different from last week, or the week before that. I take a deep breath and walk up to the mother, who I know to be a smart and cheerful woman. 'Is something the matter with Liesje?' she asks when she sees me. We're joined by her husband, who puts his arm around his wife protectively.

'No, don't worry. She's doing fine.' I look around. The sole guard in the room is too far away to hear what we're saying. Still, there are too many people around us to speak safely. 'Could you come with me to the backstage area for a second?' I say. 'It's a bit quieter there.'

'There's mice there,' her husband says. 'My wife is afraid to go there.'

'Not mice, rats!' she says. 'Just tell me. I can hear you just fine,' she says, head up high.

This is the hardest part; how do you convince someone to relinquish their child? 'Liesje is eating well, sleeping well and doesn't cry – as opposed to lots of other children.' I've toned down the volume of our conversation, standing closer to the parents. 'What I'm about to say is off the record, so please don't talk about this with anyone. We've found a place for your daughter to go so she won't have to go on the transport herself.'

'A place?' the father asks a bit too loud.

'Shhh... Yes, a family that's willing to take her in for as long as needed.'

'And where's that then?' the father asks, doing all the talking.

'I'm afraid I can't say. But it's a safe place.'

'What about our sons?'

'No, just for Liesje.' I always find this one of the hardest things to say. It's risky to take several children from the same family if they've already been registered at the theatre. Two might still work, but three is impossible. 'We don't have a place for them. Unless you'd like me to inform if we—'

'I don't want this,' Mr Katz interrupts. 'Liesje is our only daughter...'

'It's only for the time being. Until you're reunited.'

But the father won't be convinced. 'This family is staying together. We're stronger together.'

At this point, I want to scream: 'No! You're not. If you leave together, none of you are likely to survive!' But Pimentel says we have to abide by the parents' decision. I know, and it's impossible for us to save everyone, but this sweet girl... 'Perhaps you'd like to sleep on it. I'll be back tomorrow to ask again.' The chance of them deciding otherwise is slim, I know from experience. More often, it's the other way around: they'll agree initially but decide otherwise after a night's sleep. But Pimentel feels we should give the parents time for making such a major decision.

'Leave us alone,' the father says resolutely. He pulls his wife away from me, like I'm the enemy. The mother looks back at me once more. Should I have spoken to her alone? Would I have been able to convince her then? Most people don't want to, which I can perfectly understand. Would I tear my own baby from my bosom and put it in a stranger's cold arms?

Frustrated with my failure, I'm about to leave when someone grabs my arm and stops me.

'Wait.'

I look into a small, dark woman's weary eyes.

'I'll do it!'

'Sorry, what did you say?'

'I'll hand over my daughter for the time,' she says so softly I can hardly hear her. 'And her brother too. My daughter is about Liesje's age. They're friends.'

'Who's your daughter?' I ask.

'Betsie. But she was always called Napoleon.'

Then I remember: a girl with a wild head of dark curls who could really raise her voice.

'And preferably my son, Abraham, as well.'

'I'll try to arrange a place for both of them.'

'I hope you can...' the woman says. I see her eyes glisten. 'What's most important is that my children are saved.'

'We'll do everything we can,' I say softly. 'You're making a brave choice.'

The mother looks at me. 'It's the only one I have.'

CHAPTER 26

THURSDAY, 4 FEBRUARY 1943

Rumours are going round that the Red Army has succeeded in defeating the Germans in Stalingrad. Could this be true?

The orphans we hid on the evening of the transport are running around as normal the following day. Until one by one they start disappearing. Sieny and I hid three preschoolers in a large handcart full of clothes and brought them to the clothing depot on Plantage Parklaan, where Nel, an elderly woman who doesn't ask questions, takes the little ones from us as if they're parcel post packages. I also put a baby in a suitcase with air holes and brought it to Nel. When I left, the SS man Grünberg was at the door and asked me where I was going. I joked that I was fleeing to the French Riviera, obviously, winking and making him burst out laughing. Halfway down the street, the baby started to cry. Had it been two minutes earlier, all would have been lost. I told the story to my two allies, Sieny and Mirjam, and together with Pimentel we've decided to give babies a few drops of alcohol before setting out to help them escape.

Today, it's Greetje's turn. She'll be going for a walk with the
group this afternoon. Pimentel has managed to get the SS lead-
ership to let us take the children out for some air every now and
then. We're allowed to go for walks under the supervision of the
boys from the Council on the condition that all children, even if
they're less than six years old, wear a yellow star so they're
easily recognisable. This method of making children disappear
is especially suited to the slightly older ones, who no longer fit
in a handcart or suitcase. You can instruct them and make
agreements with them. They have to stand at the back of the
line, and when at a certain point the group makes a turn, they're
to keep walking straight ahead. They'll be met by a man in a
raincoat and a fedora and a woman with a red flower in her hair
who will take them from there. When the group returns to the
nursery later, two extra children are quickly added to the line
from the side entrance so the total number checks out again at
the front door. This has gone well several times already, and
Sieny assures me it's quite straightforward, but I'm not so sure
with Greetje, and I want to be there myself.

We're standing by with the group of children and a young man
from the Jewish Council, a former trumpet player from the
theatre, who'll escort us this time. The guard Klingebiel is
counting the children and writing down the number. Then it's
time for us to leave. The trumpet player isn't in on the
conspiracy and is scared to death we'll lose a child during our
walk to the playground, so he keeps on counting. I'm at the back
with Greetje and tell him to keep an eye on the front of the line
while I do the back. I tell the boy next to Greetje, who already
knows he has to keep walking straight later, that he really has to
drag her along with him, even if she doesn't want to. I've told
Greetje she has to do exactly as her buddy in line says and that
she'll be getting dried prunes, which I show her, as a reward

afterwards. The ravenous look in her eyes when she sees the prunes tells me she'll do as instructed. When the moment comes and I see the man with the hat and the girl with the rose in her hair on the bridge, I'm almost incapable of walking from nerves. The group turns right onto Plantage Muidergracht. 'Go with him,' I tell Greetje, 'then you'll get prunes. Remember?' She keeps holding onto the boy's hand without any fuss and looks straight ahead. I hurry after the group. That was easier than I'd expected. But when I look back one last time, I see them struggling to keep Greetje from running back to me.

At the park, where we give the children some time to play, I'm still so shaky I feel like I have to throw up. I try not to think of Greetje but of Pimentel's words: 'Don't get attached to any child.' When the trumpet player comes over and anxiously tells me two children are missing, I've recomposed myself. 'That's odd. I just counted two more. Come, let's go. We'll count them again in a moment.'

When we're back dawdling at the front door, Sieny quickly pushes two children out from inside. The trumpet player handling their return with Pimentel counts the children, his voice shaking, and arrives at the right number. 'Alright,' Klinge-biel says. I can tell the trumpet player doesn't understand. The guard Zündler is observing us from the other side. He averts his eyes when he sees I've noticed him. Has he seen something? I don't dwell on it. Greetje was saved, and that's what matters.

CHAPTER 27

WEDNESDAY, 10 FEBRUARY 1943

The Dutch Israelite Girls Orphanage on Rapenburgerstraat and the Boys Orphanage by the river Amstel were cleared out. Almost two-hundred children were brought straight to Borneokade, the railyard behind the station.

There's great consternation among the nursery teachers because we all know at least one child from the orphanage. When our young German colleague Cilly hears the news, she's inconsolable. Cilly lived at the orphanage herself until recently but is now staying at the nursery's community centre, Huize Frank, which served as a small nursing home until a month ago. Pimentel has set up some rooms there for girls who no longer have family. But Cilly's fourteen-year-old sister had still been living at the orphanage. I think of my own brother, Japie. Is he safe? I haven't heard from him in weeks.

Pimentel enters and says we should get to work. She takes Cilly aside.

In the evening, Cilly whispers that they were able to get her sister out. One of Süskind's aides had hidden her under a pile of old clothes by the train, and they then brought her to a hiding place.

In the days after the transport has left, orphans who've fled are coming in every day without any idea of where to go. It's important we hide them before the Germans catch sight of them. One of the orphans is old enough to pass as a nursery teacher, and Pimentel gives her a job under a false Jewish name – now I've really seen it all – which also gets her a *Sperre*. The exceedingly young nursery teacher walks around in a daze these first few days.

By now, I know the group of people from the underground who bring children to hiding places consists mainly of female students from Amsterdam and Utrecht. They're often out with a handsome male student who always wears a fedora and a dashing trench coat. Presumably, he handles the logistics. Another group of couriers is led by a cab driver called Theo de Bruin, but I'm told this isn't his real name. This group also mainly consists of young women who can pass as mothers of the children they're smuggling with them. I recognise one of them at this point. She often comes into the nursery wearing a nurse's uniform and then takes a child with her in a suitcase, rucksack or shopping basket. I act like I don't know her name, but I've seen her a few times already at the clothing depot, where I heard someone say her name: Semmy Glasoog. She's a frail young woman who likely isn't a nurse as her uniform is far too large, and she's secured the headcloth on her head with a safety pin.

I run into her in the staff room, where she's in her coat, arms crossed and wearing her rucksack, looking at the photos on the wall.

'Can I help you?'

'No, thanks,' she says anxiously. She shifts her weight from one leg to the other, then looks away again.

'Do you have an appointment with the director?'

'Errm, yes, but she's in a meeting.'

I hesitate whether to say it. 'Your headcloth, that's not how you wear it.'

She looks at me, startled. 'No?'

'It's easy for children to pull out the pin. You need to tie it.'

'It's too small to tie back,' she says, still suspicious.

I take off my own. 'Here, take this one. I'll get myself another one.'

I thought she'd appreciate the gesture, but she doesn't take the cloth.

'Don't worry, I don't have lice.'

She holds back a smile because I'm on to her, then takes it from me anyway.

I show her how to tie the headcloth behind her head, and I'm about to get on with my work, but she stops me. 'You're Betty, right? I've come to get a pack of coffee.' She utters the sentence slowly and with extra emphasis.

'You're at the wrong place for that,' I tell her. 'Real coffee hasn't been available for some time now. We only have surrogate. Do you want some?'

She stares at me with an odd look on her face, then anxiously eyes the clock. 'Is Pimentel not in?'

'She's in a meeting with Commander Aus der Fünten.'

Her eyes grow large. 'I... I have to go.' She's headed for the door already.

That's when the penny drops. Pimentel told us the couriers would be using code words. A pack of tea means a girl. Coffee for boys. 'Wait, coffee or tea. I have it all. Do you have the name of the brand for me?'

Semmy seems unsure whether she can trust me.

'Does the coffee have a name?'

THE ORPHANS OF AMSTERDAM 193

'Max Visser, less than a year old. But I need to get going. They're waiting for me.'

I go to the baby section as fast as I can and ask Mirjam which baby is called Max Visser. They're coming to get him. Even though Mirjam is a dependable person who does everything by the rules, she asks no questions now and checks the list immediately.

'I don't have a Max Visser. How old is he?'

'Old enough to fit in a rucksack.'

'Quiet,' Mirjam hisses. She glances around skittishly to see if any of the other baby carers heard it. When she checks the list again, she's certain. 'He's not here. You'd better ask Sieny.'

Sieny is in the toddler room. 'Max Visser? He's over there on the floor.' She points at a tiny boy of two, three years old steering a toy car across the floor.

'He'll never fit in a rucksack,' I whisper, more to myself than to her.

'No, he won't,' Sieny notes.

When I pass the message on to Semmy, she bites her lip. 'I'm supposed to bring him to the halfway point. There's a woman waiting at 's-Hertogenbosch Station. I can't make her wait.'

I return to the toddler room. Sieny helps me gather his things, and I tell the little guy he can take the car he's playing with. The boy seems too taken aback to protest and lets me take him to the hallway, where Aus der Fünten and Walter Süskind are just walking out the door of Pimentel's office. I give a friendly nod in passing and go into the staff room with little Max in my arms. Semmy looks surprised when she sees me enter with the boy. 'Is that Max?'

Pimentel enters. 'I'm sorry, I had an unexpected visit. Ah,

you've met already,' she says when she sees me behind the door as well.

'We have a bit of a problem,' Semmy says, nodding towards the boy. 'I'd counted on a different birth year. I'll never get him out unnoticed.'

'You'll wait until line nine arrives,' Pimentel says. 'The moment the tram stops out front, you run out and get in with the boy.'

'I'm afraid to now. I just missed it last time. Besides, you never know if there's a crooked Dutchman on the tram who'd see us coming out the nursery.'

I see Pimentel think. 'Then don't get in but follow the tram on foot to Plantage Parklaan. I'll call so that there should be a bicycle ready where Nel is.'

'Can he ride on the back already?' I don't even want to think about the child tumbling off and falling on his head.

'I'll hold him tight,' Semmy says. 'Isn't there a star on his coat?'

'Get one of the spare coats from the clothing room, Betty,' Pimentel says. 'They're "clean".'

It's only then that little Max seems to realise he'll be leaving and cries: 'No, don't wanna. Where my toitoi? I want toitoi!'

'You can have the car,' I say. 'It's much nicer than toitoi.'

'What's a toitoi?' Semmy asks.

I shrug. 'Beats me.'

Pimentel tries talking sense into the boy. She's usually able to calm an upset little child by acting both strict and understanding. But now the boy keeps crying for his 'toitoi'.

I run back to Sieny. 'What's a toitoi? Max wants his toitoi.' Sieny doesn't seem to understand what the boy means either at first, but then heads straight for the doll corner. She picks up a ragdoll that's supposed to be a cowboy. Hoping the cowboy is toitoi, I run back to the staff room.

The boy is quiet in an instant when he sees the doll. Only now he refuses to let go of my hand.

I hear the tram approach in the distance. Semmy and I are in the hallway, ready to go. Semmy is wearing Max's rucksack with all his stuff, and I have Max on my hip. It seems he senses our nerves because he isn't making a sound now. We go out when the tram has reached a halt at the stop in between the nursery and the theatre. The streets are quiet, and there aren't many passengers, so the tram starts moving again almost instantly. We walk along at the tram's speed, faster and faster, until we're running and reach the corner of Plantage Parklaan. My arms are sore from holding the child. I see a few people in the tram smiling at us. One of them even gives us the thumbs up. I pause to catch my breath, nauseous from the excitement and exertion. 'Again! Again, toitoi!' Max cries enthusiastically. This was a fun game for him.

I hear someone whistle. It's Harry putting his bicycle against the wall and walking off. 'There's your bike,' I say to Semmy.

She cycles off with the small boy on the back. 'Hold on tight!' I call after them.

'Out running, eh?' says the German guard I meet on my way back. It's Zündler. I look him in the eye; *did he see us?*

'Yes, always something,' I say, panting. 'Do this, Betty, do that, Betty. I'm constantly on my feet.'

He takes off his cap and runs his hand through his hair. 'It's important to keep fit,' he then says. 'That's right. The faster you are, the better.'

'Sure is,' I say, still reeling from the excitement. 'Especially with children.' I want to continue, but Zündler isn't done talking.

'I can't run anymore.' He points at his chest. 'They shot me here, in Danzig, the city where I was born. Lung torn to shreds. So now I have just one.'

'Oh, that makes it hard, I'm sure.'

He laughs, something I've never seen him do before and which suddenly makes him seem quite a bit younger, more my age.

'That's why they gave me a simple job, understand?' He squints for a second, as if wanting to impart more than he can say with words alone.

'I wouldn't call it a simple job,' I say. 'You have to keep a close eye on things.'

'That's what I mean,' he says, inching towards me. 'So I see exactly what I want to see, understand?'

I give a slow nod, unsure if he's offering an olive branch or making a threat.

'Good.' He puts his cap back on and trudges back to his station. *Zündler knows*. He has to. He knows what we're up to, and he's allowing it.

CHAPTER 28

THURSDAY, 18 MARCH 1943

Trains are now leaving from Amsterdam not just to Camp Westerbork, but also to the new concentration camp in Vught. The people sent here include Gypsies, political prisoners, people from the underground, drifters, Jehovah's Witnesses, criminals and black marketeers. I've heard everyone is made to wear blue overalls with a coloured triangle indicating which group of 'scum' they're part of. The most hated prisoners are the ones with a yellow triangle: Jews.

I finally hear from Japie when he calls me to say he's living in Nijkerk with a cattle farmer – a Mr Kroon – who has a hump. The address he'd been staying at before, with a half-Jewish family, had become unsafe. So he'd packed his suitcase, taken off his star and, without identity papers and keeping his fingers crossed, had boarded a train to Putten, where our family would spend the holidays before the war. I say he's mad for taking such a risk. Which is nonsense, he feels. It worked, didn't it?

He'd got the address of this hunchbacked farmer through someone who knew someone. He and another Jewish boy are helping farmer Kroon and his housekeeper on the farm. The farmer even offered for me to come too. But my brother recommends I don't. So if I ever get a message from someone to join him at Kroon's farm: 'Don't go, Betty!' Japie says the farmer is interested in Jewish girls for another reason than to help them survive. I get an awful feeling in my stomach from his story. Does the misshapen farmer limit himself to women? Is Japie actually trying to tell me he's a victim of this man himself? I tell him he'd do best to leave, but Japie says he has it good and that he wants to stay. Have I heard anything about our mother? I tell him I haven't heard a thing. Nothing at all.

Before he hangs up, I make him promise to call if he's in trouble. 'You know I'll do anything to help, right?'

'I know,' he says. 'Goodbye, Betty.'

The awful feeling lingers for some time.

The number of deportations has risen to two, sometimes three every week. In an almost routine manner, everyone is operating from their position to ensure the process is as efficient as possible. Without problems. But in the end, it's never without drama. Women no longer able to keep from panicking, men refusing to get in, children who start to scream when they see their fathers getting kicked inside. I've lost count of the number of children who've been deported by now. It's at least forty every evening there's a transport. I've also lost count of the number of children we are able to smuggle out. We hide them under capes, put them in bread baskets, potato sacks and in the food carts going back and forth between the nursery, the theatre and Plantage Parklaan each day. It's still just a fraction of the number who do end up on the trains. I know Pimentel, Süskind and his right hand, Halverstad – who supposedly is an expert at forging identity papers and removing names from the *cartotheque* – are doing all they can to increase this number. As are the theatre's secretaries helping him, the Council's couriers, the students, Theo de Bruin and his helpers, Nel from the clothing depot, and many more people. Everyone is doing their best to get more children to safety. Just like Mirjam, Sieny and I are. At first, I was particularly interested to know if the various children's escapes had gone well. Had they not been caught, had the child stopped crying, had the parents willing to hide the children received them well? Pimentel said our work ended when the children were out and that we should forget about them afterwards. It wasn't as if I wanted to know who'd delivered them, to which address, what new names they'd thought of for them... I just wanted to know if they'd succeeded. Because I'd never got beyond the point where their frightened faces were looking at me. Where they were crying for their mothers, or for me sometimes. 'Betty, don't leave!' Especially if they'd been with us for some time already and I'd got to know the children a little. 'I'll only go if Betty comes.' But no matter how I pleaded with Pimentel to tell me if they'd succeeded, if they'd been saved, I always got 'no' for an answer.

I do know a lot more about the whole smuggling system now. It's easiest to find hiding places for the babies. Younger couples unable to have children themselves are all too happy with a newborn baby. Families who've lost a son or daughter will specify particular characteristics so the child will have the same sex and appearance as a stand-in for their loss. In any case, it's easier to find places for blonde children because they look less Jewish. They're usually brought to the northern part of the country, where most people tend to have blonde hair. Dark-haired, Jewish-looking children are brought south, to Brabant or Limburg, because there they'll stand out less than in Friesland or Groningen. Girls are preferred because they're often more cooperative, and – more importantly – because they're not

circumcised. Toddlers and preschoolers are also sought after
because their memories quickly fade and they're still able to
bond with the new foster parents. Besides, they're often cute
and already potty-trained too. To 'hider parents', as Pimentel
calls them, it's important that they're still able to instil their own
religious beliefs in children at this age. But smuggling three- and
four-year-olds out is rather difficult. They don't yet understand
that they shouldn't say anything about their real name or real
parents, but they get that something serious is happening, and it
makes them feel unsafe. They're told repeatedly that they have
a different name and that they're from Rotterdam. Because
that's the story that's created in many cases: that they're little
evacuees who lost their parents during the bombing raids.
They're transported wearing signs around their necks that state
their names and that they're orphans from South Holland.

The children are usually transported by train. But sometimes, they're brought all over the country by boat too, via
various inland shipping routes. There's always the fear that one
of these toddlers will give you away. I heard a story about a
child who just started singing 'Donna, Donna, Donna', a
popular Yiddish song, while they were sitting opposite a group
of German soldiers in the compartment. The courier thought
she'd have a heart attack from fright and didn't know what else
to do but sing a Christmas song in the middle of April. Thankfully, the child began singing along. Older children pose a lesser
risk on their journey because they know what's at stake, and
they're less likely to do or say something stupid. There just
aren't that many families willing to take them in. Teenagers are
known to be difficult and pose a greater risk of being discovered.
Farmers' families are often still willing to take them in because
they can use an extra pair of hands with housekeeping or on the
land – as happened with my brother, Japie. But it can take a
while to find a place like that, which means some children are
with us for months on end, like Michael and Sal, two teenage

boys. They know exactly where to hide when deportations take place, or when there's likely to be an inspection. They even help us by also taking the younger children set to be smuggled out with them into their hiding place and making sure they keep quiet.

The smuggling system gets better each day. More efficient. There's little time to think. Much less time for being afraid. I'm scared only during my night shifts, when sleepiness overcomes me as I sit in my chair, and I end up having a vivid dream in which my family visits me. I'll be talking to my father and asking why he's no longer alive to protect us. I'll see Gerrit from behind wearing the suit he'd asked for, and I'll call his name. But when he turns around, his face has been shot off. My grandmother speaking French and telling me I'm behaving indecently, like a *putain*. One more person has joined me in my dreams these past nights. My mother. She sings and strokes my hair...

I'm woken by a loud bang that causes the windows to shake, and I sit up straight at once. It must have been a bomb that's dropped right next to our house, or a little further down the street. Somewhere near. I brace myself for another bang, but nothing comes. It's the first time in a week that it's not me but Sieny who has the night shift. I quickly pull the curling papers from my hair and get out of bed. Then I hear another bang. Screaming downstairs. I run into Sieny in the hallway.

'In the cellar, right?' We're prepared for possible attacks by the Allies, and our instructions are to take the children with us to the basement. We don't have an actual bomb shelter, but at the front of the building, in the storeroom and coal room, there are two air vents and no windows, so those are the safest places. We need to get all the children down there as fast as possible. Pimentel is in her nightgown and wearing two curlers in her hair, like a rooster's comb, which in another situation would be cause for laughter but isn't now.

'When you've brought them all down, get as many bottles of water as you can,' she tells me. 'Sieny and Mirjam, you two bring mattresses and blankets down with you.' When I cast a passing glance out the window, I'm still unable to see the source of the consternation. Light from the theatre illuminates the street as German soldiers run to the left, down the block. Orders are shouted, there's cursing and constant barking of dogs.

Divided over two cramped spaces, we sit and wait with eighty frightened children, packed like sardines. I can hear the fire truck sirens in the distance coming nearer. Pimentel gets up, which seems to take a lot of effort. A stab of pain in her back nearly makes her lose her balance. But just in time, she's able to grab onto the doorpost and stay on her feet. 'Bruni, sit!' she orders her dog, which looks up at her, expectantly. Little Remi wants to go after her too, but a pat on the head is enough to make him want to sit on my lap and wait for her to return.

'I'll be right back,' she says in a tired voice.

She's gone for at least half an hour, in which the children eventually start to calm down again. The danger seems to have passed, and one by one they start to cry or ask for their mothers or fathers. Pimentel comes back around the corner at last. Without any further explanation, she says: 'All is well. Get back to bed.'

Little Remi, who's able to walk quite well by now, crawls from my lap and runs towards Pimentel with arms outstretched.

'Hey, darling, you come with Aunt Henriëtte.' In any case, Pimentel seems to have broken her own strict rule of not getting attached to any children. 'Come, let's go back to sleep.' She kisses the boy on his forehead.

CHAPTER 29

SUNDAY, 28 MARCH 1943

We only hear what happened exactly the following day. A group of artists bombed the Amsterdam civil registry, which is located only a short way down the street on the corner of Plantage Middenlaan and Plantage Kerklaan. Their aim was to destroy all personal records. These members of the resistance went in wearing police uniforms under the pretence of having to search the building for wanted persons. They then overpowered the staff who were present at the time and sedated them with an injection, leaving them in the Artis zoo afterwards. They subsequently doused the filing cabinets with benzene and placed time bombs. The bombs exploded shortly after they'd fled, and the top floor was completely incinerated. Unfortunately, the identity cards were downstairs, and only a small number of these were destroyed. Newspapers say the Germans are offering a reward of 10,000 guilders for any information leading to the suspects' apprehension.

The children are so restless it's driving me crazy. No matter what my two colleagues and I try, it seems like they just don't want to follow rules anymore. Which isn't all that odd, considering the number of children has nearly doubled in a week. We're bursting at the seams as a consequence, and we're still short on staff, despite all the extra hands. Mirjam, who's working the baby section downstairs, enters the bigger children's playroom. 'Betty, do something!' she says. 'All this stomping and screaming is constantly waking the little ones downstairs.'

Sometimes, I don't know where I get the energy from, but there's no other solution but to go on. After all, the children don't have any other choice either.

I clap my hands. 'Hush now. All of you!'

The children are briefly silent and look at me. 'If you promise to be quiet for ten minutes, I'll promise something myself.'

'Like what?' says one smarty-pants. 'A pot of gold?'

'Certainly not,' I answer. 'You can only find those at the end of a rainbow.'

'That I can go home?' another says boldly.

'I can't promise that either, unfortunately, however much I wish I could.' I have to come up with something good or else they'll never be quiet. 'I promise...' *What in the world can I say that would make a big enough impression?* 'Errm... that I'll hoist myself down with a rope from the top floor,' I say out of nowhere. What am I thinking? Maybe it's because I once saw a film in which someone escapes from prison like that.

'But that's impossible!' says a boy with a mischievous face. 'Through the ceiling?'

'No, not through the ceiling, wise guy,' I reply, laughing. 'Through the window.'

The children run to the window to see how high it is. 'Won't you end up squashed?' asks a girl, looking concerned.

'No, don't be silly! But I'll only do it if each and every one of you can keep quiet as a mouse for ten whole minutes.'

They promise they will. Of course, they'll never manage, but trying a few times is sure to keep them busy for at least an hour.

From a monkey cage, the room turns into a silent monastery. You could hear a pin drop. Two children try very hard not to laugh out loud, but somehow they manage to keep silent. I start to get a bit nervous when eight minutes have passed. I make silly faces to get them to laugh, imitate a monkey, then an elephant, look cross-eyed, but nothing helps. They seem to have found their inner mute switch at this point. And then ten minutes have gone by. 'Out the window! Out the window!' they chant.

'Shhh, alright then. A promise is a promise. But listen up: if someone from the other rooms finds out what I'm about to do, they'll likely try and stop me. So I'll still need you to be on your best behaviour. You can only whisper to each other, or else the deal is off.'

My two colleagues come up to me. 'We don't think this is a good idea, Betty.'

'Maybe not, but I have no choice,' I say, determined. 'You two just make sure the children keep quiet!'

I've found a rope in the attic, and I'm just trying to think how to attach it to the lifting beam when I see Joop down in the street approaching on his bicycle. I rush down the stairs and stop him. 'Joop, you have to help me. I'm lowering myself on a rope from the window.'

He looks at me, dumbstruck. 'You're what?'

'I promised the children to if they'd be quiet, and if you promise something you have to do it too.'

'Right, of course, but in this case...'

'Joop, please. If there's one thing these kids need, it's trust. So they'll see that we, at least, do what we promise.'

He laughs, shaking his head, then puts his bike on its stand. 'If you insist.'

The lifting beam would have been just a bit too high because I'd have to lower myself from the attic window. But I'll just about manage from the window where the children wait in anticipation. Joop has asked Harry to help, and together they'll lower me down with the rope they've slung around a beam in the room. I get a little anxious when I'm sitting in the window and look down. It's at least ten metres down to the pavement. That might not seem so high, but you can still easily fall to your death from this height.

'Betty, don't!' Sieny, who's working the baby section together with Mirjam, suddenly comes running into the room.

'Too late!' I say.

'You're completely crazy, do you know that?'

'No, she's not!' says a boy in my defence. 'She promised!'

'See, Sieny? The children agree I have to do it.'

'Suit yourself,' Sieny says. 'Just let me first warn the guards across the street. You'll have a bullet in your bum before you know it.'

The children find this hilarious, but thankfully they agree I have to come out of this unscathed.

I've made a loop at the end of the rope to stand in with my foot; I've seen this at the circus once. I wrap my hands tight around the thick rope. When I see Sieny on the other side of the street give me the thumbs up, I let the boys know I'm ready. Joop wishes me a safe journey and pulls the rope tight together with Harry. Carefully, I lower myself over the edge. This idea of putting my foot through the loop proves to be wrong immediately because as soon as I let go of the windowsill I'm hanging horizontally. I have to hold on tight to go on. 'Yes, let me down!' I say. The thought crosses my mind that it might be easier if I'd just let go now. If, like that philosopher, I chose thin air over life on earth. To fly across the globe instead of being stomped into the ground again each day. But I can't do that to all those hopeful faces looking down at me from the window.

'Just a bit further,' cries Sieny, who's run back across the street to catch me. 'Yes, almost...'

I gracelessly touch down on the pavement with my bottom. There's cheering above us.

'What's going on here?' A woman in a nurse's uniform is standing by the front door with a suitcase.

'Nothing special,' I say, brushing the sand from my uniform. Her face looks familiar.

'Can I help you, madam?' Sieny asks politely.

'Madam? Don't be silly. I'm Virrie Cohen, the older sister of...' She then sees her sister standing in the doorway, and the two jump into each other's arms, whooping and screaming.

'My sister is from Rotterdam, where she's worked at the hospital,' Mirjam says when they're done screaming. 'She's come to help us.'

'That's my intention, anyway,' Virrie says. 'Because this place seems a bit of a mess. People being lowered from windows, good grief.'

CHAPTER 30

WEDNESDAY, 7 APRIL 1943

The trains to the east depart from Westerbork each Tuesday. The unpredictability and randomness of who are sent to the concentration camps is maddening. After your fellow concentration camp prisoners are carted off in cattle cars, it's another week until the next batch departs. Week after week. Until the moment comes when your name is also on the list. Because this is one of the few things you can be sure of in Westerbork: that a Tuesday will come when you have to pack up yourself. Until then, people live in a make-believe world with a whole industry of handicrafts, football matches and theatre evenings. Is my mother playing piano there?

One evening, when calm has returned to the nursery, I talk to Virrie. She's in the kitchen with a cup of tea and a crossword puzzle that she's cut out of a newspaper or magazine. I ask if it's difficult, and she answers she hopes so, shrugging. She has only a few puzzles left, otherwise she won't have anything to take her mind off things later.

'Is it alright if I join you?'

She gives a quick nod to indicate it's okay. 'Uprising, six letters?'

'Errm... I'm not good at crossword puzzles.'

'I was thinking "protest", but that can't be because it starts with an R.'

'Revolution?'

She looks up from her puzzle. 'Can't you count? That's ten letters.'

'Oh right, of course.' I feel like such an idiot around Virrie, who's about ten years older than me. She and Mirjam look similar in appearance. Only Virrie comes across as much more assertive and also stricter than her younger sister.

'Wait a second. You've given me an idea,' she then says. She counts under her breath. '... six. Yes, that's right. The right answer is: revolt!'

'Let the revolt begin,' I say drily.

Virrie gives me a puzzled look, then bursts out laughing. 'You're funny. I knew that already when I saw you tumble out the window.'

The ice between us is broken. Virrie tells me she did training here herself some years ago. When I take a good look, I can still recognise her from a few photos hanging in the staff room, though she's all dressed up in them. She'd had a good time with Pimentel here, but didn't want to work with children only. So she went to Rotterdam to continue training to be a nurse. Just after she'd taken her diploma and started working at the Jewish Hospital, the city was bombed. She tells me it was horrendous, and that as a young nurse she saw one heavily injured civilian after another come in. People with their limbs torn off, with grenade fragments in their body and severe skin burns. She and her colleagues had countless people die in their arms. She kept working there until the hospital was cleared out a week ago. All patients and staff were put on a transport. With her eyes turned away, she tells me she would have preferred to go herself as well. I ask why she's here then, at which she suddenly gets up and says she's here to help us. End of story. She wishes me a good evening and steps outside, forgetting her puzzle on the table.

I hear a child cry in the baby section. Such wailing usually doesn't last very long because Mirjam, being the one ultimately responsible for the very little ones, keeps a close eye on them. But now the cadence of steady crying persists, and I get up to have a look.

There's no nursery teacher in the baby section to be found. I read the card that says the little one just had a bottle of milk, so she can't be hungry. 'Hey, little girl, what's the matter?' I whisper, lifting the child from her cot. The baby lets out a belch like a sailor, which instantly answers my question. She looks at me in surprise. 'Well, it's out now, isn't it, dear?' I carefully put her back in her cot.

In the hallway, I see the front door is ajar. I go to the door and see Mirjam smoking a cigarette with Joop. 'Hey, little Y in cot number seven just woke.'

It's impossible to remember all the children's names. We call boys 'X' and girls 'Y'. I only know the names of children staying a bit longer – foundlings like Remi, orphans whose parents were already deported and teenagers we can't find addresses for. I lost track of all the children some time ago. Pimentel keeps a secret list of which children leave, and with whom. She writes it down in a little book she keeps in a secret place. I have no idea if she knows where they're all going. Maybe it's only the underground who keep records of this information, and it in turn consists of various different groups. It's important that each cell operate independently from the next so there's no risk of the whole organisation being rounded up if one branch is betrayed.

Mirjam puts out her cigarette against the wall. 'Goodbye, Joop! I have to get back to work.'

I let Mirjam pass, and I'm about to go back inside myself.

'Did I just lose all my conversation partners?' I hear Joop say.

I look around the corner. 'Looks like it, yeah. Do you have to wait here?'

'"Have to" is a phrase I hate,' Joop says, grinning ironically. I prefer to say "will". I will wait here until that fat German across the street – see him? – says I can leave.'

I try to see who's on the other side of the street, but it's too dark to make out much of anything. 'But how can he see you standing here?'

'He can't, unless he shines his flashlight at me, but they're only allowed to use those in emergencies.'

'So it's actually pointless for you to be kicking your heels here?'

'It's astounding how perceptive you are,' he says teasingly.

'Just like how persevering you are,' I shoot back. 'But besides perceptive, I'm also highly inventive. Come with me!'

I grab his hand without thinking. A bit surprised, Joop lets me drag him along.

'Maybe this isn't such a good idea—'

'Shhh!' I say. 'This door on the right.' Joop goes first into Pimentel's office. 'Wait a second.' In the dark, I walk around him to the window and open the curtains. I then pull the two chairs closer. 'We have a perfect view if there's a signal from across the street from here.'

'Are you sure this is allowed?' Joop asks, without any bravado now.

'I'm sure it's fine. Better than having to pick you up off the pavement later, right?'

. . .

I've made each of us a cup of tea, and Joop adds a splash of *jenever* from his flask.

'Don't you find it odd that two daughters of David Cohen work here now?' I ask. 'That goody-goody surely won't approve of what we're doing here.' I'm talking about the child smuggling – I avoid using the phrase to be safe.

'It is a bit odd indeed, but I don't think he knows.' I can only see the contours of his face and his two lit-up eyes.

'Really?' Maybe I'm comparing it too much with the relationship I had with my own father. I never kept any secrets from him.

'Mirjam just told me her father had to force Virrie to get off the train at Rotterdam Central. She said she stood in solidarity with her colleagues and had promised her patients not to abandon them. But her father forbade her to go along to Westerbork.'

'I don't know if I'd have been so strong that I'd sacrifice myself,' I admit. 'There's also not too much you can do once you're imprisoned there.' I think of my mother who refused to leave Westerbork and again feel anger rise up in me.

Joop snaps me out of it. 'I agree, but as David Cohen's daughter, maybe you have to do the exact opposite of what your father expects?' I get what he means. The only Jews who are still truly safe at this time are the bigwigs of the Jewish Council and their families. It shows strength of character, if you can then say: 'I don't want a position of privilege. I'm just like all other Jews.'

'Have you thought of fleeing, Joop?'

'I've given it some thought, but no concrete plans yet. I'm not just letting myself be deported, that's for sure. You?'

'Sieny and I have agreed to go into hiding together, if it comes to that.'

'Pretty smart. You're stronger together than alone, especially as a girl.'

We're silent for a moment. I feel the alcohol warming me from within. I'm not used to drinking but didn't want to admit this to Joop.

'What do you want to be when you grow up?' I ask.

He laughs. 'I want to be a fighter pilot. That would be awesome. How about you?'

'I want to be a mother of at least ten children and maybe start a shelter or something.'

'So basically what you're doing here.'

'No, not what I'm doing here. Here, I have to care for children until they're deported.'

He leans in a bit closer, giving me a better view of his face. 'But not all of them, right?'

'Why can't we help all of them?' I say more to myself than him. 'I'd do anything for that.'

'I'm sure you would.' Then, suddenly, his tone softens. 'I've never met a girl like you before, Betty. You're never afraid.'

'Being afraid is for mice,' I say. 'And cowards.'

'I'm afraid sometimes,' Joop confesses. 'Does that make me a coward?'

Our conversations have never been this personal before. 'No, not you. Or, well... I do feel it's a bit cowardly of you to stay engaged to that Christian girl.' Naturally, I'd asked Harry if Joop was already taken some time ago already. The answer was doubly disappointing.

'Is that right?' He sits up straight again. 'I seem to recall you saying "a promise is a promise" the other day. I asked her to marry me – that's not something you just throw out the window, is it?'

'Not like that, no,' I say, giving him a flirtatious look. I'd never have the nerve without the alcohol in my blood. Without the confidence it has given me, I might not have even noticed: *He wants me too. He wants me.* I take his hand and press it against my face.

Then, suddenly, the door swings open, and the lights are switched on. It's Pimentel in her dressing gown. I immediately close the blackout curtains.

'What are you doing here?'

Joop has risen to his feet. 'I'm sorry, ma'am, it was my idea. I was cold standing watch outside.'

'No, it was my idea,' I quickly say.

'Are you two going to argue over who I have to scold?'

'Me!' Joop and I say at once.

'Off to bed, you,' she orders. 'And you, outside.'

Joop gives me a quick hug in the hallway. 'It's impossible, Betty,' he whispers in my ear.

'I know.' We hold our embrace a little longer anyway, his cheek to mine. Seconds in which we don't say anything. Then, like clockwork, our faces turn towards each other, which leads to a kiss. A moment of union that lasts a few seconds at most, but which stirs all kinds of feelings in me.

My head light, I drift off to bed.

CHAPTER 31

SUNDAY, 11 APRIL 1943

Mr Van Hulst is the director of the HKS, the Dutch Reformed Training School two doors down, where students are trained as teachers. Van Hulst, whose thin, serious face and big horn-rimmed glasses make him seem not much older than thirty, has managed to keep his school open with donations from parents. The training school's garden in the back borders on that of the nursery. I occasionally see Mr Van Hulst talk to director Pimentel there. But that says nothing about whether he can be trusted. The conversations Pimentel has with Aus der Fünten seem quite friendly and relaxed on the surface too. Like they're well acquainted.

When I wake and open my attic room window, I see Virrie lifting a young girl in a red coat over the privet hedge. It's only then I recognise the child. It's little Paula, who was brought here by the Green Police some weeks ago. Because we're short on space, Mr Van Hulst has set aside a room. Each day, children are lifted over the hedge to have an afternoon nap there. I've noticed fewer children are returning than going recently.

It's impossible to take a child by the hand and walk out the nursery without being noticed because now there are often two guards in front of the theatre keeping a close eye on our nursery. But of course it's perfectly possible for a teacher or slightly older student to leave with a child from the training school entrance.

I go to Mirjam's bedroom at the front of the building and knock on the door. When no one answers, I go inside. Mirjam has made up her bed neatly, and the place smells of some kind of medicinal cream. There's a notebook on her bed, maybe her diary. I feel like an intruder in this private space, but I continue; I need to know. I pull open the skylight and pull her chair closer. I carefully climb on it and lean over the windowsill so I can look past the gutter at the street and the school's entrance. Nothing to see, apart from a man walking on the pavement. It's then I see it's 'the executioner', the NSB man in civilian clothing often patrolling the street here lately to scare off busy-bodies. And if that fails to make an impression, he hits them with the brass knuckles he conceals in the pocket of his leather coat. Local residents try to look the other way; they already know not to stand around too long. It's the people who've come here especially to see it with their own eyes. It's known that all types of things are happening in this street now, and this attracts people who are curious and looking for thrills. Is the executioner the reason they're not coming out of the training school immediately? Just when I'm about to step down again because it's taking too long, I see a young woman with a child step out into the street through the side entrance. I think it's a different child at first because it's wearing a different coat, but then I recognise Paula's spiky black hair. The red coat has been traded for a grey one. Without a Star of David.

The executioner pays no mind to the so-called mother and her daughter.

CHAPTER 32

TUESDAY, 13 APRIL 1943

When Aus der Fünten isn't present, deputy Hauptsturmführer Streich is in charge. Streich has a thing for Hetty – Süskind's secretary. I've met her a few times myself, a very pretty blonde Jewish girl who speaks five different languages. The story goes that Hauptsturmführer Streich asked her out once already, but she kindly refused. Not discouraged so easily, some time later he suggested they have dinner together without her wearing a Star of David. He also said he could help her get an Aryan certificate. But Hetty turned him down this time too. This wounded Streich's pride so much that he had her put on a transport yesterday.

I'm taking a group of children whose turn it is to play outside out to the garden when I pass Hauptsturmführer Streich, who's just leaving Pimentel's office. I kindly nod, but he doesn't even seem to notice me. He has a grumpy, even angry, look on his face.

When I've brought the children outside and I'm waiting for the group that has to go back in to gather, I see Pimentel come out her office door as well. She goes straight to the baby section opposite her office and asks Mirjam to come too. Pimentel then hurries to the back, where she pulls open one door after another. There's something about the way she's acting that frightens me, though I can't explain it. Suddenly, her blank eyes look straight at me, and she asks if I know where Virrie is. 'I think I saw her going to the storeroom a little while ago,' I say.

Little Remi comes out the open door of the director's office, walking in a wobbly way with his hands outstretched and a bib fastened around his neck. 'Remi eat?'

'Get Virrie,' Pimentel says feebly. 'Now.'

The children crowding around me ready to go to their play rehearsal ask if they can go on.

'Just wait another minute until everyone's here,' I answer, running down the stairs to the basement. 'Pimentel wants to see you,' I tell Virrie. 'I think it's important.'

Virrie hurries up the stairs in front of me. I just barely catch sight of her disappearing into Pimentel's room.

Back in the hallway, two children from my rehearsal group have hidden to play a prank on me. 'You have to find them, Miss Betty,' says a girl with mischievous eyes. 'They're definitely not in the sandpit.' At which the boy to her side nudges her.

'Why don't you go up already, children,' I tell the children, and proceed to the sandpit to get the two boys out.

Walking back inside with a little rascal in each hand, I hear a sudden screaming.

'No, no! I won't! I won't do it!' The door swings open and Mirjam comes out, immediately followed by Virrie and Pimentel.

'Mirjam, stay here,' Virrie says. 'Maybe we can still arrange something. Mirjam—' But Mirjam slams the baby room door behind her, making the babies start wailing instantly. 'Mirjam, please...' her sister says.

'Let me talk to her.' Pimentel pushes Virrie aside. 'Mirjam, come out.'

More babies are crying now; when one starts, it's joined by another, and then another shortly after.

The little boy tugs at my hand. 'Miss Betty, can we go now?'

'Yes, we're going.'

Walking up the stairs, I hear Mirjam's screams above the crying babies. 'No, I can't. No, no! I'm not doing it. No!' The children are completely silent. I swallow the lump in my throat. 'Come, let's get started.'

The awful news is going round the building. Streich has ordered the Cohen sisters to travel up and down to Westerbork to take all the orphans there in person. Including Remi. Sweet little darling Remi. Everyone has their favourites here, but Remi is everyone's favourite. Even the Germans'. It's so shocking that there are more adults than children crying today. And then there's four more orphans who have to come with Mirjam and Virrie, including two toddlers, a five-year-old girl and a two-month-old baby. But Remi has been here the longest of everyone. Why can't we smuggle him out? *There has to be something that can be done*, Sieny, Harry, Joop and I whisper among ourselves. But Pimentel won't allow it. Too many people know Remi. Streich also said that if the Cohen sisters don't fulfil their task, the whole nursery will be shut down. Our only hope is for Aus der Fünten to intervene and keep Virrie and Mirjam from getting on the train tomorrow. 'The Cohen sisters' – this is pure bullying of Streich aimed at the Jewish Council's chairman's daughters. Pure and utter vindictiveness over being rejected by the pretty secretary.

Mirjam is so devastated she hasn't come out of her room after her shift, not even at her sister's urging. She's barricaded her door.

. . .

Tensions are high the next day. Today is the day Aus der
Fünten is supposed to return from leave, and from what I
understand Pimentel will try to have a word with him. I also see
Süskind running back and forth constantly between the nursery
and the theatre to try to still make some kind of arrangement.
This transport won't happen at night but in the middle of the
day, and time is running out. A mood of utter despondency
hangs over the nursery like a suffocating blanket. The seconds
are slowly, doggedly ticking away. There's nothing we can do
until Aus der Fünten shows up. Mirjam has got back to work as
usual this morning, but it seems like she's taken something
because her movements are stiff and her pale face expression-
less. Only the twitch under her eye betrays how nervous she is.
Her older sister Virrie mainly looks angry. We don't see
Pimentel, who's in her office with Remi.

All seems lost when SS men Klingebiel and Zündler come
to ask if they're ready. Mirjam woodenly rises and goes into the
baby room. Virrie is stomping her anger into the granite floor as
she collects the bags and pushes a handcart and pram into the
hallway. Mirjam puts the two smallest babies in the pram as
Virrie loads the toddlers into the handcart. The five-year-old
orphan, a scrawny girl with a head of dark curls, puts on her
coat without complaining. There's a snot bubble hanging from
her nose, which Mirjam has her blow in a tissue. I try to make
eye contact with Zündler; *He can do something, can't he?* But
the SS man doesn't look up at me and pulls the cart of children
out the front door together with his colleague.

And then it's Remi's turn. Virrie knocks on the door of
Pimentel's office. At her 'come in', she opens the door, and we
see Remi is already in his coat and leather booties, ready to
leave. He lights up when he sees us, as always. Pimentel hands
Virrie his bag of belongings and then takes her orphan in her

arms. Some five nursery teachers go into her office to give him a kiss or hug. 'Safe journey, Remi!' 'See you back here soon.' 'Bye bye, big guy!' Then I hear a familiar German voice in the hallway. We look up, hopefully.

'Pimentel wants to speak with you, Hauptsturmführer!' I hear Virrie say. Aus der Fünten comes around the corner and is taken aback by the large group of nursery teachers he encounters.

'Well well, it's obvious who's most popular here!'

Pimentel holds Remi in front of Aus der Fünten. 'Please, Hauptsturmführer,' she mumbles hoarsely, almost inaudibly. 'Let this child stay. I'm begging you...' It's the first time I see her let go of her pride.

'What's this I hear? Is this little man just going to leave us?' Aus der Fünten booms. 'That's not right!' Remi laughs at him, and Aus der Fünten takes him from Pimentel. The director regains herself and makes a desperate plea to keep Remi in the nursery, her voice breaking.

'Oh, Madam Pimentel,' Aus der Fünten sighs. 'I wish I could, but you'll have to understand I can't go against the orders of a colleague.' He then hands Remi back to Pimentel and says: 'Where's your bear, little man? You really can't leave without your bear.' He goes over to Remi's bed. Pimentel just stands there, horrified and sobbing, with Remi in her arms. Aus der Fünten then hands him the big plush bear. 'Here, boy. Your little bear friend has to come too.'

We send them off a little later: the Cohen sisters and the orphans. They wave back at us from the open truck. The happy look on Remi's face suddenly shifts when he sees his foster mother disappear from view.

CHAPTER 33

FRIDAY, 23 APRIL 1943

Apart from a limited number of Jews in the Netherlands who have a special Sperre, *all Dutch Jews are now in Amsterdam. The Germans have declared the rest of the country 'Judenrein' today.*

I'm at a loss when I look at Pimentel and try to read her wrinkled, blotchy face for what she's thinking. It's like the map of her face keeps setting me off on the wrong track. Her frowning eyes betray anger, but the wrinkles around her eyes suggest joy instead, a life full of pleasure. The vertical grooves beside her mouth give her a hardened look. The age spots on her cheeks make her vulnerable. Her forehead is a mosaic of vertical and horizontal lines, like some secret code. Her mouth is always tense, as if she's constantly holding back the words looking to escape her lips. Her eyes are dull. This is new. I don't quite know when the spark disappeared. When she said goodbye to Remi. The child that had come her way unexpectedly, and which had clung onto her. Until it vanished just as unexpectedly.

The mood is downcast after Remi's deportation. It's as if this is exactly what Aus der Fünten had intended. He's cheerier than ever himself. Some days after their departure, he comes in to ask if we have any new foundlings yet, as he's so fond of children. 'They're like walking dolls,' he says, laughing. Pimentel gives him a blank look. She was unable to follow her own rule not to get attached to any children in particular. Maybe Aus der Fünten knows what we're up to, and this was a warning. But it's had the opposite effect. Rather than becoming more cautious or reserved, Pimentel is only more determined now.

Standing by the kitchen counter, I eat a small, unripe apple. Sieny, who's just come in, asks if that's all I'm having for breakfast. I say I'm not hungry.

'You've lost weight.' Sieny says it like she's scolding me.

'I can afford to,' I say, shrugging.

'Sure, but it's good to keep a little in reserve.'

'In reserve for what?'

She doesn't answer. Instead, she fills her mug with coffee and adds a big spoon of sugar.

'Sieny, why are you babying me?' I ask. 'Do you think I'm weak?'

'No, quite the opposite. You're brave. Braver than I am. But that's also your weakness.'

'What do you mean?'

'You know no fear. People who don't know fear tend to be less careful. That's why they're less likely to survive. I was talking to Harry about this. He recognised it in some of his friends. Because it's usually boys who are like that.'

I give her a quizzical look. What's this all of a sudden? 'I can act,' I say. 'Most boys can't.'

Sieny looks at me, then takes something from a pleat in her skirt. She slides it towards me on the worktop. 'You can't act these food coupons any more than you can act identity papers, no matter how talented you are. I know you're an expert at pretending, that you're able to charm almost anyone, and that you can lie yourself silly, Betty. But what you don't always seem to get is that one stroke of back luck is all it takes, and then you're no longer untouchable.'

'Alright, so that's why you're babying me?' I ask again.

'No, I... Never mind.' She's about to walk off.

'Sieny, wait. You're right. I should get a fake identity card myself. But we agreed to stay here as long as possible for the children, didn't we?' I toss the apple core in the waste bin.

Sieny sighs. 'There can be trouble at any moment, and you have to be prepared.'

Why is she talking about 'you' and not 'we'? She's out the door with her cup of coffee before I can ask.

I'm confused. Weren't we going into hiding together? I look at the coupons I'm holding. *Is this some kind of compensation?*

Later that afternoon, Sieny and I go to the theatre as usual. I'm still angry about what happened between us earlier today, but I've decided to play it cool. If she won't keep the promise she made before, that's her problem. She has my blessing. Only she shouldn't think I'll still consider her my best friend.

We first have to try and convince the mothers, and then we'll take the new batch of children with us across the street. I'm disappointed to see not Zündler but Klingebiel and Grünberg by the door. It's spring outside with light green leaves growing on trees, but inside it's as depressing as ever. This building knows no seasons, and certainly no spring. Besides, the artificial lighting turns every night into day. Blinking my eyes to let my eyes adjust to the yellowy lighting, I hear a scream from upstairs. Sieny and I look at each other. It's a heartrending sound that would make the hair of even the most unfeeling individual stand on end. 'What's the matter?' we ask the first boy we run into with a Jewish Council armband.

'Someone's being taught a lesson,' he says cynically. Again, we hear a ghastly scream.

I've heard these kinds of beatings before, but never this bad. 'This is outrageous!' I say. 'We have to do something.'

'If you don't want to get hurt yourself, don't get involved.' He looks at his watch. 'Süskind will be back in an hour. Things usually settle down then.'

Sieny is tasked with persuading the mother of a newborn baby, and I have to ask the Polak family if they're willing to give up their daughter. The Polak mother is easily convinced – only, when she goes to get her daughter, I see I've made a mistake. It seems there's another Sarah Polak here because it was supposed to be a girl of three, not a fourteen-year-old. Children this age are officially too old to go to the nursery, but I don't want to disappoint the mother. I hope no one will notice she's a bit older. I then locate three-year-old Sarah Polak's parents, but they want to keep their daughter with them. 'I wouldn't think of giving her up,' the girl's mother says. 'How am I supposed to protect her if she's not with me?' She's not even prepared to let us take her to the nursery until they're deported. 'You'll have to take me too,' she says in a hostile voice. The child looks up at me, holding onto her mother's skirt. The father just stands there, shoulders raised, hands deep in his pants pockets, his eyes focused on the tips of his shoes. I tell them it's unwise, but if that's what they want, fine. I'm tired of arguing sometimes.

The goodbye between the children and their parents goes off with little drama today. Maybe it's because of the beatings, which can be heard throughout the building, that the children are coming along more readily. Just when we're about to leave, a man taps me on the shoulder. 'On second thought, take her with you.' It's little Sarah's father. 'I've made a deal with my wife that she can get her back if she finds it unbearable.'

'That's always possible, of course.' I give him a thankful look. 'It's what's best, believe me.'

'I believe you, but my wife...'

Where there's doubt, there's space, I now know. I put my hand on his arm and lean towards him. 'Sir, it won't be any better where you're going... Quite the opposite. Do you understand what I'm saying? Please give her a chance.'

The man's eyes dart back and forth to think, to comprehend, to decide.

'I... I... Do it. Get her out of here.'

He doesn't wait for me to answer and kneels down. 'Hey, Sarah, you can go with this sister here. She's very sweet. Just until it's time to see Mama and Papa again, alright?' He hugs her, then walks off without giving me another look.

I take the girl's hand. 'Sarah, what do you like more? Dolls, puzzles or toy cars?'

'Puzzle,' she murmurs.

We head out the revolving door with a group of about twenty children. Sieny walks in front, and I'm at the back of the line.

'Were you just going to leave us like that?' Klingebiel says when I'm the last out the door.

'We certainly were, Officer Klingebiel. The sooner the little ones are out of here, the better, right?' I say with a big smile.

'Can I see the list?'

'My colleague took down the names.' I wave at Sieny, who's holding a baby in her arms. 'Sieny, show him the list!'

She pulls a piece of paper from her skirt with her free hand and holds it up. Zündler never checks the list that thoroughly, and I expect we'll be allowed to carry on as usual, but Klingebiel goes over to Sieny and takes it from her hand. Sieny frowns at me. No, the list doesn't check out. I know that too.

Grünberg takes a good look himself, and together they go through the list of names as if they were complex mathematical equations. Several children start wailing, which comes as a blessing this time.

I hurry to the front. 'Sir, may we continue?' I ask. 'Saying goodbye is hard enough for the children as it is.'

'A few children really have to pee,' Sieny says. She's holding the baby close and nervously rocking it in her arms.

'Then why is this name here crossed out?' Klingebiel asks at last.

I check the list with him and see there is, indeed, a name that was crossed out, though it's illegible now.

'This child will be staying with her mother, so I crossed it out, officer,' I say.

'That's odd because she was included in the tally,' Klingebiel says. 'There are more children here than were written down.' He strikes the paper with his hand, making a surprisingly loud smack.

'How silly, we seem to have made a mistake,' I say.

'Oh, I forgot this child.' Sieny nods at the child in her arms. She states the name of the baby, just a few weeks old, which Klingebiel notes in pencil at the bottom of the list.

'Then let's get going already!' I say decisively.

'No, there's still one more child missing on this list,' Grünberg says.

'You're right,' Klingebiel says in surprise, as if he didn't know his colleague could count. One by one, he starts naming every child on the list.

'Oh, I know,' I say. 'This girl is only coming to help us. She'll be back this evening.'

'Do you have permission for this?' Klingebiel asks.

I start to laugh. 'Permission to get a little help? Mr Klingebiel, do you know how busy we are?'

He gives me a surly look. 'She has to go back! Take her with you,' Klingebiel tells Grünberg.

Back in the safety of our own fortress, Sieny loses it. 'How dare they! A child of fourteen.'

'That Grünberg is just a stupid yokel who's been brainwashed by the Nazis. He has the mental capacity of a monkey. But that Klingebiel, what a creep.'

'It's the biggest chumps, the losers in school, who most enjoy the power they have,' Sieny says. She looks at the baby in her arms. 'I'd just got the mother to...'

'This wouldn't have happened if Zündler had been standing there.'

Steps have already been taken in the official records so little Sarah's name is no longer in the filing cabinet. The baby Sieny took didn't exist on paper either because she hadn't been registered yet when Sieny brought her out. But now Klingebiel has added her name on the list, we're unable to keep her from being officially registered. Pimentel tells us we won't manage to get her off the list in time. We're all feeling glum. It's hard enough as it is to get mothers to give up their children, so when you do succeed you want to be of help. Our mood is less affected by the children we're able to smuggle out than by the children we have to see put on a transport. I then have an idea.

It's not easy convincing Pimentel. She feels the plan is too wild at first, but we manage to persuade her eventually. When the question arises as to who might best perform this risky endeavour, I raise my hand. Not that I really want to, but when you come up with an idea yourself, you don't stand in back when they're asking for volunteers.

Sieny has gone to see the mother and tell her what will happen. 'When the transport takes place and we're bringing the children, my colleague will hand you your baby. But don't be surprised. The package won't weigh much.'

On the evening of the transport, we've swaddled the doll so that only a small part of its pink, porcelain face is visible. We're in the hallway ready to leave with all the children, who are so quiet it's like they're little machines. I feel jittery all of a sudden. If they catch me, I'll be given an S for *strafkamp* in my identity card, and I'll be deported straight away. *Don't think about it.* Sieny and Mirjam lead the way with the older children, and I follow at the back, holding the baby in one arm and another preschooler by the hand. While I always dread the evenings of the transports because of the violence with which people are now forced into the trucks, I'm hoping it won't be any less vicious this time, solely because of the stir this causes. The resulting chaos should suffice to divert attention from what we're doing. But today, things turn out to be rather calm instead. Then the moment comes when I say the child's name, and the mother raises her hand. I carefully put the doll in her arms like you would a real baby. Though she's prepared and tries her best to remain impassive, her face clouds over when she's given the package. Her breath stops, and she puts a hand over her mouth so as not to make a sound. She draws the attention of a woman walking past, who can clearly see it's a doll. The mother's reaction must have given this woman the impression we took her baby from her against her will. 'Say, what is this...'

'Shhh!' I look at the woman. 'We're pretending.'

I see a guard approach. *Dammit, it's Klingebiel.*

'Hold the baby close,' I whisper to the mother. 'Comfort her.'

The mother puts the doll to her chest, patting its back. I see tears run down her cheeks.

'Is there a problem here?' Klingebiel asks suspiciously.

'No, everything is fine,' I say. But it seems he senses something isn't right, and he takes a few steps closer, scrutinising the women. I look crossly at the woman who is the cause of this. *Do something!*

Then, suddenly, she starts screaming. 'I don't want to go! Please, don't make me go!' She's pretending to have a panic attack. Klingebiel grabs hold of her and calls a colleague over. The mother and the doll continue on, and I take a breath of relief.

Later, I'm complimented for how I handled the situation by my colleagues and Pimentel as well. But I'm left thinking of Sarah, the fourteen-year-old girl I was unable to save.

CHAPTER 34

SUNDAY, 2 MAY 1943

Over 200,000 people have currently joined a nationwide strike, which started four days ago in protest of the ordinance that requires all former Dutch military men who fought in 1940 to report for labour deployment.

Joop is glad he can blow off some steam with me every now and then. I understand. The mood at the theatre is much grimmer. At least here in the nursery, the drama alternates with lighter moments when we're laughing and dancing with the children. I've practiced various songs and dances to the melody of 'Peter and the Wolf' with the toddlers and preschoolers. I've assembled an orchestra of a few artists who used to perform in the theatre, like the red-haired actress and trumpeter Silvia, who also works at the nursery now. One of the children is in the small ensemble too. Sal Kool is a fifteen-year-old boy who holds the official title for being the oldest child at the nursery. He plays cello wonderfully and reminds me of my brother Gerrit, albeit a younger version. The leading role of Peter is played by a highly talented child whose father has a *Sperre* for now, and who's been with us for some time already. Harry insisted on playing the wolf. I tried to get Joop to play a small part himself, but he kept refusing. Laughing, he'd said he had many talents, only none of them musical. But he promised to come see the piece this evening.

Pimentel didn't get in our way during the preparations. She rather encouraged us. But she did find it important that we paint the 'illegal' children's faces so they'd be unrecognisable, should someone from across the street come have a look. The precaution proves justified as less than five minutes into the performance, a group of young SS men enter unannounced, including Grünberg, Klingebiel and Zündler. They giddily ask why they weren't invited to the party. They're elated, and I suspect they've been drinking. The children stop their performance at once and eye them anxiously.

'You don't have to be afraid of us,' Klingebiel says to little effect.

As the evening's host, I intervene. 'Well, you've missed a part already. But perhaps the children are willing to do the first dance one more time. Would you like that?'

'Oh yes, very much,' says Grünberg, smiling to reveal his square gapped teeth. I think he never lost his baby teeth.

Everyone starts to relax and have fun again when the children begin dancing.

After the show, the SS men in the back row are clapping louder than anyone. Then it's time for the children to go to bed.

'Well, that's a pity,' Klingebiel says in his devious voice. 'We'd have liked to celebrate this success with you.'

I see Zündler take Pimentel aside. Pimentel's defensive body language says it all. She shakes her head with her hands on her side and her chin raised, but Zündler keeps trying to persuade her. She shakes her head dismissively one more time. I have a strange feeling in my gut about this. Finally, Pimentel agrees to something and walks away from him. She stands in front of the musicians busy gathering their things.

'Alright, everyone, the children will all be going to bed now,' Pimentel says. 'Mirjam and I will help them while the rest of you stay and have a quick chat together.' My eyes cross with Pimentel's. I can tell she's anything but happy with this, but it seems she has no choice.

The glasses are topped up, people toast. 'To "Peter and the Wolf"!' I sense the boys from the Council in particular are on edge. What are these krauts up to? Harry puts his arm possessively around Sieny's shoulders. The young doctor that Virrie recently started going steady with moves in closer. Joop shoots me a piercing glance, as if to say: be careful. It's just the push I need to not sit around and wait, but to take charge. It's alright so long as the atmosphere stays light. I walk over to the trumpeter. 'Play something!'

'Like what?' he says in a panicky voice. 'I only know jazz, but that's illegal to play.'

'"Lili Marleen",' says Silvia, who's heard us. 'They love that.'

'I know that song too!' I say.

Lex plays the song's opening notes on his trumpet, and I join in on piano as Silvia sings.

'Outside the barracks, by the corner light, I'll always
    stand and wait for you at night'

Everyone starts singing along: the SS men, the boys from the Council and the girls.

'We will create a world for two, I'll wait for you the
    whole night through, for you, Lili Marleen...'

I see the SS men pass around a bottle of grain wine.

'Now for some dancing music!' Grünberg cries when the song finishes. The trumpeter gives me a helpless look. I nod: *go ahead*. Timidly, he starts to play some jazz. They don't seem to realise this is *Entartete Musik* as everyone begins dancing merrily. I'm pulled from behind the piano to join in, not by one of our boys but by Grünberg. He rocks his pelvis back and forth as he twirls me around by the hand, a wide smile on his face.

'Wow, you're a good dancer!' I say, trying to placate him. 'Do they teach you in Germany?'

'You bet,' he says. 'They teach you a whole lot more too.'

I'm unable to look at Joop, who's standing on the side, and I hope the song is over quickly. When the music ends at last, I try to make myself scarce as fast as possible. 'Thanks for this dance. I think I need a rest now.'

'Do you know I think you're the prettiest of all the sisters?' Grünberg says, drawing me close by my arm.

'Even though I'm a Jewess, huh?' I scoff. 'So yeah, that's not going to work.' I subtly free myself from his grip and I'm about to walk off, but he steps to the side and blocks my way.

'It doesn't really matter to me.' He puts his hands on my shoulders, touching me again. 'I've been watching you these past months, and you may look a wee bit Jewish, but you don't act like a Jewess.'

'No?' I say, acting surprised and trying to suppress my discomfort at his nearness. 'How so?' I know Joop is eyeing me from the side. I hope he doesn't do something stupid to protect me.

'Well, these Jews are all a bit gloomy.' He uses the German word *trübe*. 'I don't like that. You're always cheerful.'

'Sure am,' I say. 'It's important to stay optimistic.'

'What does optimistic mean?' he then asks.

'The reverse of pessimistic,' I offer, unsure if it's a serious question.

He starts roaring with laughter. I look around and see I'm not the only one getting chatted up by an SS man. Silvia is acting lively as she talks with Klingebiel, and Cilly is deep in conversation with Zündler. Thankfully, Harry is by Sieny's side. I'm just able to catch her eye: 'Music!' I hiss.

Grünberg's hands slowly drift downwards, nearly touching my breasts. 'You're so beautiful,' he says, unable to suppress a belch that he lets out in my face. 'Pardon me. So beautiful.'

Then, to my shock, I see Joop appear behind him. He taps Grünberg on the shoulder.

The music starts again, and thankfully it's an up-tempo song. 'May I cut in?' I try to signal: *don't*!

'What do you want?' the SS man grunts.

'I'd like to have a dance with this charming lady. If you'll allow me, of course.'

I hold my breath.

'Why don't we ask her who she'd rather dance with,' Grünberg says, turning back towards me. 'Who do you choose?' he asks, sniggering. He knows he's in charge here.

My eyes dart over to Joop, who's about to lose his calm. 'Well, I'd like to see if you can also dance a fast one,' I tell Grünberg. 'Sorry, Joop.'

'Ha ha ha, I knew it!' He grabs me by the waist and starts coming onto me with even more zeal. 'Oh my, you're a frisky one,' he laughs. He slides his hands down to my thighs, and I shake my hips trying to get them off. I'm afraid to look back at Joop. Grünberg then draws me close again. 'I think I'm in love with you,' he breathes into my ear. 'With that great ass of yours!' He gives me a hard smack on my bottom. In the seconds following, I try to twist my way out from his grasp as he keeps trying to pull my skirt up, convulsing with laughter, because to him it's a fun game we're playing.

Until the music stops abruptly, and Pimentel enters the room.

'Alright, we'd agreed you could all have a quick chat, but it's time now.' She says it in a tone she normally reserves for the children.

Grünberg protests. 'No, we're carrying on!'

I turn my head towards Joop. His face is red and blotchy, his eyes ablaze.

'Certainly not, Mr Grünberg,' Pimentel says firmly. 'The children can't sleep with this ruckus.'

Zündler starts rounding up his men. 'Come on, guys. That's all for tonight.' But the rest seem unwilling to cooperate.

'We're not finished!' Grünberg says, pulling me towards him and lifting up my skirt. Joop is about to intervene, but Harry stops him.

'Gentlemen, you heard her,' the trumpeter now also says. 'The children need to get their sleep, and so do the ladies.'

'Says who?' says Klingebiel, who hasn't asserted himself up until this point. The two groups of men now stand directly opposite each other. I give Pimentel a pleading look. *Do something!*

Then the door swings open. 'Good evening, everyone!' Süskind is standing in the doorway, holding up two bottles of liquor. 'I have an order here!'

Grünberg lets go of me and goes over to Süskind to take one of the bottles.

'Hey hey, calm down.' Süskind pulls back the bottle from under his nose. 'You'll have to go across the street to enjoy this excellent cognac. That's where the real party is. Not here.'

'Come, let's go!' Zündler says. Then our assailants get moving at last.

'Were you scared?' Joop asks a bit later when he's guiding me upstairs with an oil lamp. I don't answer and walk up the stairs without another word. Fear was only part of what I felt this evening. It's mainly shame that makes me lost for words.

Upstairs, Joop stands in front of me so I'm unable to enter my room. He grabs my chin and turns my face towards his. I wish I could just vanish into thin air, but he makes me look him in the eye.

'Betty, I'm sorry I couldn't protect you,' he says.

I shake my head. 'No, what you did was right. If you'd intervened, then...' I'm unable to go on. Joop runs his fingers over my cheeks, eyeing his wet fingertips as if he's never seen tears before. He then takes me in his arms and pulls me close. With my ear against his chest, I can hear his heart beating fast and regular. 'I'll never let you down, Betty. I promise,' he says softly. 'And I wish the two of us...' His words linger in the air like an unfulfilled desire. A wistful dream from a different time, a different place.

'Gentlemen, out the door!' I hear Pimentel cry from downstairs. 'We have to get up early tomorrow!'

It seems things went off the rails a bit at the theatre that evening. Klingebiel, who spurred his colleagues on to party, told Aus der Fünten about the whole escapade. And now both Grünberg and Zündler have been sent to the penitentiary in Scheveningen for the crime of committing race defilement. Klingebiel himself was promoted because of his squealing and is now in charge of the guards.

Nursery teacher Cilly is upset when she hears Zündler may be sentenced to death. She tells us he helped get her sister out the theatre after she'd been arrested again at the address where she was in hiding.

We suspect Zündler wasn't locked up because of his dealings with Jewish women but because he was helping us. So for him to be in prison is bad news for two reasons. Because now we have to be even more careful smuggling children out, as there's no longer a guard helping us. And because he can still betray us.

CHAPTER 35

THURSDAY, 6 MAY 1943

The nationwide strike was brutally supressed on 3 May. 175 people were shot and killed, and over 400 were wounded. The overall attitude of the Dutch towards the Germans is becoming less positive. The resistance is growing, and with it the number of persons willing to take people in for hiding.

A little one in bed number 14 is starting to whine. Aron Fresco, I read on the official list. Aron was born on 14 March 1943; the date he was brought into the nursery is stated as today's. A child of less than two months old, captured already. *Colic*, the card reads. *Can only drink mother's milk.* Women are allowed to come from the theatre to breastfeed their baby only in exceptional cases. The Germans felt all these mothers going back and forth was difficult to oversee. I telephone across the street to call on Aron's mother. I wasn't present today when the children were handed over, so I haven't met her yet. I calm the little man by rocking him up and down, singing for him as I walk around the room. The babies are weighing less and less when they're brought in. The mothers' malnourishment isn't the only cause –

if necessary, a child will eat its own mother, so to speak. It's also the stress causing them to produce insufficient fatty milk.

The small boy's mother enters the baby room with a face pale from exhaustion. The SS man who brought her quickly nods at me, then leaves. I don't know him. Maybe he's come to replace Zündler or Grünberg. I take her to the kitchen, tell her to have a seat and ask if she'd like something to drink. A cup of tea would be nice, she says. I boil some water for tea as she breastfeeds her son.

'Strange,' she says unprompted, 'to think my older children are here too, but that I'm not allowed to see them.'

'You have more children?'

'Two. A seven-year-old girl and a boy of four.'

'Three children, I bet that's a handful,' I say to keep things light.

But the mother won't be swayed. 'Do they sleep upstairs?'

'Your oldest sleeps upstairs, and your youngest probably sleeps in the back room downstairs. That's where the toddlers and preschoolers are.'

I see her face cloud over. 'So they're separated from each other too.'

It's a fair point. Pimentel feels we should stick with separating the smaller from the bigger children, even if they're brothers or sisters. She says it's better to have the children surrounded by kids their own age than to let them cling together.

'We play different games with them at their own level. It can be a bit difficult at first, but in a day or two they actually enjoy being around children their own age. It's like a vacation of sorts.' I'm reminded of the girl we once had here, whose mother said she'd be going to a holiday camp. That's another way to look at it, as a child. I wonder how this girl is doing now. What family did she end up with? What does going into hiding actually mean for children? That they're taken in by the family and go to school just like other children, or that they're confined to a small room they're not allowed to leave? I hear the wildest stories about people going into hiding and wonder if I could stand being cooped up and not allowed to go out for months, maybe even years.

I put a cup of tea and glass of water on the table in front of her. 'Here you are. It's important to stay hydrated. Would you also like something to eat?'

She shakes her head. The woman comes across as distressed.

'Are you here with your whole family?' She doesn't seem to understand me. 'I mean, is your husband across the street as well?'

'My husband was arrested before,' she says softly. 'We're from Deventer, where my husband ran a leather business with his brother. Well, that was taken from us, of course.'

'I know. My parents owned a textile business.'

She shrugs. 'It was a successful business once, but when my father-in-law died, he had a heart attack two years ago, our life slowly came apart.'

I sit down beside her and listen to her story, which bears striking similarities to my own. Their shop was given a *Verwalter*, and her husband had to go into hiding. After her husband once came to visit her and the children in secret, he was arrested on the way back to where he was hiding and deported. She hasn't heard from him since. Heavily pregnant, she fled to Amsterdam, where an aunt of hers lives, but this morning the doorbell was rung by Dutch volunteers from the Colonne Henneicke group, who get a bonus of seven guilders and fifty cents for each Jew they bring to the theatre. I'd heard about the so-called 'head bounties' people received for reporting Jews in hiding somewhere. The Germans know lots of Dutch people are strapped for money now, and they deliberately take advantage of that: 'You help us, and we'll help you.'

. . .

In the days after, the mother, her name is Klara, comes to the nursery each night to feed her son Aron. We talk like we've known each other for years. She says she's happy to have two sons at least, so her husband can live on in them. That is, if they survive the war. I don't say much about myself normally, but with Klara I talk about my family incessantly. It's as if we're each sharing our family histories in order to convince ourselves that they existed. So as not to lose them in mere thoughts but to capture them in words. Words that form sentences. Sentences that tell stories.

Meanwhile, she helps me change the other babies, get their milk bottles ready and pat their backs to make them burp. I allow her – against procedure – to go to the beds of her daughter and son, after which she always comes back with red eyes and thanks me with a hug. We're able to stall for time, an hour, one and a half, even two. Until the moment the guard decides it's time and comes to get her.

One evening, I talk with Klara and carefully raise the possibility of finding a place for her baby somewhere else in the country. She's adamant: 'All three of my children or none!' I only now notice how tired she looks. She has dark circles under her eyes, and her cheeks are sunken with strands of hair sticking out from the bun on her head.

'Maybe, just maybe, we could get your other son on the list as well, but all three is nearly impossible.'

'Why? Why can you take one child away from me but not the other two?'

We're not allowed to say anything about how our smuggling system works, insofar as we even know ourselves. 'Sorry, I can't say.'

'Then don't. They're children, not chess pieces that I'm

putting all in different places to spread the risk. They're either pulling through or going down together.'

Now that we're talking so concretely about their coming deportation, about the possibility or impossibility of going into hiding, the mood between us is more pessimistic than all the nights before. It's as if my question has brought her back to reality.

Even before the SS man comes to get her, she asks if she can go back. She kisses her sleeping baby son on his forehead and leaves without giving me another look. I feel guilty. Should I not have mentioned it?

I'm desperately trying to hatch a plan to save all three of her children anyway. Maybe I can give her children's identity papers to some children who aren't officially registered, and send them on the transport instead? Orphans are always given priority over children who are here with their parents. Pimentel decided this, seeing that we already know the parents of children who come here alone – whether because they were caught while in hiding or because they ran away themselves – wanted to keep them from being deported. But sometimes, these children want to go to Westerbork anyway because they've heard they have family there. What if I swap two of these children with Klara's sons? Getting baby Aron out isn't the problem. The question is if I'm allowed to do such a thing. Or would that be playing God?

I jump when there's a tap on the window. Did Klara come back?

It's a heavyset man in a police uniform at the door. He's holding a cardboard folder under his arm. I'm instantly on high alert. Who is he? What has he come for? How do I trick, charm or dissuade him? 'Good evening!' I say cheerily. 'You're working awfully late.'

'I could say the same about you, young lady.' The officer

takes off his cap and nods politely with his balding head. 'My name is Pos. Can I come in?'

'You're welcome, of course, but everyone is sleeping. Is there any way I can help you here?'

'That's not possible, I'm afraid. I have to check if the names on the list correspond with the children actually staying in the nursery. The records need to add up, of course.'

Now I'm really on my guard. No one ever comes here at night. If there's an inspection, we know in advance and make sure the illegal children are well-hidden, but there's no time for that now. At least twenty of the almost ninety children currently here aren't on the lists. 'Do come in,' I say. 'But be very quiet.' I walk in front of him, not to the baby room but to the kitchen. 'How about a cup of coffee before we make our rounds?'

'I thought I smelled something. That would be great!' He takes a seat and puts the folder on the big kitchen table with his cap on top. Then he unbuttons his coat and leans back, relaxing.

'It's not real coffee but something passing for it.'

'No problem, anything is good so long as it's warm.'

I get the kettle from the stove, pour hot water in a mug and add a spoon of coffee substitute. As we chat about the weather and the rain these past days, I rack my brain for a way to get out of this. I have to keep him from starting his count no matter what. I might talk my way out of it with the excuse that some children only just arrived, but that would mean we wouldn't be able to get these children out later.

'It's the first night that it's dry. Well, let me tell you that's a blessing for a policeman.'

'Do you always work night shifts?' I ask, feigning interest.

'Oh no. No, I could never manage that. I usually work during the day. I do the keys.'

'What keys?'

'The house keys, for when they're off to the labour camp.' It seems he doesn't see me as one of 'them'. 'They won't be needing them because they have to leave their house anyway. For the time being, at least. I collect all the keys so we can keep tabs on everything. Understand?'

I have to keep myself from acting cynical and asking if he then immediately hands the keys over to the Puls firm, which loots everything. Instead, I ask him about his job as a police officer. How busy it must be these days. And how I'm sure a lot has changed since the beginning of the war.

'You said it,' he says. 'It's all different now. The Germans are proper people, but so...' He struggles for the right word.

'*Genau?*' I say.

He finds this so funny he bares his teeth laughing. '*Genau!* That's the word! Shall we have a look at those lists now? Otherwise I'm in trouble later.' He gets up with some difficulty.

Dammit, how do I talk him out of this?

'Are they very strict with you? I mean, if you make a mistake or something?'

'It depends,' he says, slightly hesitating, as if unsure quite how open he can be with me.

'Oh really, on what? Maybe I can learn a thing or two.' I try to sound as light and naive as possible.

He then sits down again, sliding his seat a bit towards me. 'Well, I saw it coming early on,' he says in a confiding tone. 'That's why I became a member of the NSB before the war, and that's what makes the difference.'

'I get that. Too bad becoming a member isn't an option for me.' I intend it as a joke, but he doesn't catch it.

'True, true,' he says. 'But if I can give you one tip: play along, and make them feel they're important. It's worked for me.'

'Having a bit of foresight is always good,' I say. 'Some more coffee?' He's not checking anything as long as I can keep him talking.

So I continue to ask questions, smile at my most charming and share his outrage at the increasingly strict rationing. 'That's a drag, isn't it?' Yes, we're all in the same boat, supposedly. When a baby starts crying, I get up and say I have to get back to work, unfortunately. He buttons up his coat and says of course, children can't wait. He then puts his cap back on and takes the folder from the table. He'll come back another time for the lists, he says, winking at me. He suggests I go see the crying child before they all wake.

I'm left confused when he's gone. Was this a good man, or was he crooked?

In the nights that follow, he stops by the nursery more often for coffee and a chat. He only mentions the lists once more, at which I take them from him and say: 'Let me have a look.' After taking a critical glance at the names, I'm adamant: 'Everything checks out. The Germans are certainly thorough with their records, you have to hand it to them.' He never brings it up again.

Officer Pos always comes around one o'clock, when Klara has fed her son Aron and has gone back across the street already. I doubt if he's really still tasked with checking the lists. It's more likely he just enjoys the coffee and company.

CHAPTER 36

SATURDAY, 22 MAY 1943

Yesterday, the Jewish Council was told it will have to select and deport seven thousand Jews working for the Jewish Council – people like us.

The chatty officer came earlier than normal this night, so his visit coincides with Klara's. When Klara sees him enter, she turns her naked breast away from him in shame and takes the baby with her to the baby section. 'Bit sad though, a woman alone like that,' Pos whispers to me. He then looks me in the eye, squinting as he fiddles with the buttons on his coat.

'I'd like to propose something, Betty.' He glances around to make sure there's really no one else in the kitchen. I brace myself for what's to come. 'I never said this, alright?'

'Never said what?'

'No, be quiet. I still have to say it, but then you never heard it...' He raises his eyebrows so high waves of skin appear on his forehead. 'Deal?'

'Deal.'

'I've talked about it with my wife. I said: "She's a sweet and pretty girl." And you know what my wife said? "If she ever has to leave there, she can come hide at our house."

It's as if he's proposing I then also share the marital bed with him and his wife. 'Well, what do you say?' he asks, his chubby fingers still twiddling with the buttons on his coat.

'That's great, Mr Pos. That's really generous of you. And of your wife, of course,' I hurry to add. 'Please do give her my thanks.'

'I certainly will! But mum's the word.'

'Shhh,' I say, holding my index finger in front of my puckered lips.

The self-satisfied smile on the man's face makes me feel he's not doing this for me but for himself. So later he can always say: *I saved a Jewish woman.* He could save his *neshomme* with that, as Granny always said. His soul. Whichever direction the war takes, whether the Germans form a global empire or they're defeated, Mr Pos is taken care of either way. Can I blame him? Everyone's a yes-man in times like this. I have an idea. 'I suspect you have at least some influence in that club of yours.'

He nods proudly. 'I've worked my way up, indeed.'

'Suppose circumstances result in me being arrested anyway... I'm sure you know what I mean.'

'Certainly.'

'Would you also be able to get me back out?'

He looks at me, his eyes darting left to right nervously. 'I can try. But... No one can know.'

'Know what? I never heard anything,' I say coyly.

'Well, what I just... Oh right, ha ha.' He gets me. 'Very clever!'

'Coffee, Mr Pos?'

'Please. And do call me by my first name, Bartholdus.'

.   .   .

My night shifts often cause me to wake at around ten in the morning feeling knackered. Usually by the high decibels the children produce. But now it's not a child waking me but the voice of a grown man. 'Betty, Betty!' It's Joop.

'Just a second!' I yell at the door. I jump out of bed, pull the curling papers from my hair, straighten my nightgown and open the door a bit.

'Sorry, were you still sleeping?' Joop asks, politely looking away.

'No, or yes. I was, actually,' I say. 'What's the matter?'

Joop seems hesitant.

'Would you like to come in?'

'Yes. I would, actually. If that's alright.'

'Otherwise I wouldn't ask, right? Come in,' I say, gesturing for him to come in. I then open the curtains to let the morning light shine in and open the window a crack to let in some fresh air. It may be odd, but I don't feel uncomfortable around him, despite my sleepy head and that I'm only wearing a thin nightgown.

He halts in the middle of the room, wavering, his lanky arms dangling by his side, sleeves rolled up, the bag he usually carries groceries in slung over his shoulder, head bent.

'Have a seat!' I say, pointing to the bed.

He does, even though I get the feeling it's only to indulge me.

I pour myself a glass of water. 'Want a sip?'

'No, thanks. I've come to tell you something, Betty. Something awful.'

'Oh, shall we roll everything back then?' I say, laughing. 'Curtains closed, me in my bed, you at the door. And instead of knocking, you think twice and go back downstairs,' I quip, as my stomach tenses into a painful ball. 'Alright, tell me.'

'Your brother Nol and his wife Jetty have gone.'

I pull up my knees and rest my head on my arms. It's

moments like these when you wish you could freeze and turn back time to a point when nothing was said or heard. I think of my brother, who did nothing else but stay in line his whole life, doing what was asked, what was expected, and never making a fuss about anything. And now, just when his life was brightened by his wonderful wife, the baby growing in her belly, all seems lost suddenly. 'Tell me what happened,' I say without looking up.

'I don't know exactly. I only know they were on the list to be deported to Vught,' I hear Joop say. 'Maybe Nol reported himself. I know they have to select people in the Council and that they first asked if there were people who wanted to go voluntarily – they asked us too.'

I still don't understand how Nol can be this compliant. Leni says it's always been in his nature to follow the rules. And especially now Jetty is so far along in her pregnancy, he may have been willing to risk even less.

I feel Joop's hand on my back. 'Hey, are you alright? Maybe they're not too badly off over there. If I had to choose, I'd do the same.'

When the camp had just opened, people were afraid of being sent to Vught because it's a concentration camp. But now it seems you have a better chance of being able to stay there, rather than being sent on like in Westerbork, so most people would rather go to Vught.

I look up. 'You would not.'

He gives me an uncomprehending look. 'What do you mean?'

'You'd make sure you were out of there before being forced to choose.'

'Maybe you're right.' His dark eyes are serious.

'Can't the two of us go together?' I say on impulse. 'You and me on a plane together?'

He chortles. 'You're crazy, you know?'

'Crazy about you,' I say, shrugging. 'But it's no use.'

Joop casts down his eyes and takes my hand. 'It's hard for me too, Betty. You know it is.' He runs his fingers across the creases in my palm. 'Maybe if I'd met you sooner, everything would have been different.' His eyelashes form two dark fans below his broad eyebrows. The straight bridge of his nose separating both sides of his face accentuates its perfect symmetry. His wide lips below, calmly sealed.

I lean forward and gently put my mouth on his. He seems startled at first, but then he answers my kiss. As we kiss, he pushes me back onto the bed, strokes my hair, my breasts. It's as if our bodies already know each other, our movements melting into one another. I take his face in my hands. 'Promise you won't go?'

Joop abruptly frees himself from my grasp. He mumbles something like 'it's impossible', then gets up and leaves my room.

CHAPTER 37

WEDNESDAY, 26 MAY 1943

Of the seven thousand people summoned, only five hundred Jews have reported. That's why on 26 May there's a big raid in the centre and in Amsterdam East, where the nursery is located. Most people aren't squeezed into the theatre but are sent straight to Muiderpoort station.

I haven't spoken to Sieny in a while. Not just because I'm doing the nightshifts while she works during the day, but also because she spends nearly all her free time with Harry. It's annoying for several reasons, and I'm no longer able to keep my mouth shut. I enter her room and bluntly ask if she's still planning to go into hiding with me, because I'll go find someone else otherwise.

'Betty... I've talked about it with Harry, and I think we want to try together.'

The word is out. She looks a bit abashed, but they've extensively discussed this together already. I know it's getting serious between them, and that Harry sleeps with her in secret every now and then, but this serious? I can't stand how she's just breaking our agreement and choosing him over me. Weren't we going to live through all of this together?

'You know it'll be hard to find a place together, don't you? Who would want a wild couple?' I say. That might sound mean, but it's the truth. Besides, how long has she known him really? 'You'll have a much better chance if you go into hiding with me. I'm not afraid.'

Sieny is flustered. I try to impress on her how much braver I've always been compared to her.

'Yes, I know. Maybe I should after all.' She tries to sound convincing, but I can tell she's not serious.

'I understand you're in love, but would you also have fallen for each other under different circumstances?' I don't wait for her to answer and go on talking. 'I mean, doesn't he come from a different milieu than you?'

'Now, Betty!'

'I'm serious. You think it doesn't matter now, but when the war is over you're stuck with it.'

She rubs her neck and looks around anxiously, from which I surmise she's having her doubts too. Then she softly says: 'Pimentel says we should get married. Harry can get a *Sperre*, which will allow him to stay longer. I'll get one of these *Sperres* too if we're married.'

'But don't you already have a *Sperre* yourself?'

'It seems it's a special kind of *Sperre* with extra protection.' She casts down her eyes as she says it.

'So you're getting married because Director Pimentel – who never found a husband herself, for goodness' sake – told you to? You have a personal opinion too, I hope?'

'I like Harry very much.'

'Right, I like the butcher very much as well, but that doesn't mean I'm marrying him.' I scowl. 'You have to decide for yourself, of course, but if I were you...'

'If you were me?' she suddenly snaps. 'You've never had a boyfriend. What do you know about boys?'

'Nice and direct.'

'Like you're so subtle,' she says, irritated. 'You're always eager to give your opinion, Betty. Just let me be.'

'Fine, I will.' I turn around and walk out her room. Behind me, I hear her cry: 'Betty, don't be like this.' But I've completely had it.

I know I'm being mean, but what will I do when push comes to shove? Where will I hide? Who are my allies now? From pure envy, I kick the door of my wardrobe so hard a shelf comes loose and I gash my leg. 'Dammit!' I get a rag to wipe off the blood. As I rinse the rag, I take a look at my face. The mirror over the sink is so tarnished I look like a ghost, drab and blurry. I stare vacantly at my image as if I'm looking at someone else. At one of the old pictures Granny kept in a drawer, which she claimed were of her ancestors: something I never believed because some photos had family names on the back that were completely different. I could be one of those pictures now. A static image of a woman who'd been a flesh and blood human being at some point between dawn and dusk. Someone who lived no more than twenty years and left nothing. No offspring, no stories or friendships worth mentioning, no words, no feeling. Just this portrait with these dull eyes. I open the faucet and cup my hands under the cold water, then splash my face. Wake up. I'm still alive.

Klara, baby Aron's mother, is on tomorrow's deportation list together with her children. I've only spoken to her once since Aron can stomach powdered milk and no longer has to be fed by his mother. The nightly feeding and lack of sleep from the noise in the theatre have worn her out. She would now rather go to Westerbork than stay in that 'hell' any longer, she told me.

Now that she knows we won't be able to make all three of her children disappear, her only concern is to be reunited with them.

I go to the theatre to wish her the best and thank her for the hours we spent together. I find her all by herself, leaning against a pillar. Out of the blue, she says: 'Do it. Take Aron with you.'

I squat down beside her and hold her hands. 'Klara, I'm going to make sure he gets out of here safe. I promise. He'll be placed with some very loving people until you're reunited.'

'That's not going to happen,' she says.

'You shouldn't say that. Of course you'll see each other again.'

She shakes her head. 'I've been here too long to shut my ears to the stories going round. I know what's going to happen.' In her eyes, I recognise the same look I saw on myself in the mirror earlier.

'Please, don't give up yet.' I sit down beside her. 'You can't give up. Not on your children and not on yourself. There's always a chance as long as we're alive.'

'What kind of chance, Betty? After this, it's over. Only the innocents here are still able to convince themselves otherwise.' She glances into the hall, where people lie half asleep, two lovers share an embrace, a group is playing cards together and there's even laughter coming from across the room. Surely these people can't all be fools. How else could they continue to breathe, move and talk, like it's just another day and not the eve of their death? If you know the chance of you surviving is so small, why doesn't everyone rise up and revolt? Because of the small chance you'll be lucky enough to dodge the bullet? I look at Klara, who has a distant look in her eyes again.

'You have to keep your hopes up, Klara. Do you hear me?'

She doesn't respond to my words. 'Will you take good care of Aron?'

.   .   .

The following day during the transport, we have to do the trick with a doll again because Pimentel isn't able to get baby Aron off the list in such a short time. It's now a proven method of still saving very little ones from transport. But it seems there are no more dolls available at the nursery. How do we fake a baby if we don't even have a doll? Pimentel tells me to find a creative solution, otherwise we'll have to hand over the baby anyway. We can't have this whole operation fail because of one child.

I'm tremendously relieved to find one in the playroom on the windowsill after all. When I pick up the doll with the life-like face and I'm about to walk away, it's as if a siren rings. A girl watches her greatest treasure be taken right in front of her, and she's inconsolable. I can't bring myself to take what might well be the one thing this child has to hold on to. I give the doll back to her and decide to make one myself. I bundle up a bunch of old clothes, add some stones and swaddle the whole thing. For the head, I use a piece of smooth linen that I first dip in tea to give it something of a skin tone, then I draw a face on it. Finally, I put a little knitted hat on it and drape a baby blanket over it. Klara flinches when I hand her the makeshift baby, even though I warned her. She tries her best to stay strong with her two other children beside her.

'What's that?' the oldest of the two asks. The mother gives her daughter a stern look and says: 'It's your brother, can't you tell?' She then holds the so-called child close, rocking it up and down. Before disappearing into the transport truck with her boys, she looks back once more and nods at me.

CHAPTER 38

WEDNESDAY, 2 JUNE 1943

3,006 Jews were brought from Westerbork to Sobibor concentration camp in Poland yesterday, the largest transport up until this point. Initially, most trains left for Auschwitz in Poland, but now the cattle cars are also taking Jews to Sobibor and to Theresienstadt in Czechoslovakia.

I've finally received my false identity papers. My fake name is Elisabeth Petri. At least it doesn't sound Jewish. It's a perfect forgery of my old one, only this one doesn't have a big letter J on it. My sister Leni is furious when she hears I bought it with Granny's jewellery. She scolds me for not getting one much sooner; she'd bought one herself for just a few hundred guilders. Leni says Granny's jewellery was worth tens of thousands of guilders.

I shrug. 'What good are family heirlooms if we're all dead?' I ask. 'I'm not attached to anything.'

. . .

I'm in the theatre pretending to get medicines for the children from Doctor De Vries. But I know I'm not here for cod liver oil or cough syrup but for sedatives; we put a small drop of it in the little ones' bottles right before they're collected. This makes them sleep longer than with a splash of brandy.

I'm about to leave the ward when I see Leo in his doctor's coat to my left. I'm in no mood to run into him and immediately turn right towards the exit, but Leo has already seen me.

'Hi, Betty!' I hear behind me. 'Betty!'

I have to fight the childish urge to run away. Forcing myself to smile, I turn around. 'Hi, Leo, what a coincidence!'

'Not really, since I work here half the time,' he says, flashing a cheeky grin. His handsome appearance is deceiving every time we run into each other. He's standing in front of me like a Greek Adonis, but I already know how arrogant he is. How sly.

'Oh, I'd almost forgotten,' I say, feigning disinterest.

'Only I rarely see you here anymore.'

'That's right, I'm busy.' I avoid his gaze and look around nervously.

'And so you act like you don't see me?'

'I'm not!' I say, staring straight into the hypnotic blue of his eyes.

'Hey, calm down, I was only teasing.' He gives me a quick squeeze of the arm, like we're good friends. He then takes a step back and looks at me from top to bottom. 'Have you lost weight?' Without waiting for me to answer, he says: 'Looking good.'

I feel the blood rush to my cheeks. 'Guess that's the only upside of eating little and working lots,' I say. 'I need to get going. Have a great day!'

I hurry out of there.

. . .

I'm blinded by the harsh sunlight for a second, so I don't see the truck approaching from the left. Startled, I jump back onto the pavement. Instead of speeding past, the truck slows down and comes to a screeching halt right in front of me. The guard standing by the door with Klingebiel asks if they're expecting a new load.

'Every day. Until they're finished,' Klingebiel says, walking to the back of the truck. 'You've reached your destination!' he screams at the people.

I skirt around him and see the people in the open truck seated in two rows facing each other. Klingebiel lowers the tail-board, but no one is in a hurry to get up.

'Giddy up, get out. We don't have all day, people!' Klinge-biel yells. I linger a bit. There's something odd about this whole situation. Still no one is getting up. 'Are you deaf?' Klingebiel strikes the metal with the butt of his rifle and barks his orders once more. I don't want to have to see this and run across the street, where I see Mr Van Hulst, the training school director, just leaving the building. He gets his bicycle out from the rack and ties his briefcase in back, ready to cycle home. To his wife, who surely has dinner waiting. His children, jumping up to hug him. But I know Mr Van Hulst is doing what he can to help us.

'Good evening, Mr Van Hulst,' I say, passing by. He doesn't greet me back and seems to look right past me. I follow his gaze and see the people who'd refused to get up a moment ago care-fully shuffle onto the tailboard. 'Jump!' someone orders. One man jumps and collapses when he hits the ground. A woman struggles to climb off, but Klingebiel orders her to jump too. It's only then I realise: they're all blind. One by one, they jump from the tailboard into the unknown, unable to see where their fall ends and the ground starts.

'They've cleared out the institute for the blind,' Van Hulst says. The Germans' malice is perverse. They laugh each time someone falls. 'They're monsters,' Van Hulst hisses, then gets on his bicycle.

Looking down at the pavement, I hurry back inside through the side entrance. 'Are you alright?' a colleague asks when she sees me.

'No, are you?' I ask. I hear children singing inside. The high-pitched voice of a young nursery teacher saying: 'For heaven's sake, I'll give you a spanking if you scare me like that again,' which is followed by a small boy yelling 'Peekaboo!' and running off screaming.

CHAPTER 39

WEDNESDAY, 9 JUNE 1943

On 6 and 7 June, a total of almost 1,300 children from newborns to sixteen-year-olds who were staying in Camp Vught together with at least one parent were sent to Westerbork, from where they were sent on to Sobibor almost immediately. Word of these things is going round and causing dismay.

I've tried ignoring Joop, but I could only keep it up a few days. I see him too often, and I like him too much, despite everything. So now we're back to acting like we're friends.

'How kosher do you eat?' Joop asks as he helps me unpack the groceries.

'As kosher as I see fit. Why?'

'I have something you might like, but it's not entirely—'

'Let's have it!' I say even before he finishes his sentence. 'What is it?'

'Eel.'

My eyes go big, and my mouth starts watering instantly. 'Delicious! Father brought some home once. He made me promise never to tell Mother.'

'There aren't that many fish shops where we can still get some either, so keep your mouth shut about it now too.'

'Shut as an oyster,' I joke, pressing my lips together with my fingers.

Despite the scarcities, there's still always enough to eat at the nursery, so there won't be any children going hungry here. It's just so boring... Barley porridge, buckwheat porridge, wheat porridge and what-have-you kinds of porridge. We also eat beans of all shapes and sizes, most of which I don't even know what they're called. 90 percent of our meals consist of beans and porridge. The rest of our diet is made up of bread and the occasional fruit, vegetables, nuts and dairy, and meat or fish on very rare occasions. The last thing I'm concerned about is if these small treats are even kosher. Joop has kept an entire eel for me, and I'm so grateful I could kiss him. Joop watches me put the eel on a tray like it's some sacred ritual. I remove the black skin and cut a tiny piece from the long fatty fish that I fork into my mouth. The smoked, briny meat is an explosion of flavour, so soft it nearly melts in my mouth.

'Mmm, it's heavenly,' I swoon.

Joop laughs. 'I enjoy seeing you enjoy.'

'Want a piece yourself?' I ask. 'I hope not, but I'd be willing to share some of this treasure if you insist.'

'I already had some, thanks.'

'When, just now?'

'An hour ago, why?'

I hold my face close to his. 'Oh yeah, I can smell it. Then at least we both have the same taste in our mouths.'

'Errm, yes, maybe,' Joop says.

'Want a taste?' I give him a quick kiss on the lips. 'Yeah, the same.'

He laughs so hard now he doubles over, shoulders shaking.

'What? It's not that odd, is it?'

We go on joking around a little while, when suddenly Sieny enters the kitchen. 'You two are having fun, it seems,' she says in a motherly tone. The air between us still hasn't cleared since our argument, but I don't want to be the one to bring it up. If she wants to act like nothing is wrong, I'm happy to play along.

'What's so funny?' she asks.

'I brought her—'

'Shhh! Don't say anything,' I tell Joop. 'He brought me something. It's so heavenly, you just have to taste it.'

'Like what then?' Sieny asks.

'No, I'm not saying. Close your eyes and open up.' I know Sieny does in fact mind what she eats and that there won't be a single piece of non-kosher meat or fish going in her mouth. Her parents are strictly observant and have convinced her that non-kosher food will give her a stomach infection and – worse still – a corrupted soul. Let's see if she notices. 'Trust me, it's delicious.'

Joop gives me a look that says: *Are you sure about this?* But I give him a quick wink and continue cheerily. 'Go on, then!' Sieny shuts her eyes, and I carefully put a piece of eel on her extended tongue. She opens her eyes. 'Mmm, hmmm. It's unusual, but... delicious. What is it?'

'Eel!'

Sieny's face shows the full gamut of different emotions she's going through. First, her eyebrows contract, as in: Did I hear that right? Then those same eyebrows rise in disbelief. Next, her mouth tightens and her eyes go big with indignation, then even bigger with shock, and then finally anger. The corners of her mouth turn down, and her nose droops slightly too – insofar as noses can – and then she cries: 'Eel? How dare you!' She runs out of the kitchen. I can't stop laughing.

'That was a bit mean,' Joop says once I've settled down.

'So? You don't even know how mean she is to me.'

He shakes his head. 'You're crazy, Betty.'

'Right, like you're all there yourself,' I say. 'Flirting with me every day, but then staying engaged to that Christian tart.'

'Calm down, Betty, this isn't normal.'

'Normal hasn't been normal for some time now, Joop. Don't you understand? Or are you serious about having yourself castrated, if you ever even manage to marry her at all? All men married to a non-Jewish woman have to be sterilised if they don't want to be deported. To make sure no little half Jews are born. Pretty smart, those Germans. Because half rats are rats all the same.'

Joop gets his coat and is about to leave. I know I've gone too far. Much too far, but I'm no longer able to contain myself. 'Go ahead, walk away! But, Joop, you know just as well there's no such thing as moral purity anymore. Neither in what I do, or you do.'

He stands in front of me, bag flung over his shoulder, empty food crate to his chest. 'I don't have to come back here. If I want to, I can have myself transferred.'

'Then why don't you?'

'I think I just might.' He speaks these final words, then leaves.

'Get stuffed, why don't you?' I scream after him.

Even before I can sigh away my anger and my heart rate can return to normal, Pimentel enters the kitchen. 'Betty, it's very wrong what you did to Sieny!'

'Of course she went straight to you,' I say.

'Go to your room!' Pimentel has never been this cross with me.

'You're not my mother.' My harsh retort sounds weaker than intended.

'Right now!'

I leave the kitchen, knock over a toddler and bolt up the stairs to my room.

. . .

Only in the afternoon when it's time to get the children from across the street does Pimentel enter my room. 'Have you come back to your senses?'

My head bows involuntarily, and I see tears drop into my hands. The sound of my sobbing fills the room, and I hate it. The sound of my grief is unbearably ugly.

I feel a warm hand on my head. 'We need you, Betty,' I hear Pimentel say softly. 'The children need you. Baby Aron, who's getting stronger each day thanks to you.' I'd asked Pimentel to let Aron get his strength back first before we send him off to be put in hiding. I feel especially responsible for him because I got to know his mother a bit.

I raise my chin. 'Is it true about those children in Vught? Were they all taken away?'

Pimentel gives me a stern look, nodding ever so slightly.

Joop hasn't asked to be transferred, but the familiarity we enjoyed before seems to have disappeared. I haven't made amends with Sieny yet either. I tried visiting my sister, Leni, at the hospital to have a chat and feel some sense of family, which I dearly miss. She had no time for me. I feel lonelier than ever in this chaos I've wound up in. I force myself to focus on my task, which is only becoming greater because of the pressure we're under from the Germans with the deportations. The child-smuggling machine is in full swing; everyone does their part with utmost precision. We make ten, twenty children disappear each week, but all that's needed is a single slip-up and we're done for. The stress is pressing down on my stomach, tying my guts in an inextricable knot. It's fine so long as I stay active, but it's all too much when I sit down and think. On nights when I'm not distracted by babies I have to care for, I struggle to maintain hope for a good outcome. It's the small things that make it possible for me to go on, like the promise I made to Klara to find a safe place for her son.

CHAPTER 40

MONDAY, 21 JUNE 1943

Bounty hunters are catching more Jews all the time, which means the theatre is overcrowded again.

It happens very fast. I've just come back from walking Pimentel's dog, when an army truck stops in front of the nursery and two German soldiers get out. Which is odd. They usually park in front of the theatre, not where we are. I linger by the truck because I notice the driver who's remained seated isn't wearing a uniform but an army-green sweater. The soldiers ring the doorbell, and Pimentel opens almost instantly. 'We've come to get the children,' one of them says in a harsh voice. But I immediately hear the man has a Dutch accent. Pimentel looks skittishly across the street, where the guards are looking at what's happening here.

'Which children are we talking about?' Pimentel asks in a formal tone.

The soldier hands her a list. 'These are their names.' Pimentel goes inside while the men lower the tailboard. Virrie comes out with a group of children almost straight away. They

must have been all ready, there's no other way. Virrie helps one
of the men lift the children into the truck while Pimentel seems
to be checking and signing the list.

I see the two guards in front of the theatre exchange words,
still looking our way. Then one of them, his rifle over his shoulder, comes moseying towards us. It's Klingebiel.

The so-called Germans see him too and start to get nervous.
The man holding the papers runs back to help his colleague
load the children in. 'Faster!' he hisses. I catch Pimentel's glance
for a second as she stands in the doorway. She also knows this
can go wrong. I have to stall for time somehow. I quickly
unfasten the dog's leash and give it a little push. He's a fierce
one who often goes straight for those black boots. But it seems
he's not in the mood today, and he stays frozen on the pavement.
'Shoo! Shoo!' I try, but to no avail.

The last two children are lifted into the truck, and then the
board is closed. The one man hurries to the front to climb in the
passenger's seat, the other lifts himself up to sit with the children. The engine starts, and the men stick their hand up at
Pimentel to their right. They act like they don't see the SS man
approaching from the left. I see Klingebiel's facial expression
shift from unconcerned to alert. The truck starts to move, but
Klingebiel is already standing in front of them.

'Good afternoon. Could you tell me what you're here for?'
he asks the driver through the open window.

I brace myself. If they open their mouth, they're doomed.
'They've come to collect children. Orders from the Zentralstelle,' Pimentel says on their behalf.

The dog now hears its master's voice and starts barking and
running towards her.

'I'm talking to them,' Klingebiel says, raising his voice to
make himself heard, then asks the driver: 'Who sent you?'

The driver hands him the list of names. 'Chief Commander
Lages sent us,' he says, almost inaudibly.

'What's that?'

Pimentel throws something into the street, which Bruni immediately takes as meaning playtime. He runs into the street, yapping away. Pimentel and I start calling the dog at the same time, making it even harder for Klingebiel to hear much of anything.

A short 'Heil!' later, the truck starts to move, and Klingebiel watches the truck full of children drive off. He looks particularly confused and is still holding the list. 'Who were they?'

'Sir, I wouldn't know,' Pimentel says, having got her dog back.

Cursing this inexplicable occurrence, Klingebiel returns to his station.

The next day, everyone at the nursery is in a jubilant mood because of this operation from the resistance, which allowed seventeen children to escape at once. They were mostly the slightly older children who'd already been with us for some time, and for whom it was difficult to find a safe address. I hope they managed to now, and that I'll never see them back here again. It's happened several times before that we were able to get a child out, only to have it back at our door a few days – or sometimes weeks – later because it was captured while in hiding. It's frustrating.

Pimentel doesn't share our excitement. She's even a bit grumpy because her reading glasses are broken as a result of throwing them into the street for Bruni to go after. She was also questioned by Aus der Fünten for at least an hour. Naturally, he wanted a word with her, but she insisted she knew nothing and was as surprised as anyone.

. . .

During the transport that evening, the Germans are extra harsh to punish us for our small victory, as well as to show us who's in charge again. I'm happy when the trucks full of people drive off and we can go back inside. Sieny goes straight to bed and bids me goodnight. I feel bad that she keeps acting so distant, even though I apologised. How long can you stay angry about a piece of eel?

Mirjam, who's in charge of the baby section during the day, announces she's off to bed herself. We're so attuned to each other now that the shift handover takes only a few minutes. 'Bed two will have to be fed soon. Beds four and seven are teething. There's teethers in the refrigerator. Then the non-existent numbers nine through eighteen,' she goes on. She's referring to the children who aren't registered. 'Number fifteen is the child with intestinal problems. There's goat milk in the fridge for him.'

This is about little Aron. When his mother left, he couldn't tolerate instant formula again, but he's able to handle goat milk. I give him the most care out of all the children. It feels unfair sometimes that I pay less attention to the other babies. Like the girl who's here without her parents too, and who always smiles at me when I give her the smallest bit of attention. But I have to divide my time. There's usually at least one toddler who comes down the stairs at night, unable to sleep. Other times, a bigger child will be screaming in his sleep so loud that I have to wake him to keep the whole room from waking.

Mirjam is about to leave, and I tell her to sleep well, when there's a loud knock on the door. 'Open up!' I look at Mirjam, frightened.

'Distract them,' Mirjam says, then goes back to the baby room. 'Who is it?' I ask through the closed door.

'Chief Commander Aus der Fünten. Open up!'

What has he come for at this hour?

'One moment, let me put something on.' I run up the stairs as fast as I can and call Sieny.

'Hide the children. Aus der Fünten is at the door!'

I quickly unfasten the strap behind my back, open the door and see Aus der Fünten and Klingebiel standing there. 'Sorry, gentlemen,' I say, panting. 'I can't open the door in my nightgown, can I?' Aus der Fünten ignores me and walks past me into the hallway with Klingebiel. 'How can I help you? Cup of coffee, gentlemen? Or maybe something stronger?' I have to get them away from the baby room.

'Is the director not here?' he asks. He knows very well she's not here. Pimentel left right after the transport.

'She went home. Should I go get her?'

'That won't be necessary. I'm sure you can help us too. We have another seventeen empty places left in the train, isn't that right, Officer Klingebiel?' He looks to his side at his subordinate.

'Yes, they'll need to be filled,' Klingebiel says.

'Oh, but I don't know if we even have an extra seventeen children. There's not that many orphans here, really!' I hurry to say. *Seventeen, that's no coincidence. This is pure retaliation.*

'No? I think we'd best see for ourselves. Where's the list of names?'

He'll know instantly we're deceiving him if he gets his hands on the official list.

'Seventeen, you say? We might have four or five.'

'The list!' he screams right in my face, making me jump back.

'I'm sorry,' I say, my voice shaking. 'Director Pimentel always takes it home with her. If you want, I can—'

'Never mind,' he says. 'Either you have seventeen little nippers ready in ten minutes, or I'll come drag them from their beds myself.' Again, he's standing intimidatingly close and shouting in my face. 'Understand?'

'Yes, yes... Of course,' I stammer.

'What's going on here?' Sieny comes down the stairs in her nightgown.

'Well, there we have the cheeky one too! As if my day wasn't bad enough already.'

Klingebiel laughs out loud at his superior's joke.

Aus der Fünten turns towards us again. 'Ten minutes!' He then stomps out of the nursery with Klingebiel trailing behind like an obedient dog.

We have another thirty-six children here who aren't registered. Which children do we choose to be put on the transport? Ten minutes, he said. They have to be ready in ten minutes. Aus der Fünten did this on purpose! He waited until Pimentel had left and then came to us so tomorrow it's a done deal and Pimentel won't have been able to do anything to stop it. Surely he also knows things are going on behind his back. He has to! He knows we're witholding children who can't be traced and who sometimes just disappear. Mirjam, Sieny and I consult feverishly. Mirjam then goes through our adjacent garden to get her sister, Virrie, at Huize Frank community centre. Sieny and I go to the preschoolers' rooms to get children from their beds, and I'm surprised to see Harry there too. I didn't know he'd slept here in secret. Without giving it another thought, I start waking the children, cheerily saying: 'You can come along on the train after all!' I choose children I don't know. Children I don't look in the eye when I tell them to go get their stuff and not to forget their teddy bear. I suppress the nauseous feeling in my stomach, the buzzing in my head, the tingling in my hands and proceed. When I get to a girl who's wide awake in bed and tell her to get up, Sieny stops me. 'No, not her! Do him ahead.' She points to the boy sleeping beside her. A girl of around fourteen offers to go herself; she doesn't want to hide any longer. One boy protests so heavily that we have a sweet, compliant girl go in his place. The older children know where to go in these kinds of emergencies and are already in the attic. Sieny whispers she hid two children in the sandpit for the time being. Harry takes care of the remaining illegal children and brings them to the mezzanine. We come back down with nine children. Virrie and Mirjam have five babies ready in improvised carrycots made from fruit boxes and bread baskets. To my horror, I see Aron is one of them. 'Take another baby,' I say resolutely. 'They're not getting this one.'

'We only have thirteen,' says Virrie, who's writing down the names of the children we're handing over.

'We'll say there aren't any more, and that's just how it is,' I say, lifting Aron from the box.

'Then they'd better not come looking in the baby room,' says Mirjam. 'There's three more illegal babies sleeping there next to three official ones.'

Including Aron, that makes four. Where in heaven's name do we hide four babies?

There's a knock at the door. 'There they are already. Let me,' Virrie says. Holding Aron in my arms, I hurry to the baby section together with Mirjam.

'Can't you count?' someone screams. 'I said seventeen! Do I have to come get those little shits myself?'

'These are all the orphans. There's not much else I can do,' Virrie says.

Adrenaline surges through my body. *Where to hide him?* My hands are so shaky I'm fumbling about. I pull open the bottom drawer of the commode, take out one of the two blankets, put Aron in with a dummy in his mouth and push the drawer back shut. I then grab a tiny little baby of just a few days old from his bed and open the waste bin next to the commode, stuff the blanket in, put the child on top and close the lid again. The child in bed number two starts crying softly. I clap my hands right by his ears to startle the child, and the volume instantly goes up. Then the door swings open. 'Plenty of little runts in here, I see! Take those children, let's go!' Klingebiel steps into the room, followed by another SS man.

'Chief Commander, these children all have to go on the transport with their parents this coming week,' Mirjam says. 'If you take them now, you'll have empty places in the train again next week.'

'And how will you be transporting all these babies?' I add. 'Unless you want me to go as well. It's no problem, really,' I bluff.

'Don't act smart, you snot-nosed kid!'

Several babies have now woken, each crying louder than the next. I also think I hear a sound coming from the commode.

'Here's another orphan,' Mirjam says, handing over a baby. 'Take this one too.'

Klingebiel takes the child from her. 'This one smells!'

'Then he needs his diapers changed. Shall I?'

'We're done for now. Let's go!' Aus der Fünten yells over the crying babies. 'This is the last time I'll have you try and play me for a fool. Do you hear me? The last time!'

Peeking through the curtains, I watch them leave with the children. Aus der Fünten in front as his officers carry the babies. Some boys from the Council are outside, ready to help. I recognise one of them as Joop. It's as if he's looking at me, but he can't see me at all. The children are lifted into the truck.

When I turn around, I see Mirjam take one of the mattresses from the bed and lean forward to pick up a girl. She'd hidden the smiley child underneath the mattress. I open the waste bin and lift the little baby out, then open the drawer and free Aron.

. . .

Only when everything has calmed down again, when the remaining children have gone to sleep, my colleagues have gone to bed and I've started my night shift do I realise the risk we've taken. I think of the children frightened out of their wits on the train now. Not knowing where they're going or what's going to happen to them. Without any adults they know to escort and protect them. I tremble as if I'm freezing cold, while it's at least twenty degrees outside. A warm spring evening. I have to force myself not to float up and drift off again. I now know it's a danger zone up there. It's where I can see my mother again, where she'll explain why she didn't take the train back to Amsterdam. And I'll understand. It will all be clear why the lack of oxygen in that thin air is preferable over life on earth. Because anywhere is better than here at this point. I have to distract myself with work, changing diapers, giving bottles, singing songs and soothing. Because when it's quiet, I'm so afraid of what I'm capable of that my hands turn cold and my breathing quickens.

CHAPTER 41

MONDAY, 28 JUNE 1943

The Utrechtse Courant *reports: 'In the Russian town of Velikiye Luki, several tank-supported attacks by the Bolsheviks were dispersed by heavy fire or warded off in close combat.'*

The following morning, everything continues as usual. Pimentel compliments me for how we handled last night's situation, then without pausing asks if I can bring the three babies we saved to the clothing depot.

After I've bottle-fed the babies their milk with a drop of sedative for each, I swaddle them and put them in a handcart. I loosely drape some blankets over them and take it to Nel at the clothing depot. If an SS man across the street, a random policeman or the executioner who's still around here somewhere, if one of them were to stop me... I swear I'd scratch their eyes out. My fear is gone, and my overconfidence is back with a vengeance. Nothing can stop me now. I reach Nel without a hitch, and she brings the babies to the back without comment, Aron last. I kiss him on the forehead and wish him a safe journey.

'To a better life, sweet little boy!'

Harry comes storming into the nursery, looking excited. He sees me and asks where Sieny is.

'In the back with the toddlers, I think.'

Without saying anything, he heads straight to the back-room. I have no idea what he's come for, but I sense I have to be there too, so I go after him. Through the open door, I witness Harry calling out to Sieny, who's busy dressing a child at the other end of the room: 'Sieny, we can marry today!'

Sieny looks at him in bewilderment. 'Is this a proposal? This isn't how I'd pictured it.'

I'm looking at the back of Harry's head but can easily imagine his face – thrown off by Sieny's response.

'Errm, yes. We said we would, didn't we?' he says awkwardly.

I have to force myself not to laugh. Especially when I catch Sieny's eyes, which say: *Can you believe this guy?*

'On your knees, Harry,' I say.

He crouches down at once and only just manages to keep from toppling over. Down on one knee, he then says: 'Dear Sieny, you're the woman of my life. Will you marry me?'

'Yes, I will,' Sieny answers. 'But does it have to be now?'

'No, not now.' He looks at the clock. 'In two hours, at twelve o'clock.'

I can't contain myself any longer, and Sieny bursts out laughing too. The toddler with Sieny on the dressing table has no idea what this is about, but he merrily laughs along. Harry thinks we're making fun of him and looks angry. I hold both hands up in apology. 'I'm sorry, it's just really funny.'

'But romantic too, right?' Harry says in his Rotterdam accent.

'Very romantic,' Sieny says, still chuckling. 'I just don't know if I'm able to take time off.'

'I've already arranged that with your boss,' Harry says.

Without another word, Sieny goes on dressing the child. Harry glances back at me with a forlorn look in his eyes.

'I'd hurry up. You only have a few hours to get ready,' I say.

'There, you go play with the others now,' Sieny says, lifting the child from the table and putting it on the ground. She then turns towards us. 'Alright then, Harry. Let's do it.'

'Woohoo!' Harry cries. 'We're getting married!'

'Do you want to be our witness, Betty?' Sieny asks.

I look at her, dumbfounded. 'Me? I thought you were still angry with me.'

She shrugs. 'I thought you were still angry with me because I...' She unexpectedly starts to cry, hiding her face in her hands. Harry looks at me in confusion.

I walk around him to my friend. 'Hey... Are you alright?'

She lifts up her teary face. 'I'm so sorry we can't go together, Betty.'

'Oh, Sieny, you're making me cry too now,' I say, choking up. 'I understand you want to go with Harry. I was just jealous...'

Crying in each other's arms, I hear Harry behind us say: 'See that, kids? That's what happens when two people make amends. They cry with joy. Remember that for when you get in a fight with someone yourself.'

'Who'd have thought?' Sieny says in front of the mirror a little later. 'That I'd be getting married in my uniform during the worst time of our life.'

'That's precisely why you should be happy,' I say as I brush her hair. 'It shows love can still bloom, even in times so full of hate.'

'But you only marry once, Betty, and I'd always imagined it would be with friends and family, in a beautiful white dress. That Harry would come pick me up in a carriage, and that I'd say yes under the *chuppah*.'

I bend down and look at our two faces in the mirror. 'We'll just imagine that part ourselves, Sieny.' She casts down her eyes. 'Or are you having second thoughts?'

She gives a sad smile. 'Not about Harry,' she says. 'But about the moment.'

I turn towards her. 'You can still say no.'

Only now does she look me in the eye. 'What would you do?'

'What kind of question is that, Sieny? I just told you how jealous I am of you two...'

'If Joop were to ask you, would you say yes?'

I stand up straight again. 'That's not fair. You have to find the answer inside yourself, not from me. And you know just as well Joop isn't an option.'

'How about Leo?'

'Even less. Sweetie, Harry would move heaven and earth to make you happy. How many women find themselves a man like that?'

Still, she seems unconvinced. What can I do to make her stop catastrophizing? 'How about this? If you have the gall to say no, I'll make you a cake,' I say to egg her on.

She turns around to face me. 'Hmmm, it's tempting,' she says, laughing.

'Alright, I can't wait.'

At the V&D department store on Weesperzijde, there's a sign on the counter that reads: *Jews can marry here*. There's no one behind it. We ring the bell a few times, and eventually a gentleman in a tailcoat, looking a bit like a penguin, shows up from the back. 'Where's the bride and groom?' he asks the company he sees in front of him.

Sieny raises her hand. 'It's us.'

'Ah, right,' the man says.

He opens a folder and starts conducting the ceremony in an uninspired tone. Pimentel looks at me from the side and rolls her eyes. I try hard not to laugh. Especially when the officiant calls Sieny – whose official name is Schoontje – 'Schooly' several times. Pimentel shakes her head, cursing the man under her breath. Then at last, he comes to the only question that truly matters. Harry says yes without hesitating. But when the man asks Schoontje Kattenburg if she'll take Harry Cohen as her lawful husband, all is quiet in the V&D department store. Harry anxiously glances to his side. Why isn't his love answering?

The question is asked again, but Sieny keeps silent, glassy-eyed, like she doesn't hear him. Should I do something?

'What'll it be, Miss Kattenburg?' the officiant asks impatiently.

'Oh, I'm sorry. Yes...' Sieny seems to be coming back to her senses.

'Is that your answer?'

'No, I'm sorry. But I want to. I mean: yes, I want to be the lawful wife of Harry Cohen.'

She said both 'no' and 'yes' unintentionally, so I'll have to arrange half a cake.

'You had me worried for a second there, Sieny,' Harry says afterwards. He can laugh about it now that it's a done deal. We drink brandy with some colleagues to celebrate the marriage. Joop is there too. After two full glasses, I feel a bit tipsy. Daft, because I'm even less inhibited as a result, so when Joop gets up to use the restroom, I can't help but follow him.

When he leaves the men's room, I leap in front of him: 'Halt!' I say, doubling over with laughter at my silly joke. Joop laughs along with me, which I interpret as encouraging me to throw my arms around him and kiss him. But when he's freed himself from my embrace and makes up an excuse to leave, I know I've made a mistake. I go back to drink another glass of brandy. Virrie is taking my nightshift, so I can go to bed whenever I want. I toast on the newlyweds and start to sing a song: 'Make it dark, make it dark, in the dark. Even if the stars go on and spark...'

I don't know how I found my way to bed. I wake with a heavy head and find a note slipped under the door. Feeling nauseous, I pick it up from the floor and gently sit on the edge of my bed to unfold it.

Dear Betty,

I'm writing to explain again that nothing can come of this between us. It might have been different if I weren't already engaged and both our parents hadn't yet approved of our forthcoming marriage. I really like you, you know I do, and I'd like to stay friends. But if that's too difficult for you, I understand, and you won't have to see me anymore.

Love, Joop.

His choice of words makes it seem as if he didn't choose this Christian girl himself but that she was forced on him. I've never heard him speak of their relationship in terms of 'love'. But if that's his decision, there's not much else I can do. I furiously tear the note into a hundred little pieces.

. . .

I feel so awful I go to Pimentel to ask if I can get the day off. Pimentel looks up from her bookkeeping. She takes off her reading glasses and looks at me in annoyance. 'Do you think I feel great all the time?'

Taken aback by her reply, I mumble that I don't know how she feels.

'Exactly!' she says, getting up from her desk and coming towards me. 'Because it doesn't matter how I feel, no more than it matters how you feel.' She locks her arm in mine and turns me towards the window. 'Look, all those people across the street don't care how we feel either.'

I regret coming to see her and can hardly hold back my tears.

'When you come to my office, I'd like you to first think of what exactly you want to ask me before keeping me from my work. Alright?'

I nod. 'Of course. I'm sorry.'

She turns to face me. 'I'm sorry I have nothing more to offer than this, Betty. But we have to stay strong. If we lower our guard and start giving in to feelings, we're lost. Do you understand?'

I bow my head. 'Yes, I understand.'

'Take two hours off to rest, but then it's time for work.'

She's right: I have to suck it up. 'I'll do that, director.'

'Oh, and Betty,' she says before I'm out the door. 'Call me Henriëtte from now on.'

CHAPTER 42

FRIDAY, 23 JULY 1943

During the first Allied air raid on the Fokker factory, the forty-one American bomber planes missed their target and hit a residential area in Amsterdam North. A week later now, 185 dead and 104 injured have been reported. Tragedies are piling up.

Sieny tried to comfort me as we ate the promised half cake I'd baked with buckwheat and thin apple slices. She said I should forget about Joop. According to her, I can get a hundred guys who are all less cowardly and much cuter. I can imagine the first but not the second. Anyway, as if on cue, Leo appeared at the door and asked if I felt like doing something fun with him. I hadn't heard anyone use the word 'fun' in months and couldn't help but laugh. He took that as a 'yes'. That was that, then: he'd come pick me up in a few days.

Leo takes me to the house of friends of his. He says it has a beautiful courtyard that's a kind of oasis and also an interesting interior with all kinds of art on the walls. He's right: when we enter the lower floor of the house in Amsterdam South, it's like we've walked into another world where the oak furniture was chosen with due love and care and the paintings on the wall show good taste and sophistication. Leo makes me some tea and shows me a folder of illustrations from the building's Jewish owner, who's an artist. They're drawings of faces, rich in detail, which makes me feel like I personally know the people he's drawn myself. Leo says he wants to compile the drawings eventually and have a book printed. I'm surprised he's so interested in something I rarely hear men talk about. Sipping my spiced tea, I try to figure out why else it feels 'different' here. I suddenly realise: it's as if I've gone back in time to a point before 10 May 1940. I'm not confronted with orphaned children, deportations or war here. When we've had our tea, Leo asks if I feel like playing a game of lawn bowls.

In the backyard with its dry, yellowed grass, he explains how the game with the steel balls works. I'm in no such mood at first – why would I play silly games at a time like this? – but then I start to enjoy it, especially when I beat Leo. Or did he let me win to cheer me up? When we go inside to cool down, he kisses me. I try not to compare how he presses his mouth to mine and sticks his tongue inside with how it was with Joop. But I've thought of it already. It all felt so natural with Joop. Until he broke off our frenzied lovemaking because his conscience started nagging at him.

Leo drags me over to the sofa. He doesn't look at me and is solely focussed on my breasts. 'Oh my God, they're so big...'

This should be the moment when I tell him to stop, but I'm unable to.

He kisses my breasts and then lets his hand slide down towards my crotch.

'Oh, you... You want this, don't you? You want me.'

I don't know what I want or what I'm feeling. Not a lot. But I have a thousand thoughts running through my head. About

Sieny already being married now, while I'm still a virgin. About me wanting to have 'done it' before losing this war. About my mother, who always warned me not to let just anyone pluck my flower. About Father, who had to protect his daughters until a 'suitable party' came along. About Japie and farmer Kroon. About lecherous SS men with Jewish women. About Pimentel, who prefers women over men, apparently. About Remi and his intense dark eyes. About all that is lost and dies. About Granny, and all she'd endured at the hands of men she didn't like.

'*Arrête! Arrête! Arrête!*'

'What's that?' Leo's face is right above me. 'You said something.'

'Errm, yes. I don't remember.'

'Did you like it?' Leo buttons up his pants. 'Well?'

'Yes, sure.'

Leo is in the best of moods and walks me back, his arm on my shoulders. We part ways on the final leg. He has to be somewhere. We say goodbye with a last kiss. The magic is gone, insofar as it was ever there to begin with. It was pure projection of my desire for love from the very start.

Confused and miserable, I return to the nursery, where the dog is barking in the hallway. I try to grab him, but he growls at me. 'Hey, Bruni, it's me. Where's your master?' Only once I've got the dog to be silent do I notice there's no one here. No children, no adults. No one. I push open the door of the baby room. All the beds are empty, but for the rest it seems like nothing has changed. Everything is in its right place in Pimentel's room as well. The tables in the back room are set for dinner. I go into the garden, where the play area is scattered with little bicycles and the shovels and moulds are in the open sandpit. I feel a nauseating panic rising. *This can't be! Everyone is gone. Where are they?* I go up the stairs, my legs stiff from fear. I check each room, one after another. Empty. They're all empty.

Hyperventilating, I call out: 'Hello? Is anybody here? Where are you? Hello?' Another flight of stairs takes me to my own room, where nothing has moved since I was there this morning. I'd left it exactly like this, as if time was frozen. I jump when I see my own reflection and start frantically gathering my belongings. That's that. I need to get out of here. Only then I hear someone whisper my name. I creep into the hall, where the sound came from. 'Hello?'

'Up here.' I see the timid face of one of my younger colleagues above me, in the hatch to the attic. 'Are you alone, Betty?'

'Yes, I'm alone. What happened? Where is everyone?'

Before answering, my colleague lets down the ladder. I take it from her and secure it on the wooden floor, after which she climbs down, followed by a colleague and then another six children. Their faces are tight with fear.

'What happened?' I ask again.

'The SD came in and then...' My colleague is unable to continue.

'Then they took everyone,' says Sal, the oldest boy in the nursery. 'All the children, all the nursery teachers and Pimentel.'

'Everyone?' I ask in disbelief. The girls nod.

'What about Sieny?' I ask, my throat constricted.

'I'm sorry...' one of them weeps.

I hear footsteps in the attic. 'Is there someone else?'

A pair of men's legs appear in the hatch, and Harry climbs down with a small girl in his arms.

'Sieny wasn't on the list to be taken,' he says. 'She had that special *Sperre* from me. And of course Virrie didn't have to go because of her father. But because these two idiots hid themselves...' He points at the two young nursery teachers. 'They were short two people, so they took my wife and Virrie anyway.'

So this is it then? The end of the nursery? Now what? What's going to happen now? Should I flee with my false identity papers, all by myself? Or should I just report myself and join my friend and Pimentel?

We're all in the staff room feeling devastated, when suddenly Joop turns up at the door. 'Thank God,' he says when he sees me. 'For a second I thought you'd also...' Süskind appears behind him. The man with the constant fake smile on his face looks serious.

'This is a very tragic day,' he says. 'I'm doing what's in my power to get them all back, but I really don't know if I'll be able to.'

'Sieny has a special *Sperre!*' says Harry, showing his Rotterdam fighting spirit. 'Otherwise, I'll go get her myself!' He gives the younger colleagues a spiteful look again, and they immediately start sobbing.

Süskind joins us at the table. 'One person isn't worth any less than the next, Harry. Besides, they didn't know your Sieny and Virrie would be made to go instead.'

Harry gets up from the table, fists clenched, and paces up and down the room.

'In any case, what I did manage to arrange is for the nursery to stay open. They've brought some more children to the theatre again this afternoon, so Aus der Fünten feels the annexe can't be closed yet.'

It's eleven o'clock at night when I hear someone knock on my bedroom door. I'm wide awake immediately. Have they now come for me as well? But when I see who enters, I jump straight out of bed. It's Sieny. I open my arms and hold her close. Her body is shaking like a leaf.

'It was awful,' she weeps. 'Awful.'

I wipe the tears from her face with the sleeve of my night-gown and have her sit down.

'I thought... I thought it was over...' she stammers. 'I'd even accepted it. Maybe I'd see Mother and Father again. We were lying there on the dusty ground with all our colleagues and the children close together. We'd stick together and couldn't lose each other. There were hundreds, maybe thousands of people waiting for the trains in that vacant lot right by the railway. Until Frau Cohen was called to report. I thought it was about Virrie, but they meant me. I got up to go to the commander, and then I heard they were sending me back to the nursery to be appointed as the new director. I said I was too young to be in charge and that I needed Director Pimentel's help. But they refused. I wasn't even allowed to say goodbye to Pimentel.'

'Henriëtte...' I whisper.

The nursery just kept going as if Director Henriëtte Pimentel, head nursery teacher Mirjam Cohen, sixteen other fellow carers and tens of children hadn't been arrested and deported. The morning after, only Virrie Cohen returned from the rail yard from where the trains had left. She was older than Sieny and also had a nursing diploma. Aus der Fünten had decided she would be in charge of the nursery from now on. And so it went.

CHAPTER 43

TUESDAY, 28 SEPTEMBER 1943

The Jewish Council is finished negotiating, insofar as their negotiations ever resulted in anything to begin with. All Sperres, *the regular, the special and even the most exceptional of the highest members, have been declared invalid. Everyone is summoned to report.*

You wonder where they got the Jews from at this point, but they just kept packing people into the theatre this last month. Their resistance seemed broken, their morale crushed. We kept caring for and smuggling out their children, sometimes thirty a week. Virrie is doing what Pimentel had so brilliantly set up. The whole operation works like a well-oiled machine, and human emotions have to be kept in check as much as possible. 'When it comes down to it, your feelings only get in the way,' Virrie also says. She's right. Feelings make you think when you have to act, make you weak when you have to be strong, make you cry when your face should be smiling. We can't have that. If this were a piece of music, us nursery teachers take care of the prelude, the female students taking the children all across the country are the cadence and the families taking them in are the final chord. The theme is always the same, and there's no beautiful melody in most cases. But anything is better than the immense requiem the Germans are performing.

The shrill sound of the bell rings through the hallway. I jump. *Not now, we're not done yet!* Shaking, I get up and look towards the heavy front door at the end of the hallway. We've been ordered to get all the children ready for departure: the nursery has to be cleared out. Haubtsturmführer Aus der Fünten came to tell us in person: 'Get those damn children out of here!' he'd said. '*Abtransportieren!*' We already brought the babies to the Hollandsche Schouwburg theatre yesterday. The rest of the children will follow today.

'Betty, could you get that?' Virrie calls from Pimentel's director's office.

I stick my head around the corner. 'What should I say?'

'That we need more time.' Virrie barely looks up from her paperwork; she's busy getting the official records to add up. Again, the bell makes its screeching sound.

Still trying to think of a reason to stall for time, I pull open the heavy door. I'm surprised to see not an SS man at the door, but a woman with an enormous bosom. It's the first thing I notice. A brown hat casts a shadow across her face. Drops of sweat glisten on her upper lip. She pulls the collar of her high-necked dress, pulling a thin necklace with a gold cross along with it.

'Can I help you?'

Her eyes dart around nervously, looking for someone or something. 'We can't keep him.' She's almost panting her words, like she's out of breath. It's only then that I notice the picnic basket next to her worn-down boots. The red chequered ribbons used to fasten the lid dance in the wind. 'This is the nursery, right?'

'Yes, but we're closing.'

Despite my clear message, the woman doesn't seem ready to give up on her mission just yet, and using her foot she pushes the basket towards me. 'Please, it's an easy baby.'

'Madam, you really need to keep him yourself. There's no more room for children here.' I say it with added emphasis, hoping to convince her.

'But where else can I take him?' Her voice shakes. And then, leaning towards me, she whispers: 'He's circumcised, you know.'

'Christians also have their children circumcised. I'm sorry, you'll have to take him back with you.' I pick the rectangular basket up from the pavement. 'Please.' I want to hand her the basket, but the woman won't take it from me.

'No, no. It's too dangerous.' Her hat wobbles on her head. 'You're not taking a risk. You're Jewish, but I...' She doesn't finish her sentence.

I feel the anger rise in my throat. 'It doesn't really matter for me anymore, is that what you're trying to say?'

My remark seems to change her demeanour. She puts her hands on her waist and sticks out her chin. 'I fed this child like it was my own flesh and blood. You're not telling me I haven't been good for your kind. But my husband thinks the risk is too great now. I don't... I...' She reaches for the basket momentarily, but right before her fingers touch the wickerwork, she retracts them and turns around abruptly.

'Wait a second. What's your name?' I call after her.

'I'd rather not say.'

'And the child's name?'

'There's a card that'll tell you everything you need to know.' She then hurries off.

I see Klingebiel staring at me from across the street. I casually hook the basket over my arm and go inside.

The heavy front door closes with a sigh. Without the street noise, I hear a soft murmur coming from the improvised carrycot. I hurry to the empty baby section, where the smell of talcum powder and faeces still lingers. I put the basket down on one of the changing tables. The empty white cribs around me feel like silent witnesses.

The moans become louder. I start singing softly as I untie the straps and daylight enters the basket. As soon as he sees me, he starts bawling. His little hands swing at the air, and he opens his mouth so wide a saucer could fit inside. *Dammit, we don't need this. Not now.* With one hand under the soft downy hair and the other under his buttocks, I lift him up. The cotton of his diaper feels moist. I sing a little louder to mask his crying. 'Little robin by the window, tap tap tap. Let me in, let me in.' I hold his jittery body close to my chest, gently pushing his little head against my shoulder. He's now screaming so loud my ears ring. Undeterred, I continue to sing.

I shift my weight from one foot to the other, rocking the new child up and down. 'Shhh, quiet now...' His muscles start to relax, and his beady eyes look at me quizzically, as if wanting to ask: *Who are you?*

'Good boy, there you go.' I offer him my pinkie, which he starts sucking on eagerly straight away.

Then I hear the determined sound of approaching footsteps in the hallway. The door swings open. 'Who was at the...' Virrie doesn't finish her sentence when she sees me and the little one. Her nurse's cap sits tilted on her head. 'Betty, where did you get that?'

I give her a helpless look. 'From someone who got cold feet.'

'We can't keep him! They're coming to take the beds later.'

'I know, but I was thinking, maybe I can bring him to Nel.'

'There's at least another ten children hidden there who still need to go too!' Virrie straightens her cap. As if everything that's crooked can be straightened out just as easily. She follows with a sigh. 'I'll see if I can reach someone. Is this place empty for the rest?'

'Yes, we just checked.' Children can hide in places no one would have thought of. Behind the slanted walls in the attic, under the remaining coal in the cellar, in the pile of linen slowly rotting away, under the sofa.

'Keep him with you meanwhile and make sure no one sees him. Or hears him!' She rushes back out the room like a whirlwind.

The card the woman mentioned isn't in the basket. No name, no birth date, no address, nothing. 'Hey, little man, who are you?' I say, to which the baby gives me a toothless smile in return. His broad mouth glistens with saliva. It looks like his eyes are laughing too. I'm unexpectedly overcome with a feeling of happiness so deep it almost hurts. 'Dear child, what are we going to do with you?' His eyes tighten for a second, followed by a puzzled expression, but then that radiant smile appears back on his face. Was it fate for me to take this young boy, I think all of a sudden? It's usually Virrie who opens the door, not me. Could this be a sign I should keep him with me? The idea comes to me in a split second: what if I tried escaping with him? What do I have to lose? He has the same dark hair colour as me, the same straight nose. He could easily pass as my son.

The baby has fallen asleep on my bed. The indecision when I was sorting through my clothes to take with me earlier now gives way to resolve. I gather some underwear, a dress, stockings, an extra pair of shoes and the shawl Granny gave me and put everything in my suitcase. I add a stack of cotton diapers, the baby clothes and a feeding bottle. I tuck my forged identity papers in the lining of my uniform together with the only pair of earrings I didn't pawn. Now to find the right moment to escape. I hear footsteps downstairs, furniture being moved around, doors opening and shutting, men's, women's and children's voices. I gently lift the sleeping child off my bedspread and put it back in its crib.

'I'll be right back. Be good!' I close the lid and slide the basket under my bed, hoping he doesn't wake. I smooth down my uniform and slip out the door.

As instructed, I helped Sieny put all the toys in burlap sacks. When we're finally done cleaning up the playroom, I run into the kitchen to make a bottle of porridge. As I'm walking back, I see two SS men standing in the hallway with lists in their hands. I hide the bottle under my skirt and run up the stairs to the attic.

Even before I get to my room, I hear him. I quickly close the door behind me and pull the basket out from under the bed. I'm shocked to see he's turned purple. He's been crying his poor little eyes out.

'It's alright, little man. Shhh...' The crying stops as soon as he smells the milk and starts sucking on the bottle. 'Easy now. Drink slowly...' Gripping the bottle with his little hands, he wolfs down the porridge in minutes. For a moment, he seems exhausted from the intense series of highs and lows in his young life, but then he starts moving restlessly. He stretches and bends his legs in turns and grimaces. I hold him up straight and gently pat him on his back. Right after he lets out the burp that was troubling him, my door swings open. I'm not the only one who jumps, and just when I'd got him to be quiet the baby starts wailing again.

It's Sieny.

'Virrie says he has to go immediately,' she says hurriedly. 'There are too many Germans coming in and out. Come, I'll bring him.' She wants to take him from me.

'No, I promise he won't make a sound, really.'

'Betty, you can't guarantee that.' She raises her voice to make herself heard over the crying.

'Shhh, hush now.' I hold him closer still and try to muffle the sound. 'I put some strong stuff in his milk. Just a few more minutes and he'll be sleeping like a rock.'

Sieny's eyes are full of pity. 'I had to promise Virrie I'd take him.'

'No, please. I can swaddle him and put him under the roof.'

'They can also hear him there if he's crying hard. Be sensible, Betty.'

'Letting them take a baby to a concentration camp, that's sensible?'

'But what then?' Sieny asks. 'We've done what we can. It's over.'

'It's over tomorrow, not now.'

It's as if the baby senses we're talking about him because he slowly starts to calm down. Sieny stands beside me. Instead of comforting the baby, she puts her arm around me.

'You're right. We can't give up. But where in heaven's name do we leave him?'

I look out my attic window at the nursery's garden. It's deserted, without a single child playing there anymore, just a few tricycles, little wheelbarrows and other playthings. The sandpit, where castles were built each day, is still open too.

'Can't he go to the school next door?'

Sieny shakes her head. 'The school is abandoned. Did you want to leave him there all by himself?'

I sit down on my bed and look at the little man in my lap. Not even half a year old and in so much trouble already. And again, the child smiles at me, looking at me sideways.

'I can escape with him.'

She looks at me in disbelief. 'With a screaming child?'

The baby's head suddenly tilts backwards. The alcohol is starting to kick in. 'Sieny, we have to give him a chance until tomorrow morning. Maybe there'll be a place for him then. I swear he'll sleep all through the night.'

I see her hesitate. 'But, Betty...'

'I'll be responsible for him. If they discover him, I'll take all the blame and swear none of you had anything to do with it. I can hide him in the sandpit. We've done that before.'

'Yes, with a couple of six-year-olds, and that was a close one.'

'It'll be easier with a baby. When all the children are gone and they've inspected the rooms, I'll go get him out and keep him in bed with me.'

'And what if they come back unannounced this evening? That's always possible.'

'They won't. Clear is clear.' I give her a pleading look. 'Please, Sieny.'

'Alright then, I'll keep watch.' She gets up from the bed. 'I'll give you a sign when it's safe to go out.'

I can smell he's soiled himself. 'Wait,' I say to Sieny, who's just about to walk out the door. 'Give me two more minutes.'

I've made the improvised crib as comfortable as possible, with an extra blanket, a hot water bottle I filled with water from the kettle in the kitchen, and even a small plush bunny. I then wrapped a thin cloth around the basket to prevent insects from entering. When I see Sieny wave at me from the garden, I close the lid and tiptoe down the stairs with the basket. Sieny is waiting for me by the back door. We exchange a glance, then I continue to the back, where Sieny has already removed the buckets and shovels from the sandpit. I dig a hole with my hands and put the basket in it. Finally, I carefully put the cover back on the sandpit. As I brush the sand from my knees and go back inside through the garden, an awful feeling I just buried a child alive comes over me. *Don't think about it.*

In my room, I scrub the sand from under my nails and grab the soiled diaper to toss in with the laundry downstairs. Walking into the basement with the laundry room, I nearly walk into Virrie. Opposite her are the SS men I'd seen in the hallway earlier. I notice Aus der Fünten last. I jump.

'There we have Miss Betty.' Aus der Fünten, glistening with sweat, gives me a condescending look.

'I was just telling these gentlemen that these cooking pots may be quite useful, but that we've been boiling diapers in them,' Virrie says, involving me in the conversation.

'That's right. I wouldn't eat soup out of those anymore,' I say off-hand.

Aus der Fünten laughs out loud at my quip. The two SS men copy him.

'No worries, we've never eaten from these,' Virrie assures them. 'Hygiene has always been our highest priority. But perhaps you can use them for something else? The coal stove is still useable too, just like the stacks of cloths, the drying racks and waste bins.'

I then become aware of the dirty diaper in my hand and realise I could give away that there's still another baby here. Just act like nothing is wrong and walk away.

'Well, I'm sure you'll figure it out for the rest,' I say kindly. 'Have a good day!'

'Wait a second, Betty,' I hear from behind me. My heart speeds up. Virrie's eyes dart towards my hand, which is holding a big white wad. 'Come closer.'

What does he want from me? Is he really so perceptive as to

see I'm holding any old white cloth in my hand and recognise it as a baby's diaper? A diaper that proves the plague of Jewish children wasn't yet fully eradicated here...

'Come on, we don't have all day.'

I drag my feet but keep my head up high, holding my hand behind my back.

When I'm right in front of him, he throws a fatherly arm around me and turns me towards his subordinates. 'This is the wench Officer Grünberg was so stuck on. However objectionable, I can somewhat understand Officer Grünberg. He had good taste,' Aus der Fünten says. His breath smells of alcohol. 'But in the end, she's still a Jewess.' He lets go of me again.

'She smells like a Jewess too,' one of his subordinates jeers, waving his hand in front of his nose. The laughter that follows makes me turn red. Not from shame, but from anger. But I'm able to contain myself.

'Oh dear,' I say coyly, 'you just have to let one out sometimes.'

'I apologise, Commander,' Virrie says, embarrassed, then turns to me and says: 'Betty, get your smelly behind upstairs!'

As I clear out the older children's room together with Sieny, I hear Aus der Fünten and his retinue stomp through the building. Sieny and I look at each other, wide-eyed, when we see them enter the garden, followed by Virrie. I stay low and try to see what's happening from the window. After they check the shed, a few SS men try to climb on a children's bicycle for laughs. Aus der Fünten looks at them, laughing as he lights a cigarette. The other SS man has found a ball that he keeps up with his foot a few times but then kicks over the hedge into the training school garden. They then, all at once, look at the sky. It's starting to rain, so they hurry inside.

· · ·

The building has been searched now, but the SS men are still in the director's office. Perhaps knocking a few back, but I don't dare get the baby from the sandpit until they've actually left. It's still raining outside. I'm worried it's leaking through the cover and the basket. Why did I think it was a good idea to hide a baby in the sandpit? What if the blankets in the basket are soaking wet, and it's my fault the child gets hypothermia? Or suppose I've given him alcohol poisoning with the generous splash of brandy I put in his milk. Suppose he's choked on his own vomit. The third time I walk past the office door, I can't take it any longer. I have to know if the child is okay. I hurry outside and leap over the puddles towards the sandpit. My limbs are stiff from worry as I slide the wooden cover to the side. I see the sand is still dry. There's no sound coming from the basket.

I get a fright when I open the lid and untie the cloth. He's just like I left him, only his face is white as milk. A child in his coffin. I hold my trembling finger under his little nose. Did I feel a small breath of air or am I just imagining it? I touch his hand: his body temperature is normal. Then a spasm turns into a grimacing face. He's alive. I breathe a deep sigh of relief, my head spinning from the extra oxygen. *Everything's alright. He's doing well. In half an hour, an hour at most, the danger will be over.* As soon as those krauts leave the nursery, I'll get him from his hiding place and warm him in my bed.

Once more, I go through all the steps in reverse order, very careful not to wake him. I then slide the cover back over the sandpit and brush myself off. Lost in thought, I get up, and I'm about to go back inside when I see the silhouette of a man in uniform in the doorway.

'What are you doing there?' I recognise the voice as Aus der Fünten's.

'I'm tidying up. That's what we were supposed to do, right?'

I walk towards him as casually as I can, but his voice is high and shrill: the sound of someone no longer in control of his nerves.

'Were you making sure all the sand is in its proper place?' He sounds drunk.

'No, Hauptsturmführer. I was putting all the toys inside.' My acting isn't very convincing.

'Perhaps I should check if that's so, don't you think?'

'You could.' I clear my throat. 'If you like sand moulds and shovels, you can even take them with you. There's no one coming here anymore anyway.'

'Does that cheeky mouth of yours ever stop talking?'

'Not if you keep asking me questions. Have a good evening.' I want to walk past him and even have the nerve to look him straight in the eye and nod kindly. But then I'm pulled by the arm. 'Show me what you've hidden there!'

'In the sandpit? What can you hide there?'

'Let's go see!' Aus der Fünten drags me by my arm to the backyard. 'Open it!'

I catch a glimpse of Sieny upstairs behind the window with her hand covering her mouth.

'What's the hold-up?' he drawls.

I need to pull myself together. There's still a chance. I clear my throat. 'Could you please step aside for a second?' I say. 'It won't work otherwise.'

Aus der Fünten takes a few steps back. 'Hurry up!' Instead of sliding the cover off, I lift it up.

'What's that?' Aus der Fünten says when he sees the basket.

'A picnic basket. I'm sure you've seen one before. I confess, I've hidden some goodies,' I say.

'I want to see what kind of goodies,' Aus der Fünten says, pointing at the basket.

'Look for yourself,' I say. 'I don't have any free hands.'

He eyes me suspiciously but then decides to stoop down anyway. A few more seconds and he'll know my secret.

Arrested, shot or sent to a concentration camp. Those are my options. Unless...

I've already decided. I flee like a hunted mouse that also doesn't weigh the pros and cons before it scampers into a hole. I let go of the cover and my legs start running before I know it. Not to the nursery, but over the hedge to the garden of the training school.

'Dammit! Hey, where are you going?' The glasses of *jenever* have slowed down Aus der Fünten's reaction speed. I run as fast as I can down a small path through the gardens to the back of the training school and duck into the bushes. 'Come back right now! That's an order!' Aus der Fünten roars.

I frantically try to think of a place to hide. The training school garden is a bit bare, apart from a stack of wooden boards and two birch trees. I weigh my options. I can take the fire escape to the first floor, or climb over the wooden fence to the adjacent garden, but it's nearly impossible to escape unnoticed like that. Then I see the grating on the pavement, close to the back wall of the building. I move towards it, staying low, and with a bit of force pull out the grating in one go. I duck into the hole and gently slide the grating back in place.

Covering my nose and mouth with my hands, I try to slow my rapid breathing. I hear high-pitched women's voices, screaming, German cursing. More noise, a loud bang. A crying child. My child? A gunshot. Then Virrie's voice: 'Betty, come back! Do you hear me?' I know when she means something and when she doesn't mean it. She doesn't mean this.

'Sturmführer, forget about her. There's nowhere she can go, anyway,' I hear Virrie say.

'She's done for. I'll see to it myself. That swine is finished.' Then the sound dies down and calm slowly returns. Through the grating, I see the two white birch trees swaying back and forth in the wind. I stay in the hole until I get a cramp in my buttock. When I shift my position, I feel a cold glass surface

behind me. I take a better look and see it's a window to the basement. I pull at the wooden frame to see if it'll open, but it's
locked from the inside.

I kick the window with my shoe, and the glass breaks, shat-
tering on the floor. Again, I hold my breath. *Keep quiet. Don't
move now.* I sit there for minutes, stock-still in a cramped position, alert to any sound. Then I gather the courage to start
moving again. I take the cloth from my hair, wrap it around my
hand and carefully pull the glass shards from the window
frame. I put my headcloth in my apron pocket and inspect the
room with my head through the broken window. There's a small
desk under the window. As carefully as I can, I step through the
window frame onto the desk. I don't bother looking if I've cut
myself and jump off, then walk to the only door in the room and
push the handle down. The door leads to a dark hallway.
There's more light on the right side. That's where I have to go.
Tentatively, I go down the hall, around the corner, and end up
at a stairwell. Do they know about my escape route? Are they
waiting for me upstairs?

I cautiously walk up the stairs. This has to be the entrance
hall. It looks deserted, and holding my breath I scurry along the
wall of this big open space. The front door is just a few metres
away. I briefly consider running out the door to freedom. But I
know this front door is also clearly visible from the theatre. It
would be the same as turning myself in. No, I have no other
choice but to stay here and lie low. I tiptoe up the wide staircase
in the hall. I open a random door and jump at the terrible
creaking that pierces the silence. The closed curtains in the
classroom make it hard to see the room's contours. I'm not
scared easily, but the building is eerily empty. Every time I pull
open a door, I'm afraid I'll find something or someone that'll
frighten me to death.

I know time is running out. Aus der Fünten sounded set on
punishing me. The training school is surely one of the first

places they'll come looking. I anxiously wander through the dark school building. I need to find a good place to hide. The rooms are full of desks and seats, but they're otherwise empty. The built-in cupboards are too small for me to hide in. The teachers' room is locked, as are the storerooms. The toilets smell so awful I can't stand it.

I see there's a space under the ridge of the building, just like at the nursery. I'm not going to find a better place to hide here, and I hope it's good enough. I climb up the shaky ladder, pull the heavy thing up with some effort and close the attic hatch. Thankfully, there's a small window that lets daylight in. The space under the collar beams is filled with junk: building materials, shelves, paint, some straw mattresses and wool blankets. I'm about to lie down on the blankets, but when I fold one open a bunch of moths fly up. Looks like I'll have to do without a soft surface to lie on. I crawl to the other side of the low-ceilinged space and into a corner behind a stack of shelves. With my knees pulled up and my head resting on my arms, I feel a tingling on my leg. There's a small trickle of blood coming from my shin, slowly dripping on the floor and colouring the wooden floorboards red. I pull a shard of glass from the skin below my knee with my fingernails, then press my apron on the wound to stop the bleeding, and stay put.

CHAPTER 44

TUESDAY, 28 SEPTEMBER 1943

LATE AFTERNOON

I don't know how long I've been here. Was the boy I hid in the sandpit saved? Or did my ineptitude rob him of the chance of ever having a full life? My stupid move of going to check up on him right when we were having an inspection...

My body aches from the hardwood floor I've been lying on. Cold wind slips through the roof tiles, and I'm numb with cold. I look out the small window. It's getting dark out, which means I've been hiding here for two, three hours already. If I wait a little longer, it'll be pitch dark and the curfew will have started. There are too many raids to be wandering aimlessly around Amsterdam now. They'll ask questions that trace me back to the nursery, and my name is now surely on a wanted list. But I decide to take my chances anyway and flee the building. I get up feeling sore all over, brush the dust from my uniform, tie my hair back and put on my nurse's headcloth. Just when I've gently opened the attic hatch and I'm about to let the ladder down, I hear creaking footsteps coming up the stairs. I stop what I'm doing at once and hold my breath, waiting to see who it is.

'Hello?' I hear a man's voice whisper. 'Betty? Are you here somewhere, Betty?'

I know that voice. I lean forward cautiously and peek through the opening, catching a glimpse of his dark hair.

'Joop, I'm up here.'

He instantly tilts his head back, and I look into his astonished eyes. 'Monkeys got nothing on you,' he mumbles. 'How'd you get up there?'

I slide the ladder over the opening. 'With this, how else?'

Climbing down, I feel his hands on my legs. 'I've got you, just a few more rungs.'

'It's better if you just hold the ladder,' I say deadpan. 'If it falls, holding onto my heavenly legs won't do much good.'

'You can't help but talk smart, even now,' he chuckles.

'If I ever stop, it's likely because I'm dead,' I say, stepping off the ladder onto the floor. More than ever, I feel an urge to throw myself into his arms, but I contain myself. How many times can someone reject you? 'How did you know I was here?'

'Harry said you might have hidden here. And he'd heard it from Sieny.'

'Was the child saved? The baby?'

'I think so.' His twitching eye betrays otherwise. I feel the tears burn behind my eyes.

'You can't go back, Betty. You know that. Do you have a place somewhere?'

I shrug. 'I think so, or else I'll think of something. You know me.'

'Here – I don't know if it's any use to you.' He hands me my identity card. 'I'm afraid I couldn't bring much else.'

'I don't have much else.' I put the document in the slit pocket of my dress together with my fake card.

Joop leads the way through the labyrinth of hallways and stairs. We end up at a side door that opens out into the cold outside. 'Do you want to take my coat?' he asks.

I shake my head. 'Thanks, I'm not cold.'

'They're so busy with the logistics of all those people who were arrested that they're no longer busy with your disappearance. Aus der Fünten is trying to get promoted, so what counts isn't the deportation of a single Jewish nurse but that of all the Jews in the Netherlands.'

'What will you do?' I ask.

'I'm going to be a fighter pilot. Didn't I say so already?' he says. 'So, if you're ever in trouble, just give me a call and I'll come flying your way.'

He's decided not to trust me with where he's actually going. 'I'll keep that in mind. Goodbye, Joop. Take care.'

'Goodbye, Betty. See you around.'

'So long. And give my thanks to Sieny.'

'I'll do that.'

'Have a good flight.'

'Bye.' Then he's off.

Overcome by shame, I lower my head. I'm ashamed of myself and everything I did and didn't do. All my screw-ups and failures. I even feel shame for my apparent gains and successes. For my false pride, my misguided arrogance, my supposed intelligence. I'm ashamed of the jokes I thought I had to make and every action I ever took. Of the sound of my voice. Of the child I'd wanted to save.

'Hey, are you alright?'

I thought Joop had left already. 'Sure,' I croak.

He pulls me close, running his hand over my hair, his sweater prickling my cheek. I smell axle grease, sweat, wool and a hint of aftershave. 'I'm so sorry. I wish... and might rather have...'

He doesn't finish his sentence.

'It's fine, Joop.' I let go of him. 'Thanks for coming to get me here.' I make myself look him in the eye and put on a broad smile.

'I thought it's best if you go first,' Joop says. 'Then if they see you, I can try to distract them.'

'Alright.' There I go. Back into war. Into Plantage Midden-laan, where suitcases are being loaded onto trucks. Where a procession of number 9 trams is waiting. Where throngs of people wait to go to their final destination. Where barking dogs and German orders vie to be the loudest, and where children try to hide between their fearful parents' legs. I force myself not to look which children they are, or if I know them, so I won't unintentionally stop and draw attention.

It was unbelievably stupid of me not to accept Joop's offer to take his coat. I'm freezing. When I walk into Plantage Kerklaan and pass Nel's clothing depot, I hesitate whether to knock on the door for something warm. I don't see anyone through the shop window of what used to be a dry cleaners'. The place looks deserted. I turn the door handle and find the door isn't locked. I decide to take my chances. Immediately when I open the door, the bell rings. It's not Nel but Virrie who comes from the back. 'Betty, what are you doing here?'

My sense of duty is so great I feel caught in the act. 'I... I'm not coming back to work.'

'Of course you're not coming back to work. They're looking for you. Not just because of the child in the sandpit; you're on the list.'

The information barely registers. It's the end of the line for me either way. 'I, errm... I was thinking: maybe Nel has a coat or a stole for me?'

'They came to get Nel yesterday.' Virrie keeps talking as she sifts through the bags of clothes. 'The theatre is a madhouse now. I think there's been an ultimatum from Berlin. They're in a hurry and everyone has to go.'

'You too?'

She gets up with a grey wool cape in her hands. 'Yes, me too. But I'm not going, and neither are you. Someone has to return these children to their parents when the world comes to its senses.'

'I don't know if that'll ever happen,' I say, resigned. 'I sometimes wonder what the use is anymore. Why not just turn myself in?'

'Then you might as well hang yourself straight away.' Her sharp eyes peer at me from behind her round-framed glasses. 'I have Pimentel's notebook with where each child was placed. It's going to be a lot of work to track all those children down again. I'll need your help, Betty.'

I didn't know there was a notebook with all the hiding addresses. So, it turns out Pimentel was in charge of the whole organisation! She knew everything, including where each child had been placed.

'You have a duty to survive, Betty!' She puts the cape on me and grabs me by the shoulders. 'Alright?'

I nod unconvincingly. 'The boy in the sandpit. Is he...' I don't finish my sentence.

'They took him. Don't think about it. Oh, I almost forgot: I got this from someone, who got it from someone else. It's from your sister.' She hands me an envelope.

'Did my sister get away?' I ask hopefully.

'I can't say for sure,' Virrie says. 'I heard that someone saw her after they cleared out the hospital. But if she was also able to escape, I don't know. Go now, Betty. You should leave. You're no longer safe here.'

I put the envelope in my apron and walk out into the dark blue evening light.

You should leave. You're no longer safe here. Virrie's words echo in my head. Unambiguous, a clear message. It sounds so simple, but what does 'leave' mean in neighbourhoods that are surrounded, in a city where we're hunted day and night? Of course I should go, but where to? I'm all alone. I no longer have anyone here. I'll never reach the Baller family before the curfew starts, even if I'm not arrested before then. There's no Star of David on the cape, but there's one on my uniform. As a precaution, I've made some snap fasteners on it. I quickly pull off the star and put it in my apron. Instinctively, I've gone to Van Woustraat, to my family home. It's already pitch dark outside, and while I can hardly see where I'm going, I know each cobblestone, each pole and each step. I could find my way home blindfolded. From across the street, I look at the house where I once had such a happy, carefree childhood. But the white letters on the shop window, KOOT, are hard to miss. Even if the moon didn't exist and not a gleam of light shone down on earth, I'd still recognise those hideous four letters. Didn't this story begin with that awful family? With Koot's death?

All of a sudden, I know. My legs start to move, as if my body got the idea even before it entered my head. *Ein Brera* – there's no other choice.

I take a deep breath and ring the bell. On the first floor above me, someone pulls open a curtain. The window opens and a woman sticks her head out. 'Yes, who is it?'

'Betty Oudkerk,' I say softly.

The window closes immediately. I don't know if this means she's coming down or if she wants nothing to do with me anymore. Thankfully, the front door soon opens and Mrs Overvliet, our old neighbour, pulls me inside. 'Did anyone see you?' she asks as she closes the door behind me.

'I don't think so.'

'What are you doing here, girl?' she asks with a face that says she already knows the answer.

'I don't have anywhere to go, and since you said—'

'Yeah, yeah. That was then. We've been through a lot since then, sweetie.'

I get the sense it was a mistake to come here, and I feel like just turning around. The problem is I have no alternative. 'Please, I don't have anywhere to go.'

'No, sorry, Betty.' She's already opening the front door to gently push me out again.

'I'm begging you, Mrs Overvliet. Wasn't my father always good to you? Didn't he often slip you things for free? Surely you haven't forgotten?'

'Quiet down!' Mrs Overvliet says, panic in her eyes. 'They might hear us.'

I take her hand. 'I promise I'll be quiet, but don't put me out on the street. I'll sleep in the cellar if I have to.'

My plea seems to have an effect.

'Well alright, come upstairs with me. We'll discuss it with my husband.'

She leads the way up the stairs to their home and keeps saying: 'Dear, what a mess, what a mess.'

When I enter the living room, the husband looks up from his newspaper, annoyed.

'Hello, Mr Overvliet. Remember me?'

'Is someone ill?' he asks, deadpan.

'Oh, you remember Betty, don't you? She's a nursery teacher, and she's now looking for a place... We can help her, can't we?' It's as if she's hoping for an answer like: 'No, I think we'd best not.'

But showing little interest, the husband says: 'Fine, so long as she doesn't sleep in my bed.'

'See, I told you we'd help,' his wife says, triumphantly now. 'Have you eaten?'

. . .

After I've had a piece of dry bread with some cheese, she leads the way to the cellar. 'Here's the light,' she says, switching on a lamp. 'Blankets are over there. We don't have a mattress here, but at least there's a bed.'

I look at the steel bedframe with the mesh base and wonder how I'll manage to sleep on this.

'Well, sleep tight. And remember: don't make a sound. I'll come get you out tomorrow.'

My whole being screams not to stay in this dark cellar. But before I can react, Mrs Overvliet walks out the room and, to my horror, locks the door behind her.

CHAPTER 45

WEDNESDAY, 29 SEPTEMBER 1943

There are no longer exceptions for anyone. All remaining Jews will be deported to Westerbork immediately. Only mixed marriages will be spared, provided they have themselves sterilised.

I haven't slept a wink in this cellar, where the bedsprings nearly perforated me, and the cold has gone deep into my bones. But that's not the worst of it. The idea that she'd locked me up made me constantly have to distract myself from my thoughts, sing songs and recite rhymes to keep from hyperventilating. I've had to suppress these terrifying thoughts in my head all night just to keep myself from having a panic attack. Like a bomb that can go off at any moment and all at once wipe out what courage I still have.

I bolt out as soon as Mrs Overvliet opens the door. 'Oh my, what's the rush?' she says. 'There's some food for you upstairs.' I was planning on heading straight for the door and leaving immediately but then reconsider. Best not to hit the road on an empty stomach.

Lo and behold, I smell real coffee upstairs. The butter cake I get with it is an unexpected treat. It would seem this couple doesn't have it all that bad.

'It's bizarre, isn't it?' the wife prattles in a tone that's more like thinking out loud. 'How we used to rent from your father, and now you're here with us, sleeping in the cellar. Who'd have ever thought?'

I never knew the house they lived in was my father's.

'Not your father, anyway. He was a good man. Even if he was Jewish. I'd always tell my husband: that Oudkerk sure has a talent for business. We could learn a thing or two...'

'Who do you pay rent to now?' I ask, interrupting her.

'Don't you know, Betty?' she says, surprised. 'To your *Verwalter*, Mrs Koot.' Just hearing that name makes my stomach turn. 'Did you know Mrs Koot went to visit your family?'

'What's that? Visited where?' I ask, alarmed.

'In Westerbork. She thought your mother and grandmother had taken gold and jewellery with them to the camp. Which wasn't allowed, obviously.'

I feel a sharp pang in my chest. 'What do you mean, exactly?'

'Well, that gold was officially Mrs Koot's. However unfairly, of course. I remember telling her: I can't imagine Jet Oudkerk would just sneak off with it.'

'Did you hear this story from Mrs Koot herself?'

'Yes, we still have coffee together sometimes. Not too often though. In any case, her visit assured her your family wasn't keeping anything from her. Mrs Koot threatened to report them to the camp officials if they didn't give her everything.' Mrs Overvliet pours more coffee into my cup. 'Bit sad that she reported them anyway, even though your family didn't have a penny to their name. It seems they were transferred the following day. Well...'

I get up, dizzy and shaky.

'What are you doing, child?' I hear Mrs Overvliet say.

I puke everything out in the sink, a slurry of real coffee and butter cake.

'Oh dear, that's not nice now, is it?'

Downstairs, the doorbell rings. The wife runs to the window.

I grab my cape, stunned, and I'm about to go down the stairs. But she stops me. 'Not that way. Quick, under the table!' she says. 'My husband is coming with his German colleagues.' She pushes me under the table and drapes the tablecloth over it so just a crack of light comes through beneath. Then she hurries downstairs. Huddled under the table, I feel like I'm in some kind of farce. Meanwhile, my thoughts go round and round. All I can think is that it's my fault. It's my fault my family died. I'd taken the jewellery from our home shortly after they were arrested. Gold and diamonds, which Mrs Koot might otherwise have found. But now Koot found nothing in our home, so she assumed my family had taken everything with them to Wester-bork. As revenge for having to make an unnecessary train journey, she personally ensured Mother, Granny and Engel would be sent on to Auschwitz. Koot killed them for the gold I used to buy false identity papers.

'What can I get you, gentlemen?' the wife asks with fake cheer when she returns to the kitchen. The sound of her nimble women's heels is followed by heavy footsteps.

'I'll have some coffee,' I hear Mr Overvliet say. He then switches to German. 'How about a cup of real joe, Herr Schneider?'

I smell them first and only then see them under the table-cloth: the German's black leather boots. He's an SS man.

'How about you gentlemen go sit and talk business in the

living room, and I'll come bring coffee in a moment,' the wife says.

'Sure thing, sweet cheeks!' her husband cries, and then the voices disappear into the living room.

'I knew this was a bad idea,' Mrs Overvliet says, lifting up the tablecloth. I walk out the kitchen without saying a word to her, run down the stairs and rush outside. I walk down the street as fast as I can and turn off at Sarphatistraat. Past the bridge, I pause to catch my breath, when in the distance I see people being forced from their homes. I turn around immediately and go onto Amsteldijk.

Now what? How do I get to Amstelveen from this ghetto? I follow the Amstel river, when I see a group of Jews walking in front of me. They're young, students. Their faces are indifferent. As if they knew all along this moment would come. They're being held at gunpoint by German soldiers. We're all the same age: the students, the soldiers and I. In another world, we wouldn't be pitted against each other, we wouldn't have been enemies. In another world that no longer exists.

'This way! We won't use force if you cooperate,' someone shouts. Like a hunted animal, I scurry into a side street.

I wander through Amsterdam without knowing where to go. *Elisabeth Petri, Elisabeth Petri,* I think to myself, practicing my new name. 'What's your name?' 'Elisabeth Petri, officer.' 'And what about the uniform?' the officer will ask. I'll have to seduce him with my eyes, my smile, bluff my way to freedom, to life, but I don't know if I can still do it: *Acting. Feigning, pretending I'm fine. I can't... Not anymore.* I'm walking through a labyrinth with no way out, with no solution. *Sick, beaten, broken. Should I surrender? That's not who I am, is it?* Betty never gives up. Only I don't know where that Betty went. The girl who says she's never afraid.

I reach for the star in my apron pocket. If I put it on, I'm done for soon enough. I then feel something else: the letter Virrie gave me. I'd completely forgotten the white envelope. *For Betty*, it reads. I tear it open and pull out a tattered postcard with only grey pencil scrawls on it. I then get another shock that almost knocks me off my feet when I recognise the scrawls as my mother's handwriting. Supporting myself against a wall, I read her words:

DEAR CHILDREN, YOU WILL NEVER SEE ME AGAIN BECAUSE WE'VE BEEN DEPORTED. WILL YOU TAKE GOOD CARE OF JAPIE?

I look up at the sky. *This is it. My game is up.* The winner was known before we began. The sky is a perfect blue, apart from a small cloud that drifts in front of the sun. The rising wind slowly blows it on its way, and sunlight warms my face. I think of how children draw the sun, with big yellow points. Then I know what I have to do. I take the yellow star from my pocket and attach it to my uniform. Then I get rid of my cape so everyone can see: I'm a Jewess.

It happens faster than I'd expected. 'There's one over there!' I hear a policeman cry in a breaking voice like my little brother's. I don't try to hide anymore, don't run away. I stay where I am until the officer reaches me. 'Identity papers!' I hand over my card and wait for him to conclude what I already know. 'Get in line!' he then says. Just like that, I merge with the group and disappear.

They've brought us to Amstel station. Everything happens in a daze, like I'm not really here myself. The crowded train station, the cacophony of voices, hundreds of people waiting to be transported to their deaths. Standing, sitting or even lying down on the cold floor. There are tables at the front of the hall where the organisation sits. The Jewish names that are called out echo against the tall space's tiles, after which new batches of people move towards their oppressors. The executioners at the scaffold.

I hear a child beside me tell her mother she's finally going to see Daddy again. Only children haven't given up hope yet in this place. Only children. I'm so dizzy I have to support myself against a pillar to stay on my feet.

My name is called out. It's my turn. This is it. Stupefied, I head towards the row of tables. I'll be getting on the doom-bound train soon. No one can say I'm naive anymore. Mother also knew what was going to happen. She'd have preferred to take her own life – she had the heart.

'Are you Betty Oudkerk?' asks one of the system's lackeys from behind the tables.

'Yes, that's me.'

'Papers!'

I reach in my pocket for my identity papers and feel two cards. How do I know which is the right one?

'What's the hold-up?'

'Yes, I'm sorry.' I think the paper of my real card is a bit flimsier and pull that one out. It's the real card indeed.

The man copies my details and then hands me back my card. 'You'll have to hand in your house keys over there to the left.'

I'm sent to a different table. There's a bin on the floor with thousands of shiny keys. I stare at it as if mesmerised. 'Miss Oudkerk, your keys,' I hear someone say.

I look up. 'Beg your pardon?' It's odd, his face looks so familiar.

'Can I have your house keys? You have to hand them in here.'

'I don't have any house keys.'

The guy gives me a piercing look. Only then do I see who it is: Mr Pos, the policeman who had coffee with me some nights at the nursery. He of 'mum's the word' and 'you didn't hear this'.

I'm distracted by the beads of sweat on his forehead. 'Can I see your identity papers, Miss Oudkerk?' I hand over my card, wondering how it's possible Mr Pos is here. Doesn't he come visit me in the nursery every evening? It's like my brain has stopped working. As if it got stuck on some complex mathematical equation. I see Mr Pos's chubby fingers write something on my card and then put a stamp on it.

'That line, please,' Mr Pos says, giving me back my card. It feels like a labyrinth of tables and identity cards.

I get in line with a group of people. 'Not that line, Miss Oudkerk. Over there!' I'm startled and almost lose my balance. Mr Pos has a loud voice. I let someone push me in the right direction. When I look over my shoulder, I see Mr Pos is already dealing with the next person.

Shuffling in a short line, I'm getting closer to yet another man behind a table. When I'm right in front of him, I think I recognise his face from somewhere as well. I feel like I've fallen into a dream. A nightmare I can't wake from, though I know it isn't real.

'Move along!' the man says. I have no idea if he's talking to me or someone else. 'And what's with this pretty swine?' I'm surprised by the volume coming from the man's skinny body.

'She's in a mixed marriage!' Mr Pos shouts from behind his table.

Hey, is this about me? Mixed marriage? I've never been married, let alone a mixed one.

'Card, please!' the commander says. For the third time, I hand over my identity card and see him take a disdainful look at it. 'Betty Oudkerk, mixed marriage... That's wonderful.' He then gives it back to me. 'You can go.' All of a sudden, I realise: I recognise him from photos in the newspaper. *Isn't he the top boss? Willy Lages, Aus der Fünten's superior.* 'What are you waiting for?' he screams in my face.

A soldier ushers me out. 'Beat it!' Dazed and confused, I walk away from the station. My mind still can't keep up with all these steps, the chronology of events. I rub my face trying to lift the dense fog, the unfathomable chaos in my head. What's happened? I look at my identity card and see a red J was stamped diagonally across the black J. The realisation comes with a delay. *Mr Pos saved me.* He kept his word that I could fall back on him. Is it possible there are actually good people on the other side? Is this an opportunity? Or is this another deceit to distract me from my goal of following the tracks to my family? I'm so tired of fighting. Exhausted, numb. If only I could lie down and close my eyes for a bit. Rest forever. Sleep without dreaming. Nothing. I think of Sieny, my best friend, and of Harry. If only I'd joined them in time. They'd have dragged me along to something better. To the light. I still have a chance. Think, Betty. Don't go soft now. I have to keep moving, but where to?

Wandering about, I try to come back to my senses, to logic and reason. Without noticing, I've found my way back to the city centre via the Amstel river. I'm at Kloveniersburgwal. All of a sudden, I remember something Tineke once told me. Her uncle is supposed to have a stove manufacturing business here. I check the frontages for names, from front to back, but I can't find a stove maker anywhere on Kloveniersburgwal.

I stand on the bridge and watch the boats passing through the canals. A pleasure boat, a boat with scrap metal, a boat with children fishing. Pedestrians, horse carriages and cars pass by on the waterside. You can hardly tell our country is under occupation. People are laughing, and it's a beautiful day. This is how it should be, and how it will be for years to come. Only without us Jews.

. . .

A stylish, hunchbacked lady with silver hair, just like Engel's, approaches and stands right beside me. She puts her walking stick against the bridge railing and takes some bread crusts from the bag she's holding. Small birds and ducks come flocking instantly. The bread bag seems to be quite full because she keeps grabbing a handful from it. My staring gaze makes her look up. 'Would you perhaps like some bread yourself?'

'Isn't it for the birds?'

She comes a little closer. 'Are you alright, dear?'

Lost for words, I only manage a faint, 'I don't know.'

'You look a bit pale. How are you feeling?' She reaches in her bag and hands me a piece of bread. 'Here, chew on this.'

I impassively take the brown crust and put it in my mouth.

'Are you a nurse?' she asks, her head slanted and looking up at me.

I shake my head, unable to speak with my mouth full, and hold my hand at waist level.

'Ah, a nursery teacher?' I nod.

'That's great work,' she says, satisfied. 'It makes you never forget that you were a child yourself once. Here, girl, take this.' She hands me the bread bag. 'Promise you'll eat it all?' She then grabs her stick from the railing and is about to walk off.

'Excuse me, madam. Would you happen to know if there's a stove maker called Baller anywhere around here?'

The woman looks astonished. 'There sure is. You're right next to it.' She points to the nearest building on the quayside. The frontage reads: BALLER FIRM, STOVE MAKER.

I feel anxious when I'm at the door. What if they lock me up in a cellar again? The woman who gave me the bag of bread crusts waves her stick at me in the distance. It feels like encouragement. I grab the leather strap and ring the bell, which is louder than I'd expected. I instinctively look around to see if anyone might have heard me. Being alert is now second nature to me, even at moments when there's no immediate danger.

'Come in!' I hear someone cry.

I walk through the door, uncertain about what next catastrophe awaits me this time.

'Can I help you?' asks the man in the workplace. He looks exactly like Karel Baller.

'I'm Betty Oudkerk,' I say, 'a friend of your niece Tineke.'

'What a pleasure,' the man says warmly. 'Have you come for a stove?'

'No...' I hesitate for a second, then say: 'I'm Jewish.' I hold my cape to the side and show him my star.

Mr Baller's face tightens. '*Meine Güte,*' he says.

'Your brother always said he wanted to help me... But I can also leave.'

'No, of course not.' Behind me, Mr Baller locks the door of his shop. 'There, just to be safe. Come with me... Betty, you said?' He smiles kindly and opens the door to the stairwell. 'We need to find a way to get you out of this rotten city as soon as possible. Follow me and I'll introduce you to my wife.' He leads the way up the stairs.

I hear singing from upstairs. 'When the lights go on at Leidseplein. And there's good times in the city streets, and Lido's blinds are up again...'

'Honey, can I introduce you to Betty?' Mr Baller says to his wife in the kitchen.

She looks up from a bucket of soapy water, slightly embarrassed. 'Hi, Betty. I like to sing when I'm scrubbing.'

'My mother always used to sing too,' I say, even though Mr Baller's chubby wife doesn't look anything like my mother.

'Singing soothes the soul,' she says as she dries her hands. 'And if you're good at it, you can earn a pretty penny with it too.

But that's not for me, unfortunately.' She looks at me, smiling kindly, and extends her hand. 'Vera Baller, nice to meet you.'

'Betty is a friend of Tineke. She needs help,' Mr Baller says with a meaningful glance.

'Oh, child, what are they doing to you people?' Mrs Baller strokes my arm unexpectedly. 'How about I first heat something up for you to eat. You must be hungry.'

My breathing speeds up suddenly, and I'm getting spots in front of my eyes. I want to apologise but can't make a sound. Just in time, I'm able to grab onto the table.

'Hey, kiddo, don't fall now,' Mr Baller says, helping me onto a chair.

It seems I haven't lost, not yet. The fog is slowly lifting from my head, giving me a new outlook. Mr Baller gives Karel a ring as his wife serves me a bowl of thick pea soup. Half an hour later, we leave in his car, which smells of coal and metal. I look out the window at the roads slowly leading us out of the city I once loved so dearly. Stone gradually gives way to meadows and forests. The low autumn sun casts an orange glow on the land as a train passes in the distance. Maybe it's the train I was supposed to be on. How is it possible I'm now here, and not there? Life is making less sense all the time.

Was it the hate that gave me the strength to go on? Or was it the love for the children that made me think I was untouchable? Was the comic act I put on what saved me until now, or was it pure luck that I eventually met the right people to send me in the right direction and put me in the right line? I have too many thoughts going through my head to find the answers. Torn between one extreme and the other, I now no longer know what is true or what has value. All I'm certain of is that that the others, my brothers Gerrit and Nol, my mother, Granny and Engel, my Jewish friends, colleagues, Madam Pimentel, Remi and those hundreds of other children... that I was unable to save them. Didn't they have a right to live just as much? I wrap my arms around my shoulders and lean against the door as we drive along the bumpy road. I hold myself tight and try to keep from falling after all.

AFTERWORD

AFTER THE NURSERY

The number of children saved through the nursery is estimated at six hundred. This was around a quarter or a fifth of all the children who were at the nursery between July 1942 and September 1943.

Most children's names have been changed for privacy reasons, as have the names of the two young men Betty had a crush on. However, these characters are based on real people and events.

I've kept the names of most people who played a major part in this story, such as Sieny, Mirjam, Virrie and Henriëtte, in order to keep their heroism alive. But in order to connect the facts together, I've interpreted these characters in my own way.

After a turbulent and difficult time in hiding, Betty started taking care of orphans again immediately. She married Bram Goudsmit, and the two had five children. Betty would have liked to have had many more. But for a long time, she didn't want to look back at what she had experienced; the pain she felt about all the children she wasn't able to save was too great. Until, advanced in years, she met a man at one of her children's party who had been saved as a baby by the nursery's carers. It felt like a miracle that their paths should cross again through their children. This encounter was of great significance to Betty: only now did she become aware of the impact her deeds had and was she able to look beyond the children she hadn't been able to save. 'Now I know why I went on living,' she said. Gradually, she started to share stories about what had happened to her.

In 2019, during the 4 May Remembrance Day ceremony in the Netherlands, Betty placed a wreath on the National Monument on Dam Square in the name of all the children who couldn't be saved, her family and all the other Dutch Jews who had died. After laying the wreath, she told her son and grand-daughter: 'I can now finally put it all behind me.'

After their arrest in France, Gerrit and Lous were brought, via Tours, to Drancy, from where they were deported to Auschwitz a few months later. Nol and Jetty were in Vught until October 1943, after which they were brought through Westerbork to Auschwitz. Betty's mother Jet Oudkerk, Granny and Engel were sent to Auschwitz after Koot's visit. They were sent to the gas chambers immediately upon arrival. Leni, Japie and Betty survived the war.

Baby Remi spent a month in Westerbork, after which he was deported to Sobibor together with 2,510 other Jews, which included 601 children. Not one of this transport survived.

Greetje survived the war and ended up at a family care home afterwards.

At Westerbork, Henriëtte wrote a detailed plan for expanding the nursery after the war. She sent this to the nursery's management in Amsterdam. In September 1943, she was deported to Auschwitz, where she was sent to the gas chambers immediately upon arrival.

Virrie Cohen went into hiding after the nursery closed. She

survived the war, as did her sister, Mirjam, her father, David Cohen, her mother and her brother. The nursery was reopened in 1950 under the new name Huize Henriëtte, where Virrie was put in charge. Her sister Mirjam was never able to process her wartime experiences and became ill.

Harry and Sieny survived the war in hiding together and stayed together for the rest of their lives.

There were more 'helpers' of Pimentel besides the main characters, such as Fanny Phillips. She also played a major role in convincing the parents and smuggling children out. Several young men from the Jewish Council were involved with this as well.

Nursery teacher Cilly Levitus had asked the SS man Alfonds Zündler to save her sister Juta, who was set to be deported from the orphanage. Cilly was under the impression Alfonds had died during the war, but Zündler survived his captivity and returned to Germany. Shortly before his death, Cilly was able to thank him in person. A group of Dutch people who'd been saved by him tried to nominate Zündler for a Yad Vashem distinction, but this faced too much protest.

Ferdinand Aus der Fünten and Willy Lages were part of the Breda Four, who served a life sentence in the Breda Koepel-gevangenis prison. Aus der Fünten died shortly after his release in 1989.

Walter Süskind was eventually also summoned to Wester-bork, where he had travelled to regularly to negotiate with camp officials about prisoners and to visit his wife and daughter, whose deportation he had been unable to prevent. While his contacts with the resistance in Amsterdam offered him possibil-ities to free himself and his family, he rejected the plan at hand because he didn't want to endanger his fellow prisoners. On 3 September 1944, he was put on a transport to Theresienstadt, from where he was deported to Auschwitz a month later. His wife and daughter were sent to the gas chambers upon arrival. Süskind survived the camp but finally died of exhaustion during the death marches.

Walter Süskind's right hand was the economist Felix Halverstad, who was good at drawing, painting and forging identity papers. He had children disappear from the records and provided new identity cards. His wife, who was a secretary at the theatre, actively assisted him with this. They survived the war together with their daughter.

Hetty Brandl, Walter Süskind's secretary, was deported to Bergen-Belsen after she turned down the advances of Deputy Chief Commander Streich. She died on 1 April 1945.

Karel Baller was active in the resistance and provided many Jews with hiding addresses, among them Betty, Leni and Japie. For this, he was given a Yad Vashem distinction after the war.

Betty's great love, who is called Joop in this book, actually became a fighter pilot. Betty was friends with him for the rest of her life.

A LETTER FROM ELLE

Thank you so much for reading *The Orphans of Amsterdam*. If you'd like to keep up to date with all of my latest releases, you can sign up at the following link. Your email address will never be shared, and you can unsubscribe at any time.

www.bookouture.com/elle-van-rijn

My interest in this book's subject began more than two years ago, when by chance I heard about the Jewish Nursery and director Henriëtte Pimentel after the death of resistance member and professor Johan van Hulst. I was only vaguely familiar with the story and had never heard of Henriëtte Pimentel. But I knew a director friend with a nearly identical last name: Pollo de Pimentel. When I asked him if there was any relation between him and the nursery's director, he told me Henriëtte Pimentel was his great-aunt, a sister of his grandfather. We decided to link up and develop a drama series or film together. The more I learned about the personal stories of the Jewish nursery teachers and the children in the nursery, the more this remarkable history affected me. I couldn't let it go. I was awed by the network Henriëtte Pimentel had secretly set up in her nursery, which ended up serving as an annexe to the Hollandse Schouwburg theatre, the main place where Dutch Jews were gathered and deported. After much research and with some detours, I decided to write a historical novel about the subject that would tell the whole story in an empathic way.

And I knew early on that the only nursery teacher still living, Betty Goudsmit-Oudkerk, would have to be the main character of my novel. During my research into the nursery's history, I had come to love her most.

I visited her together with Pollo de Pimentel two days before the nursing homes closed because of the COVID pandemic in March of 2020. It was a remarkable meeting that made a big impression on me. Her thoughts weren't as clear as they once were, but she still had so much humour, pride and love. Lots of love, especially.

'The children,' she said, 'they can't touch them. Children can't do anything about what adults get up to.' She also emphasised several times how she had to act in order to save herself and others. 'I've always acted, and I continue to do so.'

'Do you act?' she asked me. I told her I'd gone to theatre school and did lots of acting afterwards. She liked that a lot. She'd learned how to act herself from real life, with Plantage Middenlaan as the set, in the autumn of 1942, when she was a wide-eyed seventeen-year-old nursery teacher working at a place from which many people would be sent to their deaths. She put on an act of courage, charm, naivety, fearlessness and perseverance. Until at a certain point she started to believe her own performance.

Only later did she realise how much she'd repressed, how many losses she'd had to mourn. The ghosts that kept her up at night had children's faces. They clung to her with fearful expressions. She kept hearing their voices in her head. 'Why won't you save me, Betty? And me. Me...' She only started to talk about this when she was eighty years old, still with an air of lightness and in a light-hearted tone, but with hard, cold facts.

This past June, as I was finishing the story about the Jewish Nursery, I received the sad news that Betty had passed away. She'd had a fall shortly before, and her suffering was becoming unbearable. She was through. At that point, Betty had been on my mind for months already, so it felt like she was a part of me. Can you speak of mourning when you've only met someone once? When you were only able to look into those piercing eyes a single time? When you felt the energy of her beating heart only once? Maybe not. Still, I was left downcast and numb by the loss. A heroine had died. The greatest souls on earth don't have eternal life either.

Betty's death further convinced me this novel had to be written. Her story has to be passed on. Naturally, I felt uneasy at times – I'm not related to Betty, and while my youngest two children have a Jewish last name, I'm not Jewish myself. Nor do I have any link to the resistance through my family, so who am I to write this story? Still, with this historical novel, I hope to provide a complete picture of all the individual stories surrounding the nursery, and in doing so bring this history closer to home. The theme is timeless. The story is about courage, about hatred and exclusion. It raises dilemmas each of us might face at some point. And then what do you do? Do you choose fear or courage, decide to run away or stand your ground, or choose yourself over the group?

In my novel, I've tried to do justice to the history of the nursery and all the people who were involved. The family stories and dialogues I describe go beyond what I was able to discover. The novel form allowed me to fill in what might have happened and have been said where I was unable to find out.

The story of Betty and the other resistance women teaches us an important lesson: joining forces makes us strong, especially when it comes to protecting our children. In Betty's words: 'You keep your hands off the children! They can't do anything about what adults get up to.'

 twitter.com/ellevanrijn

HISTORICAL NOTE

In this novel, the heroic story about the child smuggling from the Hollandsche Schouwburg theatre takes place around the nursery, where the carers operated with the help of the Jewish Council's couriers. Henriëtte Pimentel led this complex operation together with Walter Süskind, but they also maintained the network of different organisations that took care of the children after the nursery. The children had to be transported throughout the country, a high-risk operation that was usually done by young women. They were also constantly looking for suitable hiding addresses – taking Jewish children into your home was a risky decision; all non-Jewish people in this escape chain risked being deported as well if they were caught.

The non-Jewish resistance groups involved with rescuing children were groups that were formed spontaneously and came from all layers of society. Groups who got the most children out of the nursery were:

- The Utrecht Student Committee and the
  Amsterdam Student Group, young people who
  would stop at nothing, led by the student Piet

Meerburg. He worked together with Iet van Dijk, Mieke Mees and many others.

- De Naamloze Venootschap ('the nameless partnership') from the working class, with more communist leanings. Joop Woortman and his wife, Semmy Glasoog, were in charge from Amsterdam.
- The Trouw group, which formed the resistance newspaper *Trouw*, was an intellectual Christian group led by feminists Gezina van der Molen and Hester van Lennep, who came into contact with the nursery's operations through Johan van Hulst and the Kweekschool teachers' training college.

ACKNOWLEDGEMENTS

My special thanks go out to Pollo de Pimentel, who went on this search with me. I also wish to thank Martijn Griöen for his confidence in me, Lenneke Cuijpers for her careful work and great suggestions, and Christine and the whole marketing team for their enthusiasm. Marion Pauw also helped take the book an enormous step forward with all her concrete feedback. Thank you, dear Marion!

My greatest support in this process was Elco Lenstra, my publisher. I thank him for his commitment, expertise and words of motivation at moments when my confidence was low, like: 'Elle, writing is like bicycling, you never forget how to do it.'

Finally, I want to thank my husband and children, who I deprived of many hours of my time while working on this book.

BIBLIOGRAPHY

For writing this historical novel, I have made use of the sources below.

BOOKS

Alles ging aan flarden. Het oorlogsdagboek van Kaartje de Zwarte- Walvisch, Klaartje de Zwarte-Walvisch

Atlas van een bezette stad, Bianca Stigter

Betty. Een joodse kinderverzorgster in verzet, Esther Göbel and Henk Meulenbeld

Dag pap, tot morgen. Joodse kinderen gered uit de crèche, Alex Bakker

Harry & Sieny, Esther Shaya

*Omdat hun hart sprak. Geschiedenis van de georgan-
iseerde hulp aan Joodse kinderen in Nederland, 1942-
1945,* Bert Jan Flim

*Onder de klok. Georganiseerde hulp aan Joodse
kinderen,* Bert Jan Flim

Silvie, Silvia Grohs-Martin

*Walter Süskind. Hoe een zakenman honderden Joodse
kinderen uit han- den van de nazi's redde,* Mark
Schellekens

ARTICLES

'De helden van de Joodsche Creche', Anita van
Ommeren and Ageeth Scherphuis (*Vrij Nederland*)

'De Hollandsche Schouwburg. Theater, depor-
tatieplaats, plek van herinnering', Frank van Vree,
Hetty Berg and David Duindam

'De kinderen van de Joodsche Crèche', Harm Ede Botje
and Mischa Cohen (*Vrij Nederland*)

AND ALSO

NIOD Institute for War, Holocaust and Genocide
Studies, various archives

Jewish Cultural Quarter, various films and sound
recordings

Shoah Foundation, various interviews

Sound recordings of interviews by Bert Jan Flim with Virrie and Mirjam Cohen

De Hollandsche Schouwburg

Joods Monument

Verzetsmuseum

Various journalistic articles from newspapers and online information sources

CPSIA information can be obtained
at www.ICGtesting.com
Printed in the USA
LVHW052315180722
723792LV00020B/290

9 781803 140292